Praise for Shannon McKenna

"Sensual, hard-hitting love scenes, and underlying themes of hope, faithfulness and survival."
—*Romantic Times* on *Extreme Danger* (4 starred review)

"A passionate, intense story about two people rekindling lost love in the middle of a dangerous, heart-pounding situation. Intricate story-lines give the book depth and power, tying in the edge-of-your-seat ending with flawless ease."
—*Romantic Times* on *Edge of Midnight* (4 ½ starred review)

"Wild boy Sean McCloud takes center stage in McKenna's romantic suspense series. Full of turbocharged sex scenes, this action-packed novel is sure to be a crowd pleaser."
—*Publishers Weekly* on *Edge of Midnight*

"Highly creative, erotic sex and constant danger."
—*Romantic Times* on *Hot Night* (4 ½ starred review and a Top Pick!)

"Super-sexy suspense! Shannon McKenna does it again."
—Cherry Adair on *Hot Night*

"[A] scorcher. Romantic suspense at its best!"
—*Romantic Times* on *Out of Control* (4 ½ starred review)

"Well-crafted romantic suspense. McKenna builds sexual chemistry and tension between her characters to a level of intensity that explodes into sexually explicit love scenes."
—*Romantic Times* on *Return to Me* (4 ½ starred review)

SHANNON McKENNA

ULTIMATE WEAPON

BRAVA

KENSINGTON PUBLISHING CORP.

www.kensingtonbooks.com

BRAVA BOOKS are published by

Kensington Publishing Corp.
850 Third Avenue
New York, NY 10022

All Kensington titles, imprints and distributed lines are available at special quantity discounts for bulk purchases for sales promotion, premiums, fund-raising, educational or institutional use.

Special book excerpts or customized printings can also be created to fit specific needs. For details, write or phone the office of the Kensington Special Sales Manager: Attn.: Special Sales Department. Kensington Publishing Corp., 850 Third Avenue, New York, NY 10022. Phone: 1-800-221-2647.

Brava and the B logo Reg. U.S. Pat. & TM Off.

ISBN-13: 978-0-7582-1189-7
ISBN-10: 0-7582-1189-9

First Kensington Trade Paperback Printing: November 2008
10 9 8 7 6 5 4 3 2 1

Printed in the United States of America

This book is dedicated to my magnificent critique partners Elizabeth Jennings and Lisa Marie Rice. Thank you for being my adjunct brains! Couldn't have done it without you.

Chapter
1

Find the weak spot. Then exploit it.

The brutally simple directive repeated in Val's head until it was meaningless babble. Val pushed the white noise to the back of his mind and clicked "play" on the footage he'd collected that day.

For the twentieth time, he watched the woman unload the wriggling toddler from the SUV and head toward the waterfront park playground. He had memorized their every move—the swings, then the slide, the merry-go-round, the jungle gym. Then came a horsie ride on the woman's shoulders through the trees. And the moment when she held the child up to swipe and grab the brown leaves that clung to the branches. He had memorized every nod, every smile, every hug.

The jeans, hiking boots, and shapeless down jacket the woman wore did nothing to hide the feline grace of her slender body. Her brown hair was twisted into a loose, thick dark braid. She wore no makeup. The child reached higher to grab for the leaves, giggling.

Children were always a weak spot—but not one he could bring himself to exploit. He hated when there was a child involved. It made him tense, anxious. It destroyed the hard-won professional calm that usually rendered him such an effective operative. Had he known about the existence of the child, he would have refused the job, no matter how Hegel blustered and threatened. The worst they could do to him was kill him, no? Let them try. Others had already, several times. Eventually someone would succeed. It wouldn't matter a damn who had done the deed after he was dead.

The job had seemed straightforward when Hegel presented it to him. Locate this woman who was in hiding—one of Val's specialties, considering his hacking abilities and his skills at social engineering. Deliver her to Georg Luksch, willingly, if possible, under false pretenses if not. Failing that, by any means necessary. Coercion. Abduction.

He did not like working for Luksch or having any dealings with the mafiya. Too much history, too many ugly memories. But Hegel had pulled rank, yanked strings. And Val had convinced himself that he could stay cool and just get the job done. Wrong.

The first thing he had done was to send out feelers to all of the best sources for fake identities. Using a judicious blend of threats and bribes, he had obtained a list of the passports that Steele had procured for herself and her daughter. A few telephone calls and some discreet hacking into Homeland Security databases had ensured that Steele was never going to be traveling with any of those documents, at least the ones he knew about. Now he wished he had not been so efficient.

He wanted her to escape. Damned unprofessional of him.

The room was cold, growing dark with the onset of the early January sunset. He wore nothing but a pair of baggy sweat pants, but he stayed motionless on the floor in a meditative position in front of the computer monitor, trying in vain to settle his mind down to the stillness necessary to perform his personal technique of data processing.

It was based on the way Imre had taught him to play chess years ago as a boy. Deceptively simple, but requiring profound concentration. He put the information, no matter how irrelevant or superficial, into a floating construct in his mind that Imre had named "the matrix" and held them suspended in a transparent form that he could rotate, turn inside out, dissassemble, reassemble, contemplate from every side. Then he detached from it, floated away, and quietly observed.

Take three steps back and breathe, Imre had said.

That distance was the key element. It kept his mind loose, soft and open, leaving space for insights, solutions, realizations to arise.

Not tonight. He'd sat there motionless for hours while dark fell, and muscles cramped in protest. Solutions and insights were not forthcoming. He could not take three steps back. He was distracted. Angry that there was a child. Anger derailed the process. He had to stay cool.

And God knows, staring at Tamara Steele for days on end was no way to get or stay cool. He had never seen a woman so vividly beautiful. Her beauty was intensified by something burning inside her, a bright light, a driving force. She disturbed his dreams, unsettled his thoughts, stirred his body. And utterly destroyed his concentration.

Imre had earnestly explained that the matrix process worked for solving ethical problems, too, but that sermon had been wasted on the young Vajda, cynical, thieving hoodlum that he'd been.

Hmmph. An irrelevant thought. It had no place. It would not serve. He dismissed it, waving it away in his mind like a stinging insect.

He knew every detail of Steele's schedule, all centered on the child. Weekly visits to the pediatrician and child psychologist, trips to the Children's Museum, story hour for toddlers at the library, the Mommy & Me swim class, the playground at the riverside park. No variations to speak of, except for that unwary visit to Conor McCloud's house that had given him his opening.

She had her groceries delivered. No doubt she did her personal shopping via Internet. She spoke to no one but her daughter's doctors, visited no one, never went to a coffee shop or restaurant. He did not blame her. The child's schedule was already a dangerous level of exposure for her. As demonstrated by the amount of data he'd gathered on her in the two weeks since he'd finally pinpointed her residence.

It had taken weeks of data analysis and tedious waiting before the passive surveillance he'd been conducting upon the McClouds had paid off. Steele showed up one day on the long-range telecamera mounted to a tree in the park across the street from Connor and Erin McCloud's residence. With a toddler on her hip, to his blank astonishment.

The tech who was monitoring had called him, and by chance, he'd been near enough to hand tag her SUV with an RF device while she was still on the back porch having barbecue with her friends.

He had not mentioned the child in his reports. He was not sure why. There was no hiding her. Once the satellite had trained its cold eye on the woman's residence, everyone at PSS who was interested knew that the woman was caring for a child. They could see her with their own eyes, loading the kid into the car, playing with her on the beach.

Now that he'd found Steele's mountaintop home outside the small coastal town of Cray's Cove, his challenges were different. It would have been easier to conduct surveillance in a bustling city, although he'd need a team. But no one could follow her undetected in a place like Cray's Cove. Which was, he supposed, the whole point of hiding there.

As soon as he had tagged her SUV with the nearly undetectable RF device, things had proceeded smoothly. He analyzed her schedule, installed tiny surveillance cameras at key points in her trajectory. A wireless receiver in a series of rental cars parked a discreet distance from the establishments in question, and he could watch and listen to her in real time on his laptop, or even his Palm Pilot.

He'd forgone tech support, being as competent with the electronic equipment as any of PSS's tech specialists. He wanted no one breathing down his neck on this job. No spectators, suggestions, criticism. He preferred to work alone whenever humanly possible.

In fact, he preferred to do almost everything alone. It was easier to take those crucial three steps back without the noise and the chatter.

It had been an easy matter to breach security at the psychologist and pediatrician's offices to obtain copies of the child's clinical charts. He'd hacked into the database of the agency handling the adoption proceedings. He knew the entire dramatic story of the child who was soon to become Rachel Steele, and thanks to the remotely activated bugs under the psychiatrist's and pediatrician's desks, he now knew more than he had ever cared to know about the child's bowel habits, food allergies, rashes, hip and ankle malformations, vision problems, chronic ear infections, sinus problems, and sleep disruptions.

And he knew a great deal more than he was comfortable knowing about how much Steele cared about the child. It was important information for the matrix, but he resisted it. It disturbed him.

He knew what his target wanted the world to know about Tamara Steele, which wasn't much nor was it true. Her multilayered identity held up well to prolonged scrutiny. He would have had no reason to question it had he not already known that the woman was a con artist, thief, and killer. Skilled at bank fraud, real estate scams, money laundering, and various other criminal enterprises too numerous to count. And a talented liar.

Then again, what was truth? He was not judging her. His own life was a tissue of lies so thick and complex he no longer had any idea what personality traits he could actually claim as his own. It was all false scaffolding and beneath, blankness. Paper and cardboard.

He batted the distracting thought away, irritated. This kind of self-pitying reflection was stupid and irrelevant. He had no time for useless philosophical musing.

If the doctor's and psychologist's security was inadequate, Steele's own fortress was not. He knew the layout of her property from satellite images provided by Prime Security Solutions, the private security company for which he worked as a covert operative, but he could get no closer to her state-of-the-art security systems without being nailed.

What he needed now was a pretext for approaching her. With someone so paranoid and reclusive, that was impossible to devise.

He wondered what had possessed a career criminal like Steele to adopt a toddler. If it was a cover, it was a cumbersome, inefficient one, and the woman presently calling herself Tamara Steele had never shown herself to be anything but ruthlessly efficient in the past.

He let out a sigh, acknowledging defeat, and got up, bending his knees and shaking his bare feet to get blood moving. He snapped his fingers under the sound-sensitive lamp, illuminating the hotel suite. Val padded silently into the kitchenette and pressed the hot spigot of the water machine over his cup to brew a cup of smoky

Lapsang Souchong tea. It occurred to him as he fished the tea bag out that he'd bought the same brand as he had last week, having liked it. The detail was seemingly banal, but lapses like these could kill a man.

He had to stay rigorous. He should have bought coffee, fruit juice, Red Bull. Anything else. *No habits.* It was one of the first lessons he'd learned as an operative. Habits were deadly. They soon became needs. An operative could not afford needs or even preferences. He had to be a blank slate, ready to be anyone, anything. Light and empty, flexible as a gymnast. Ready to jump in any direction. Imre's training helped.

But Imre had never meant for him to be a man made out of blank paper and cardboard. An empty man who could call nothing his own.

He breathed in fragrant steam, feeling oddly rebellious. So he was getting sloppy, but no one was watching. He was just a fly on the wall in the ass end of nowhere, watching Steele play with her new daughter, and inexplicably fascinated by it. If not for the fact that she would almost certainly kill him if she knew what PSS wanted from her, and that he might be required to abduct either her or her little daughter, he might almost have been enjoying himself.

That was the most alarming development of all.

Detach, he reminded himself. The woman was deadly dangerous. Some years ago, Steele had become involved with Kurt Novak, Daddy Novak's son and heir to his mafiya empire. During that period, which had led up to Kurt Novak's spectacular and theatrical death, Georg Luksch, Kurt's lieutenant, had developed a burning obsession for her.

Steele had not returned his regard. In fact, she had vanished like smoke on that bloody day and had shown no desire to be found.

Val had found her, but now he wished he had not. He didn't want to deliver her to Luksch, who was at best a criminal grown rich by trafficking in drugs, humans, and everything else, and at worst, a psychotic freak. But PSS was not inclined to criticize a client so immensely rich.

Val carried the cup back to the laptop glowing in the middle of the wood floor and sank down in front of it. His naked chest was covered with goosebumps, but the tea would warm him, and he didn't want to bother finding a shirt or turning on the heat.

He clicked the footage he'd obtained yesterday. The toddler's swim class. He took a sip of the hot, bitter tea and skipped through the footage to his favorite part. Here he was again, allowing himself to have favorites. Like the tea. An uncharacteristic indulgence.

From one moment to the next, it would distort into a need. And from that, an obsession. He had always wondered what an obsession would feel like. It would seem that he no longer had to wonder.

She came out of the women's dressing room, silent and graceful as a slant-eyed female panther among the crowd of chubby, chattering women with their squealing offspring. She led the wobbly-legged, huge-eyed little girl carefully by the hand.

Her body was stunning in the black maillot. He always watched the exit from the dressing room, having grown addicted to the hot rush of delighted surprise that it gave him no matter how many times he saw it. He skipped through the class, which he had already watched ad nauseam, to the moment that she lifted the dripping child out of the water and vaulted out in turn onto the pool's edge, poised in the perfect equilibrium of a predator's crouch. The curves and hollows, the highlights and shadows of her wet body. High, lush breasts, the discreet mandolin curve of hips and ass. Endlessly long, strong, shapely legs.

He'd seduced many women in his career, and some of them had been very beautiful, but he'd never reacted like this to mere visual stimuli. Or any stimuli, in truth, visual or otherwise. He liked sex, but he took his usual three steps back from it—particularly in the context of a professional operation. From the beginning of his career with PSS, they had required him to use his looks and body as a means to an end. His sexual technique was flawless, but he stayed cool. Always.

So why was he sweating now? Panting like a hormone-intoxicated teenager? There was no logical explanation. And no excuse.

The thought of that woman soiling herself with that prick Georg Luksch made his hands clench. It made his gorge rise. A bad sign.

Ah, here it was, the best part. The women's changing room. He had seen a hiding place for the tiny camera behind the fluorescent light fixture in the shower area the night he'd broken into the place. He'd been unable to resist. After all, a long look at the target's naked body could yield useful data.

Ah, no. Unfortunately, he was not as adept at lying to himself as he was at lying to the rest of the world.

That footage was incredible, though. High breasts, water coursing around her taut, protruding brown nipples as she soaped herself. The child was wrapped in a towel after her own bath, playing with a rubber frog, unaware of her mother's nudity. Tamara rinsed. The suds sluiced into the minuscule swatch of decorative pubic hair over the smooth, depilated cunt, filling the alluring hollows of her groin.

Steele ignored the other women in the room, who sneaked slack-jawed peeks at a body the likes of which they'd only seen in their husbands' airbrushed men's magazines.

His cell phone rang. Val was savagely irritated at the interruption, and yanked off the earpiece clipped to his waistband.

He hung it on his ear. "What?" he asked, with ill grace.

"So?" It was Hegel, his direct superior at PSS, the man who had recruited and trained him. The tone in the man's voice put Val's teeth on edge. Tough. Resentment was another thing that he could not afford.

"So what?" Val countered.

"It's two weeks since you located her. The fat cats are breathing down my neck. Stop sitting on this thing like a fucking hen. Have you got the kid yet?"

Val's jaw tensed. "That is not the correct approach."

"It's quick," Hegel said. "We need results."

Val was silent for a moment. "I cannot be sure that she even cares enough about the child for her to be an effective lever," he said. "I'd prefer to try a subtler approach first."

"Subtle. Hah." Hegel made a doglike growling sound. "Come on, Janos. One of Daddy Novak's ex-thugs should be more professional. What is your brilliant alternative plan? Knock her on the head and put her in a box? That works for me, as long as you do it soon."

Val clenched his jaw. *Three steps back*. Hegel loved waving Val's old connection to Novak's organization in his face, but it could only irritate him if he allowed it to. "I'm working on it," he said finally.

"Hmmph. Work harder, Janos. I hope you're not having an attack of scruples about the kid. That was what fucked up your performance last time. Patience is growing thin up here. Damn, I should have called Henry for this job. He would have been done and gone by now."

Val was stonily silent. Hegel liked to sow discord, believing that a situation that he had destabilized himself was more easily controlled. But Hegel could not control him. He could have him killed, yes, perhaps. But he could not control him.

Nor could he interfere with Val's bond with his closest friend and fellow operative, Henry Berne. In fact, Henry might well be his only friend. The person known as Val Janos had "friends," but none of them knew about his double life. Only PSS staff knew, and of them, only Henry could be counted as a friend.

One friend, in all the world, unless he counted Imre. But Imre was in a category all his own.

"This job is your ticket to retirement," Hegel ground out. "Do not fuck it up, Janos. I am tired of your superior attitude. I would love to see the ass end of you head off into the sunset, because the alternative would be stressful and bloody. And my personal responsibility since I was the dick who recruited you. Think about that." Hegel hung up.

Val pulled off the earpiece. It flew across the room and hit the wall before he could even try to grasp for his elusive, detached calm again.

God. Twelve years of sweating blood and taking bullets for those ungrateful bastards, and still they waved their fucking threats at him.

Scruples. Another thing he could not afford. His scruples had been a problem for most of his life. Ironic, considering the career destiny had in store for him. Imre's influence, no doubt. He could hear in his mind's ear exactly what Imre would have had to say about that, but he blocked the lecture before it could start to play in his head. He had no time or energy to spare for guilt.

He had told Hegel that he didn't know if Steele cared enough about the child to use her as a lever, but he had lied. No woman of her type sacrificed an hour of her life to suffer through the tedium of Mommy & Me, or spent hours rolling a ball back and forth across the grass in the park except out of love. She cared, intensely.

From the point of view of expediency, it was difficult to justify not doing what Hegel had urged. Take the child, and start negotiations.

But he disliked hurting children. Kidnapping that child would hurt her. It would hurt any child. Particularly a small, wounded one.

That child was wounded. He knew her story, he'd seen her files, read her charts. He would not be the one to inflict the next blow in an endless series of blows. To say nothing of the practical logistics of caring for a small child with medical problems. He would need a team. It would be chaotic, complicated, messy. A state of affairs he took pains to avoid.

In the course of his career, he'd managed to finesse his dislike of hurting children, and still obtain successful outcomes. He'd relied on luck and cleverness, but his luck had run out last year in Bogotá.

The problem had been glaringly evident to the powers that be at PSS. Which explained the long vacation they'd given him. Aside from the small matter of the bullet wounds he'd sustained.

He'd been out of favor ever since, expecting them to put him down like a rabid dog at any moment. Vaguely surprised every morning that he woke to find himself still alive. They hadn't gotten around to it yet.

He'd begun to hope that they would simply ignore him for the rest of his life, but no. They had called him to locate Steele—and behold, she had a baby daughter. It was a test he could not afford to fail.

He clicked automatically on the shower footage, thinking to distract himself with that dance of wet female flesh. It did not help, to watch her play with the toddler. It made him squirm, it made him sweat. He could not think straight, could not detach, could not take the three steps. Nothing had ever shaken his self-control to this extent.

Find the weak point. Then exploit it. The rule droned in his head.

Vaffanculo, he responded mentally, banishing it.

The beeper attached to his pants chirped at him. He took a look, and his gut clenched. It was a numeric code, sent by Imre's house-cleaning service in Budapest. They were supposed to inform him of any change in Imre's health and welfare. They had never beeped him before.

The code informed him that he had an urgent message to retrieve from the computer bulletin board. Something had happened to Imre.

His heart accelerated without his permission. There was a tremor in his hand as he entered passwords, clicked the message, decoded it.

A few terse lines informed him that the woman who was paid to cook, clean, and do Imre's shopping had come in that day and found the door forced, the apartment ransacked, and Imre unconscious on the floor, badly beaten. He was in the hospital, his condition grave.

Val stared at the text on the screen for approximately three seconds and sprang to his feet, overturning the cup of tea. He groped for his phone, splashed and slipped clumsily in his bare feet through the steaming puddle in his haste to dress, pack, go, go, *go*.

He was breathless, dizzy. Panicking. *Calm down*. Three steps. Panic was another luxury that he could not afford.

Find the weak spot. Then exploit it.

His gut churned nastily. It seemed someone had just found his.

Chapter
2

Adrenaline kicked her right across the barrier of sleep.

Tam jerked up in bed, every nerve screaming, and instantly put every mental trick she had into action to block the dream that had provoked it. If the images didn't sink their claws into her conscious mind, the feelings faded more quickly. Though never quickly enough.

Tonight, she couldn't block it. The crackle of rifle fire. Hard, clutching hands holding her down under a bruised white sky. Dark silhouettes, mouths screaming, but she could not hear what they said. She was deafened by those rifles popping.

She squeezed her eyes shut and saw their stiff white faces, blank eyes staring up from the trench. Dirt showering into their open eyes. She had tried to close their eyes. Tried, and tried, but she'd had no coins to weigh their eyelids down. They would stay open forever. She could not hide what she'd become from those staring eyes.

And the fear, the shame. Burning, corrosive hatred for that evil leering monster. For what he'd done to them, to her. *Stengl*.

Her hands itched to kill him, even after sixteen years.

She pressed her hands against her face, and tried to breathe deep, but her lungs seized up halfway through each breath in a painful hiccup that jolted her whole body. Ah, God. She hadn't dreamed about Stengl and his secret police squad, or the horrors of Sremska

Mitrovica for years. She'd deep frozen it, buried it, rolled huge rocks over it.

But something was rolling the rocks away, one after the other. Something like Rachel. Fancy that.

Tam wrapped her arms around her knees. Her body ached, every muscle rigid. Her heart felt like it was going to explode, it raced so fast.

Moonlight streamed in the huge windows of her bedroom. She had chosen every detail of the room to calm, to soothe, having pictured an uncluttered, tranquil haven where she could feel safe and peaceful. What a fantasy. Sleep was a dangerous place for her to go.

The electronically programmed blinds would automatically close shortly before dawn to keep the room dim so Rachel would sleep longer, but the moonlight seemed blinding to her, casting shadows as cold and sharp as knives.

Tam looked down at the lump in the bed beside her. Rachel stirred, fussed in her sleep. Tam laid down alongside her, and stroked the child's back. She wasn't sure it was appropriate to take her nightmares into bed with the innocent toddler, but Rachel wouldn't sleep on her own for love or money.

When she was being honest, though, she recognized that excuse for the cheap justification that it was. She just liked to be close to Rachel. She loved to watch her sleep, see the rise and fall of her little chest, the beatific relaxation in her face. To touch and snuggle that warm body. And she liked to be there when Rachel reached for her in the night. Right at the child's fingertips. Instant gratification. The least she could offer, considering what Rachel had been robbed of up to now.

Just watching her was restful. Maybe she couldn't get a decent night's sleep herself, but watching Rachel get one was the next best thing. Tamara could lie there and feel that miraculous sensation that had taken her hostage in the aftermath of the organ pirate adventure. That hot softness in her chest. The melting.

The problem was, the rest of Tam's emotional defenses were melting right along with her heart, and she was by no means ready to live without them yet. Scary.

Rachel rolled over and reached out, flinging a skinny but surprisingly strong arm over Tam's neck, dragging her into a strangling, baby-soap, sour milk, and toothpaste-scented hug.

Tam grabbed the little girl, comforting herself with the warmth of that snuggly, wiry body. Rachel vibrated with life, glowing like a little sun. Being close to her fed something inside Tam that had been starving. Something she had thought was stone dead.

Rachel needed her so badly. Or rather, Rachel needed someone, and it had been the toddler's questionable luck that Tam had been the one standing there, at the crucial psychological moment. Snap, click, and hey, presto . . . the kid was stuck to her like glue. And out of nowhere, Tam had suddenly come to crave being needed in return.

So strange. Where did that come from, after a lifetime of deliberately not giving a shit? After making not caring into a high art?

Rachel was barely three years old, and she'd had more crap luck than a lot of people pulled in an entire lifetime. Tossed into a sty of an orphanage at birth, scooped up by rapacious organ pirates to be broken down for parts, locked in a stinking windowless pen with a pack of desperate kids for months—it didn't get worse than that.

Until you added in the fact that somehow, she'd managed to pull Tam Steele out of a hat for an adoptive mother. Yippee, what a prize.

And if that wasn't enough, the mother she had chosen was getting twitchy and paranoid. Which was to say, more twitchy and paranoid than usual, which was really saying something, given her impressive list of mortal enemies. It was a strange sensation, but she couldn't shake it. For weeks, she'd felt her grunting reptile brain looking back over her scaly reptile shoulder, telling her she was being watched.

Paranoia or genuine danger? Impossible to tell. Her instincts were good. But the emotions that had broken ranks and gone nuts inside her might have knocked even that out of whack.

She might never get it all wrenched back obediently into line. Chaos ruled, inside and out. She just had to get used to it.

Tam petted the fleece-covered back of the sleeping toddler, stroking the warm curve of the child's head. Her fingers marveled at the spider-silk ringlets, the swell of her soft cheek, that flowerlike pink mouth, half-open, shiny with baby spit in the moonlight. Such a pretty little girl. Her breathing deepened, her heartbeat slowed, steadied. And then, that incredible feeling unfurled in her chest, like it always did.

Hot and soft . . . and so alive.

Alive. God help her. There was something alive inside of her, after all. She regarded that development with mingled terror and awe, not quite sure yet if it was good news or bad.

Moonlight crawled over the wall with agonizing slowness. Tam stroked the child's back and just breathed. The crackle of gunfire still echoed stubbornly in her head, the shrieks of pain and terror floated up from the basement cells and reverberated through her memory. But if she just concentrated on Rachel, on how beautiful and small and perfect she was, she could get enough oxygen. She could walk that narrow line through the bad memories without falling headlong into a stress flashback.

It was hard. The dream images weren't fading tonight. They'd sunk in deep. She'd be hearing that gunfire, those screams, all night long. But she would endure. She was all right. Just . . . breathe.

Part of her missed the cold numbness she'd felt before Rachel. It was a pain in the ass, being continually tossed and flung around by her emotions like a twig in a flash flood. She hadn't expected that when she took the child. The impulse had taken her by surprise. She hadn't had the presence of mind in the turbulent aftermath of the organ pirate adventure to consider what Rachel would do to her equilibrium.

Hell, she'd thought she could handle anything. She'd been keeping it together fairly well, after all. Flying under the radar, turning a nice profit with her business, paying her taxes, not getting in anybody's face. Her current identity was holding up nicely, even under the pressure of drawn-out adoption proceedings, which was a testament to her unusual skill set. She'd been a bit bored, yes, after her supremely eventful former career, but the raid on the organ pirates had helped with the ennui. That thrill ride had been calculated to keep her going for a while.

Enter Rachel. Talk about adventure. Hah. Bye-bye, ennui. She had no time for boredom now. She was fried, trying to stay on top of it all. Blitzed by the hugeness of the responsibility. The massive snarl of bureaucratic red tape that comprised an international adoption. The appointments, the special foods, the allergies, the naps, the illnesses, the medications, the baths, the fits. The fears.

And even so, life without Rachel was now impossible to contemplate.

The miracle happened so quickly. Sneakily, too. That skinny monkey of a baby girl wrapped her arms around her neck and hung on for dear life, and the place where her heart was theoretically supposed had gone all hot and soft out of fucking nowhere. Something twisted, swelled, went *pop* inside her and—

The kid just *got* to her. Those huge, liquid brown eyes, so much like little Irina's—ah, no. No. *Don't.*

Tears were slipping down her face, hot and fast. Her chest vibrated with sobs so fast, they were a seamless, silent shudder.

God, she hated crying. She gently detached Rachel's clinging arm, and slid out of the bed and down onto the blond bamboo floorboards.

Fuck this. She did not want Rachel to wake up and see her this way. *Pull yourself together, Tamar.* The kid had enough to feel insecure about already without watching her mamma come apart at the seams.

Tamar. She'd slipped into calling herself by her childhood name. And that stern inner voice had sounded so much like her mother. Odd. She'd been insane, to use something so close to her real given name for her alias. A suicidal impulse? Or just pique? Or simply a need to claim something real for herself. To make herself feel more coherent.

A tall order. But she was stalling. *Up, Tamar. On your feet. Be the fucking grown-up here. There's no one else to do it.*

She dragged herself to her feet, stumbled into the bathroom and leaned over the big marble sink. She splashed her face, glanced into the mirror. That proved to be a mistake. Her sight of her own thin, hollowed face, her red, staring eyes, her blurred, shaking mouth—it did not help. Eeeuw. Bad. But once one of her crying fits started, there was no way out but through. She leaned over the sink again, ran water into her hands, gulped it. Splashed water over her face. Rinsed away tears, snot.

That mission accomplished, her legs decided that no more was currently required of them. She pressed her back against the wall and slid bonelessly down. Her ass bumped onto the chilly floor tiles.

She curled into a shaking knot. She hadn't cried in years, before Rachel. Over a decade, maybe. Hadn't missed it, either.

She pressed her palms against her eyes until they hurt. Poor Rachel. Tam should never have touched the kid in the first place, considering who and what she was. But she had, and the damage was done, to both of them.

Rachel needed a mother so desperately. A real one, someone committed, smart, sane. Only an idiot would take on a hard luck case like Rachel, considering the child's background, but an idiot would never survive the experience. The idiot would give up as soon as her pretty fantasies about how sweet and compassionate she was got dashed. And a kid like Rachel would be sure to dash them.

Rachel needed so much. She was a vortex of need, physical, emotional, financial. She'd been deprived since birth. Sveti, the older girl who had been penned up with Rachel in the organ pirates' shithole, had been the first one to be tender to her, and Rachel had glommed onto the girl and sucked it up like a thirsty sponge. Just like she did from Tam.

Tenderness. Of all things to be required of her. Of all feelings to be entertaining, voluntarily.

Sometimes she missed the hours of quiet. The splendid, barren solitude. Absorbed in her jewelry making, bothered by no one. Needed by no one. And then, out of nowhere, the bleakness, the silence, the blankness of her life before Rachel hit her. And staggered her.

Rachel was over a year behind in development. She was three, but she looked, talked, and had the motor skills of a shrimpy twenty-month-old. And that was the good news. It could've been worse. She could have been a drooling vegetable. Or turned her face to the wall and died.

It was a miracle that she hadn't. And Tam took that miracle to mean that she wasn't meant to die. She was meant to survive, and to thrive, too, damn it. She was meant to shine, to bloom. Against all odds.

Rachel had made big progress in the months that she'd been with

Tam. She no longer looked like a shriveled little monkey. She was walking better, talking better, babbling in three languages; the Portuguese of her babysitter, her own native Ukrainian that Tam was determined that she maintain, and English, of course.

Tam was proud of what she'd accomplished with the kid. But with the fear of stalking predators dogging her, with screams and rifle fire from her dreams ringing in her ears, she couldn't get away from the thought of how selfish, how egotistic she'd been, to take the child just because she couldn't resist the way Rachel made her feel. Because she looked like Irina. Because Rachel made her feel so unexpectedly alive.

As if she could offer the child some sort of normal family life as a fair exchange for that feeling. She had no such thing to offer in trade.

Normal? Tam had no parameters, no fucking clue what normal looked like, felt like. Her own early childhood had been good, but it was a million years away, and inaccessible behind that big stone wall in her brain that she'd erected herself. No models to work from there.

She'd been all alone in the wilderness for most of her life. Camped out on Planet Tam. Or not even a planet. It was more like a space station that orbited normal reality, with thousands of miles of vacuum at Kelvin zero temperature as a safety buffer.

What had made her think she could take a fragile, wounded little girl into exile on that space station with her? For company? What kind of egotistic madness was that? A selfish, solitary bitch like her with all her wires crossed? She wasn't fit to mother a toddler. She was a thief, a crook, a scam artist, a swindler, even a sometime assassin when the situation called for it, although always in self-defense. And everyone she'd ever wasted had richly deserved it. No innocent victims. She was all too aware of what it felt like to be an innocent victim.

But she wasn't innocent now, by God. She was wanted for a list of crimes too long even for her own steel-trap mind to keep straight. She was in hiding from international law enforcement agencies and the global mafia both. She was fucked, left, right, and sideways. In every way. On every level.

And yet, here she was. Mamma, for a problematic toddler with special needs. Everything was guesswork with Rachel. Tam just kept blundering forward into the dark, desperately hoping every little choice she made would work out.

And of course, there were all the vengeful, dangerous people out there who would love to grind her into paste. Daddy Novak was number one. Georg Luksch was a close second on that list, though he wanted something other than her blood. A chill shudder of disgust racked her at the thought.

She'd been horrified to discover that he was still alive, after the Novak bloodbath. She'd been unforgivably sloppy that day, not to have killed that venomous snake while she had the chance. He'd been hauled off to prison after they patched him up, of course, but she knew how that went. No prison could hold a man with his contacts.

There were plenty of other enemies. The list was long. Tam could be run down, taken, killed, or worse at any time. She could not guarantee a safe home for Rachel, even though it hurt like hell to imagine turning away from the child now that they had bonded.

Rachel would see it as yet another abandonment. Try to explain "for your own safety" to a wigged-out, scared little three-year-old who had never been able to count on anyone in her life. See how far you got.

Still. Arrangements had to be made for Rachel. And soon. Worst-case scenario. Tam tightened her gut, and grimly forced herself to consider the various options.

She could ask one of the McCloud women or Raine to take Rachel, or at least to be her guardian, should she get herself wasted. They were the only women friends she had, if one defined friendship loosely. Or if it wasn't friendship, it was the closest Tam had ever come to it. They all owed her. They'd all gone through the fire, having found themselves on some scumbag's hit list at some time or other. But not due to their own arrogance or bad behavior, as was the case with Tam.

Those women weren't fools. They knew the score. They had no problems with tenderness, either. It would be hard and exhausting for them, and their men would be unthrilled, but whatever. Expensive, too, with the surgeries that Rachel had in her future, but Tam had plenty of money socked away. Money was never going to be a problem for the kid, for the rest of her life. That, at least, was a non-issue.

Any of those women would do it. Not one of them would say no to her. She knew that in her bones.

And still, she cringed to think of asking a favor that huge. Truth to tell, she was uncomfortable dealing with women friends at all. The bother of it, the noise, the time sink. Having them in her face on a regular basis. Having them care, for some strange reason. Their questions, their concern, their laughter, their chatter, it drove her nuts. Their very femaleness grated on her, unfair though that was. Estrogen overload. She could only take so much. She was a solitary creature. Atypical, asexual, asocial. Royally screwed up, yes. She had no illusions about that, and she made no apologies for it. She was what she was, and if someone didn't like it, tough shit for him. Or her.

Not that their men were much better than the women. The Mc-Cloud Crowd menfolk were relatively intelligent, as men went, but they were all alpha dogs to the last woof, and as such, they all had that fog of testosterone obscuring their brains. Which made them prone to the usual arrogant, posturing male bullshit, for which she had no time or patience.

And yet, there they were. Underfoot all the fucking time. She couldn't get rid of them. They felt protective of her, of all crazy things. Nick, too, now. After the organ pirate adventure, he'd landed himself squarely on that short list of people with controlled permission to annoy the living shit out of her without getting killed for it. Maimed, maybe, but not killed.

Their efforts to be her friends were puppyish and earnest. She was charmed by it—sometimes. Amused, even, when she was in the mood. Which hadn't been lately, with all these nightmares she'd been having. They were way too much like the stress flashbacks she'd suffered back in her younger days. Before she'd turned herself into a human icicle. Robot Bitch, her alter ego.

She wasn't an icicle now. Particularly not when she pictured Margot, Erin, Liv or Raine parenting Rachel. A jealous, vengeful and totally disproportionate rage blazed up inside her when she pictured one of those women sweetly, gracefully, effortlessly being a better mother to Rachel than she could ever be. *Fuck* that.

It wasn't their fault. There was nothing wrong with those women. Oh, no. That was the exact problem. Everything was right with them. Damn them to hell. She would have laughed at herself for being so silly and crazy, if she were not mortally afraid that it would start her up crying again. Only in these naked moments in the wee hours before dawn did she let herself acknowledge humiliating truths like this. She was a jealous bitch. Bitterly envious. Not of their men, God forbid. The last thing she wanted was to be bothered with their silly, pointless, attention-hungry men, although all of those women had relatively good ones—insofar as any man could be called good. That being, after all, a blatant contradiction in terms.

No, it was because their lives made sense. They were hooked into the world, they functioned well, they thrummed, they glowed. They threw out vibes of sexual fulfillment strong enough to knock a celibate like herself back on her scrawny ass at fifty meters.

And they were so unafraid of motherhood. At least the ones that were well into it, and she had no doubt it would be the same for the others when their time came—Liv, and Becca, Nick's fiancée, soon to be wife. All of them had that feminine, motherly vibe, just like Margot and Raine and Erin. *Moo.*

For them, motherhood was all joyous cuddling, spiritual fulfilment. Wallowing in bliss with a proud daddy looking on. Glowing at baby's amazing progress and sparkling genius. Raine was almost due, and glowing like a full moon. Erin's boy was a year old and Margot's little redheaded girl was seven months old. Fat, uncomplicated babies, rolling on the rug, gurgling and laughing. In the top percentile for height, weight, good looks, intelligence and happiness. Tra la la.

Not like Tam's intense, clinging Rachel with the fits of rage, the screaming nightmares, the developmental delays. Bone malformations in her ankles and hips, eye problems caused by months of confinement in artificial light with nothing to focus on farther away than a concrete wall in front of her face. The doctors were always muttering about possible brain damage from abuse, neglect and malnutrition, but Tam was privately convinced that it was bullshit. All they had to do was look Rachel in the eyes, and it was clear that the kid was as sharp as a brass tack, tracking at all levels. She was just a stubborn, hard-headed, suspicious little pissant who did not appreciate being cognitively evaluated by strangers wearing white lab coats. Tam could relate to that perfectly. The doctors just didn't get it.

Rachel was determined to make up for every last bit of what she'd missed in love and affection, and no one could blame her, but her craving for attention made Tam feel she had the kid wrapped around her head sometimes. Rosalia helped, the sweet, stolid Brazilian lady who came in every day to provide Tam with a chunk of quiet time for work, but that precious chunk was always chipped away at each end by some daily emergency or other, if it wasn't eaten up entirely, and in any case, it just wasn't enough. She could barely hear herself think. God, she could barely breathe.

And even so. Even so. That kid was hers. Everyone else had failed her, but Tam would not. No fucking way. She would make it work. Tam pressed her eyes against her knees until the pressure made them ache, and still she saw that dusty trench in the ground they'd thrown her mother and her baby sister into. Irina had been two. Their faces, so pale and stiff and still. Their eyes, so wide. Dirt showering down on top of them. Tossed away like garbage.

The image was stamped on the inside of her eyelids.

Ah, God. Her least desirable memories, crashing into her like a runaway train. This was the price she had to pay for dredging up tenderness out of the depths of herself for Rachel.

She'd dreamed of revenge all her life, not tenderness. She didn't process tenderness well. It crossed her wires, blew her circuits. It confused and rattled her. Revenge was so much more simple and comprehensible. Revenge she could wrap her highly functioning mind around and feel it start to buzz and hum and work.

She was a well-tuned revenge machine, programmed to locate and kill Drago Stengl, and put the ghosts of her past to rest. And now look at her, trying to manufacture tenderness for Rachel out of a revenge machine. It was like making cookies with a rocket launcher. Like making lemonade with grenades instead of lemons. Problematic as hell.

Rachel's shrill, teakettle shriek suddenly sounded, and Tam

sprang up like she was on springs and bolted for the bedroom. The kid always freaked out when she woke in the dark and found herself alone.

She slid under the covers and curled up around the rigid little body. After she had soothed the child back to sleep, she nuzzled Rachel's neck, inhaling the fragrance of no-tangles shampoo. Feeling the magic happen. The tension, easing inside her. That soft, hot place, blooming open. So sweet. She couldn't resist. She was strung out.

Now that the dream images were easing off, her habitual obstinacy was rearing right up to take its place. She was glad. That was much more comfortable.

Hell with it. Rachel might not have a normal mom, or a normal life, but she'd have pure screaming hell on wheels to protect her if anyone ever tried to hurt her again. That was worth something. That counted. It had to count.

So Rachel was damaged. Big fucking deal. So were they all. She was also tough, and strong. Tam would try everything money could buy to help her. Anything that might give her back some small measure of what those murdering pieces of shit had stolen from her.

Rachel was not so damaged that she should be tossed like garbage in a hole. Buried with indifference and bureaucratic bullshit. Rationalizations about points of diminishing returns. Poor allocation of resources. Black holes.

Fuck that. Rachel was not so damaged as that. And even if she was, fuck anyone who didn't want to waste his or her precious time and energy on black holes and damaged goods, anyway. Fuck them all.

Tam snuggled the child and inhaled the scent of her hair as if it were pure oxygen in a vacuum. Rachel murmured in her sleep, and grabbed a hank of Tam's long hair in her damp little fist.

She thought of Novak, Georg, all the rest. She thought of the prickle on her neck. Reptile brain, warning her she was being stalked.

The resolve burned itself into Tam's mind like a brand.

Just try and take her away from me. Go ahead, try. Watch who dies, and how fast.

Budapest, Hungary

"Are you keeping him under strict surveillance, András? Your men should not take their eyes off him for a second. Vajda is a highly trained secret agent. He can melt into thin air before you know it. Who do you have watching him? When did they last report?"

András sighed, inwardly, folded his massive arms over his barrel chest, and carefully modulated his voice. It would not do to display impatience when mafiya boss Gabor Novak used that fretful, querulous tone. "Bede and Gálas reported to me exactly six minutes ago," he repeated. "He is at the Országos Traumatólogiai Intézet, and he has not moved from the old man's bedside, except to piss, for three straight days. Csobán hacked into the patient database, and it tells us that Imre Daroczy is due to be discharged from the hospital at midday. We can make our move this evening, when they are back at Daroczy's apartment, if you like."

"If I like?" Novak repeated. "If . . . I . . . *like*? What do you mean, if I like?" Novak turned his poisonous green gaze upon his second in command, purplish lips drawing back from long, yellowed teeth like some fanged beast. "You think this is a matter of liking, András? You think this is a fucking *whim*?"

András schooled his face to utter impassivity. "No, boss. Not at all," he soothed. "Of course, we will act as soon as possible, but the Országos is too public a place to abduct them. We must be patient. We must wait until they—"

"Patient? Don't talk to me about patience! He told me she was dead!" Daddy Novak spat the words out. "Georg told me that treacherous snake Tamara Steele choked to death on her own blood the day Kurt was killed. He lied to me! Why did he lie, András? Why?"

The gazes of the other men standing around the table shifted, darted, uncertain where to land. The boss had been dangerously unpredictable since his son's untimely death a few years ago. People died without warning when he used that tone of voice.

The intercom buzzed, and András leaned over and punched it, intensely grateful for the diversion. "Yes?" he barked.

"It is Jakab Lajtos," the sentry said. "Georg Luksch sent him."

"I told Georg to come himself! Not to send one of his useless butt-lickers!" Novak snarled.

The sentry hesitated, nervously. "Should I, ah, tell him to go?"

"No. No. Send him in, send him in," Novak muttered. "I want to talk to him."

Luckless dog, András thought. It was Jakab's shit luck to happen upon the boss in one of his moods. There would be a mess to clean up today. Not that he was complaining. Better Jakab than András. Oh, much, much better.

The door opened, and Jakab paused at the threshhold, sensing mortal danger. His polite smile faltered as his gaze darted from Novak's wild grimace to the stony caution on the faces of the rest of the men. "Ah . . . Luksch sent me to see what you needed," he said warily. "He could not come himself. He is in Odessa, attending to some problems at a munitions plant. There was a problem with the delivery of a load of—"

"Do you see this thing, Jakab? This filthy thing?" Novak stabbed a skeletal finger toward the huge teak table that dominated the room. A golden torque, displayed in a black velvet box, lay upon it.

The sentry shoved Jakab from behind. He stumbled forward into the room. "Ah . . . ah, I, ah—"

"This thing is an insult to my son's memory!" Novak's pointing finger shook with the violence of his emotions. "That woman's existence on this earth is an insult to his memory! And you knew about her, did you not, Jakab? Did you not?"

"No! I know nothing about this!" Jakab protested desperately. "Nothing! I am just a messenger! I was sent to find out what you wanted—"

"I want her blood," Novak hissed. "I want her entrails, spread out upon the ground. That is what I want."

Jakab swallowed repeatedly. He was gray-faced, shaking. Novak reached out, and stroked a finger along the ropes of gold that twined and twisted, snakelike, in an ancient Celtic design. The finials of the crescent were adorned with cabochon rubies. The piece pulsed and glowed in the light from the library lamp, as if it were somehow alive.

Novak pushed one of the rubies on the finial. It came loose, and a tiny blade slid out. "Do you see this? It's a miniature of the dagger that opened my son's throat. It is an exact reproduction of the torque Kurt gave McCloud's woman. My Kurt's foul murder is immortalized in a cheap bauble for a brainless whore!"

Jakab jumped as Novak drove the small blade into the table. It stuck, vibrating. He cleared his throat with a dry, nervous cough.

Novak picked up the card in the black velvet box. No logo, no address, just bold letters.

DEADLY BEAUTY
Wearable Weaponry by Tamara

And below, a cell number. Inactive, of course. Nothing so simple as that.

"A direct message," the boss muttered. "A slap in my face."

In fact, the message was hardly direct. By pure chance had András noticed the torque on the mistress of a business associate at a party in Paris some weeks before. It had caught his eye, since he knew the odd manner of Kurt's death. The woman had demonstrated her torque's special properties when András got her alone, and helpfully shared the name of the broker who had sold it to her lover, but she'd been unwilling to part with the piece when András offered to buy it. Happily, no one noticed that the jewelry was not on her broken body when she was found shortly thereafter, having flung herself from the penthouse terrace.

Drugs, of course. A useless life, a meaningless death. So sad.

The broker had been most forthcoming, with András's knife digging into his carotid artery. He'd provided the business card and a physical description of the torque's designer. A stunningly beautiful, mysterious young woman who could only be Kurt's lying, murderous ex-mistress.

Whom Georg Luksch had sworn was dead. How very strange.

"Help me understand this situation, Jakab." Novak's voice was deceptively gentle. "I spent a fortune to have Georg freed from prison. I spent another fortune to have his face and body put back together. I groomed him to be my successor, to take Kurt's place at my side. I made him rich, powerful. Now I discover, by pure chance, that this filthy whore is alive and flourishing? And that Georg has contracted a PSS agent to locate her? Without informing me?"

"He . . . how did . . . but how do you—"

"How do I know this?" Novak's smile peeled back from long, yellowing teeth. "I have my ways, Jakab. I know everything, sooner or later. I know that it is my old protégé, Vajda, who is charged with the task of looking for her. A good choice. A whore to catch a whore." He wrenched the dagger loose. It left an ugly divot in the gleaming table. "I have been used," he announced. "Lied to. Where is she, Jakab? Where is Steele?"

András braced himself. Lied to, Novak's pet hate. The words "lied to" always ended in a bloodbath.

Jakab reached out an entreating hand. "Boss. I don't know! I swear! They don't tell me these things! And I am sure that Georg did not mean to mislead you. Perhaps this is a misunderstanding. The situation is complex. The woman is—"

Thunk. There was a choked gasp from Jakab. The dagger had pinned his hand to the table. The man's jaw sagged. Blood pooled under his palm.

"Complex, did you say?" Novak's voice had gotten even gentler. "I think it is quite simple, Jakab. Nothing like a knife through the hand to simplify things."

Jakab had begun to shake violently. "But . . . but I cannot . . . I don't—"

"Where?" Novak put his hand on the jeweled finial. "Where is she? Or shall I twist it?"

Jakab gasped, breath hitching. Novak wrenched the blade out. A shriek of agony jerked from Jakab's throat. "Tell me, you useless bag of shit!" the old man rasped. "What has Vajda discovered? Where is the bitch? Tell me! Now!"

But Jakab could no longer answer. Something was very wrong with him, something more serious than a minor puncture wound. His mouth began to froth. He pitched forward, eyes wild, face squashed against the table, blood pouring from both nostrils.

His twitching slowed, gradually ceased, while they all watched, in silence.

Novak blinked, and examined the dagger in his hand with renewed interest. "Poison," he commented. "Interesting."

András stared at the meat that was now his responsibility to remove, with an inward sigh.

"Get rid of this garbage, András," Novak ordered. "Cut off a few identifying pieces and send them to that lying pig, so we all know where we stand. Then get Vajda for me. He had no business working for Georg in the first place. We will remind him of where his real loyalties lie."

"I will take care of it, as soon as Daroczy is discharged from the hospital," András repeated, with grim patience.

But Novak was no longer listening. The boss's eyes burned as he turned the dagger in his hand. "He will bring her to me. And I will use this blade," he mused, his voice almost dreamy. "This very blade, once the poison is removed, of course. It must be slow. She will watch, in the mirror. And I will save her eyes for last."

Georg bucked and heaved grimly against the body of the sex professional who writhed against him on the bed. She was making too much noise. It was spoiling his fantasy.

He was annoyed. He'd thought she'd do so perfectly when he'd seen the photographs of her. The initial effect was striking: the long red hair, the perfect body. She'd had extensive cosmetic surgery done to her face to make her look as much like Tamara Steele as it was possible to look. The surgeons had done a good job.

It was her voice that was the problem. He remembered Tamara's husky alto voice all too well. It made him shiver with raw hunger.

This woman's wailing squawks of feigned appreciation were high-pitched, strident, stupid. They ruined the effect.

It was disappointing. Boring and exhausting, too, but there was no question of stopping, not with three of his men standing over the bed watching him, as was his custom. He could no longer conclude a sexual act without an audience.

Fortunately, Georg had no lack of willing spectators.

He tried to close his ears, picturing Kurt Novak's pale, crazed eyes watching him as he possessed Tamara. Sweat broke out on his forehead. The most erotically intense moments he had ever experienced.

The thought detonated something inside him. He jerked, convulsed, came.

He collapsed for a few panting seconds upon the woman's damp body. He could hear the heavy breathing of the men watching. Her perfume was unpleasantly strong in his nostrils.

He clambered off her body, fastened his pants, buckled his belt. The woman propped herself up on her elbows. He did not look at her, but he saw out of the corner of his eye her miffed expression. Arrogant bitch. Expecting to be praised and petted for doing her job.

One of his men cleared his throat. "Uh, boss?"

"What?" He sat down at the desk and powered up the computer, already putting the experience out of his mind.

"Can we . . . ?"

Georg glanced back at the three men who'd stood slavering over the bed, and then at the growing outrage on the masklike Tamara face superimposed upon the redheaded woman reclining on the bed.

He shrugged. "If you like. I don't want this one again."

She folded herself up defensively. "That wasn't in the contract! There's nothing about taking on four men in my contract!"

"So you'll be paid quadruple," he said indifferently. "In cash. And I can refrain from mentioning this bonus to the agency."

Her red lips pursed and her eyes narrowed, calculating.

Georg turned back to the computer, bored with it, and pulled up the file of digital photos he had collected of Tamara. He clicked through them with dreamy concentration, studying her from every angle. The whimpers, grunts, and muffled laughter that began to emanate from the direction of the bed faded away, and he was alone on the earth with her. No one else existed. Perfect beauty. Beauty, strength, perfect symmetry. The only fit mate for him. She just didn't know it yet. She had no idea of the vast empire he would offer her, the power, the wealth, the luxury.

A voice intruded on his reverie. He turned and found one of his men, Ferenc, holding a waxed cardboard box in his arms. Out of the corner of his eye, he noticed that the woman was now on her knees, rocking vigorously as she serviced two men at once, one with her mouth, the other with her backside. The man holding the box did not appear to notice the pornographic tableau behind him.

That alone was remarkable enough to snap him to full attention.

The man's eyes were frozen wide, his skin greenish gray. There was a greasy sheen of sweat on his forehead.

"What is it?" Georg demanded. "What's in the box?"

"Jakab," Ferenc said hoarsely. "Or . . . some of him."

Georg pushed aside the packing material. A blood-drenched, severed head and hands were wedged inside. Jakab's eyes stared up at him, wide and startled. He looked perplexed at his fate.

It would seem that Novak had discovered Tamara was alive.

Georg grabbed the blood-stiffened hair and lifted out the dead man's head. Ferenc jerked his gaze away, throat working. Soft, Georg thought scornfully. Useless. He dropped the head into the box, and pulled out his phone, waving the man away. "Dispose of it."

The man scurried out, stumbling in his haste. The panting and gurgling from the bed was beginning to annoy him. "Shut the fuck up," he snarled at the writhing knot of limbs. "I'm working."

The heads of his men swiveled. They gave him assorted nervous glances. The head of the woman could not easily turn since she had a penis in her mouth, but her eyes rolled toward him. Her face, distorted by the act of fellatio, no longer looked even remotely like Tamara's.

He turned away, letting it fly out of his mind while he concentrated on this puzzle. The operatives at Prime Security Solutions would never let slip any details about their search for Tamara Steele. The reputation of their organization depended upon it.

Which meant that there was a traitor in Georg's own midst, in contact with Daddy Novak. He stepped out onto the balcony, pulling up the number for Hegel, the PSS agent on the case, as he ran through the roster of his staff, one by one, trying to imagine which one deserved a slow dismemberment.

The man picked up on the first ring. "Yes?"

"There's been a new development," Georg said. "I have discovered that she is in danger. I need her brought to me immediately."

The man hemmed. "Ah, I will get in touch with the operative—"

"Immediately." Georg dropped the phone into his pocket and looked up at the moon. It hung full and bloated on the horizon.

So he was no longer Novak's chosen surrogate son. He did not really mind, he realized. He had developed his own power base by now. He preferred the role of avenging conquerer anyway. It suited his personality better.

He was tired of kissing the old man's mummified ass.

A new era was beginning. His heart thudded with excitement.

He could hardly wait.

Chapter 3

Val shifted in the old wingback chair, restless and agitated after spending three days next to Imre's hospital bed. He'd forgotten how it felt to fidget and tap his feet. He'd been living in a state of cool, floating detachment for so long. Years, in fact.

Twilight was fading, leaching the light out of Imre's shabby study and leaving only dull shades of gray. In the shadows, Imre's lean, seamed face was as unrevealing as an ancient statue, despite the bruises and the swelling from the attack mere days before. He had been discharged only hours ago, against Val's disapproval.

"Stop twitching," Imre said calmly. "You're distracting me."

The elderly man ignored Val's automatic murmured apology and contemplated the chessboard with sphinxlike gravity. No triumph, despite how blatantly he was winning.

But the magic of a challenging game wasn't working on Val. It was strenuous mental work, maintaining a shifting matrix of probabilities, strategies, choices, and consequences, but it was also an excellent buzz.

Imre's gift to him. One of the many. He'd been craving it like a drug, though it was stupid to rely on anything for comfort or refuge.

But there was no buzz, no magic tonight. He could not hold the matrix in his thick head. It kept collapsing in on itself. The heavy, antique chess pieces sat squatly on the board: the white carved of yellowing ivory stolen from African elephants in another century, the black carved of aged, cracked ebony. Inert, revealing nothing, suggesting nothing. No solutions, just a puzzle he was too stupid to solve. Like the puzzle of what to do about Steele and her daughter.

"Knight to king five." Imre's cracked voice dragged Val's attention back to the game just in time to see the old man checkmate him. "Too easy, boy. No sport."

Val studied the carnage on the chessboard, trying to analyze in a glance what error in judgment had brought him to this. He quickly abandoned the effort. Fuck it. It was too hard, he was too tired. Too many stupidities piled on top of one another to count them all.

He scooped up the pieces, and stood, rolling his shoulders as he gazed out the window into this decaying back alley of Józsefváros. He was stiff, from days of sitting.

Technically, he was not supposed to be here. One condition of his employment with PSS had been that he stay away from Budapest. He had violated that order from the start to visit Imre. He had alternative identities, both PSS-sanctioned ones and ones he had obtained secretly for his personal use. He was skilled at disguise. It had been easy.

But the periods of time that passed between those visits had grown longer and longer as the work he did for PSS pushed him farther from himself. He didn't want Imre to know what he did or have the old man examine too closely what he'd turned into because of it. He didn't want to bear Imre's disapproval. What was the point? Imre could not help him find his way. He had done everything he could for Val.

He was reluctant to feel again at all after years of cultivating chilly detachment, but here he was, twitching. Embarrassed at what he had become. Angry for feeling that way. Bracing himself for judgement.

He sensed the old man was quietly waiting for him to talk, but he was no longer accustomed to explaining himself. It had been years. He had lost the knack of speaking the truth, even to one who had a right to hear it.

After all. His stock in trade for his entire adult life had been lies.

"You are distracted," Imre observed carefully. "Agitated."

Val shrugged. "I was worried about you."

"I am fine," Imre said firmly. "I had many tests in the hospital. Bruises, contusions. Nothing serious. You overreacted, Vajda."

Val just looked at him. After days of bullying doctors for details of Imre's cracked ribs and internal bleeding, he was in no mood to be cajoled with bullshit. "Don't call me that," he said. "It's dangerous."

"Yes. It is. You should not come back here at all," Imre scolded. "This city is dangerous for you. I am dangerous for you. You must turn your back on the past."

"Turn my back on you?" Val demanded. "After what happened?"

The old man gazed from his chair, his face unreadable. The ugly bruises were obscured by deep shadow. "If you must," he said quietly.

Anger wrenched him like a cramp. The old bastard cared so little, then. He was promptly shocked at himself. Getting his feelings hurt like a spoiled little child. So much for his cool detachment.

The phone rang. Imre stared at it, puzzled. Two rings, three, four.

"Who would call me at this hour?" he murmured. He reached for the phone. "Yes?" He listened. His sharp eyes glinted in the dimness as he looked at Val. "I'm sorry. There is no Valery Janos here. You must have misdialed."

Val shifted into high alert as Imre listened to whatever the man was saying. "Perhaps you were mistaken in the person you saw entering the building," Imre countered stubbornly. "He is not here."

There was no point in this charade. Val reached for the phone and pried it out of the old man's gnarled fingers. "Who is this?"

"What the fuck are you doing in Budapest, Janos?"

The rasping voice raised the hairs on Val's neck. *Fuck.* Hegel, again. He had been found. "How did you find me here?" Val asked.

"Don't start with me, asshole. You had a job to do. You ran away from it," Hegel said curtly. "The car is waiting outside the door of the building. Come immediately. I need to speak to you. Right now."

"I have other plans for the evening—"

"Shut up and move your ass." Hegel hung up.

Val replaced the phone in its cradle. Hegel could have called the dedicated line on Val's satellite phone more easily. The fact that he had reached Val through Imre's phone was a message. Not a friendly one.

Imre was a dangerous weakness. Val had been aware of that since he was a child. He'd done everything he could to keep the man's existence secret from those who might have a desire to manipulate him.

Everything had evidently not been enough.

"So," Imre said slowly, "you are still with PSS, then?"

"Off and on," Val hedged. "I haven't done anything for them for almost a year. There were disagreements about my last assignment. I thought they were done with me. Then I was called for one more job. I interrupted it to come here when I heard about what happened to you. They aren't pleased."

"It would seem not." Imre's voice was uncharacteristically hard. "So you are being called to heel, Vajda? Like a good hound?"

Val swallowed the anger, with effort. He forced himself to take the three steps back. There was no point in getting his fur ruffled over the flat truth. "Don't call me Vajda," he said stiffly.

Imre's eyebrow twitched upward. "It is hard for a tired old man to change the habits of a lifetime," he complained.

What horseshit. Even at eighty, Imre's mind was as flexible as a circus contortionist. "Try to remember," he said. "Vajda is dead. I am Valery."

"Are you indeed?" the old man murmured. "And who is this Valery? Do you even know, boy?"

His anger flashed up again, sharper and incandescent. He clamped down on it grimly. "As well as anyone," he snapped.

"I think not," Imre went on, relentless. "I thought that PSS would be better than Novak, but they are not. Not for you. Novak may have stolen your life and your future, but PSS took away your whole self."

Very abruptly, Val was all too aware of why he had come back to Budapest so seldom in recent years. Imre's tendency to speak the raw, unpalatable truth had always been annoying.

"I'll go into hiding," he said on impulse. "Fuck them all. It's the only way to be rid of them."

Imre blinked and looked politely doubtful. "You told me yourself how vast PSS's resources are. It would be so easy?"

"Easy, no. Possible, yes," Val said. "Expensive, yes, but that is no problem. I have money coming out my ass now."

Imre looked pained. "Please, Vajda. And your business?"

Val hesitated. In point of fact, it would hurt to give up Capriccio Consulting. The business had come into existence years ago as a cover while he wormed his way into the inner circle of a drug smuggling ring, but since then, and almost by accident, it had evolved into a profitable legitimate enterprise that he truly enjoyed. Fulfilling whims. Finding and obtaining objects, treasures, information. He was good at it.

He was secretly proud of himself for having created something that functioned so well; something that was not a scam, cover, or lie. His business did what it promised to do, with an excellent success rate. God, how he liked that. The simplicity of it, the dignity. Was it so much to ask to mind his business, satisfy his clients, make his money?

But like everything else, it was dangerous to be attached.

He let out a long breath and tried to take the three steps back, but he didn't feel the click of disengagement, the floating feeling.

"I'll find something else to do," he said, after a moment. "I'll buy you a new passport. Come with me. We'll go someplace hot. A desert would be good for your arthritis. I could keep a better eye on you. We could play chess every night."

But Imre was already shaking his head. "This is my home," he said. "Near Ilona and little Tina."

Stubborn old sentimentalist. Trotting out his wife, dead thirty years, and his daughter who had died in infancy, buried together at the cemetery. Val rubbed his face with a groan. "For two mossy graves, you stay in this moldering dump? I can look after you if you're close to me!"

"You already look after me." Imre's voice was tranquil. "I will stay here. And I will die here. It's all right to die, Vajda."

"Spare me the cloying platitudes," Val snarled. "This isn't one of your fucking philosophy lessons."

Imre regarded him for a moment, his thin shoulders stiff. "Calm yourself, please," he said haughtily. "I will make us a pot of tea. Or should I bother? Do you have to scurry off to lick your handler's feet?"

Val let out a long, slow breath before he allowed himself to reply.

"I'll make the goddamn tea," he said before Imre could rise. He needed a moment for his self-control. And he didn't want to watch Imre's pained, arthritic shuffle toward the kitchen.

Hegel would be furious to be kept waiting. Val did not care.

The kitchen was dirty. The dishes in the sink stank. He made a note to scold the agency he paid to send someone to cook and clean for Imre. Lazy cow. It would never occur to Imre, the perfect gentleman with his head in the clouds, to scold the stupid woman for slacking off.

Perhaps she'd been too upset by finding Imre in such a terrible state, but even so. This was accumulated weeks of mess, not days.

He put the kettle on, dumped some cookies onto a plate. The chipped, stained porcelain teapot unleashed a flood of memories.

The first time he'd seen that teapot, or sat at that table was twenty-two years ago. He'd been Vajda then, a tough, slit-eyed twelve-year-old, small for his age, trolling the streets for a trick, a pocket to pick, any way to make his quota for that prick Kustler, and avoid the beating or cutting or cigarette burns that were his punishment if he didn't. He'd seen the man, shabby clothes flapping on his thin body, staring from across the street. He had an intense look in his deep-set eyes, as if he recognized the boy from somewhere.

Vajda thought he knew what that look meant, so he sauntered over and tried to bum a cigarette. The man had told him sternly that he was too young to smoke, which made Vajda practically choke laughing.

Then the man had invited him up to his apartment, which was a stroke of luck, as it was beginning to snow. Kustler had taken his coat that morning. Vajda hadn't had a chance to steal a replacement yet.

The apartment had seemed luxurious and rich to him at the time, lined with books, crowded with antique furniture. He'd expected the man to open his pants, tell him to undress. Imre had not done so. He'd just summoned the boy into the kitchen and poured him cup after cup of sweet, milky tea while he soaked bread in egg and fried it in butter. The first food Vajda had eaten that day, perhaps longer. Delicious.

It had disoriented him. He'd told Imre angrily that if he wanted tail, get the fuck on with it, because he had places to go, things to do.

Imre had beckoned him into the parlor, lit the lamp, sat him down and proceeded to teach him the rudiments of chess. The place was so warm. The snow outside so cold. It was strange. He had stayed.

When he started to nod off, the man gave him a blanket, and let him stretch out on the divan. He'd slept like the dead, and wakened in the morning, confused and scared. Imre sat across from him, staring at him, and Vajda thought then, with a rush of bitterness, *Here's where it starts. He's just like all the others. He just needs a lot of lead-in time.*

But Imre had only dug some money out of his pocket, more or less what Vajda might have earned in a good night. "Up with you," he said. "You may use the bathroom. There is milk and bread in the kitchen, and then you must go. My first music student will arrive shortly."

Vajda stared at the money in his hand. "Why . . . ?"

"I don't want you to suffer when you must account for your time," Imre said, matter-of-factly. "I enjoyed your company."

Vajda had pocketed the money, speechless. He inhaled every crumb of food Imre had put on the table and left the place with his belly sloshing with hot milk, pockets bulging with tea biscuits. A warm, worn jacket on his back, sleeves rolled up four times to find his hands.

He'd gone back another wet, cold night. Crept up to the fourth floor, listened outside the door to Imre playing his grand piano while he summoned the courage to knock. Imre had let him in again, fed him again, played Bach inventions for him. He offered the divan, although this time he insisted that the boy take a bath and change into Imre's own threadbare pajamas. The boy had left a seething nest of fleas and lice the last time he had slept there.

Imre had regretfully explained that he enjoyed the company, but did not have the funds to finance every visit. So Vajda found his own ways to budget time, and crept to his odd haven whenever he dared.

He had barely been able to read, but Imre would have none of that. He was a demanding teacher. History, philosophy, mathematics, languages, Val sucked it all up like a hungry sponge. Besides Hungarian, he already spoke the Romanian of his infancy, and the gutter Italian that he'd learned from Giulietta, his mother's roommate. Imre taught him more. English, French, Russian. He even tried to teach the boy to play piano, but after some effort, he had to concede that Vajda had no musical talent at all.

As Val grew bigger and vicious enough to intimidate in his own right, when he'd been promoted from picking pockets and selling tail and smuggled cigarettes to heroin dealing, he returned the favor the only way he could—by making it known on the street that anyone who bothered Imre would be gutted like a fish.

Fucking idiot that he'd been. He should have kept his mouth shut.

"Good God, Vajda! Wake up!"

Imre's indignant voice jerked Val out of his reverie. "Huh?"

He turned to see the old man scowling from the kitchen door, leaning heavily on his cane. "That kettle's been wailing like a cat in heat for five minutes!" Imre shouted over the din. "Are you drugged? That would explain your chess game, at least!"

"*Ah, cazzo.*" Val jerked the shrieking kettle off the gas flame.

The familiar ritual of brewing and drinking tea restored a cautious equilibrium between them, but the long silences made Val uneasy.

Finally Imre set down his cup with a decisive click and threaded the tips of his swollen, arthritic fingers together. "Vajda."

The heavy, preaching way that he pronounced the name made Val brace himself. "Don't call me that," he repeated grimly. "I told you."

Imre waved his hand, impatient. "When I die, you must—"

"You're not going to die," Val cut in.

"Don't be childish," Imre said sternly. "Let me finish. When I die, do not expose yourself again to come here and bury me. Mourn my death in any way you like—from a distance. I will be safe and happy with Ilona and Tina. Swear it, Vajda."

Val sprang to his feet, rattling the teacups on the cluttered table, inexplicably furious. "No," he said. "I swear nothing, to anyone."

Imre stared at him. His grim mouth was swollen and scabbed at the corner from the split, battered lip his attackers had given him.

Val stalked into the foyer, shrugged on his coat, seething. Imre did not come out of the kitchen to bid him good-bye. It was just as well. There was nothing more to be said, and if Val spoke at all, he would start shouting. He ran down four flights of steps and out into the frigid night air. Snow was falling thickly, just like the night he'd met Imre.

Images rushed unpleasantly back when he saw the black BMW idling on the curb, the driver an anomymous dark shadow. The lock popped as he approached. His stomach clenched. For a horrible half-second, he was eleven years old again, shivering on the curb.

No choice but to get in, and go wherever the car took him.

He hesitated. *Detach*. He was not that helpless boy anymore.

He spat into the gutter, yanked open the back door and got in. He was big, strong. He wore fine clothes, had an expensive haircut, good shoes, a cashmere coat, money in his pocket and far more in the bank. He'd forgone his guns tonight because they distressed Imre, but he had the knives. He had years of fight training. Eyes in the back of his head.

No, he was far from defenseless. Few people on earth were better equipped for that. And still, getting into that fucking car felt like climbing into a fucking crocodile's mouth.

Fortunately, that phase of his life hadn't lasted long. He got his growth fast, and became too big, too scary looking for Kustler's stable. But they found other uses for him soon enough, on the heroin supply chain.

He hated dealing drugs, with his mother's track marks and hollow eyes haunting him. He had found her body one day when he was eleven years old, sprawled on the bathroom floor. Choked by her own vomit.

That was the same day that fuckhead Kustler, his mother's pimp, had come by, looked him over and decided that all was not lost.

Vajda was unfortunately dark-complected, but pretty even so. Kustler had decided that the son would do nicely to take over his mother's job.

He flinched from the memory of that day.

Yes, he hated drugs. But one did not say no to Daddy Novak, or to anyone who answered to him. Not if one liked staying alive.

Though "like" was perhaps the wrong word. He had clung to life out of spite. Staying alive was a fuck-you to the world. Anger kept him alive. Imre had been the only one to show him something beyond it.

It was ironic how the best way to protect Imre would be to not care about him at all. Whatever Val dared to care about was liable to end up dead on the bathroom floor. The more he cared, the higher the probability. He wished he could detach completely. Just float away.

The snow fell thickly now, flakes fluttering through the air, obscuring the cityscape until it was a blank, swirling no-man's-land. Val stared out the car window, trying to orient himself with childhood landmarks. Each one he identified sparked bleak memories.

As he grew older, without really meaning to, he'd come to the attention of Gabor Novak, the big boss, having distinguished himself as a bright young man with unusual language skills and an aptitude for computers. Useful as Novak's business expanded and went global. Soon he was exiled from Budapest and sent off to Novak's country palace on the Danube, far from the distractions of the city, to work on encryption software, Internet marketing, front company documentation, etc. The work was endless. But at least it was not bloody.

On the surface anyway. There was always blood at some level.

Gabor Novak was formerly from Ukraina. He had married a Hungarian woman, taken her name and nationality, and proceeded to set up illicit businesses in cities all over eastern Europe: Budapest, Riga, Prague. Before he murdered her, or so the legend went.

Imre tried to persuade him to break free of Novak's organization, but Val knew in his bones what Imre would not understand—how far men like Kustler would go to protect their territory. Imre would have had his balls cut off and his throat slit for interfering, if he was lucky. If not, there were things that lasted much longer. Val had seen them with his own eyes, unfortunately. He wished he had not.

No, there was no way out. Until he found PSS and Hegel. Or rather, they found him, eleven years ago, after the orders had come down from Daddy Novak to groom Vajda for arms deals. Vajda's English was quite good, thanks to Imre. Useful for doing business in West Africa. Sierra Leone, to be exact. His first gunrunning assignment.

The car stopped outside a small café in Belváros. The driver sat without turning or speaking. Val got out of the car and went in.

He found Hegel in a corner, tucking away a large steak tartare, and a heaping plateful of spicy goulash and potato croquettes. He gave Val an unfriendly look as the younger man approached.

Hegel was not a handsome man. He was grizzled, thick and square. His coarse, pitted face was heavy-jowled and scowling.

"You're late," he growled, wiping his mouth.

Val sat down without explanation or apology, and Hegel ignored him as he shoveled food into his face.

Hegel was an American ex–Special Forces helicopter pilot, Vietnam vet, and covert operative with Prime Security Solutions since its inception. Val had met him eleven years ago in Ouagadougou when he arrived with thirty tons of small arms and ammo, antitank weapons, surface-to-air missiles, RPG tubes, and warheads from a Ukrainian arms manufacturer, destined for the rebels of the Revolutionary United Front.

He was to trade them for a fortune in smuggled diamonds.

A plane waiting for them began to discreetly ferry the weapons to Monrovia, where the final transaction would take place.

Hegel was one of the helicopter pilots who flew the weapons into the rebel strongholds in the jungle. Val discovered afterward that he had been working undercover, investigating sources of arms that flowed to the rebels. Hegel had invited him to go on a weapons run, and out of curiosity and boredom, Val had gone along. They stopped because of mechanical difficulties in Moidu, a small town in the jungle.

By chance, they were there when rebels attacked the town.

It was a massacre. The rebel soldiers were children and teenagers themselves, crazed out of their minds on palm wine and cocaine, armed with the assault rifles and rocket launchers he had just sold to them. They sliced, hacked, and gunned down everything they saw.

Val had seen a great deal of violence in his life, but when he saw the young pregnant girl ripped apart before his eyes by two young thugs with machetes, something tipped inside him. He didn't remember the dynamics of the fight, how it went or how it ended. It was just a blur of noise, blood. Hegel had dragged him out of it. Alive, amazingly.

He'd awakened in a hospital bed in a fog of agonizing pain and saw Hegel beside him. The man's metallic gray eyes were looking him over. Coldly, appraisingly. As if considering his purchase.

Hegel told him about Prime Security Solutions, a private mercenary army equipped with armored fighting vehicles, gunships, fighter planes, all manner of weaponry. It provided its clients with military training, VIP protection, airline transport, offshore financial management services, intelligence, infrared photo recon, satellite imagery. PSS could deploy a battalion-strength force anywhere in the world in hours. It was well equipped, sleek, powerful. And it paid well.

Hegel made him an offer. Vajda could be reborn with a new name, a new life—in exchange for service as a covert operative.

Vajda explained that leaving Gabor Novak's employ was more complicated than it seemed, but Hegel just shrugged. Money would solve that problem, and Vajda was well worth the severance fee Novak would charge them. It would all be taken care of—if Val said yes.

At the time, it was an attractive alternative to his former servitude. He soon realized that there was no difference that mattered. PSS's agenda was brutally simple: to help their wealthy, powerful clients amass more wealth and power by means of pulling strings all over the world. Openly or secretly. Legally or not. To that end, PSS wanted a killing machine. Killing was killing, whoever you did it for.

So it was that he had become Valery Janos, Italian citizen, resident of Rome, born in Italy of Hungarian parents. The first of many aliases and his best developed innocuous civilian identity.

It was his favorite identity. On paper and on the Internet, Val Janos lived the life he secretly longed for. A hardworking businessman who lived quietly in his lavish apartment on Piazza Navona in Rome.

He loved his adopted country and city. He had absorbed his adopted language as if he had been born to it. He lived in it, thought in it, dreamed in it even, far more so than in the Hungarian he had learned at the age of six when his mother brought him to Budapest or the Romanian he'd been born to. He liked being Val Janos, the perfect, cultured gentleman who minded his business, and bothered no one—unless one counted his disgruntled ex-lovers, of course. The Val Janos persona was a voracious ladies' man, who bored easily.

But even after investing a fortune in his training, even though he was one of their best operatives, PSS never let him forget what he owed them. He was a tool, like a grenade, bomb, gun—but ultimately, he was just mafiya scum to them, to be kept under careful control.

Vajda was still on the street, just with a more powerful pimp.

Hegel belched and wiped his face on the checkered napkin. "What the fuck are you doing in Budapest?"

"Why even ask?" Val said. "You already know everything."

Hegel grunted. "I thought you were more professional than this. Although your performance on that last operation gave me doubts."

Val imitated Imre's air of impenetrable calm.

"Tight-assed bastard," Hegel muttered. He grabbed a shot glass, sloshed a generous amount of palinka into it, and shoved it across the table at Val. "Relax, for fuck's sake. You're giving me gas."

Val made no move to taste the liquor. Hegel grabbed the glass and downed the shot himself in one noisy gulp. "If I meant to kill you, I wouldn't do it in a restaurant," he announced. "And poison's not my style. Woman's weapon. I don't do chick tricks."

"You have no style. You do whatever is expedient. It's the first thing you ever taught me," Val said. He reached for the shot glass, sniffed it, and set it down, untasted.

Hegel glugged more palinka into his glass. "You want to know a secret, Janos?"

"I'm not sure," Val said. "Do I?"

"You were supposed to die that day, eleven years back, in Sierra Leone. Did you know that?"

"Really." His response was emotionless. He was feeding data into the matrix, observing from within a core of utter silence. Waiting until he knew where Hegel was going with it. It was no surprise, in any case.

"We were monitoring the arms suppliers to all of the African conflicts. It was concluded that you were dangerous, young as you were. Better to kill the poisonous snake right out of the egg, right?"

"I see," Val said.

Hegel shook a cigarette out. "Then I saw you fight in Moidu. You were a fucking maniac, even without any formal training. Natural talent, languages, and brains. All the makings of a brilliant operative. I decided to take a huge risk. For you."

"I'm touched," Val said coolly.

Hegel lit his cigarette and took a drag. "That day could have gone one of two ways. Either I held your nose shut, or I offered you a job."

He gazed at Val, breathing out a long stream of smoke.

Val stared back, expressionless. What did the man expect? Gratitude for not killing him? He'd spat blood for PSS for years.

Hegel's lips pursed around his cigarette. "I'm starting to regret that decision."

"I am devastated," Val murmured.

"Don't mouth off to me. What happened in Moidu was damn lucky." He grunted. "For you, anyway."

Val was not sure that his life over the past eleven years was that much more desirable than a bloody but mercifully quick death.

Hegel made an impatient sound. "Get your ass back to work, Janos. You made me look like shit, going incommunicado for three days. Luksch is riding my ass. He wants that woman now."

"Sorry," Val said, unrepentant.

"This is your last chance to redeem yourself for that Fuentes disaster," Hegel went on. "Do not fuck this up."

"That op went by the book," Val argued wearily. "Every member of the Fuentes cartel was dead at the end of the day. What's to criticize?"

"Emilia Fuentes," Hegel snarled. "Don't play dumb with me."

Val saw the girl in his mind's eye. Puppy fat, school uniform, eyes huge behind thick glasses. In shock. Spattered with her parents' blood.

"She was eleven," he said tightly.

"Yes, and she was the daughter of Francisco Fuentes, and she saw everything. You knew she had to die. You fucking *knew* it."

"I don't . . . do . . . children." The words dropped out of him, heavy and clanking and cold. And so fucking futile.

"You can't afford a code of conduct," Hegel hissed. "We own your ass, Janos. We tell you what to do with it. Who to kill, who to kiss, who to fuck. And I don't appreciate being forced to clean up your shit."

"Is that what you call that car accident?" Val retorted. "The one that killed her grandmother and her two cousins and her pregnant aunt, too? That is what you call 'cleaning up my shit?' You hack."

Hegel's eyes narrowed to puffy slits. "That was damage control. And you can chalk the grandmother, the aunt, and the other kids up to your own incompetence, since you didn't have the stomach to do your job. God knows who she talked to in that forty-eight hours—"

"She couldn't talk," Val said, his voice hard. "She was catatonic."

"Shut up. Your sulking has been remarked upon, Janos. Your usefulness has been put seriously into question. Understand?"

Val poured some palinka into the glass and took a reckless swallow. "I'm bored with the threats. What puzzles me is why you haven't killed me yet. Do it, if you can. Since retirement doesn't appear to be an option, death is starting to look very restful."

Their eyes locked. Seconds ticked by. Val saw death in the other man's eyes. He smiled at it with all his teeth. Unintimidated.

"You owe us," Hegel grated. "You owe us your fucking life."

Val shrugged. "I've paid and paid. Enough."

Hegel rose to his feet. "All right, then. Time for the big guns, old friend. You might be hard to kill, but your shriveled old grandpa is not."

Something froze inside him. Hegel sensed it and smiled. *Fuck*.

Hegel peeled bills out of his pocket, and tucked them under his plate, grinning. "Never knew you had a sentimental side. Dangerous to your health. Like principles. Ditch them if you want to survive."

"Fuck off." Val's voice was strangled.

Hegel chuckled, genial now that he had won. "Aw, don't take it so hard. Consider this. If you'd followed instructions and stayed away from Budapest, you wouldn't be in this position right now. There's a flight for London that leaves in three hours, with a tight connection back to Seattle. Be on it. I want that uppity bitch fucking Georg's perverted little brains out within forty-eight hours. If you have to stick pins under the baby's fingernails to make her do it, that's your problem."

Val stared after Hegel's broad, blocky back as he stumped out of the restaurant. He was unable to move for several minutes.

Finally, he lurched to his feet and left the place. He turned his face up to the sky. Snow brushed his face, caught in his hair. The car was gone, of course. There were no taxis to be seen anywhere. Snow was piling up. Cars were crawling, skidding in the slush.

He tried to think it through on the long, cold walk back to József-város. He and Imre were leaving the country tonight, if he had to club the old man over the head and carry him over his shoulder.

And when they were safe, he just might discreetly contact Tamara Steele and warn her about whoever Hegel might send next. Why not?

It was strange. He had never even physically met the woman, but he had begun to feel almost responsible for her. And her child.

Then his neck began to crawl, as he approached his rented car. His stomach sank. He looked around himself, wishing he'd called a cab.

A mistake. His last mistake. A culmination of an infinite series of mistakes, false moves, errors in judgment that stretched back over generations. To his stupid mother, who should have stayed with the boring pig farmer from the country she'd married after she got pregnant with Val. Who should have been grateful to live a life of hard-working respectability in Romania rather than coming to the big city with nothing but her beauty and her young son, to meet men, drugs, ruin. And her son's ruin.

That and other irrelevant details flashed through his mind as the flickering shadows converged upon him in the deserted street. He pulled his knife. He should have brought a gun. Another mistake, he thought.

Time to stop thinking. He spun to meet them, staying in constant twirling motion as they came at him. Four men. Five. More.

Lunge, spin, duck, kick. The heel of his boot crunched through the bridge of someone's nose. Blood spattered the dirty snow. A high parry blocked a blade that slashed through the thick wool of his sleeve. He lunged low, a stabbing blow, blade punching through cloth, piercing flesh, grating on bone. He saw blue eyes widen, stringy blond hair swirl and flap as the man spiraled back, shrieking. Val lost his center of balance as he followed through on the blow, lunging too far forward to jerk back and evade the blackjack that whipped down—

An explosion, all white, all black, and pain blotted out everything.

Chapter
4

Val had been drawing reluctantly nearer to consciousness for a pain-blurred eternity. The bucket of ice water clinched the job. He gasped, choked. The realization was a hammer blow. He tried a slit-eyed peek, gasped at the searing pain in his head.

There was no need to see. He knew the nightmare smell of the place. Bleach, disinfectant, humidity, mold. Beneath all that, a deathlier smell. Old blood, shit, worse. Novak's secret torture chamber. Designated for executions, interrogations. No need for luxury here, just privacy, soundproof walls, and a drain in the floor for easy clean-up.

His past had caught up with him altogether. Its fanged jaws clamped down, crunching his bones.

He braced himself against the pain and nausea, and forced himself to look up at the blazing fluorescent lights. Eight men stared down at him. Seven held guns. All were pointed at him.

It had been eleven years since he had seen Daddy Novak. He'd been hideous then. He was a death's head now: bulging eyes, jaundiced skin, long teeth. An old, pitted skull dipped in yellow wax.

Novak dug an ungentle toe in Val's kidney. He flinched. Someone had already found the place and given it a thorough pounding.

"Wake up, fool," Novak said. "We have business to conduct."

Val ran a quick damage assessment as he rose carefully to his feet.

A couple of teeth loose. Ribs cracked but probably not broken. A knot on his temple, sticky with blood. Hot red pain pulsing in his head with every heartbeat. Bruises, a shallow slash across his forearm, clotted and black, oozing fresh blood through the white sleeve.

Not so bad. He'd taken much worse on other occasions. They hadn't meant to hurt him, just subdue him.

He looked around. He recognized András from the old days. That hulking, beady-eyed sadist had been Novak's main man for years. Three more he remembered from the old guard, the rest were fresh blood. The blue-eyed blond man he had stabbed was not there. Dead, perhaps, or close to it. Several were marked. By him, he surmised, glancing around at the crushed noses, the split lips, the cold, murderous eyes.

New enemies. God. As if he needed more of them.

His eyes flicked back to Novak. He coughed to clear his throat and tasted blood. "This drama was not necessary," he said. "You could have e-mailed or called."

Novak smiled. "You would have ignored me, as you have done for eleven years. Now that you have risen so high in the world, you have forgotten your old friends, no? And besides, important business is best conducted in person."

Dread settled deep inside him, heavy and greasy and cold. "We have no business," he said. "I work for another organization."

Novak steepled his skeletal fingers, smiling thinly. "Yes, of course. PSS bought you from me for a tidy sum, but I always suspected that I accepted too low a price for you. But this is special. I have a business proposition that you might find interesting."

"I'm out of this business," he repeated.

"Yes, yes. We know the success story. Vajda, prostitute, drug dealer, and gunrunner, who repented his wicked ways and now conducts a glamorous double life—covert operative by night, pampered entrepreneur and gigolo playboy by day. I follow your cover career on the Internet, you see. Very inspiring. Makes the boys weep with envy, particularly all the women you fuck. Bad for discipline, Vajda."

"I do not want to—"

"What you want does not interest me." Novak's voice cut

through his. "You've forgotten your manners. Must I re-educate you?"

Val shut his eyes against the light, the pain, and Novak's probing gaze. The man's hot, foul breath was inches from Val's face, like gas escaping from a decomposing corpse.

Val hardened his belly to iron to control his gorge. He'd endured worse. In fact, he would endure worse tonight. Far worse, before this was all over. No way out. He tried to wrap his mind around it.

He swallowed. "What do you want?"

Novak seized Val's shoulder, spun him around, and shoved him, stumbling, against a long, dented metal table. A file lay open upon it, a sheaf of photographs fanned out across it. "Her," he said.

Val stared at the photos. They were of Tamara Steele. The one on top showed her in a bikini, on the arm of a hairy middle-aged man on the deck of a yacht. She was laughing, holding a champagne flute. Blond hair swirled out in the wind like a pale flag.

The next was a closeup. She wore a silvery evening gown. Her hair was red, coiled close against her head. She was looking over her shapely shoulder, listening to a man whisper in her ear. He recognized the blond, tight-lipped, pale-eyed young man. Novak's son, Kurt. Her crimson lips curved in a secret smile. Jeweled earrings dangled low. Her huge eyes looked past the man, almost directly into the camera.

In another, she was getting into a black Jaguar, beaded with rain. The place looked like Paris. Dark hair, long against her white raincoat.

The next was unlike the others. It was black and white, shot by a long-range camera. She was oddly unglamorous, wearing a simple black dress, rendered elegant only by the intrinsic grace of her body. Her hair was drawn back in a severe roll. Her face was free of makeup. Pale, stark, and sad. People milled around her, but she did not notice them.

She was leaning over to drop a bouquet of small wild daisies and lavender in front of a bronze plaque on a big marble slab. He turned it over. The photo was date stamped. Five years ago.

He reached out, rifled through the rest. No pictures of her with

Rachel. All of them must be from the Kurt era, four years ago or longer.

Perhaps Novak didn't know about the child yet. He refused to let himself hope for that much grace. "Who is she?" he asked.

Novak backhanded him with his fist on the temple. The hard blow knocked Val against the table. Bloody spittle flew from his mouth, and spattered the silver evening dress photo. His head spun, his vision blurred. The old man was much stronger than he looked.

"Don't even try," the boss hissed. "I know that you are the one investigating her. That you know where she is."

He pushed the pain aside, forced himself to concentrate. *Three steps back.* "Why do you care?" he asked.

"She was Kurt's last mistress. The whore who delivered my only son up to his death."

"Ah." He kept his voice neutral. "So you want her dead then?"

"Nothing so quick. I want her chained to a table. I want to teach her what happens to a lying bitch who betrays my son."

He let out a long breath. "And what do I have to do with this?"

Novak smiled. "You will bring her to me, Vajda. I know that you are looking for her, for PSS and Georg Luksch. But you will not bring her to Georg. You will bring her to me. Simple."

The prospect of pain was getting more and more imminent. Val's knees felt watery at the prospect. Chilly detachment only went so far when it came to torture. He closed his eyes. "I cannot—"

"Oh, but you can." Novak's voice oozed insinuation. "With your looks, your charm, your pretty body. Your respectable identity as a rich Roman business consultant. Your reputation as a gigolo and bon vivant. Any contract killer could blow her head off from a distance, but that does not satisfy me. I want her seduced. I want you to gain her trust. I want her to fall in love with you. I want her betrayed, turned inside out, as she did to Kurt. One pretty, lying whore to catch another."

Val kept his face carefully blank. "Gain the trust of an assassin?" He paused. "A difficult proposition."

"I did not say it would be easy. That's why I am seeking out such rare bait for my trap, no?" Novak snagged the file with a thick, yellowed fingernail, and dragged it toward himself. "Everything we know about her is in these files. Her origins are obscure. She burst on the scene in 1997 on the arm of Sheikh Nadir." Novak stabbed the yacht photo with his nail. "Said to be skilled with drugs and poisons, excellent with weapons, trained in hand-to-hand combat. Famous for bank, computer and credit card fraud. Skilled sexually, when she is not plotting her lover's death, of course. She uses a dozen aliases that we know of, and certainly more that we do not. And now we have this." He flipped open a jewelry case that lay on the table. "She designs jewelry."

Val stared at the torque. It glowed against the black velvet.

"Interesting," he murmured.

Novak pushed a red stone on the finial, and the piece slid out, revealing a small dagger. "This was poisoned. It was found on the neck of one of Vassily's women in Paris."

"Does she know who the—"

"No, she does not. The woman is dead," Novak snarled.

Val sighed. Dealing with madmen was exhausting. It was difficult to pry useful intelligence out of a corpse, but explain that to a man like Novak. The lack of simple logic made his brain ache.

"That is unfortunate," he said through gritted teeth.

Novak held up the business card. "It is a reproduction of an ancient Celtic relic that my son gave to a woman in the Seattle area, an antiquities expert. Erin Riggs and her husband were also involved in Kurt's death. They will pay for their share, too, when they least expect it. But first, I deal with this treacherous slut."

Val peered at the card in the old man's shaking yellow claw.

Deadly Beauty. He recognized the name. He had moved some of those pieces before. They were very popular with many of his clients. Clever wearable weaponry with exquisite design and workmanship. They commanded handsome prices, and the mysterious anonymity of the artisan was part of their allure. He had not known that his target was the creator of Deadly Beauty. Interesting.

"Why haven't you taken her before?" he asked.

"I was told that she was dead," Novak hissed. "I was lied to."

Val hesitated. "I have a previous commitment."

"You wound me, Vajda. But I have the perfect motivation." Novak's smile widened. "Bring the man."

Val went immobile, like a man regarding a snake that was poised to strike. Two of Novak's men left. Minutes ticked by. The door burst open, and Novak's men came back in.

Imre dangled between them. He looked terribly small and fragile. He had been beaten again. One of the lenses of his spectacles had been shattered. His head dangled, blood streaming down his chin.

The world receded to an unimaginable distance, leaving Val suspended in a vacuum. No air to breathe. No place to stand.

Imre lifted his head and looked at Val, breathing heavily. His eyes watered, but they were calm. One was swollen almost shut. New cuts and bruises were superimposed over the old.

"You thought we did not know about your pet?" Novak's voice was a crooning taunt. "Your favorite client? You think no one wondered who taught you English, French, fucking existentialist philosophy? Cretin. I kept him aside for years for just such a moment, Vajda."

Yes. He was a cretin, for not moving Imre closer to him. Criminally stupid, for not guarding his weak spot with more care.

"You thought you were too good to serve me?" Novak said. "You are a whining dog begging for scraps, Vajda. And this old pervert gave you scraps, did he not? When he was not buggering you?"

Novak made a sharp gesture. One of the men holding Imre elbowed him viciously in the face. Fresh blood spattered onto Imre's white shirt, joining the dried spots.

Valery lunged toward them. Several guns swung up, trained on him. Someone wrenched his arms back violently and slammed a metal pipe across his throat. He barely felt it.

He stared at Imre, shaking. Unable to speak, to think.

"So." Novak caressed Val's chin with a clawlike hand in a hideous parody of tenderness. "I hope, for your old friend's sake, that you are not going to tell me you are incapable of undertaking this."

Blood was filling his mouth again, but Valery could not swallow. The pressure across his throat was strangling him. His ears roared.

"No," he choked out hoarsely. "I am not saying that."

"Good." Novak made a gesture to the men holding Val. The pressure on his throat eased. His arm was released.

"And now, a demonstration of my resolve," Novak said briskly. "We will remove a piece of your friend—a small piece. A finger, an ear, so we all know where we stand. Keep the piece if you are feeling sentimental. Did I hear your friend plays the piano? A teacher at the conservatory? Once a concert pianist? Charming. A finger, then."

"No," Val broke in. "Do not touch him. Or it's no deal."

"You do not set the terms of this deal." Novak's smile stretched out over his long, discolored teeth. "I set them. All of them. You have forgotten the rules, my boy. A few of his fingers should remind you."

Val's mind raced desperately like a rat in an electrified maze. He groped in his shirt pocket with his hand, felt a small, smooth cylinder.

He yanked it out, with a flourish. "The rules just changed."

The snickering and muttering abruptly stopped. All eyes went to the ampoule in Val's hand.

"And what is that?" Novak asked.

"Poison gas," Val said. "If I break this, everyone in this room dies before they can reach the door."

Novak chewed the inside of his sunken cheek. He shot a look at András. "Whose responsibility was it to search this man before he was brought into my presence?"

One of the younger men's eyes went wide. He began to back away.

András lifted his gun and shot the man in the face. He hit the wall and slid to the floor, the swath of gore vivid against white cement blocks. Imre made a choked sound. He sagged between his two captors.

"Everyone dies, including yourself?" Novak's tone was light. "And your friend?"

"Of course," Val said. "It's worth it to me. I dislike being bullied. You and I can continue this conversation in hell."

Novak chuckled softly. "Do you always carry poison gas on your person? What an odd accessory."

Valery's eyes locked on Novak's. "Life is so uncertain," he said. "Death is much more reliable."

The chuckles turned to wheezy gasps of laughter. "Ah, Vajda, I have missed you since I sold you on the auction block to those PSS dogs all those years ago," Novak said, wiping his mouth. "So. Tell me. What do you hope to accomplish with your poison gas?"

"We talk terms," Val said. "My terms."

"And they are?" Novak's voice had a humoring tone.

"The kill fee, to start. Five hundred thousand euro, expenses excluded."

There were assorted snorts and snickers from the men assembled. Novak looked amused. "You think well of yourself, Valery. But why a kill fee? It is not necessary to kill her. I will take care of that personally."

"Bringing her to you alive is more difficult than a straight kill," Val said. "I require no interference, no backup team. Live webcam conversations with him upon request." He gestured toward Imre. "As well as your solemn word before witnesses that he will not be harmed."

Novak's pale, poisonous gaze narrowed. Val kept his face impassive. His heart thundered.

This was a wild gamble. Novak had a pathological hatred of being lied to. There were whispers about what he had done to his wife years ago to punish her for lying to him. It was said he'd cut off his own son's finger when he was a child as punishment for lying about some trivial childhood sin. The underlying message was brutally clear. *If the boss did that to his own son, what might he do to a piece of shit nobody like me?* It had been a very powerful deterrent to lying.

But the corollary was that in his own twisted way, he considered himself a man of honor. If Novak gave his word not to harm Imre in front of his men, he would consider himself bound by it. Val hoped.

On the other hand, the man was utterly mad, after all.

"Vajda." Imre cleared his throat, coughing. "You cannot—"

"Shut up, old man," Val said harshly. "I did not ask you."

Tense moments crawled by. Novak pondered, rubbing his chin. "The demand for money is absurd," he said. "But I do appreciate a man who gives good sport. For this, I will spare the finger—for tonight. And in return . . ." His voice trailed off, eyes sparkling with amusement.

Val waited, not allowing himself to swallow or breathe.

"You will provide me with video footage of your affair with Steele," Novak said. "Something juicy and explicitly sexual, something to entertain the men on dull nights. You will have a few minutes of communication with your friend. If at any point the video rendezvous is missed, I will start to remove pieces of him. I require my first installment—let me see—Monday. I am giving you a few extra days of grace, to allow for travel time," he concluded, his tone magnanimous. "After that, I will expect something every three days."

Val's jaw ached with tension. "I cannot guarantee—"

"Then I will start with his fingers," Novak said lightly. "Do not try to intimidate me, Vajda." His grin stretched wider. "Look into my eyes. Do I look like a man who has anything to fear from your poison gas?"

Val's fingers tightened on the ampule. The faces of the other men in the room were rigid with terror. Novak's was alight with triumph.

"Do we have an understanding?" Novak asked.

Val nodded. Novak jerked and wheezed with laughter. He gestured to one of his men. "Give him his things."

The man jerked into movement, producing Val's wallet, cell phone, Palm Pilot. He dropped them onto the table.

Val pocketed the items. He seized the file that held the photographs, and shoved the case that held the torque under his arm.

"I need this," he said. "For pretexting an approach."

"As you wish." Novak's voice was oily with satisfaction. "Be sure to bring it back when you deliver her. I wish to kill her with it."

Val gave Imre one last look. The old man's eyes were hollow and bleak. Val felt helpless. "We will speak on the videophone," he said.

Imre did not reply. Novak's men shrank away from Val as he made for the door, their eyes on the ampule. No one accompanied him as he made his way out of the labyrinth of subterranean passageways beneath the warehouse district in Köbanya. He remembered the way. The fully functioning businesses above were money laundering fronts for Novak's other, more profitable businesses. He had organized the front company documentation for some of them himself many years ago.

The men at the guardposts stared at him as he stumbled out into the frigid night. He had left his coat behind. Snow brushed his battered face. It felt good against inflamed flesh. The water in his hair and shirt promptly froze solid. He shuffled aimlessly through ankle deep slush. Whoever saw his blood-spattered face scurried away, unnerved.

So they should. He was soiled, corrupt. Sent out to play roles he could not shake, despite all his desperate effort. Whore, liar, betrayer.

Killer. Worse. Delivering Steele alive to Novak was more cruel than the swift mercy of a bullet through the nape. Far worse than delivering her into Georg Luksch's hands. Killing her outright would be kinder.

And he had to make her trust him. Hah. If not for Imre, he would not know the meaning of the word. But if he could not do it . . .

He seemed to stumble and shuffle for hours through the pelting snow. He stopped on the Széchenyi Chain Bridge, and stared up at the pitiless, implacable stone face of one of the lions. Wind whipped his breath from his mouth. He saw Imre, hunched in his cramped kitchen, frying egg-soaked bread for him as he lectured on Socrates, Descartes.

Imre, with blood streaming from his nose and mouth, his eyes full of mute suffering. Imre, with mutilated hands, dripping blood.

Val lurched to the side, and vomited up his guts. The heaving went on long after his stomach was empty. His eyes streamed, his nose ran. The dark water of the Danube roiled sluggishly below. He longed for the icy, airless darkness of it. Not for the first time. He thought of his mother.

No. It was not his nature. Fuck them. He was too angry to give in.

He straightened, wiping his face with a sleeve stiff with ice, and resumed his shambling way to the hotel, the jewelry case and file of photos clamped beneath his arm. The conversation with Hegel flashed through his mind. It seemed so long ago.

He began to laugh. At least he no longer had to worry about Hegel hurting Imre. His friend could only be savaged by one villain at a time.

Laughter hurt his cracked ribs. He stopped it.

At least Novak did not know about the child. He clung to that.

He was still clutching the ampule in his hand, he realized, though his numb fingers barely felt it. His hand tightened on the hard cylinder. He broke off the tip and inhaled deeply.

It was a sample vial of a new scent, blended exclusively for him by his personal *parfumeur* in Provence. An extravagant affectation, but fuck it, he had the money. Why not? He liked good smells.

The scent was voluptuous, hints of sweet wood, fleshy depths of forest mushrooms, the warm, spicy tang of pine, lavender and sage. A pathetically small victory in the face of the leverage that Novak wielded on him, but he would cling to any minor triumph.

Three more days of safety for Imre's finger, for a vial of perfume.

He rubbed some on his skin, inhaled. His body was too cold to release the scent, and the inside of his nose felt frozen solid, but still, he smelled it, just barely, and the earthy, sensual essence warmed him.

It made him think of Tamara Steele. The way her red lips curved in that secret smile in the evening gown photograph. The picture of her in the black dress, wildflowers in her outstretched hand. Lavender and daisies. Her pale, beautiful face, filled with ancient sadness.

But the image of Imre's mutilated hands battered at him.

He was unaccustomed to the sensation of fear after years of cultivating detachment. It was intensely unpleasant.

If they killed Imre, that was it. There was no other reason for Val to remain even remotely human.

You are a whining dog begging for scraps.

True. His stock portfolio had a net worth in the millions now, and look at him, still living on scraps. A chess game every few years. Distant memories of egg and bread fried in butter, Socrates and Descartes, Bach inventions played on the grand piano. That lumpy, dusty old divan.

And soon enough, a mossy grave in the cemetery with Imre's name carved on it.

Scraps. All that he would ever be allowed to have.

Chapter
5

Tam muttered something foul in some half-remembered language as she tore off her goggles. She wiped her hair back off her sweaty forehead and flung down the troublesome pendant with disgust.

She hated it. The colors weren't melding. She had envisioned a tangle of bronze and green-tinged copper clockwork bits layered with delicate filigreed gold to hide the mechanism that housed the little hypodermic, but it wasn't fitting together right, and the semiprecious stones she'd chosen looked dull and blah. The piece didn't throb or hum, or whisper seductive, ominous things; it had no menace, no driving intensity, no sex appeal. It was a necklace that a funky college girl with a pierced nose might buy from a pothead vendor in a Seattle open-air market for fifteen bucks. Not Deadly Beauty.

She was losing her touch, her eye, her concentration. In a word, everything. Lack of sleep, maybe. Not that she'd ever slept much.

The light over the door strobed. Rosalia was intercomming her. She pulled off the earphones, thinking wistfully of the twelve-hour-long trances she used to go into to work. Absolute concentration, no distractions. Miles inside the sweet privacy of her own twisted mind.

Those days were gone. And she had no one to blame but herself.

She stabbed the button that stopped the savagely melancholy

Spanish gypsy lament howled out by broken wine-and-cigarette-roughened voices. A sentimental choice. Unusual for her. Usually she went for hard rock. Something feverish and raucous, to burn out the fog in her head and help her get to the faraway place where the images of the jewelry came to her, glowing and glittering and twisting in her mind.

She hit the intercom. "Yes, Rosalia? What is it?"

"A visitor," Rosalia replied, in her native Brazilian Portuguese. "The red Volkswagen. I think it is the dark lady with the boy baby."

Tam dropped her face into her hands. No. Please. Not Erin again.

It had only been a week since the last concerned visit, full of great examples of beatific madonna-style mothering and tit-sucking and cooing and crooning and gentle, well-meant, incredibly irritating advice.

She tossed down the goggles and punched up the security program onto her studio computer monitor. Sure enough. There was Erin's red Volkswagen Bug, parked outside the outermost line of defense. Waiting to be beckoned in. Tam switched to another camera angle, and made out the car seat in the back, with Kev's chubby, heavy-cheeked profile. Probably already hungry for his liquid lunch. She was in for it.

Her sigh felt almost like a growl as she deactivated the various devices. Time to brace herself for the irritating questions. Had she done a fucking blood test to check for anemia? Was she taking a fucking multivitamin and mineral supplement? Did she want to do another fucking barbecue lunch on Sunday with the McCloud Crowd? To which the answers were *always no, no, no*, and *leave me alone, already.*

But Erin was tough. Thick-skinned. She didn't back down easily.

Erin's car started up again, and Tam watched it glumly as it advanced up the road. The McClouds made big fun of all her security doodads, but she could care less. Daddy Novak would probably love to kill Connor and Erin and their spawn too, for their part in Kurt Novak's death. But if they wanted to paint targets on their asses and hang them out in the breeze, that was their affair. She wanted no part of it.

She washed her hands and headed down the stairs to the entrance. Rachel was heaping towers of blocks with Rosalia on the floor in the big living area. The instant she saw Tam, she dropped everything and hurled her little body in Tam's direction, squeaking, arms outstretched. Tam scooped her up and hugged her hard. She hefted the toddler, gauging her weight. A little heavier this week. Thirty grams, maybe, depending on whether the diaper was wet. Since taking on Rachel, Tam had become a human precision scale.

Erin was parked in the garage and getting little Kev out of his car seat when Tam opened the door. Kev was almost as big as Rachel was, even though he was two years younger, the snorting little piglet. Tam tried not to hold that against him. It was difficult sometimes.

Tam ran an appraising eye over Erin as she hoisted the chubby kid onto her hip. The other woman was finally slimming down from her baby weight, though she was still very soft and squeezable. Tam suspected that Connor liked his wife just that way. Whatever. To each his own.

"And to what do I owe the honor of this visit?" There was no way to modulate the bitchy edge in her voice, so she didn't try.

Erin ignored her completely, saving her smiles for Rachel. "And how is this pretty little sweetheart today?" she crooned. She bent forward and gave Rachel a kiss on the back of her tousled, black-curled head. Rachel clutched tighter, buried her face in Tam's neck, fingers digging in like little kitten claws.

Progress. Four months ago, that brief kiss would have sent Rachel into screaming convulsions of fear. She was mellowing. Her little body was tense, but not trembling much. As Tam reset the alarms, Rachel even lifted big dark eyes a little to peek out at the baby on Erin's lap. Little Kev returned her regard with grave, oddly adult curiosity.

"You're not quite so thin this time." Erin's voice was full of motherly approval. "That's really great. You look better already. Much."

Tam suppressed a sharp reply. Her appetite was as crappy as ever, but Rachel had this annoying new mealtime game without which she would not eat, called you-take-a-bite-and-then-I-take-a-bite. So, by brutal necessity, a certain quantity of butterfly pasta, banana slices, crackers, fish sticks, Cream of Wheat, yogurt, and turkey burger patties were introducing their fat and calories into her system.

She supposed it wasn't so terrible. She'd been looking pretty damn haggard, not that she cared much. Rachel didn't give a damn what her new mother looked like. Beauty had just been another weapon in Tam's arsenal, but it was not one she cared to ever use again. It was only useful to attract and maniuplate men, and she'd aggressively phased that necessity out of her life. After that last revenge stint with Kurt Novak and Georg, she was so, *so* done with that groping, sweaty drama. She swallowed down a greasy clutch of nausea at the mere thought of it.

Rachel consented to being put down on the kitchen floor, where Rosalia was laying out coffee things and a plate of shortbread cookies. Cookies, for God's sake. While Tam wasn't looking, her house had morphed into a cozy, fluff-lined nest. That was what came of letting other people into it. Tam watched with something akin to horrified fascination as Erin dove face first into those lethal cookies. Look at the girl go. Cellulite city. No fear, no shame. It boggled the mind.

"Stop looking at me like that," Erin said, reaching for her second cookie. "You make me feel like a captured space alien whose feeding habits are being studied by scientists. If you don't approve of amazing homemade shortbread cookies, why serve them?"

"I didn't," Tam said, casting a speaking glance toward Rosalia. "She did. Can you see me baking cookies? I don't do cookies. I'm not even on speaking terms with cookies."

"True enough. I can see you cooking up deadly poisons to dip hairpins into, but not pastry," Erin admitted as she unrepentantly poured a heart-clogging quantity of half-and-half into her coffee.

Tam winced. "Jesus, Erin. Watch it with that stuff."

"Don't be afraid for me," Erin soothed. "Nursing makes you fearless. The cookies are fabulous, Rosalia. Can I have the recipe?"

Rosalia smiled her thanks and nodded as she herded the little kids into the adjoining room. Tam abruptly missed the noise and distraction. The sudden silence and Erin's sharp, amber brown eyes made her twitch. After an endless string of stress nightmares and largely sleepless nights, she was too raw and rattled and frustrated right now to keep her shields properly up. She hated that.

"Are things going any better?" Erin asked gently.

Irritation made Tam lash into attack mode. "Is what going better?" she snapped. "What the hell are you referring to?"

Erin shrugged. "In general. Your health. Your sleep, your appetite, your daughter. Since you won't tell me any specifics, I have to ask general questions."

"You don't have to ask questions at all. Where is it written?"

"I ask you because I care," Erin said, quietly stubborn.

Being shamed into feeling like a spoiled, sulky bitch did not do any favors to her mood. Tam felt her irritation ratchet up a couple notches. "I didn't ask you to care," she said.

Erin gave her a reproving look. "Cope," she said dryly. "I know you may find this hard to believe, but I actually came here today for a reason other than just to torment you and waste your time."

"Oh. Astonishing," Tam muttered.

Erin was silent for a long moment, her mouth pressed into a thin line. Tam could actually hear her, in the ether, counting to ten and praying for patience. It gave her a pang of mingled guilt and satisfaction. She'd pierced the protective layer of Zen-like, cow-hormone-induced calm. Zing, she'd scored a point. Tam tried hard to enjoy it.

Erin let out a long, slow breath that she had surely learned in a mellow new-age yoga class. In with the good vibes, out with the bad. "It's about this really weird thing that happened to me at work yesterday. It might be a business opportunity for you," she said.

Tam blinked. That was, in fact, utterly unexpected. "Huh?"

"At the museum. I did a consultation for this guy. He came all the way from Rome. He wanted an expert opinion on a replica of a piece of Celtic-themed jewelry he'd found. He's trying to locate the designer, and he had a lead that she was in this area. So he opens up the case, and I look in, and I just about drop my teeth. It was one of your designs."

Tam felt a cold, unpleasant chill spreading from the pit of her belly outward through her limbs. "Which one?"

"One of the torques. The one you named for me. The Erin."

Tam drummed her fingers and stared down into her cup of black coffee. The Erin. A piece she'd done to help exorcise the demon of Kurt Novak, not that it had helped much. "Describe it," she snapped.

Erin looked puzzled. "I just did. It's part of the series of—"

"No two pieces are alike," Tam said. "Tell me which stones were in it, the number, the color scheme, the number of gold threads in the braid, the size of the finial. Rubies or garnets? Amythyst or sapphire?"

"Oh." Erin thought for a moment. "It was similar to the original," she offered. "But the stones were cabochon rubies, I think. Not garnets."

"Gotcha." Tam filed that into her database, made a mental note to call the broker in Marseilles who had handled that particular sale, and went back to drumming her fingers, silently processing data.

She was alarmed. And unnerved. Someone who had been able to connect Erin to the creator of Deadly Beauty had access to information that could only spell trouble for all of them. She had passports and multiple alternate identities set up for herself and Rachel, and various emergency bolt-holes already prepared in remote parts of the globe, but those identities weren't as ripe or well constructed as her current one. And a woman with a child was more visible, more memorable.

More vulnerable.

Besides. She liked this home. Rachel liked it, too. And she liked her work, a lot. If she changed identities, she would never be able to do metalworking again. The very thought of it made her furious.

Plus. The McCloud Crowd might bug her, but they were the only safety net Rachel had. If she took the kid to South Africa or Sri Lanka, their space station would be that much farther from solid ground and normality. Relative safety, maybe, but not a life. Not an extended family.

Still. If her identity was compromised . . . she should get those extra passports out of the safe, pack up Rachel, and go. Right now.

Erin waited, and waited, growing visibly impatient. "What?" she prompted sharply. "What are you thinking?"

Tam hesitated for a moment before replying, her voice hard. "I think you and Kev and Connor should take a very long, quiet vacation somewhere. Like an uncharted island in the Pacific, maybe. By private boat. I think Seattle just got a whole lot more dangerous for everybody."

Erin's gaze darted nervously to the kitchen entrance to her son, who was flopping and rolling enthusiastically on the carpet in the other room while Rachel giggled her appreciation and egged him on. "Um . . ." She swallowed, visibly. "Aren't you overreacting a little?"

"No," Tam said bluntly. "Not even a little."

"Damn," Erin sighed. "I have this verbatim conversation all the time with Connor and my brothers-in-law. Not you, too. Isn't it remotely possible that a thing can sometimes be exactly what it seems?"

"It is exactly what it seems," Tam said. "A trap."

Erin's mouth tightened. "I can't keep looking over my shoulder for the rest of my life," she said rebelliously. "I just can't. It drives me nuts."

Tam shrugged. "So don't complain when you get stabbed in the back, honey."

"Oh, shut up. You are hopeless," Erin snapped.

"Literally and figuratively," Tam agreed. "But come on, Erin. What are the odds? Of all the experts on Celtic antiquities to consult with about this piece, he picks you? Granted, you're good, and a lot of people know it, but you're far from the only one, far from the most famous one, and certainly one of the youngest ones. Five years ago you were finishing grad school, doing unpaid internships."

"But he has consulted other experts," Erin said stubbornly. "He mentioned some of them. He even talked to my old thesis advisor, who's the head of the Antiquities Department at—"

"Did you call and corroborate?"

"Yes, I did!" Erin's voice was defensive. "And yes, he'd been there. They all admired the workmanship of your piece, by the way."

Tam grunted. "How gratifying. So this guy's prepared. And awfully motivated, don't you think? Scouring the world to locate the maker of some obscure jewelry reproductions? It smells, Erin. Like a dead dog."

"I would hardly call your stuff obscure," Erin countered hotly. "It's original and beautiful, and according to this guy, in certain circles, it's getting famous. Your pieces are hot investments. They acquire value incredibly fast. This Janos told me one of the Deadly Beauty spray hairclips sold at auction for triple what the original owner paid for it, which was no small sum to begin with. If I remember your prices correctly."

"Janos?" Tam narrowed her eyes. "Never heard of the guy."

Erin dug out a business card and handed it across the table to Tam. "Valery Janos. He says he has a bunch of interested buyers. He'd like to arrange a private showing. His consulting business hunts objects for people who have too much money and don't know what to do with it, if I understand correctly. Wish fulfillment, that kind of thing."

Tam studied the card. "Capriccio Consulting," she murmured. "Valery Janos. Not an Italian name. Rome, huh? I'll check him out."

"I'm sure you will," Erin murmured. "I sure did."

The odd note in her voice made Tam look up abruptly from the card. There was a sparkle in her eye and a sly curve to her smile that put Tam on alert. "What's that supposed to mean?"

Erin bit her lip and dropped her gaze coyly. "Oh, I don't know. He just so happens to be insanely, unbelievably gorgeous."

"Oh, really?" Tam said slowly.

Erin's shrug was elaborately casual. "Breathtaking."

"Bet you didn't mention that detail to Connor," Tam said.

Erin rolled her eyes. "What, you think I'm stupid?"

Tam waited for a beat. "Tempted?" she asked sweetly.

Erin's brow creased in a thoughtful frown. Tension shivered for a moment in the air. Erin broke it with a burst of whispery laughter.

"Um, no," she said demurely. "Not in the least. I noticed him, of course. I'd have to be dead not to. But I've got my hands full, on every level, in the best way possible." She left a pause. "So . . . don't worry."

"Why the hell should I worry?" Tam snapped back. "What the hell business is it of mine?"

Erin lifted an eyebrow. Tam turned away. The other woman's occasional razor-sharp perception bothered her. She didn't like anyone's gaze to pierce that deep. Nor was she interested in examining why it rattled her to think of Erin's bond with Connor being threatened.

It actually made her . . . well, disquieted. Kind of angry.

Please. That was deadly stupid. Alarming, too. It meant she was needing something she couldn't have. Relying on things that were unreliable by their very nature. Desire, trust, honor. Love. Hah. When a woman started pinning her already shaky psychological security on that kind of crap, she might as well just open her veins and be done with it.

"Truth is, I wasn't thinking of this Janos for me," Erin went on. "I was thinking about you."

"Me?" Shock was replaced by disbelief. The tension in Tam's chest was released with a harsh bark of laughter. "Oh, please. As-fucking-if."

"Six four, huge shoulders, barrel chest, chiseled cheekbones, perfect jaw," Erin said dreamily. "Olive skin, great eyebrows, sexy little accent. Nice cologne, and I'm not even a fan of man scents. Fathomless, liquid black eyes with long, inky lashes. Beautiful, big, manly hands. Deep, mellow voice. Tight ass. Long legs. Eight hundred dollar shoes."

Tam snorted. "You should have gone into advertising. You'd be richer. All I need right now is some spoiled Eurotrash clotheshorse to waste my time."

Erin looked hurt. "Hey. All I said was that he was handsome and charming. Hardly a basis upon which to automatically despise him."

"He's a man, isn't he? If he's pretty, he'll expect to be worshipped. Who has the energy to kneel down and lick some man's swollen ego?"

"Hmm." Erin looked quizzical. "I don't know. Connor's handsome, and he doesn't expect to be worshipped. Except when he . . . ah, well, never mind." She subsided, a blush rising up on her face.

Oh, please. The innocent, pink-cheeked milkmaid routine made Tam's teeth hurt.

"I was thinking, you don't have a date for Nick and Becca's wedding, do you?" Erin said. "Why not ask this guy if he's free on—"

"Erin. You are kidding, aren't you?" Tam demanded. "Because if you aren't, you're scaring me."

Erin looked at her with that sharp, narrow gaze that Tam disliked intensely. "There hasn't been anyone for you since . . ." Her voice trailed off, but they both heard the name. It echoed through their worst nightmares, linking them together. *Kurt Novak.*

The sharp, instinctive gesture Tam made to ward off evil surprised her. One of her great-grandmother's tics. One of the few things she remembered about the old woman. She'd died when Tam was small.

Strange. The man was stone dead, after all. No doubts about it. She'd seen pretty much every last drop of his heart's blood decorating the walls, thanks to Erin's amazing courage under fire. Which continued to surprise her years later. Girl nerds. You never knew.

"You can't let him poison that for you forever." There was a tight, vibrating intensity in Erin's voice. "It's just not right."

Brittle laughter would have been the best response, but Tam's chest was screwed too tight to move. "There is no 'that' for me, Erin."

"But you can't just shut it off like a faucet and—"

"I can do whatever the fuck I want. My choice."

The edge in Tam's voice put a hot flush of hurt embarrassment on Erin's face. She sprang up and turned her back, sipping her coffee as she stared out the window into the forest. The children's laughter and Rosalia's low voice murmuring encouragements in Portuguese floated in.

Tam stared into her coffee. Angry for feeling guilty. Guilty for feeling angry. What a crock of pointless shit this was. Who needed it.

"I guess I should go." Erin's voice was tight. "It's almost naptime for Kev, and I should take advantage of—"

"Why do you put up with me, Erin?" Tam asked abruptly.

Erin was startled into turning. "Huh?"

"I'm a rude, abrasive bitch. That's not likely to change, ever," Tam said, her voice stony. "So why? Why do you bother?"

Erin opened and closed her mouth a few times. "I—I—"

"Is it pity? Because I don't need pity."

"You certainly don't deserve it," Erin observed tartly, crossing her arms beneath her ample bosom. "But you did save my life, you know. And my husband's life. That makes up for a few behavioral quirks."

"You saved mine right back, so we're even," Tam said. "And besides, it was an accident. I wasn't in that shithole with any heroic plans to save anybody. I just wanted to wipe out that psycho son of a bitch, get my revenge, and save my own skin. You owe me nothing. So why?"

Erin shook her head. "I don't know," she said slowly. "It's true. You're awful. You're the rudest, most irritating, pain-in-the-ass friend I've ever had, or even imagined having. But you'll also race off at the drop of a pin and risk your life to save a bunch of helpless little kids from organ thieves. That kind of behavior racks up big points fast."

Tam made a derisive sound. "Oh, horseshit. That was just for fun. I was bored, OK? I needed some action."

"Oh, yeah. Right. Bored," Erin scoffed. "You are so full of shit. So you took Rachel on because you were bored?"

Tam choked on her coffee. "No, I took Rachel on because I was insane," she muttered. "But I want to know, Erin. You've got Connor. Margot and Raine and Liv now, too. They're so much nicer. You don't need me, for anything. So why the hell do you bother with me?"

Erin seemed to grow five inches. Her face glowed hot pink with anger. "You know what I think?" Her voice rang. "I think you should see a talented shrink since you don't have the guts to talk to your friends about whatever godawful bug is up your ass. I've seen this before. You try to drive everyone away so that the view outside matches the view inside. Nobody likes me, everybody hates me, I think I'll eat a worm. Well, fuck that, Tam. And fuck you, too. I'm *sick* of it."

Tam blinked, startled into fascinated silence. It was fun to get Erin worked into a lather. She was slow to start, but once she got going, watch out. Blood spattered the walls, left and right. Wow.

"You cannot afford that self-indulgent, scorched earth bullshit anymore," Erin fumed on. "You've got a child! Kids need family!

Lots of it! Community. Aunts, uncles, cousins. And so do you, whether you'll admit it or not, you stubborn, snotty bitch! So just grow up already!"

Tam let out a low whistle, impressed. "Whoo-hoo. Feisty."

"Do not condescend to me. You know what else? We're it, whether we like it or not. We've been through some bad shit together, and that makes you family. Congratulations, you get to be the scary aunt that everybody's afraid of. Every family's got one."

"I could change my name, go into hiding," Tam mused.

"Oh, shut up," Erin snapped. "I've had enough of your crap."

Tam's mouth twitched. "You're cute when you're mad," she murmured throatily. "Rosy glow, heaving bosom . . ."

Erin slammed her cup onto the table. "Don't even start. You can't convince me that you're a lesbian, either, so don't jerk me around."

Tam hid her smile in her coffee. "Aw, come on. It keeps 'em guessing. Gives me more space."

"You have plenty of space," Erin snapped. "And we're tired of guessing."

Tam suddenly thought to peek over at the door, where Rosalia's wide-eyed fascination suggested that her English comprehension far outstripped her verbal skills. Rosalia's gaze slid away guiltily, and she nudged the kids deeper into the living room.

"It's hard to find a category for you," Erin bitched, dropping into her chair. "How do you define a friend like Tam? Well, if bloodthirsty terrorists were threatening my family with a dirty bomb, she'd be there to rescue us in a blaze of glory with diamond-studded hand grenades. But would she give me a ride to the airport? Fucking forget it!"

The smile sneaked out before Tam could stomp it. "Why should I? What a freaking bore. That's what men are for. What's the point of putting up with their crap if they don't provide abject servitude?"

Erin harrumphed. "Speaking of men and abject servitude and all that good stuff, what am I supposed to tell the pretty boy? That you only do big business with ugly, smelly, badly dressed men?"

Tam picked up the card Erin had given her, and scowled at it. "Don't tell him anything. Don't even take his calls. I'll check him out. Since chances are good that all he wants is to stick a knife into my eye."

Erin made a frustrated sound. "Why can't anything ever be just normal or nice for you? A business opportunity, a cute guy to flirt with? A date for the wedding? Why is it always blood and guts, life or death?"

The inane goofiness of the question and Erin's sad, plaintive voice touched her buried tender spot. Tam's voice came out so gentle she barely recognized it herself. "There's no normal or nice for me, Erin," she said. "There never has been, never can be. But don't sweat it. I just do the best I can. I'll be OK. Really."

Erin looked doleful. "But I want better than that for you."

Tam stopped the automatic sarcastic reply that rose to her lips with tremendous effort, and stayed silent. "Well, I appreciate that sentiment," she said, stiffly. "In my own way. For what it's worth."

Erin looked down, blinking hard. Several agonizing seconds passed, each more fraught with tension than the last.

Tam snapped under the strain. "Don't you dare start sniffling on me! One tender moment is enough, all right? I can only take so much!"

Erin sniffed her tears back aggressively. "Oh, fuck you."

Tam let out a sigh of mock relief. "Thank God. That's more like it," she said. "Back on solid ground."

Erin stalked past her, muttering under her breath, and collected her kid. Kev complained about being separated from his new captive audience, and then, oh joy, then Rachel got cranky too, at having her brand new live toy taken away, and so commenced the mad maelstrom of shrieking and flopping and writhing, then the changing of diapers, the distribution of cookie bribes, the reloading of bags, bottles, binkies, bibs, wipes, snacks—Christ alone could remember what all. Tam was on the verge of shrieking with frustration by the time Rachel was calmed down in front of the boob tube, zoning out on Elmo, and the donkey laden Erin and her baby were finally heading down the stairs.

God help her. She'd helped execute blood-drenched coup d'états in third world countries that were less freaking complicated.

She started down after Erin. "I'll go down and disarm the—"

"I can do it," Erin cut in. "I learned the goddamn codes. All eight of them. Good-bye." And off she flounced without looking back, offspring howling and wiggling, diaper bags swinging angrily. Pissed as hell.

"Leave them off," she shouted down after Erin's stiff, retreating back. "It's about time for Rosalia to leave anyhow."

Erin muttered something rude, and slammed the door to the security room. Tam shrugged inwardly. What the hell. Narrow-eyed, she stared down at the card that lay on the table. Picked it up, fingered it.

She actually felt curious, in spite of her apprehension. Tempted to check it out. Maybe . . . maybe she wouldn't dismiss this out of hand without investigating further. Very, very carefully, of course. She'd been so wound up in dealing with Rachel's problems, it had been a long while since she'd organized any sales. The coffers could always use a fresh influx of ready cash. She liked cash.

She stared at the cookies that were left on the plate in the middle of the table. She could smell the butter from the other side of the room.

Some perverse impulse prompted her to grab one. She examined it from every side, sniffing all its glittering, sugary, cholesterol-laden, artery-plugging, insulin-resistance-causing, cellulite-provoking glory.

Deadly in its own way. Like one of her jewelry creations.

Rosalia appeared in the kitchen entryway. Tam's cookie-holding hand dropped down under the table as if she'd been caught stealing.

Too late. She could tell, by the discreetly delighted smile the older woman tried so hard to hide. "Nine o'clock tomorrow?" Rosalia asked.

Tam mumbled an affirmative. "Go right on out," she said. "The security's disarmed. Erin left it open."

Rosalia nodded toward the cookies. "Enjoy," she said. "Next time I do the caramel leche cookies. You try, you like for sure, hmm?"

Tam winced inwardly. She'd created a monster. "Tomorrow then."

Rosalia clumped down the stairs, humming cheerfully. Tam stared at the cookie in her hand. It seemed to stare back, smug and impassive.

Oh, what the fuck. She was destined to die anyhow. She took a bite, chewed. Sugar fireworks went off in her brain. Wow.

She chewed it very slowly and realized with surprise that she was genuinely curious to see just how handsome and charismatic a guy had to be to dazzle a woman as gooey-in-love with her husband as Erin was. He had to have some mojo. He probably thought he was God incarnate, which was a big freaking bore. Or else he was a merciless hired killer engaged to take her out. Which was much more interesting, but a big, fat, dating disadvantage. And mortal danger tended to be a sexual turnoff. She took another bite of deadly bliss, staring down at the card. Janos. Hungarian, maybe. If the name was real, which was doubtful.

She realized she was smiling at the irony of it. Demure little Erin, earnest girl nerd, trying to fix her up. Trying to get her laid, of all crazy things. Hah. Cute. Misguided, wrong-headed, insane . . . but very cute.

She tossed it into her mouth, wallowed in the sugar orgasm, let the buttery, sugary sexuality surrogate melt on her astonished tongue.

Huh. Go figure. She felt . . . inexplicably better. Scary, that.

The only way to know for sure if her current identity was truly compromised would be to suss the guy out, do her X-ray eyes routine on him. Men were easy to read, particularly for her. A few well-placed words to strip them bare, cross section them, and the thing was done.

After all. She'd hate to throw away everything she and Rachel had here out of sheer paranoia. She would have to be careful, but hey. She'd always liked risk. Though she could no longer afford to like it, not with Rachel to factor into the mix. She reached for another cookie.

It might even be kind of entertaining to cut this guy down to size.

Chapter
6

Val stepped into the building that housed Shibumi, an exclusive private dining club, and gave his name to the security personnel at the desk, secretly vibrating with unprofessional excitement while they called up to see if he was expected. They verified that he was and he proceeded up to the sixteenth floor. Shibumi was the meeting place stipulated by Tamara Steele on the computer bulletin board, the only way she would deign to communicate with him after her initial phone call the day before. She had posted the meeting location a half hour before. A cautious woman.

He still could not believe his luck.

He wrestled his mind back into matrix mode. Cool, detached, and watchful. He must not betray himself by demonstrating urgency or fear. He couldn't even think about Imre, sitting slump-shouldered and alone in a dark, locked cell. Or about what could happen to the child in Novak's hands. Or the fate that awaited Tam Steele if he carried out his mission. The things he'd seen, in Novak's underground chamber.

Things that still haunted him.

Don't. He pushed the memories aside. Tonight's job was simplicity itself. Buy Imre more time until he could think of a fucking plan. That was all. Tonight, he was a rich Roman entrepreneur, on a mission for profit. A confirmed playboy who loved wine, women and money. All he had to do was charm her . . . and seduce her. On film. Hah. Easy.

He would deal with all the rest of it one fucking minute at a time.

He had identified a short list of priorities as a basic framework to work from. One, keep Imre in one piece. Two, keep the child far from the action. Three, spare the woman. Four, stay alive himself, if at all possible. If not, *pazienza*. He died. So what? He hadn't really expected to live all that long anyway.

The elevator opened onto an elegant, tasteful room decorated with Japanese paneling and screens. He informed the impassive Asian man behind the desk of his appointment. The man picked up the phone, murmured into it in Japanese. Moments later, two tall, very broad men came out. One was fair and one was dark. He recognized them both from the surveillance cameras he had mounted outside the McClouds' homes. The blond man was Davy McCloud, the dark one was Nick Ward.

Their muscular bodies were dressed in surprisingly good suits, discreetly tailored to make room for their shoulder holsters. They had the requisite flat, watchful look of security personnel on their faces.

"Mr. Janos?" said McCloud. "Come with us, please."

McCloud led the way, while Ward fell into place behind him. Val had been surprised to hear the man pronounce his name correctly. Yah-nosh. They returned to the elevator, and proceeded to the next floor, which evidently housed the private dining rooms. A key card opened one of the doors. A small, paneled anteroom had a closet for his coat. The security men watched him while he hung it up.

"Ms. Steele does not want to meet with anyone carrying a weapon," McCloud said.

Val thought about that for a moment. "Ironic," he murmured.

The man's expression did not change. He waited.

"Will she abide by the same terms?" Val asked.

The two men glanced at each other and shrugged. "Not our business," said Ward. "Ask her yourself. See what she says."

"You're free to leave, if you don't like it," McCloud added.

He crouched and pulled the knife out of his ankle sheath. It was just as well that he'd left the pistol, considering it out of character for a wealthy businessman. He'd figured that the knife was an accessory that any man abroad in an unfamiliar foreign city might choose. He felt naked without it. But his hands and feet were weapons themselves after years of intensive training in various martial arts disciplines.

McCloud took his knife. Ward stepped up, gesturing for him to lift his arms. "Excuse me," he said, sounding far from apologetic.

Val submitted to a thorough pat down. "Do you two work for the club or for Ms. Steele personally?"

"We do our job," Ward said. "We don't talk about it."

Fair enough. McCloud opened a door to an adjoining room, and gestured for him to enter. It was large, candlelit, a table positioned next to a floor-to-ceiling window with a spectacular view of the evening cityscape and the expanse of Elliott Bay.

"Wait here," Ward said. "Ms. Steele will be in when she's ready."

The door clicked shut behind him. Val looked around at the beautifully appointed room. On one side was a long conference table with chairs around it. Against the opposite wall was a lavishly stocked bar, a bottle of champagne in a bucket of ice, a bowl of fruit, a crystal carafe of water, an assortment of glasses. The beige carpet woven of sand-grass had a suble, complex pattern and a sweet, earthy scent. Low, intimate chairs faced each other over the dining nook. It seemed a spot for a lovers' tryst, not a business meeting.

He wondered at the choice of place. Probably for the privacy, the controlled atmosphere. Ease of monitoring entrances and exits.

He wondered if he was being watched, and sat on the urge to look around for the surveillance equipment. If these people were as professional as they appeared, he would not find it, and he would reveal too much about himself by searching. Val Janos, the pampered Roman *uomo d'affare*, was not paranoid. He had no reason not to simply pour himself a drink, sit down, and enjoy the view.

Val did exactly that, but he let his foot tap with the jittery impatience of a rich man not accustomed to being kept waiting. It was not good to seem overly controlled, either. That, too, was incongruous.

He stared out at the city lights and added data to the matrix. Watched it shift and turn as he prepared his mind to take in more. To observe all, forget nothing.

The door opened. The anteroom beyond was brighter than the

room he was in, and Steele was poised in the door with her face in shadow, backlit for maximum effect. Her slender, gracefully curved body was clothed in black, sinuous as a cat. She held a large leather case. He'd asked her to bring a wide range of designs.

He rose to his feet as she walked in. She gave him a brief nod of greeting, turned to lay her case upon the large conference table, and crossed the room toward him with that loose, feline gait that had fascinated him on the video footage.

She stared into his face. The matrix flashed, sparked and melted in his mind into soup under her direct, unflinching gaze.

He kept a bland smile on his face as he regrouped. He hadn't been prepared for the physical effect of her upon his senses.

The sheer, raw, electric force of her. He was buzzing, breathless.

Her costume was elegantly simple. Snug black trousers, gleaming, spike-heeled black boots and a tailored black silk blouse, to set off a dazzling array of collars, pendants, earrings. Her hands were loaded with rings, her wrists with bracelets. Her hair was slicked back with gel, plastered to her head and twisted into an intricate knot, which was stabbed through by cruelly sharp sticks, adorned with a snarl of silver and obsidian beadwork. The look was severe and striking.

Her gaze did not waver. His heart quickened. His cock stirred.

Don't, he told himself. His dick had no say in this. *Detach.* Three steps back. Seduction yes, but controlled seduction.

Her face was both flawless and unique. Elegant bone structure, each feature bordering on perfection; her lips lush and full and yet delicate in a way that bee-stung silicone lips could never be. The jut of her cheekbone was echoed by the sweep of her eyebrows. Her piercing eyes were huge, tilted at the corners. Her lashes were long and curling.

Hazel green. Not her original color. His lust to know their real color startled him. She wore no makeup on her fine-grained, flawless skin, and needed none. Just a slick of colorless gloss on her lips.

"Mr. Janos." She also pronounced his name correctly. Her voice was low, husky, but intensely feminine, full of rich colors, spices, smoky sweet overtones. It went straight to his groin, like a bold caress.

"Ms. Steele." He held out his hand. She hesitated, just long enough to make him consider dropping it, but instinct prodded him to persevere.

She took it, finally. Her skin was soft and smooth. The chilly, textured hard metal of her jewelry was a sharp contrast. A shock of electric awareness shot up his arm from the physical contact, zinging through his nerves, making lights flash, bells ring inside him.

She felt it, too. He sensed her sudden stillness, the way her smile tightened. He released her hand reluctantly. The silence between them felt suddenly awkward, too long. Charged with meaning.

"Would you prefer to conduct our conversation in Italian, Signor Janos?" she asked him, in flawless Italian. "We could, if it would be more comfortable for you. It's all the same to me."

Interesting that she would let him choose the language. He could sense her mind-set shifting in a way that wasn't American at all. Very civilized, very European. Concealing far more than she would ever reveal.

"I am tempted," he replied in the same tongue. "Italian sounds beautiful on your lips. I usually prefer English for business. I appreciate its clarity. For pleasure, however, perhaps later . . . ?" He let his voice trail off suggestively. Let his eyes gleam with discreet hunger.

"English, then," she said crisply. "I see you have already made yourself comfortable." Her eyes flicked to his whiskey glass.

He acknowledged the subtle slap-down with a rueful smile. "May I get you a drink?" he asked. "I chose the Macallan."

"You are a connoisseur, then. The Macallan is a favorite of mine, too. Mr. Takuda put it out for me especially."

He seized a tumbler. "Straight up?"

"Of course," she murmured.

He was grateful to have a moment with his back turned, to collect himself. A few seconds of relative privacy to get the matrix re-established, the data feed started back up. He had a method. A good one. Stick to it, *testa di cazzo. Detach.*

He handed her the glass. Candlelight sparkled on her rings and bracelets, off the cut crystal tumbler, the amber swirl of liquid, the bright awareness in her eyes. She lifted the glass to her lips.

He dragged his eyes away. He was sweating, for the love of God. His collar tight, his face hot. This was absurd.

He stared down at her hands and nodded at their glittering load. "A one-woman arsenal, I assume?"

Her lips curved. His lungs suddenly stopped working, his heart speeding up. Her smile was a weapon in itself, spiced with danger and challenge, hinting at unheard-of delights. "I enjoy the feeling of a secret advantage," she said. "It is the spirit behind all of my designs."

"They are beautiful," he conceded. "*Complimenti.* Forgive me if this is an invasive question, but do you never create a beautiful thing just for beauty's sake alone?"

She sipped, her eyelashes mysteriously lowered. "Never. And besides, dangerous secrets are beautiful. Don't you think?"

He thought about that. "They can be, I suppose," he said dubiously. "It depends on the secret. And your point of view."

She smiled. "And what is your point of view, Mr. Janos?"

He lifted his glass to her in a silent toast. "That of a man whose lone secret weapon was confiscated by your security staff," he said.

"Ah. That." She tilted her head to the side, amusement gleaming in her eyes. "Did the boys alarm you? They are very protective. Touchingly so. But I hardly consider you defenseless."

"No?" He swirled the liquor in his glass and inhaled the rich, complex smell of it. "With such deadly beauty, so many dangerous secrets massed against me?"

"No. The way you move says it all," she said. "Shaking your hand confirmed it. The enlarged knuckle joints and the calluses on your first and second finger are those of an experienced judoka. And your hands are electric, Mr. Janos. You are accustomed to channeling vital energy with them. You are an experienced martial artist with a high level of interdisciplinary training."

He was startled into a split second of blankness, but rallied quickly. "I do enjoy martial arts for exercise and recreation," he said. "And I belong to a martial arts club near my home in Rome. But I would not presume to call myself a master. And I miss my knife."

"Your knife, I think, is overkill."

He injected a calculated hint of seduction into his smile. "I like overkill," he said softly, letting let his gaze drop to the tangle of complicated jewelry at her cleavage. "And so do you, I think."

She conceded this with a brief nod.

"I am tempted to procure some of your dangerous secrets for myself," he said. "To combat my male insecurity."

"Bullshit," she said softly. "You do not have a single insecure bone in your body, Mr. Janos."

He blinked. "Ah. Thank you . . . I think."

"Don't thank me," she said. "It was not a compliment, just an observation. And in any case, I do not design jewelry for men. Ever. It is against all my principles." Her smile turned predatory.

He knew when to back off. "Of course. I was surprised at your security procedures. Was all this elaborate choreography necessary?"

She lifted her shoulders. "Who knows? I never do. Hence my caution." Her smile widened. "Welcome to my world."

"I am honored, to have penetrated even the outermost defences."

Her eyes flickered. "*Che galantuomo*," she murmured. "Erin told me about your old world charm."

"I try to please," he said. "Are you immune to charm, Ms. Steele?"

Her smile tightened. "We shall see, hmm?"

He had evidently overstepped his bounds by flirting with her. Val Janos allowed himself to be cowed.

"Excuse me for getting straight to business, but would you show me the torque that you showed to Erin?" she asked. "Before we begin, it makes sense to verify that it really is one of my designs."

"Of course." He opened his case and lay the flat black leather case on the conference table. Steele flicked it open and gazed down at it.

Her head was inches beneath his face. The mingled scents of her perfume and her hair gel tickled his nose. The coils of her hair were gleaming and slick as varnished mahogany, gelled sternly into submission. No wisps allowed. Part of her armor.

But he had seen her without it. He had already seen the thick, disheveled braid swinging down her back as she played with the child. He had seen it wet and loose, clinging to her neck, to her slender, naked back and shoulders. The damage was done.

She looked up, rocking him with the sudden, blazing force of her eyes. "The provenance?"

He looked politely regretful. "As is often the case in my business, the piece came to me by unofficial channels. I bought it from a woman in Rome who had received it from a mysterious foreigner in Prague on a mad weekend love affair—after which she could never contact him again. He evidently gave her a false name and cell number. She sold the piece to me out of pique. The card was with it. I recognized your name, since I've dealt with some of your pieces before. I have received many offers already. The price rises daily, you will be gratified to know."

"I see." She stared down at the torque, a tiny dent marring the smooth skin between her perfect brows. "Were you aware that the last known owner of this piece died three weeks ago in Paris? She fell to her death from a penthouse terrace. Thirty-four stories."

"I am shocked to hear it," he said, his voice respectfully subdued. "Was it . . . ?"

"Suicide?" Steele's elegant shoulders lifted. "Murder? Who can say? Perhaps she saw or heard something she shouldn't, perhaps she slept with the wrong person. I imagine it's best for you that the story not be widely known. People might consider the piece cursed."

Val made a noncommittal sound. "Forgive me if this sounds calculated, but considering the type of people who are most drawn to your work, it may enhance the torque's value. Risk makes people feel alive. Danger is an indulgence for many of them."

"Yes, of course. Carefully controlled danger. Like an amusement park ride." Her tone was delicately contemptuous. "Do you like danger, Mr. Janos?"

"I am here, am I not?"

Her chilly smile pushed him away. She lifted a telephone set into the wall near the table. "Have you eaten? The food here is excellent."

"I rarely eat in the evening," he said. "But rules can be suspended. When temptation beckons, it is wasteful to resist."

She ignored his flirting. "I had originally thought to invite you to a place that specializes in Italian food, in case you were homesick for *ragú*, or *gnocchi*," she said. "Then I changed my mind, decided to range a little further afield."

"You did well," he said. "I seldom eat Italian food outside of Italy. No matter how talented the chef, *la cucina italiana* loses much of its magic out of context."

"I agree," she said. "Well, then. Your choices are the classic Japanese haute cuisine of Mr. Takuda, or that of his wife and associate, Mariko Takuda, who specializes in a more modern style of pan-Asian fusion dishes."

"Choose for me," he said gallantly. "I put myself in your hands."

"Ah, you do enjoy risk." She picked up the phone and spoke at some length in what sounded like fluent Japanese to whoever was on the other line.

"How many languages do you speak?" he asked.

Her gaze slid away. "Oh, I lost count long ago," she evaded. "The question becomes irrelevant at a certain point. Shall I show you the pieces, while we wait for dinner?"

He assented. She turned on a light, and laid out her pieces.

Her work was stunning. The designs were bold and yet delicate, imbued with a sense of simmering danger, and the hidden weapons were as cunning and ingenious as they were effective. He understood why Steele's work was becoming a hot investment. It was unique, timeless. The businessman inside him that desperately wanted to be let out was intrigued, already calculating the profits that could be had by organizing a private auction to select clients of Capriccio Consulting.

He tried not to dwell on how badly he wished his act was real.

A discreet knock indicated that their meal had arrived. Two attractive Asian women entered, clad in skintight, jewel-toned silk brocade dresses, pushing a rolling tray full of fragrant, steaming dishes.

Dinner was essentially a duel. He continued his attempt to flirt with her. She would lead him on for a few dance steps and then slam the door in his face. She ate little, despite the savory perfection of the food, and preferred the steaming green tea to the sake that accompanied the meal. He was pouring her another cup when her cell phone chimed.

She pulled it from some hidden pocket in her pants and glanced at the display, frowning. "Please excuse me for a moment."

She retreated to the far corner of the room, and stood with her back to him, muttering in Portuguese, in a tone he wasn't meant to overhear. ". . . yes, I told you she needs a bath . . . well? So? She always has a cold! If I only bathed her when she didn't have a cold, she'd never be bathed at all . . . so heat the bathroom, and dry her hair . . . Cristo Santo, Rosalia, you'll survive if she screams. I survive when she screams . . . no, not the yogurt. She's constipated. Give her the fruit, and the bran cookies if she wants another snack . . . how should I know where the fuzzy pink blanket is? Look in the laundry room, or under the covers of my bed . . ."

The hot buzz that had been building up in his balls vanished.

The child. He'd been so titillated by his seductive role, he'd let his lies and his lust become almost real.

And this was his chance when she wasn't looking. Her jewelry carrying case sat on the floor within arm's reach. He had no idea if the room had hidden cameras. He weighed the risks and made his choice.

He poked the tiny, missile-shaped RF beacon needle tip right through the black leather of the case and insinuated it beneath. It left a tiny misshapen bulge, but by the time she noticed, it would no longer matter. It would only monitor her for maybe thirty-six hours, having so little battery power.

But Imre only had a couple of days, in any case.

". . . so tell her I'll be back soon. And only Elmo, or Pooh. The other ones give her nightmares. Yes. Just a couple of hours. 'Til then."

She clicked the phone shut. He sensed rather than heard her sigh of frustration.

"You have a child?" he said quietly.

She whipped around, alarmed. "You speak Brazilian Portuguese?"

He shrugged. "Romance languages," he said lightly. "Spanish, French, Italian, Romanian. You learn one, you learn them all."

"Hmmph." She gazed at him, eyes wide. He had scared her.

"Tell me about your daughter," he urged.

Her haughty chin lifted. "I do not discuss my private life with strangers."

He gave her a coaxing smile. "I am still a stranger?"

"Let's focus on business," she said crisply. "Why am I here, Mr. Janos? Talk. And be succinct, please."

He displayed appropriate good-humored disappointment at being frozen out. "Very well. I am interested in organizing a private auction. Many of my clients are already eager to acquire your work. Once I put out the word, there will be a quiet stampede. And I have the perfect setting for it, too. A friend of mine owns a restored medieval *masseria* in San Sebastiano, near Naples, where we could organize a weekend event, and if you came—"

"Why the hell would I come?" Her voice was sharp.

"Your presence would be a huge draw," he assured her. "Your mystery, your secrecy, your beauty."

She gave him a disdainful look.

He persisted. "I am serious. Nothing stimulates people to spend money more than feeling part of an exclusive club. The commisions you will get for future pieces will keep you busy for years. You could earn hundreds of thousands, Ms. Steele. Perhaps seven figures."

She crossed her arms over her chest and pondered him. "And you?" she asked. "What do you earn, Mr. Janos?"

He shrugged. "A modest percentage, of course."

"Modest," she purred. "A dangerous word. Very subjective, especially when it comes to money."

"Never mind the money. We can hammer out the financial details later. For now, think about it. You come to San Sebastiano, enjoy a sensual, profitable weekend, and then disappear again to your secluded privacy with a sack of money. Why not?"

"It sounds dangerous," she said.

"Not at all," he assured her. "The place is private, the guests hand-picked, the security good, the time interval brief."

"It's dangerous because *you* are dangerous," she said.

"You are more than what you seem. Or less. Shall I tell you why?"

Her words chilled him. "I beg your pardon?"

"Let me tell you all about yourself." She gave him a coaxing, overly sweet smile. "Then tell me if I hit the mark. Think of it as a get-to-know-you game. Wasn't that what you wanted? To know me better?"

He sensed a trap, but threw up his hands, *galantuomo* to the last gasp. "How can I refuse a lady?"

Chapter
7

Tam cupped her tea in both hands and inhaled the steam as she studied his face. She didn't like to admit it to herself, but it was taking more energy than she'd expected to withstand the gale force of this man's sex appeal. Not just the language but even the way she talked changed in his presence.

Erin had not been kidding. For some reason, Tam had been expecting a generic, male-model sort of handsomeness. Which was unfair. Erin was married to Connor, after all, and even Tam could appreciate his craggy, fierce good looks. Even at her moodiest.

But still. She was utterly unprepared for . . . well, him.

Lethal. It was the first word that came to mind, even though it embarrassed her. He was so solid, so hard looking. Dynamic, and yet calm and focused. Nothing soft about him, except for the gloss of that thick brush of black hair. She wanted to touch it, just to see if it really was as soft as mink. Gypsy dark eyes, inky brows and lashes. The planes and angles of his face were starkly masculine, arrogantly sensual, but that smile was pure temptation. She'd considered herself impervious to men's lures, so why was she marveling at the lines carved into his cheeks when he grinned, or that blinding flash of teeth against his dark skin? *Get a fucking grip, Steele. This is unacceptable.*

His face looked hard used for a rich business consultant. There were bumps on his slightly crooked nose, a white diagonal scar sliced through one thick, slashing eyebrow, and subtler scars that only a trained eye accustomed to evaluating the effects of cosmetic surgery could catch. And the hands, of course. He'd fought in his life. Fought hard. Won, more often than not, judging from his vibe.

And what a vibe. It blasted out of him, full force. It was out of human range, a frequency that only a fucked-up freakoid with a weird, checkered past like hers could perceive. But so different from the danger waves that had throbbed out of the sicko madmen she'd had the misfortune to get close to before, like Novak, Georg, Drago Stengl. Their vibration had made her recoil.

Not so with Janos. In him, the danger was blended like a cocktail with seductive, predatory male sexual energy that assaulted her at every level. It silently said, beneath the smooth veneer of perfect gentlemanly courtesy, that he wanted to fuck her, left, right, up, down and sideways. And that it would be well worth her while.

She didn't doubt it. But she wasn't going to listen, not even with her nerves jangling, her skin prickling, her heart thudding. Back off, boyo. This was business, and that was how it was going to stay.

"You're not what you try to appear," she said. "You are charming and flirtatious and inscrutable, Mr. Janos, but tiny details betray you. Your hands should be soft from handling nothing heavier than a pen and a computer mouse, but yours are scarred and callused. And your face. Your nose has been broken. Several times it wasn't set. You can't blame the martial arts club. If it happened during sparring, why would a rich, image-conscious businessman neglect to get his nose set? Of course he would not."

"I did not see the point of—"

"So it happened when you were a boy," she went on smoothly. "No one set your nose then, either, which implies poverty, neglect, or both. I'm thinking an urban environment, judging from your basic vibe. And those scars on your face, the tiny one above your lip, the one cutting through your eyebrow, the one on your forehead that you almost hide with your hair, it makes me wonder what other scars you hide with the beautiful six-thousand-euro suit you're wearing. You've had laser treatments, dermabrasion, but the ghosts always remain."

"I'm glad you like the suit," he said blandly.

"You're no country boy," she went on. "But you're not from Rome. You don't have the accent of the Roman periphery. Your Italian has a Roman cadence, but to my ear, it is a studied one, not a native one. You grew up somewhere else, speaking something else, and learned your perfect Italian later. And you grew up rough. Very rough."

He stared back at her, frozen into stillness. His eyes were chips of black, opaque glass. "Go on," he said.

She set down the teacup, threaded her fingers together, and rode the swirling current deeper into wild speculation. She felt like she was drifting on a boat into a night-dark cave of mysteries, and only the currents of air, the echoes, the flutter of distant bats' wings could hint at its true vastness. It was dangerous. And . . . exciting.

She pondered his stark face for a moment, and went on. "You are a ladies' man, and your charm is practiced. You are accustomed to controlling women with sex, but unlike other men with that ability, your ego doesn't rest on it—although your looks and your body would entitle you to—"

"Thank you," he murmured.

"I'm not complimenting you," she said, her voice impatient. "This is an analysis, Janos. Not flattery. Not flirting."

"My error," he said, after a brief, startled pause.

She did not acknowledge his sarcasm. "Sex is a tool for you," she said. "But when seduction does not achieve its goal, you just change tactics without getting your pride hurt and try again, and again, and again. This suggests a lack of machismo not normal in a man from any culture I know—particularly not one who professes to have grown up in Italy. Italian men aren't known for their humility, or their self-control. This coolness, this calculation regarding sex is a trait I associate with high-end sex professionals."

His gaze flickered.

She pounced. "Ah. I've hit a sore spot," she murmured. "Have you ever been a gigolo, Mr. Janos? Do you have a more colorful past than you lead people to believe? Some dirty, dangerous secrets of your own?"

He stared at her. His eyes burned.

"Tell me something, Janos," she whispered. "Can you make your cock hard on command?"

His mouth was a hard, flat line. "Yes," he said. "But in your vicinity, no effort is necessary."

"What a lovely compliment. Should I be gratified?"

"Reach under the table, and take the measure of your future gratification right now," he said.

"Oh, my." She pretended to be shocked. "The veneer of the perfect gentleman is cracking."

"You should not wonder at it since you shattered it yourself with an ice pick. See what lurks beneath the veneer. Go on, feel it. It's yours for the asking. I do not think you will be disappointed."

She stared at him, her heart pumping. The game had slipped out of her control and taken on its own life. She realized that she was tempted to do exactly as he invited. To grasp his cock, test his heat, the hardness. Feel the vital energy of him pulsing against her hand.

Currents of silent communication swirled between them, dangerous eddies of challenge. She dragged herself back from the brink.

"No," she said. "I'm not finished yet."

"On the contrary, Ms. Steele. You are. The subject is closed." He rose to his feet. The hard tone of his voice and the coiled tension in his body suggested that he was reaching the end of his self-control.

Good. Exactly where she wanted him. Adrenaline pumped through her. She got up and moved in behind him. "Everything you told me is a lie," she challenged him. "Capriccio Consulting is a lie, your smooth style, your ego-stroking offers. I can't see inside you, Janos. All I see are smoke and mirrors. Which makes me think that perhaps there is no one inside at all. Just a gutted, blackened hole. Which means . . ."

She seized him from behind, pressing the tip of the tiny dagger from the ruby-studded horn necklace against the throbbing pulse point in his throat in one swift lunge. "Who the fuck are you, Janos?" she asked softly. "Who sent you?"

His throat worked. "I will warn you only once," he forced out. "Release me. Now."

"I'm warning you, too," she said. "This blade is coated with a poison that works with incredible speed. If the dagger breaks the skin, within seconds your convulsions will be so violent, they will probably snap your spine."

His larynx moved beneath the blade. "Cut me then."

That was so unexpected her brain wouldn't process it for a second.

"Go on," he prompted. "Why should I fear death? I am a gutted, empty hole, no? Death holds no terrors for me. So cut me."

She opened her mouth, not sure of what she was going to say, and in that moment of hesitation and doubt—

Holy . . . *shit.* The dagger flew, bounced. She was spun and flipped. Pain flashed white hot through her body, and *oof,* her breath was knocked out and her head hit the floor, painfully hard.

She was flat on her back, staring up at the bottom of the table, at the carved leg of his overturned chair, seeing stars.

Janos pinned her, blocking every point of leverage. Her arms were stretched high, both wrists clamped in the manacle of one of his enormous hands. His steely forearm pressed her chin up and put intense pressure on her windpipe.

How . . . ? God, he was fast! No one had gotten the better of her like that in years, not since she'd learned to fight like a hellion. She fought the panic, the fury. "What happened to your death wish, you lying snake bastard?"

His face was inches from hers, a taut mask of fury. "I reconsidered it. I do not like a poisoned blade at my throat."

His forearm lifted, enough to let a stream of air rush through her bruised throat. It rasped, making her cough. Their eyes were locked.

"Let me go," she coughed out, without much hope. "Get off me."

"Ten seconds ago you were about to kill me. Why should I?" he asked. "Do I look that stupid?"

She coughed again. "Who are you?"

"You are in no position to ask the questions. Enough about me. Let's talk about you. Turnabout is fair play, no?"

Panic swelled inside her. Spots danced before her eyes. Being pinned reminded her of . . . *no.* She would not think of it.

She struggled harder. "Let . . . me . . . go!"

"No." He countered every move, keeping her flat to the floor. "Where to begin? I am a more ordinary man than you gave me credit for being, so I will start from the obvious place. Your beauty."

"Oh, shut up. I'm not interested in your bullshit—"

"Too bad. You are afraid of your beauty?"

She snorted. "Wrong."

He ignored her. "You are too afraid to destroy it, in case you might need it. Too vain to hide it completely. But you are afraid to use it as you could if you wished. Look at you, all in black, every inch covered. Hair dragged back, face bare of cosmetics. You hate men. You love to confuse them, attack them. Punish them for treating you like a thing—"

She convulsed. "Let go of me, you twisted son of a bitch!"

He bore down, squashing her to breathless immobility. "You knock everyone who gets near you off balance," he went on. "It is the only way you feel steady yourself. You are always braced for a blow, always angry, always afraid. You are too thin, with purple shadows under your eyes. You sleep badly, eat little. You weep secretly in the darkest part of the night."

She stopped moving, chilled to her bones at his supernaturally good guesses. "Shut up," she whispered. "Just . . . stop, Janos."

He moved in smoothly for the kill. "Your jewelry says so much, I am amazed that you dare to make it. Sensuality clashing with violence, beauty clashing with paranoia. The contradiction is like a bleeding wound. For you are wounded, no? Mortally wounded, maybe. But you are taking your own sweet time to die, hmm?"

No. She mouthed the word. There was no breath behind it.

"Even the name you've chosen reflects this longing for hardness. You wish you were forged from steel, no? The only thing that gives you pleasure is working with metal. Sharp blades, needles, drugs and poisons. Secrets to armor you. You dream of invulnerability, but it is just that . . . a dream. You are curled around unhealed wounds."

Her throat ground against the crushing pressure of his arm as she turned her head away. "No," she croaked. "It's not true. It's not me. None of it. You asshole."

His eyes narrowed. "You hide behind the child." His voice took on a tone of discovery. "You need the child. What other reason do you have to keep living? Why else wake up in the morning, put food in your mouth? You need her to claw your way from one day to the next. No?"

"Leave her out of this." Tam squeezed her eyes shut. With her hands confined, she couldn't cover even her shaking mouth, her leaking eyes.

Nor could she reach the panic button strapped to her thigh, the one that would summon Nick and Davy, guns drawn. They had begged and urged and lectured her to mike the room so they could monitor the conversation, but know-it-all bitch that she was, she hadn't wanted their noses that deep in her business.

"Poor little girl," he murmured. "Too innocent to understand how she is being used. And still, in the middle of the night, you are terrified at what you have done to yourself. The vulnerability, the work, the time, the noise. The awful responsibility. Do you wonder if survival is even worth it? If death would be less frightening? Less effort?"

Her body shook in his hard grasp. "Fuck you," she whispered.

"I would," he said. "Right here, on the floor, until you whimper with delight. You like strength. You crave it, as much as you fear it. And I am strong enough for you. I would put it all at your service. Everything you fear, everything you hate, everything you fight so hard against dedicated to your pleasure."

Her eyes popped open at that absurdity. "Oh, please. What a pile of melodramatic shit."

"I could force you," he said. "Part of me wants to. But you are so fragile. You would close up completely, and I would find myself fucking a beautiful doll."

She laughed. "That's enough for most men," she muttered. "They never know the difference."

He stared into her eyes. "I know the difference."

She felt too weak to lift her ribcage beneath the weight of his body. But that was all right. She didn't really want to breathe. Her chest felt too unstable. Pulling air in could ignite it like dry tinder, make it burst into flames. Her brain kept trying to form responses to what he said, but they didn't make it as far as her shaking mouth. She could make no sound without air anyway. She was muddled, flushed with a strange, hot power that pumped up from some mysterious hidden spring inside her. Speeding her heart. Her skin felt weirdly sensitive. Hairs prickling up.

Almost as if she was . . . oh, dear God. Why, that sneaky bastard. How dare he. As if she had no clue, no defenses. He'd gotten so deep in her mind, fucking with her head, making her . . .

Hot. She shifted. He anticipated the movement, canting his hips so the whole hard, hot length of his cock was cradled in the cleft between her legs. His hips swiveled, a slow, rocking, grinding push.

She gasped. She was turned on. Out of nowhere, and like never before. She'd thought it was all burned out of her, after Novak.

But no. She was on fire. Hot and soft and shivering. He'd made her . . . wet. He was a sorcerer, a shaman.

His face was a mask of concentration. "You feel it," he said.

She did. There was no point in lying. It took her a moment to reply. "And? So?" Her tone was ragged, wobbly. "What of it, Janos? Happy with yourself now? Get off me. Go carve another notch on your gigolo belt. What the fuck do I care?"

"Not yet," he said. "I aim higher. I want a bigger prize before I carve my notch. Feel how good it would be." He stretched her trapped arms higher. Swiveled his hips, and pleasure throbbed through her, from groin to nipples, flushing her face, making her thighs clench, her knees contract, her toes curl.

This had to stop. "Good for you, maybe," she shot back.

"I know," he murmured. "You would never let me please you the way I know that I could. You would never open yourself so wide, let down your guard so much. You have not been fortunate in your lovers?"

Hah. What a joke. Novak flashed through her mind, Georg, Stengl. "You think you could please me?" Her voice shook. "Men always think they have the answer to women's prayers bouncing between their legs. It makes them pathetically easy to control."

His smile faded. "You're afraid. You have been abused? By who?"

"Fuck off, Janos." She renewed her struggles, but with a deft shift of his weight, he immobilized her again.

"It is a terrible crime to hurt a woman in this way," he said.

The gentleness of his voice both infuriated and embarrassed her. Condescending son of a bitch. How dare he feel sorry for her. "Do not presume to understand me, you prick," she hissed.

His face was somber. "Ah, yes. I see. Compassion. The biggest insult of all."

"Compassion, my ass. You're a cold fish, Janos. You're just jerking me around at random until you find out what strings and buttons make me jump. I'm bored with the game."

"I don't believe you're bored." His low voice rumbled, caressing her. "Your body is hot and soft. It vibrates under me. Your face is pink, your lips are red. Your eyes are lit up, shining. You're having fun."

Laughter jerked out of her, the words were so incongruous. "Fun?" she squeaked. "You call this fun? Having a muscle-bound lout throw me on the floor, sit on me, and fuck with my mind?"

"Since you have not invited me to fuck with any other part," he said philosophically. "And yes. It is fun, for a complicated woman like you. How long has it been since anyone challenged you? Since someone gave you anything real to push against? You have to play hard to find your pleasure, no? How long since someone brought you to orgasm?"

Years. She shut her eyes, as he rocked against her. She shuddered with the hunger, and the snarled, painful memories and shame that came with it. "Stop," she said. "I don't want it."

"You are lying," he said. "You are so close. Fight me. Throw me off. You're strong. The strongest woman I have ever known. Try harder."

"Arrogant dickhead." She writhed desperately, and before she knew it, he was kissing her, his lips dragging over hers. He tasted good, so smooth and hot and fragrant. So strong and sensual, his muscular body hard and unyielding. She wanted to flip him over onto his back and devour him. But he was too big, too heavy. She couldn't control him. It was driving her mad, the helplessness, the heat.

She struggled. Every desperate jerk, he answered with his hips, his tongue. He murmured low, sexy words of encouragement, nudging her closer to . . . no, her shattered nerves weren't up for this kind of voltage, she was going to explode, disappear, die . . . no . . . *yes.*

Yes. The wave broke, crashing through her. The fear, the fury, all blended with a pulsing pleasure so sweet and hot and deliciously endless, widening out to a shimmering glow . . .

The crash of a door being slapped open broke through her floating languor. Janos went tense with readiness on top of her.

"Holy freaking shit. What the—Jesus, Tam!"

Tam turned her head. Davy and Nick stared down at her, mouths agape, guns pointed at Janos. Janos looked at her, and silently raised his eyebrow. He did not let go of her hands.

Tam licked her lips. "Ah . . . um," she said, inanely.

Davy slowly lifted his gun. "Help me out here, Tam," he said carefully. "You hit the panic button, right? So what's the deal?"

Panic button? Oh. Yes. The button. Tam's gaze dropped to her thigh where the band with the panic button was strapped. In the throes of heaving on the floor with her legs clamped around Janos's thighs, the button had tripped itself. Against the floor most likely. Very funny.

It took effort, under Janos's weight, to suck in enough breath to speak. "M-must have gotten pushed by accident. Sorry for the adrenaline rush, boys. Thanks for the speedy response. Nice to know you care."

"So, uh, I assume then that everything's cool then?" Davy's voice was wary. "We can, er . . . leave you to it?"

She smiled coolly. "Yes, gentlemen. Thank you for your concern, but I have the matter completely in hand."

Davy's eyes flicked to her wrists, still clamped in Janos's unwavering grip, and cleared his throat. He was trying not to grin without much success. "Yeah. We'll just disappear. Right? Bye."

He slunk out the door, but Nick lingered, a huge, shit-eating grin on his face. "Man, I take my hat off to you," he said to Janos. "You must have monster cojones to tangle with this hellcat. I suggest you watch out for 'em."

"Oh, but I will," Janos said.

"Piss off, Nick," Tam snapped.

Nick ducked out the door, still chortling. The door swung shut.

Tam forced herself to meet Janos's gaze, and realized, with intense discomfort, that she could think of nothing to say. That earthshaking orgasm had wiped her brain clean.

"A panic button?" He smiled. "No microphones? I'm glad to know that our conversation was private, at least."

"You can let go of my hands." She felt, oh God, almost shy.

"You're wearing sixteen different kinds of death draped over your body," he pointed out.

"I won't cut, spray, scratch, or stick you with any of them," she said. "At least, not without fresh provocation."

He gave her a cautious smile. "How do I know you'll keep your word?"

"You don't," she said. "You have to risk it. Didn't you just strip me bare, read my mind, make me come? Don't you trust your instincts?"

He grunted. "No. I do not trust anything. But I will trust you, Tamara . . . this once. Just because I want to. No other reason."

Tears stung her. Ridiculous. She was going soft. This was probably just a deeper level of his clever games, but if so, it was subtler than she was. "That's dangerous," she whispered.

"I know." His words sounded heartfelt. He let go the steely grip he had on her wrists and rolled off her body.

Tam rubbed her sore wrists as she sat up. Heat lingered in her face and glowed in her body. She felt so light, without him on top of her. Like she might float away. A silly, frivolous girl. Insubstantial.

And vulnerable. She hated feeling vulnerable.

He got to his feet. She hastened to follow. No way was she staying crumpled on the floor, huddled in his shadow.

She stumbled, and Janos caught her instantly. His move was so slick, so graceful, it felt inevitable that she should end up in his arms, kissing him again. His lips were so pleading and soft and hot, his body throbbing magnetic male energy at her, through her.

Panic cramped the sweet swell of longing, and she fought free of the kiss. "No," she said breathlessly. "Don't push your luck."

"My luck?" He grinned, and she was dazzled by the devastating white teeth, the deep dimples. "The luck was yours, *bella*. I want to push *your* luck. As far as it will go, and I think it can go very far."

She pushed at his chest. "No. Stop," she said shakily. "Enough."

"Let me." He sank to his knees, sliding his hands under the loose black silk of her blouse. "Let me please you. For hours."

She shuddered as the warm, rough rasp of his calluses scraped over the sensitive skin of her belly, and pushed at his face, feeling the strong bones, the hot velvety skin of him. "You are not going to get lucky tonight, you oversexed son of a bitch, so back off!"

He rose gracefully to his feet, looking resigned.

"Tell me your real name, who sent you, and what the hell you want from me," she demanded. "That's all I ever wanted from this meeting. I'm not leaving until I get it. And neither are you."

All the playfulness went out in his face. The energy of the room changed. It felt colder. Darker.

Oh, no. Oh, shit. Whatever it was that he had to tell her, it was something she would not enjoy hearing, she realized with a sickening flash of insight. Her belly began to hurt.

He tried to smile, but the effort was hollow. "Promise me you won't kill me," he said.

She did not smile back. "I make no promises."

He stared down at the remainder of their meal. "I don't have any name other than Val Janos to give you," he said. "The name I was born with means nothing to anyone, so you might as well stick with Janos. It's one of several identities that I use. In my work."

She swallowed and braced herself. "Fine, then," she said tightly. We'll stick with Janos. What work? Who sent you, Janos?"

His Adam's apple moved, as if he were trying to speak, but couldn't bring himself to get the words out. Her neck prickled, her skin crept. Suspicion hardened into cold, blunt certainty. She knew.

The two people who had most cause to actively search for her were Daddy Novak and Georg Luksch. Novak wanted her dead. Georg wanted her, period. This man was not here to assassinate her, of that much she was sure. Which meant . . .

"Georg," she whispered.

His face did not change, his eyes did not drop. And he did not contradict her. The stony coldness spread.

"I am an operative for PSS," he said. "Prime Security Solutions. It is a—"

"A private army for hire. Yes, I am familiar with PSS," she said, tonelessly. "So Georg hired you? How did you find me?"

It took him a long time to reply. "The McClouds," he finally said. "I planted cameras outside their homes weeks ago. One day you showed up at Connor McCloud's house. I got there in time to put a GPS locator on your SUV. It was a stroke of luck."

She put her hand over her eyes. "I can't believe this." She wanted to shoot herself for being so sloppy. Putting everyone in danger, especially Rachel. She'd just wanted so badly for Rachel to have a semi-normal life. She might have known that it wouldn't be possible. Not with Tam Steele and her reality-warping force field anywhere nearby. Forget normality. Forget anything clean or healthy. Just give up the effort.

"It took a while," he offered, almost if he were trying to console her for fucking up. "If it weren't for the McClouds—"

"Shut up. Just shut up," she said through clenched teeth, and another unpleasant thought jolted her. "Hey. What about Erin?" she demanded. "You involved Erin. Stay away from my friends, understand? If you mess with my friends, I will cut you into bloody little pieces."

"I will not bother Erin, or any of your other friends," he soothed.

A worse thought occurred to her, with a wrench of stomach-turning fear. "Rachel," she whispered. "Oh, no. I'll kill you. I'll gut you, put out your eyes, break every bone if you've done anything to my—"

"No, no," he said hastily. "I have not touched her. And I will not. Though those were my original orders. To use her as a bargaining chip."

"Oh yes? We're not bargaining, Janos. Whatever Georg wants from me, the answer is fuck you very much, but no. I don't want to see you ever again, you scumbag pimp. Get lost."

She slapped the door open and confronted a stupefied Davy and Nick. "Escort this lying piece of walking shit off the premises," she ordered them, her voice shaking. "If you ever see him again, kill him."

She stormed out of the room, eyes full of furious tears. She despised herself for wanting him. When all he intended was to pass her over to Georg, that slobbering pervert.

After sampling the goods himself first, of course. Why ever not?

If there was one thing she hated more than anything else in the world, it was feeling stupid.

Chapter
8

He'd failed. The world as he knew it had ended.

Val stood in the middle of the room, staring at the hole in which she had just stood. She'd left abruptly, distorting space, sucking the air out with her. Leaving a vacuum that made his lungs burn. The one time in his life as a professional liar in which he gave a shit, and the woman had seen right through him, effortlessly. Smoke and mirrors. A gutted hole. A lifetime of training good for nothing. Now what?

McCloud came in, looking baffled. "Hey, Janos," he said gruffly. "Look alive. You heard the lady. Move it."

He just looked at the man stupidly. His throat ached. His brain stalled out.

McCloud made an impatient gesture. "Your business here is finished. Go on back to where you came from. And don't come back."

Val roused himself, retrieved his briefcase. In the anteroom, Nick Ward silently handed him his coat and knife. He shrugged the garment on, sheathed the knife, moving stiffly, like a robot.

Ward cleared his throat. "Hey, uh, don't take it too hard."

Val looked at him, utterly blank. "I beg your pardon?"

"A woman like Tam..." Ward waved his hand helplessly. "That's, like, her way of showing that she likes you."

Val felt a crazy urge to laugh. "Likes me? Me, the lying piece of walking shit that you have been ordered to shoot on sight?"

"Oh, don't take that personally," Ward encouraged. "At least you made an impression. And let me tell you, that chick is hard to impress."

"True," McCloud interjected dourly. "You're still alive, so you must have something going for you. Now move it. This isn't a fucking therapy session."

The men flanked him, escorted him down the elevator and walked him out of the club in stolid silence. They left him a few hundred meters from the building and strode briskly away without looking back.

With an extreme act of will, Val gathered his wits and looked around. There was a bar across the street, a seedy place with few people inside. He would take refuge in a glass of scotch. He might as well continue to act like Val Janos until further notice. He had no better persona to assume. Certainly none he could call his own.

He ordered, and sipped morosely at the shot of Glenfiddich, hunched over the scarred wooden table in the backmost booth. The flavor reminded him of those gleaming, tilted eyes, taking him in, sizing him up over the rim of the cut crystal tumbler.

Piercing him through.

He could not hide from those bright eyes. Empty, paper nonentity that he was after all those years of killing and whoring for PSS.

He rubbed his face. The woman had power, he acknowledged silently. To make him creep into a bar with his shoulders hunched, to suck liquor and feel sorry for himself. But he did not have that leisure.

In forty-eight hours, Novak would start to cut. Val could not acknowledge defeat. Not yet.

He got his laptop out of the briefcase, unfolded the collapsible liquid crystal monitor into a twelve-inch screen, unfolded the tiny skeleton keyboard, and booted up. He took another swallow of scotch, let it burn its way down his gullet, and opened the file of Novak's photographs that he had scanned into his computer that morning.

They shone, turning in the matrix. It never bored him to meditate upon them. There was always something new to discover in a photograph of Steele, even while squirming under Novak's boot heel.

He clicked through them until he found his favorite, the most mysterious and enigmatic of them all. The black dress, the sad face. The bouquet of wild daisies and lavender laid on the bronze plaque. He put it in the matrix and took three steps back, letting it turn and shine.

A shiver went up his back as an idea took form. He began to magnify the photograph, enlarging the plaque until it filled the screen.

Other bouquets were piled below the plaque, obscuring what was engraved on it. He barely made out the word *Zetrinja*, a date, *1992*, and some quote in a language he did not know. Then a list of names.

It was a very long list. The names were indecipherable, at least with this program, at this pixelation.

The memorial plaque and the names suggested a mass grave. There were crowds of people. Men in suits, television cameras.

A memorial service, honoring the dead from some wartime atrocity. His mind raced. 1992. The Serbo-Croatian conflict. Not his area of expertise, but Henry had spent time in the Balkans and spoke the language well. PSS had many operatives deployed there. And Henry was the only person he had spoken to about this mission.

He pulled out his phone and called him. His fellow operative was currently at the main PSS headquarters outside Paris. The phone rang six times before his friend answered, his voice thick with sleep.

"Fuck this, Val. It's five in the morning," Henry complained.

"I need a favor," Val said without apology.

"Don't you always," Henry grumbled.

"Ever hear of a place called Zetrinja?"

Henry thought about it. "Rings a bell. Croatia, I think."

"Go into the archives. Find what you can about what happened there in 1992. See if you can get me a list of the girls and young women from the age of, say, ten to twenty who might have been involved in it."

Henry whistled. "You think Steele is Croatian?" he said finally.

"Could be," Val said. "Or this could be completely irrelevant."

Henry was silent for a long moment. "What's going on?" he asked quietly. "Something off?"

Val hesitated. He'd been trying to decide whether or not to involve Henry in this snakepit ever since he had left Budapest. But if he needed to mount a rescue mission, he was not going to be able to do it alone. He needed backup, and Henry was the only one he trusted.

He took the plunge. "Something's off," he said.

He detailed Imre's hostage situation to Henry in a few terse phrases. His friend was grimly silent afterward.

"That rots, buddy," he said. "You are truly fucked."

"Ah. Thank you for the encouragement. I am heartened."

"What next?" Henry asked.

"I don't know," Val said. "I'm improvising. I may come up with something extremely dangerous and crazy. Can I count upon you?"

"Don't insult me, asshole. I live for dangerous and crazy. Want me to come to—"

"No. Stay in Europe. I'll let you know what I need. And check on Zetrinja for me as soon as you can. I need a hook into this woman."

They closed the call, and he pulled up the phone numbers.

Time to start bothering her. In a couple of hours, Steele would know exactly who was putting it to her. With luck, she'd get angry enough to try to track him down and kill him. That old schoolyard attitude: negative attention was better than no attention at all.

He would do anything to make her notice him. Anything at all.

He should have told the boy.

Regret for not having done so ate at him worse than the physical pain. Imre tried to breathe, to relax into it, but he could not. His lungs had contracted, clenching like fists that would not relent.

He rocked back and forth on the small, hard cot, gasping for air.

The room was small, stinking. Squalid and desolate. A dim cube of concrete blocks with no natural light. Day and night were artificial constructs, defined by a brutally bright, jittery fluorescent light on a timer that was switched on for twelve hours, and off, to utter blank darkness for the other twelve. The room was filled with dismal, hopeless graffiti from its previous inhabitants, most of which appeared to have been written in human blood, or other substances even less appealing.

Imre tried not to look at it. Not wearing his spectacles helped.

The pain was grinding, unrelenting. He'd had his share of aches and pains even before the doctor's revelation, and there were the two beatings, but the worst now were his bones, degenerating inside him.

He desperately missed the morphine tablets the doctors had given him. He missed even more the other techniques he used for pain control. Bach was his favorite. The suites for violoncello, or the partitas for violin. Music could make the mind take flight from a failing body. Also poetry, philosophy. Even just the pigeons cooing outside his apartment window, the clouds turned pink by sunset. A cup of tea and a game of chess with his old neighbor down the hall. Humble pleasures. They seemed so precious now.

He tried to call to memory his favorite psalms for comfort. He had tried to pray. He had even called on Ilona for help, and her sweet memory was always a blessing. But he was no saint, no superman.

He was terrified out of his wits.

It had been hard enough, to face up to his own impending death even before the abduction. Pancreatic cancer, they had told him. Advanced stage. They had offered him the usual treatments, but he read the look in the eyes of the doctors, he listened to what they said about infiltration, lymph nodes, metastases to liver and bone. He understood the futility of fighting it. Three months if he did nothing. That was almost a month ago now. And he had not told Vajda.

It wasn't that he was afraid of death. He was almost eighty. Thirty years of his adult life he had lived without his darling Ilona and little Tina. He was ready—he had faith—he was almost certain that he would find Ilona and Tina on the other side of the veil, but death was still a great unknown. It was hard to let go. But it tormented him that his poor Vajda was being ground up in this monster's infernal machine for Imre's sake when Imre was practically a dead man already.

Not that the cancer would matter to Vajda. Seeing his foster father tortured would hurt the boy terribly. Vajda was so brittle, so vulnerable and alone. He had established no other ties, from what Imre could see, tenderhearted though he was beneath his defenses. Imre had always sensed the depth of the boy's love for him. His need, too. Though his proud Vajda would surely rather die than admit it.

Vajda was the son he had never had. And what a son. Such intelligence, such potential, abandoned in a sewer. Pearls before swine.

He had failed his foster son. He had not succeeded in freeing him from this pigsty. Imre had wanted so badly to see Vajda bloom and grow, to see him take his rightful place in the world. He was wasted as a mercenary soldier, just as he had been wasted as a mafiya thug's minion. That cruel, stupid waste angered him. Ate at him, for years.

Now, at last, he understood why Vajda had always insisted that he had no choice but to continue working for Novak. How ignorant, how arrogant Imre had been to scold the boy, call him foolish, defeatist. He realized now that Vajda's caution was just a calculated bid for survival. He'd simply been displaying the pragmatic realism that had kept him alive against all odds. He owed the boy an apology.

More than an apology. He owed Vajda everything. But this was a price that the boy could not afford to pay. This would cost him his soul.

He should have told the boy. He'd been so afraid that Vajda would dig in his heels, insist on staying near if he knew Imre was ill. Budapest was a dangerous place for him, full of bitterness and painful memories. He'd thought it best that the boy stay away from his past. But the past had overtaken them with a speed no one could have foreseen.

Only Imre's death would liberate Vajda. But how? The room was empty but for the cot, the blanket, the metal toilet sticking out of the wall. They gave him food twice a day on a plastic plate, a plastic tray, with a single flimsy plastic spoon to eat it with. There was no metal in the room to file to sharpness, no glass to break.

He shrank from the idea of taking his own life, but surely it would not be a sin if it was done for love, out of desperation. At the very least, it was less of a sin than the one that Vajda risked for his sake.

If he could only find a way.

Tam still shook with rage when the camo'd doors ground open out of the mountainside to let her into the underground garage.

She'd hoped the drive would calm her down, but she was nowhere near calm. She was utterly freaked out. So angry she wanted to vomit.

Perhaps the lure of overtime pay and some abject begging would persuade Rosalia to stay for another couple of hours so Tam could throw herself onto the computer and start thrashing out a plan.

That hope vanished when she heard Rachel's wails. They had that nails-driving-straight-into-the-brain quality that always meant a very bad night. *Shit*. Why now? Tonight, of all nights. She was meat.

Tam had barely put down her purse before Rosalia thrust the shrieking toddler into Tam's arms and lunged for the closet to re-trieve her coat and purse.

"Hey, Rosalia, hold on," she protested, pitching her voice to slice through Rachel's howls. "I was going to ask you if you could stay a little bit longer tonight, just until I have a chance to—"

"No! I have to go right now! My boys just got arrested over in Olympia! I just got the phone call, a half an hour ago, and I was going to call you, but the baby was crying and I didn't have a chance. I have to go to my boys right now!"

Tam was startled out of her own problems, finally noticing the ashen cast of Rosalia's face, the stress sweat on her forehead, her rolling, reddened eyes. "But—but how . . ." Her voice trailed off.

A terrible suspicion dawned. Oh, that evil, evil son of a bitch. Suspicion grew instantly into certainty. He would suffer for this.

"I don't know! They were working in that restaurant, and the cops come in and say they are dealing drugs out of the kitchen!" Rosalia's voice vibrated with outrage. "Drugs! It's a dirty lie! My boys don't deal drugs! They're good boys! Roberto was going to get married next month, and Francisco, he was enrolled in night school at the community college! He's going to be a pharmacist! They are good boys, both of them! I have to go, right now! I am sorry."

Tam's heart sank. "From this, I gather you won't be able to come in for a while," she said.

Rosalia threw up her hands. "I don't know! How can I know when I can come again? I tell you, I am sorry! This problem, I have to fix it! I don't know how long it will—"

"Yes, I know," Tam said, through clenched teeth. "I understand perfectly. Hold on, Rosalia. Don't run out just yet. Let me get something for you." Tam tried to put Rachel down, but the kid stuck to her like she was smeared with superglue, so Tam wiggled into the pantry closet with Rachel still clutching her neck. She shoved cereals and cans carelessly out of the way and pried a board out of the wall to reveal a hidden safe. She tapped in the codes until it swung open and grabbed a few packets of emergency cash. Enough to help the hardworking Rosalia out with whatever came up, but not so much that it would frighten her.

It was the least she could do, since she was terribly afraid that Rosalia's problems were Tam's own goddamn fault anyhow.

She came out into the kitchen again. Rosalia waited, clutching her purse with white-knuckled hands. Tam held out the wads of cash.

"Take this," she said brusquely. "It might help. Bail, and all."

Rosalia took it and hefted it gingerly, her eyes big. "This . . . this is clean money?" she asked timidly.

Hmph. Rosalia was no fool. She had a nose for anything outlaw, despite the language barrier. "Clean enough," she assured the older woman. "I didn't steal it. I earned it with my jewelry business. I even paid taxes on it, wonder of wonders. Go on, get out of here, and go see to your boys. I'll call you to see how it's going."

Rosalia shoved the money into her purse and grabbed Tam in a tight, impetuous hug. Tam stiffened, unprepared for it, but Rosalia didn't care. She just chucked her on the chin, gave the whimpering Rachel a fervent kiss, and scurried down the stairs.

Her exit was another upset to Rachel's already precarious emotional balance. It touched off a brand-new screaming, flailing fit. The kid had supernatural endurance and vocal technique that would put a Wagnerian opera diva to shame. An hour went by, and her wails were still so loud Tam didn't even hear her alarm. Only the red strobing light over the doors informed her that there was a breach of security.

She'd installed the system so she could keep an eye on her domain while rocking out at high volume on headphones, never thinking she'd need it for dealing with a three-year-old's high decibel tantrums. Life was funny that way.

She carried the shrieking child over to the security monitor and stared at it, a sour, sinking feeling in her belly. A police cruiser idled outside the apparently falling-down barn that camoflauged the entrance to her driveway. Two men were inside. One lifted a cell phone to his ear and talked into it, scowling. A bad sign, that they had found her at all. Someone had blown her cover. Her teeth gritted.

That filthy rat bastard. Fucking with her. Again.

She chewed her lip, barely hearing Rachel's shrieks. If she ignored them, they would get huffy, go away, and come back in force. A siege she definitely did not need. That was a game she could not win.

She hit the button that activated the intercom hidden in a hollow tree right next to the police cruiser and typed one-handed, changing the audio settings so their responses would be loud enough to hear over Rachel's noise. "Good evening, officers," she said into the mike. "What can I do for you?"

The guy behind the wheel, the beefier one, jumped hearing her voice and Rachel's coming out of nowhere. His window buzzed down, and he leaned out the window, scowling. "Ms. Steele? Is that you?"

So they knew her name, too. Worse and worse. "Yes, I'm Tam Steele," she said. "May I ask what this is about?"

"May we come up to the house?" the man asked. "We'd like to speak to you."

Shit, shit, shit. "May I ask what it's about?" she asked again.

"Ms. Steele, may we come up to the house and speak to you?" the man repeated doggedly.

She mouthed a vicious curse against Val Janos's ancestors back to the seventh generation and hit the buttons that would open up the barn passage. So much for her clever, costly camo job. It would be a public sideshow from now on. She might as well call Seth's workmen to come and dismantle the fucking thing. What a pain in the ass.

Maybe she could sell it. Right. At an assassin's garage sale.

She used the few minutes of grace that she had before they reached the house to dress the wiggling, shrieking Rachel in a coat and shoes, and she was waiting for them with the toddler wailing on her hip as the cruiser pulled up to the garage. A grizzled, burly older man and a skinny younger one got out, looking avidly around.

"Good evening, officers," she said. "What can I do for you?"

"Good evening, Ms. Steele. I'm Sheriff Meechum, and this is Deputy Licht," said the older man. "Can we come in?"

She considered asking if they had a search warrant, just out of principle, but decided on the spot that it would be counterproductive. Besides, they would never find anything incriminating. She was careful that way. "Certainly," she said, resigned. "Follow me."

It irritated the shit out of her, being bullied into letting strange men into her private space when she and Rachel were alone. She was reasonably sure she would be a match for the two of them, even armed as they were, but not one-handed, with Rachel clinging to her neck.

Rachel changed everything. All her formulas, all her rules.

Rachel was redoubling her efforts. She always flipped out in the presence of strangers, men in particular. It had taken her many months to get used to the McCloud Crowd's male contingent, and she was letting it be loudly known that those policemen were not on her security list. The noise grated on Tam's sanity. She was good at blocking out unwanted sensory data. She'd had intensive training in biofeedback, but Rachel's fits challenged her skills to the utmost.

She led them through the security room, up the stairs and into the kitchen. Between shrieks, she heard the TV. Winnie the Pooh singing about how much he loved honey.

Rosalia had left a pot of coffee, bless her. "May I offer you some coffee, officers? Cookies?" she asked politely.

"No, thank you, ma'am," Meechum said. "We'll get right to the point. We've received a tip that you are using controlled substances here. Making illegal weaponry. Drugs, explosives and . . . whatnot."

Tam widened her eyes in feigned shock and shook her head, switching the flailing Rachel from her exhausted right arm to the left and hoisting her higher. "No, I'm just a jewelry designer," she said.

The guy cleared his throat. "Hmph. Well. Can you think of any reason why this accusation might have been made against you?"

"I'd better look over my list of jealous ex-lovers," she said. "Their wives, too. You never know. The green-eyed monster."

The officer grunted and eyed Rachel. "Ma'am, is there by any chance someone else who can look after the kid while we have this conversation? It's, uh, hard to talk over this racket."

"No," Tam said. "There's no one."

The two men shot each other pained glances. "Couldn't you just, you know, put her in a playpen in the other room, or something?" the younger one suggested hopefully.

As if. She'd tried that only once, and learned her lesson but good. In fact, once she thought it through, she'd felt like an insensitive idiot for trying it. Like she could put Rachel in a pen and leave her alone. A flipped-out, scared little kid who'd spent the first two and a half years of her life locked in a fucking cage.

Not in this lifetime, buddy boy. Certainly not for your convenience.

She gave them a big smile. "No," she said. "I can't."

Licht blushed, his Adam's apple bobbing, and his eyes slid wildly away. They darted around to try and find a place to rest, always drawn back to her face. She let him flop on his hook for a few seconds and decided that this stupid sideshow was too fucking tedious to prolong.

Best to make it mercifully quick. She sighed. "Care to come up and see my laboratory?" she asked.

The two men stumped heavily up the stairs after her. There was nothing for them to object to. The questionable substances she had on the premises were hidden in such a way that the house would have to be knocked down to get at them, or she herself drugged or tortured to reveal their locations. Meechum and Licht didn't look like they were up to electrodes or waterboarding.

There wasn't much of the stuff, in any case. Just a little stash for her own personal emergency use. She did not arm the needles, sprays, daggers, grenades, or bomblets before she sold them. It was too risky. Too much exposure, too much accountability. The most she did was to post recommendations for arming them in a private, password-protected place on the Internet. The rest was up to the buyer.

No doubt disseminating even that much deadly information was illegal, but what the hell. Her conscience was a callused, leathery one. It had seen some hard use in its time.

Fortunately, she had an innocuous dummy line of jewelry without any hidden weapons to show, if necessary. The wearable weaponry pieces were kept in the safes camo'd into the walls.

Tam juggled, coaxed, and vainly cuddled Rachel while the two policemen poked around her laboratory. They squinted at the dummy pieces laid out on the display table for their benefit, poking gingerly as if they expected them to bite, and examined the heavy equipment, looking bewildered. Men usually were when they dealt with her. What a bore.

They were soon ready to leave, having found no plastic bags filled with pills or powder, no bricks of hashish or explosives. Just a working studio. She politely gave each of them one of her Deadly Beauty business cards. Meechum stared at it.

"Why the 'deadly' part?" he demanded.

She gave him her most mysterious, lash-fluttering smile. "Oh, that's just a little inside joke I had with an old lover, years ago," she said, throatily. "It was his nickname for me."

Licht chortled a little too loudly. "Must've been a real interesting relationship," he blurted.

She turned a wide-open, limpid gaze on him. "Oh, yes. It was."

He blushed, and started the squirrely eye dance again. She had to force herself not to groan and roll her eyes. Callow twit.

"Hmph. Well, then. Please don't take any long trips. You'll be hearing from us again, Ms. Steele," Meechum said.

"I'm looking forward to it," she said.

She and Rachel saw them out. The men climbed into their squad car with an air of relief. Thrilled to get away from the human ambulance siren, Tam reflected glumly as she watched their taillights recede into the night. Lucky them.

It took the better part of an hour to get Rachel calmed down, into pajamas and cuddled to sleep. At that point, she was too tired even to work up another fit of righteous anger at Janos's malicious meddling.

What a cruel joke. Whenever she let down her guard, she got screwed. But did she learn? Never.

Seldom did any of her lovers crack through her armor and startle her into genuine excitement—and not surprisingly, every single time it had happened, it had proven to be a disaster.

The last time had been with Victor Lazar, Raine's uncle. He'd at least been as fucked up as she herself, and every bit as shady, but so strong. He had radiated strength . . . like Janos did. That was the attraction, she reflected. Janos was right. She liked strength. A lot.

But Lazar had gotten himself killed before she even had a chance to enjoy him. Deservedly so, but still, it hurt. She'd wanted to punish his killer. Which was what had gotten her mixed up with Kurt Novak.

She shuddered. She'd considered herself up for anything, but that guy had been way over her head. Brilliant, sadistic, psychotic. Then there was Georg to add yet another flesh-creeping element to the mix.

Stop. She had more than enough fodder for nightmares in her head without dwelling on those guys.

She went down to the kitchen with a vague plan to stare out the window at the dark while sipping a shot of single malt when she noticed the light flashing on the answering machine. A rare occurrence, considering how few people had the number. She stabbed "play."

"Ms. Steele? This is Emma Carew from the adoption agency. There's been a hitch in the adoption proceedings. We really must talk about this in person, but I'm afraid that we may have to review the case. I'm not sure I should be calling you like this, but after all our conversations, I feel I owe you a personal explanation before we have to . . . well, this is terribly embarrassing, but we've received some alarming information regarding possible criminal activity in your household, and, er, your own unstable psychological condition. It may be necessary for us to take Rachel into protective custody pending a full investigation and psych evaluation for you, just until we can clarify that this—"

Rip. Tam yanked the machine right out of the wall. She flung it at the blank brick wall across the room. *Crash,* it fell to the ground in pieces. She stared at it, face red, heart revving.

Yes, very nice, Tamar. Lovely demonstration of your maturity, your fitness for parenting, lectured a dry, academic voice in her head. *All ready for your psych evaluation, aren't you?*

It was her mother's voice. It gave her a pang. She hadn't thought or even dreamed in that language for years. Hadn't known that she still remembered the sound of it. She hadn't heard it since she was fifteen.

Certainly not. How could you, knowing exactly what I would say about your carryings-on? For the love of God, Tamar. Really.

Oh, shut up, she silently said back. The voice did. Another one of her mother's dirty tricks. Haughty retreat. The silent treatment.

She instantly regretted having banished the internalized ghost, snippy though it was. The room seemed so empty without it.

She'd never suffered from loneliness before. She'd never minded solitude at all. On the contrary, aloneness meant safety, quiet, peace from the greedy, grabbing demands of other people. Aloneness meant cleanliness, freedom. She craved it.

That was why she loved working with metal and gemstones, beyond the natural love she had inherited from her goldsmith father. They were hard, shining, nonporous substances, impervious to stain. They did not absorb filth, they did not rot or corrupt. They were clean, stark, inviolable. She loved that. Longed for it.

Janos had guessed it. He'd put his finger right on it. And yet, he was the one who they sent to pimp her out to that scum Georg. He was the one charged with the task of throwing her back into the sewer.

Bastard. Putting Rachel's safety at risk. She would pulverize him, eviscerate him, iron-maiden him. She punched in his number.

He picked up swiftly, even at this late hour. "Ms. Steele?"

"Don't you Ms. Steele me, you stinking turd," she hissed in Italian. "How dare you?"

"Ms. Steele." The velvety amusement in his voice infuriated her. "I'm pleased to hear from you again so soon—"

"Shut up," she snarled. "Mess with me and my daughter again, and I will annihilate you."

A thoughtful pause on the other end. "Try to calm down," he said gently in Italian. "Let's meet and talk about this like two reasonable—"

"Fuck you," she snarled. "You make me sick."

She hung up on him and burst into tears.

Chapter
9

Tam raced feverishly through the house. No time for blubbering or second thoughts. She'd practiced this routine in her mind hundreds of times until it was as automatic as a martial arts kata.

First, the big suitcase that was always packed, and updated every single week on Sunday evening after Rachel was in bed, inventoried to make sure it was up to date on Rachel's constantly changing survival gear. The nose aspirator, the aerosol machine, the cortisone drops, the emergency antibiotics, the Tylenol syrup, the allergy ointments, the wipes, soaps, and anti-allergenic toiletries. Changes of clothes, diapers, underthings. A few bare essentials for herself tucked in around the corners. She pulled it out into the hall.

Then it was off to the kitchen, to grab some kiddie snacks. Crackers, carrot sticks, yogurts, cheese sticks, boxed fruit juices. The pantry safe, to yank out all the money and the envelope of bearer bonds. Her stash of passports. She thumbed through them, picked out her favorites, sealed the rest in the bag, and took them too. A tiptoeing pass through her bedroom to gather up emotional survival items; pink fuzzy blanket, curly-haired Sveti bear, battered blue binkie.

That son of a bitch. Her Rachel would never see her beloved Sveti again because of that meddling scum. She was alarmed to notice that tears were streaming down her face. She hadn't known how much she valued what she had built here. Her comfortable house that felt almost safe. Her drop-dead beautiful view of the Pacific. Her beach access to a secluded cove that no one else could reach except by boat. The outrageous sunsets she could see from her kitchen, living room, studio and bedroom windows. Her fabulously equipped studio, the best she'd ever had. Her work, which she loved.

And her friends, too. No matter how much they irritated her, it hurt to let go of that sense of almost belonging. A group of people who knew her more or less for what she was and still accepted her—she wasn't going to find that again, not in this lifetime. She mourned it even more for Rachel's sake. All those aunts and uncles and cousins, lost.

Goddamn him. But she had no time for this. She knew when she'd been outmaneuvered. Poor little Rachel, who counted so heavily on habit for her emotional equilibrium. She had to give up her home, her name, her nanny, maybe even her language, depending on where they ended up. And dragging a three-year-old on a high-stress, illegal cross-continental adventure was not going to be fun.

But she had no one to blame but herself for complicating her life beyond all reason. Enough bitching.

She packed as many of her Deadly Beauty designs as would fit into the carrying case she'd taken to Shibumi. Not that she would be able to sell them again, not without announcing her location to her enemies with a trumpet fanfare. She had the time it would take to drive to the airport to think of a brilliant plan to dispose of them. She couldn't risk trying to carry them onto an airplane, at least the ones with hidden blades. If she put them in a checked bag, they would go through X-rays too, and a possible inspection by some airline employee would be too dangerous.

She threw her own personal favorites into her travel carrying case, sorting out and discarding the ones with explosives. Bad mix, airports and explosives. Just soporifics, and a couple of poison needle and spray pieces, for her physical person. The amount of dangerous substances in their reservoirs were small enough to risk going through airport security with them. She'd designed them that way on purpose.

Traveling could be dangerous. A woman always needed options.

Then, the computer. Dried tear tracks tickled her cheeks as she pinned down the first e-tickets she could find. Seattle to Hawaii, Hawaii to Auckland. Fine for now. Nice and far. She and Rachel could play on a warm beach and try being Kiwis. She closed her laptop, packed it.

She packed everything into the fogeymobile, an antiquated, butt-ugly beige Ford Taurus that the McClouds' computer geek buddy Miles had sold to her some time ago. Invisible cars came in handy sometimes.

And then the hard part. Waking Rachel, dragging her out of a warm bed, dressing her, wrestling her into the car at this ungodly hour of the night. It would be an insult to anyone, let alone a toddler.

Rachel was as unhappy about it as Tam had anticipated, but once she got the kid strapped into the car seat, the worst of it was over. There was nothing like earsplitting wails of rage to keep a woman awake and alert on the road—and incidentally, to distract her from any impulse to look nostalgically back over her shoulder, as the closest thing to home she'd had since she was fifteen receded into the distance.

Back to zero again. What a bore. And she couldn't even vow revenge on that goat-fucking bastard.

Her stomach burned, her chest was tight, her throat ached. She'd considered herself detached, but she needed a pair of bolt cutters to detach from all this. Snip, snip. Watch her bleed.

After a half hour, Rachel had shrieked herself into an exhausted doze, leaving Tam in blessed silence. She had less than two hours to come up with a clever plan for stashing her jewelry, other than the trunk of the car, abandoned in the long-term parking lot. There were worse places. No time to do anything else with them and still make the flight.

Either she'd get back to them, or she wouldn't. Let it go. It was only hundreds of thousands of dollars invested in pure gold, platinum, precious gems, and creative designs that she'd spent years of her life developing. No biggie. Snip, snip with the bolt cutters. Let it go.

Rachel was sleeping when they got to the airport. Tam tucked her into the stroller and watched her breath fog around her pale, tiny face as they waited for the shuttle. Long in coming at this desolate hour.

The lines weren't bad once they got to the terminal. She willed Rachel to stay asleep until the security gate. Not a chance that the kid would sleep through getting pulled out of her stroller, having her shoes removed and going through the bomb-puffing portal, but if Tam could hear herself think up until that point, she would count herself lucky.

Things went smoothly at the e-ticket kiosk as she put Rachel's ticket info through, but it choked on her own. Tam hissed through her teeth as the message on the screen told her to talk to a ticket agent. Now for an interminable fucking wait in a long, slow line. The back of her neck was crawling madly as it was.

She spent the time in line analyzing everyone she could see, including the airline personnel, identifying potential attackers. One never knew. She wished she could have disguised herself, but then again, why bother? Rachel was a dead giveaway. It wasn't as if she could pass the kid off as a bag lady or a Hasidic banker.

When she got to the head of the line, Rachel was awake, and starting to fuss. The apple-cheeked woman at the counter looked over their passports, tapped into her computer, and frowned.

She tapped some more, blinked, and shot a furtive glance at Tam. The woman's eyes slid quickly away. Tam's stomach clenched.

This, too. Janos must have accessed her computer, intercepted the data somehow. He'd red-flagged her. *Shit.* Tens of thousands invested in travel documents for Rachel and herself squashed in one deft move, and now what the fuck was she going to do?

This meant that Janos and God knew who else knew exactly where she was right now. Her heart sped up. She looked over her shoulder and reassessed everyone she'd studied before.

"Um, ma'am? I'm sorry, but there's a problem with your passport." The woman blinked nervously, as if expecting Tam to sprout horns. "I'm afraid you'll have to, um, talk to security."

"Security?" Tam made her eyes innocently big, and pulled Rachel out of her stroller. The toddler wrapped her arms around Tam's neck in her octopus hug. "What seems to be the problem?"

"Oh, I'm sure it's just a little glitch in the system," the lady assured her. "But if you'd just step over there to the side and wait, I'll have 'em come right on over and sort this out for ya right away, OK?"

Tam exchanged big, fake, golly-gee-aren't-these-machines-a-pain-in-the-behind smiles with the woman and walked the way she'd been pointed. Leaving behind the survival suitcase full of medicines, toys, equipment. Leaving behind the stroller and the compromised passports. Keeping only the diaper bag, her purse, and Rachel. Snip, snip went the bolt cutters. She walked past the place the woman had indicated.

"Um, ma'am? Wait right there, please," the woman called out anxiously. "Security'll be right with ya!"

"Sorry, but my daughter needs the bathroom," Tam called back. "Urgently, or we'll have an accident. I'll be right back, OK? Gotta scoot!"

She ducked around the corner, circled a crowd of Japanese tourists being herded into the ticket line by a harrassed tour operator, and sprinted down the escalator to the ground transportation area. There were several people in line for the taxis, and no taxis to be seen. She could not wait in that line. They would be on her in minutes.

The shuttle to the other terminals and the long-term parking lot was in the far lane. She darted across the road and climbed aboard the short bus, slumping down in the seat to be less visible. A minute or so later, a tall guy in an army jacket with a battered knapsack, long tangled brown hair and a bushy beard climbed aboard. She'd seen him in the terminal, asleep in one of the chairs, legs sprawled, mouth hanging open. Shaded John Lennon glasses covered his eyes.

He slouched promptly down into his seat and fell asleep again. The reek of his patchouli and marijuana filled the shuttle. He must be going somewhere in Asia, to smoke massive quantities of weed and dream his days away in the Himalayas, or the sun-drenched beaches of Phuket. The lucky bastard.

"Is this bus leaving?" She couldn't control the edge in her voice.

"Two minutes," the guy said.

Two minutes were a goddamn eternity. The next passenger to board was a tall, burly guy with a square chin, and a thick neck, and a swollen, reddened face that screamed *steroids*. Late thirties. Long, layered blond hair. Big white teeth. Hulking shoulders. No suitcase, just a knapsack. He slumped into the seat opposite hers. His thick thigh muscles bulged, straining his tight jeans.

Tam's neck crawled. She had no guns or knives. They were out of the question for anyone hoping to fly. She had nothing helpful on her except a topaz-studded sopor-spray barrette with a very small reservoir. A one-squirt deal. Maybe two squirts, if she was lucky.

Rachel was starting to tug at Tam's coat and ask questions she could not focus on sufficiently to answer. Two more guys got on the shuttle, both suspiciously young, fit and unencumbered. One was a lanky black man with a hooded sweatshirt, a duffel bag over his shoulder. The other was a crewcut jock type in polar fleece with a backpack. Both of them had cold, hard faces. Neither looked at her.

That, in itself, was strange enough to warrant alarm, even at an airport at the crack of dawn. In the normal universe, any straight man who saw her looked at her and then looked again. It wasn't vanity, just a simple fact of life. The fact that three men in a row had not done so was a very bad sign.

In the very second in which Tam decided that throwing herself on the mercy of airport security was preferable to the ominous possibilities of these strange men, the bus lurched abruptly out onto the road.

She leaped up. "Hold on. Wait! I'm getting off here!"

The driver accelerated and cleared the end of the terminal, easing the bus into the chute of an exit ramp. No escape.

"Too late," he said, his voice faintly triumphant. "You can get off at the next terminal, or you can make the loop."

Tam sank back down into her seat, jaw clenched, and fought with the urge to panic. She murmured something senseless but soothing to Rachel's inquisitive babble, and she started rummaging in the diaper bag for her jewelry case. Her hands were cold, shaking.

She was an idiot for having put Rachel into this situation. For not finding a solution sooner, not doing the hard, necessary thing before it came to this. There were some possibilities in her purse, but she disliked the thought of spraying toxic substances in an enclosed area near Rachel. She identified each by touch, discarding one after the other as too risky. The barrette she currently wore was her best bet. It was a small dose, and just a soporific, not a poison or a corrosive, if Rachel should accidently take a hit.

She pulled it out of her hair, positioned it between her fingers.

Maybe she was being paranoid, she thought. These men might just be mercenaries off to Iraq or Afghanistan. Men like that tended to have that hard, suspicious vibe. They kept to themselves, traveled light.

Yeah, right. Her stomach churned. Rachel picked up on Tam's unease, and went very quiet, clutching Tam's collar with damp, clammy kitten claws.

Thick Neck slid across his seat, across the aisle, and into the seat behind them. He leaned on the back of their seat, grinning.

Adrenaline ramped up in her overloaded system. Her hand tightened on the barrette. Thick Neck fluttered blunt, bolt-knuckled red fingers at Rachel. "Hi there, cutie," he said in a hoarse voice.

Tam gave him a big, sweet, sudden-death smile. Rachel dove for cover in her bosom. He watched appreciatively. "Nice," he said.

"She doesn't like strangers," Tam said.

"She'll like me when she gets used to me," Thick Neck said.

The hell she will, shithead, she told him with her eyes. "Why don't you just piss off?" she suggested sweetly.

The segue into doom had been so smooth, she wasn't even surprised when the SIG with the silencer rose up, cleared the top of the seat, and pointed at the back of Rachel's curly head.

The guy clicked his tongue. "Rude," he whispered. "Now listen to me, bitch. Do exactly what I tell you. Move real slow, and don't make a sound. I'll let you just imagine what'll happen if you don't, because I don't want to have to say it in front of the little cutie-pie. Got me?"

Tam's eyes darted around the bus. The men who'd gotten in after Thick Neck watched what was happening with expressionless faces. Patchouli Pothead dozed blissfully on, head lolling, mouth slack.

"Listen good. Put the kid down real slow on the seat," Thick Neck whispered. "Then stand up. Turn your back to me, and put both hands behind your back. Slow . . . slow. Barker, get over here with those cuffs. Wow, they didn't tell me you were so hot. Look at those tits. We're going to have to get to know each other, beautiful. Those tits are special."

Tam put Rachel down on the seat, detaching tiny, clinging hands from her hair. "Listen, baby," she whispered in Ukrainian. "These men are bad. Slide off the seat and onto the floor, and stay way down. Can you do that for Mamma?"

"Shut up, bitch. Speak English," Thick Neck growled.

"Shut up, and speak English?" she murmured. "Neat trick."

He scowled. "I said, shut *up*!"

Rachel stared up into Tam's face, her dark eyes huge, and slid like a boneless little eel down into the dark well between the seats. *Brilliant, smart, good girl, yes, yes, yes.* Tam silently cheered. To hell with the stupid doctors who'd warned her that Rachel probably had brain damage. The kid was smart as a whip. She made Tam proud.

"What's the kid doing?" Thick Neck whispered furiously. "I didn't tell her to get on the ground! Get her back up onto the seat. Now. Hey!"

Patchouli Pothead exploded into movement with a shout. A silenced gun went off—*thhtp.* Tam took advantage of Thick Neck's distraction, whipped her arm up under his gun hand, knocked it upward. She squirted the barrette straight into his face.

Thick Neck's gun went off. The window next to them shattered. The shuttle veered on the road, bounced against the guardrails, scraping and fishtailing. "What the flying *fuck*?" The driver lurched to a shuddering, squealing stop. He turned, and gaped.

"Drive, you dumb fuck!" Polar Fleece guy snarled. "Move!"

Thhtp. Another silenced gunshot. Thick Neck blinked stupidly, started to sag. One down, thank God.

"Get down!" Patchouli Pothead was shouting frantically, and she realized, startled, that he, too, had a gun. "*Mettiti giù, cazzo!*"

Holy shit, it was Janos. He squeezed off another shot, ducked as Sweat Shirt popped up and took a shot at him. *Crash, tinkle,* another window. She dove into the aisle. *Thhtp.* The driver looked surprised, put his hand up to the hole that appeared in his throat. Blood welled thickly through his fingers. He flopped forward at the waist and dangled like a doll over the gearshift.

Two more shots. What seemed like a panting eternity of silence followed them. She huddled, plastered to the plastic carpet runner.

"Get up, Steele. You have to drive."

It was Janos's faintly accented voice. Calm, cool, and even.

Profound relief rushed through her. She kicked herself for feeling it. That man was not her friend or her savior, no matter how things looked right now. On the contrary, he was probably the prime reason she was in this fix to begin with. And she might be obliged to kill him.

Like it would be so easy.

She let out a shuddering breath, peering into the darkness under the seat to seek out Rachel's tiny hunched form in the dark. She reached out, groped until she snagged a handful of Rachel's coat.

"Are they dead?" Tam asked Janos. The question sounded shaky, stupid and scared.

"I'll make sure. You drive the bus."

"You drive the fucking bus, Janos," she snapped. "I've got Rachel to take care of."

Janos snarled something in Roman dialect about the sexual depravity of her dead sainted ancestors. She ignored him, shimmying under the seat to drag Rachel out and up into her arms.

The sickening crack of a man's neck being broken took her by surprise. Ouch. *Grow up, Tam*, she scolded herself. She'd gotten soft.

Janos leaned over, peering down through those goofy round glasses at Thick Neck, who was slumped sideways on the seat. "How long will the drug you sprayed on him last?" he asked.

"Not long," she said. "Ten minutes, maybe fifteen. Small dose."

Janos put his gun to the nape of the guy's neck.

She jerked upright. "Don't you dare!"

He gave her an incredulous look. "Excuse me?"

"You asshole!" she hissed. "Not in front of the child! Are you crazy?"

He rolled his eyes but let Thick Neck be and proceeded to the front of the van. He gently lifted the bloody, dripping head of the dangling driver and peered into his eyes. He reached for the man's wrist, felt for a pulse. His eyes flicked to hers. He shook his head.

He grabbed the driver's big, heavy body under the armpits and heaved him into the first passenger seat without apparent effort. The man's legs draped obscenely across the aisle. Tam hugged Rachel's face to her chest. Not that the kid was noticing anything. She was locked in her own inner world, and from the looks of her, it wasn't a pretty one.

Janos slid into the driver's seat and put the vehicle in gear. They peeled out onto the road, tires squealing, and picked up speed.

"Where are we going?"

"The lot where you parked," he said.

"How do you know where I—"

"Later," he cut her off brusquely. "I'm thinking."

Oh, indeed. God forbid she should keep a man from actually doing that. She almost said it, but until she knew exactly what the fuck was going on, even she knew how to keep her big mouth shut.

On a temporary basis, anyway.

It scared her that Rachel wouldn't speak or make eye contact. Nor was she clinging to Tam's neck as she usually did when she was terrified. She was limp, clammy, and pale, which frightened Tam more than the bullets had. She preferred a screaming, writhing meltdown to this total withdrawal. Cold air blew in the bus's shattered windows.

The van slowed, slewed into a sharp turn, and bumped over the barrier into the long-term lot where she'd left her car. The bar rose for the shuttle automatically. The guy in the window didn't even look up from his magazine.

No one was waiting for a ride when Janos braked at the bus shelter. Unheard-of luck. She'd been bracing herself for a nasty public scene when the bus stopped, and she hadn't been looking forward to it.

Janos looked over at her. "Get out," he said. "I'll deal with the last one when you and the child are clear of the bus."

She slung the diaper bag and purse over her shoulder, pressed Rachel's face to her chest, and clambered over the legs of the driver.

They climbed out of the death bus into the fresh morning air. Dawn wasn't far off. She dragged in a breath.

Thud. She felt the silenced gunshot vibrate in her gut as Janos's bullet punched into Thick Neck's nape and finished off the job.

Janos came out, jerking his chin for her to follow him.

She clutched Rachel more tightly to her chest. "I'm not going to let you take me to Georg Luksch," she said, suddenly exhausted. "I would rather die." It was a pointless declaration, but she made it on principle.

He stared at her, eyes narrowed. "I'm not taking you to Georg."

She blinked at him, bewildered. Her eyes burned and stung in the breeze that kicked up. "Ah . . . no? Then what are you doing here?"

"I am helping you," he said curtly. "Follow me. Quickly."

After a second, Tam followed him, for lack of a better plan.

"Somebody's going to get a nasty shock this morning when she tries to get the shuttle to her flight," she said.

Janos walked quickly, not looking at her. "Not our problem."

"It will be when they dust for prints, and investigate that god-damn passport," Tam said sourly. "Just what I need. A murder rap, and I didn't even have a gun. Like I don't have enough problems."

"Faster, please. Do you want to talk to the police about it now, while half the world is trying to kill you, or later?"

She speeded up to a shambling trot. Rachel wasn't heavy at all, but those oft-repeated adrenaline zaps were taking their toll on Tam's motor control. "Later is fine," she said. "In the next lifetime, maybe."

"We're in agreement then."

They hurried along. Tam panted, the muscles in her arms trembling with strain. Legs wobbling. She could not crash yet, god-damnit. "How did you know where I was?" she demanded.

He let out a sharp sigh and slanted her an irritated glance. "A radio frequency transmitter. In your jewelry case."

She stopped in her tracks, mouth open. "How did you—"

"Later. Move." He yanked her arm, getting her going again.

She noticed that they were passing the fogeymobile. "Stop," she said.

"We're not taking this car," he said. "Hurry. We don't have time for—"

"I have to get Rachel's car seat," she told him.

The blank disbelief on Janos's face bugged the shit out of her.

"It's the law," she said more loudly. "Children have to be properly restrained. You can't let them rattle around in a vehicle. It's not safe."

That you-have-got-to-be-fucking-kidding-lady expression pushed her raddled nerves right to the snapping point. "Look, asshole, I have left everything behind!" she said, her voice shrill. "My home, my stuff, my friends, my work, my stroller, Rachel's Tylenol and diaper wipes and allergy medicines! I left our entire fucking identity behind, thanks to you! I am not leaving Rachel's car seat, so get the fuck out of my way!"

Janos lifted both hands in the air, eyes wide behind the weird glasses. "*Calmati,*" he murmured. "Keep it down. And hurry, please."

He looked incredibly different with that hair and bushy beard and that stupid-ass knit cap stretched over it. Tam stared at him for a second, shook her head, and stuck Rachel right into his arms. What else could she do? No way was the kid capable of standing on her feet.

She dug keys from her purse with stiff, shaking fingers, opened the door, and struggled with straps, clamps and tethers until she got the car seat out of her vehicle.

Then she wrenched open the trunk and grabbed the jewelry case too. What the hell. It didn't look like she was going to be taking a plane trip anytime soon, and the way things were looking, some of this stuff might well come in handy. And she could always melt it down for gold and gems later on if she got desperate. Which was looking more and more likely, the way she was running through money.

She had to get her hands on a gun. Preferably more than one. The McCloud Crowd could help her, but she hated to involve them. They were so inquisitive, so damn protective. She didn't want to put their families in danger. But she would, for Rachel. Oh, yes, she would.

She'd gotten out of the habit of packing heat, having a curious three-year-old crawling all over her, but what happened in that bus was a brutal reality check. She'd gotten sloppy. She gave herself a mental slap as she jogged alongside Janos, clutching the heavy seat.

Rachel was as slack as a doll. She looked so small, curled up against his huge chest. He stopped at a black van with tinted windows, and opened it without the benefit of a key. "Is this your car?" she asked.

He gave her a significant look. "No."

She flung open the back door, and hoisted the car seat into place, again struggling with tethers, belts, and straps. "Stolen?"

Another *duh* glance from behind his shaggy fake locks. "Borrowed," he said. "We will take it back now to the mall parking lot where I found it, and the owner will need only to fix the locks and the steering column. Perhaps I will even leave money for repairs."

"How civil of you." She grabbed Rachel from his arms. "Not often one meets a car thief and killer who's such a good citizen."

He lifted an eyebrow. "I do my best."

"How did you get from the parking lot to the terminal?" she demanded. "You weren't on my shuttle. You weren't in the lot."

"I had a motorcycle in the back of the van," he said. "And that is the last question I am answering for now, so shut up. Try not to leave prints on the van, no? Things are complicated enough. Do not put the child in the seat yet. Stay down on the floor until we are on the road."

That sounded wise, so she placed Rachel on the floor in front of the backseat and huddled beside her until she felt the van stop. The window hummed down, the exchange was made. The turn, a smooth acceleration, and they were off. She went limp with shivering relief.

"All clear," he said.

Tam hoisted Rachel up into the car seat and strapped her in. She grabbed the clammy, chilly little hands and chafed them. It alarmed her, the way the child's head lolled. Her heartbeat was frantic, like a little bird. It made her feel horribly helpless.

"Janos, do you have a plan?" she demanded. "And does it include telling me what the fuck just happened back there?"

"Yes and yes." He was using that super-cool, even voice again. "We leave this van in the mall parking lot, retrieve my car, and go straight to a comfortable hotel where we can rest safely, and talk at great length about many things that will interest you. That is the plan."

"Why don't you tell me about the things that will interest me now, and then I decide if I'm interested in going to this hotel with you?"

"No," he said. "I am driving now. Not talking."

"What bullshit," she said sharply. "You appear to be a very talented multitasker. And I am curious right now. Not later."

"You will be just as curious later. How is the child?"

Hah. The master of diversion. She stroked Rachel's clammy cheek. "Ice cold, racing heart, won't talk to me, won't make eye contact. Shocky. Why? Don't try to tell me that you care."

He caught her glance in the rearview mirror and gave her a reproving frown. "That is unjust."

His aggrieved tone set her right off on a rampage. "Oh, is it? None of this crazy shit would have happened to her at all if you hadn't fucked with our lives and put us on the run, you meathead moron."

"It would have happened," he said. "Be glad it happened here and not at your home, where I would not have been able to help."

"I'm supposed to be grateful? Spare me. Rachel, baby, are you in there? Anybody home? Talk to Mamma. Come on." She patted Rachel's cheeks, gulping back tears. Now was not the time, damn it.

Out of the corner of her eye, she noticed a large dark splotch high on Janos's coat sleeve. She leaned over the seat to take a closer look.

"Hey. You were shot," she said in an accusing voice.

He grunted. "It is nothing."

Macho cave man talk. Nothing, her ass. "Nothing meaning what?" she demanded. "Meaning there's a bullet embedded in your arm, but it's really nothing?"

"It is not embedded. It grazed me only. It is nothing," he reiterated, his voice hard. "Please do not try to tell me that you care."

Was he for real? "I most certainly won't and don't," she informed him. "Go ahead, Janos. Bleed. Do you need me to drive?"

"No," he growled.

"Do not, I repeat, *not* faint behind the wheel with my kid in the car," she warned. "Or I will rip your head off your neck. Is that clear?"

He made a frustrated sound. "Be silent. We will talk later."

He stopped responding to anything she said after that, maintaining a silence that drove her insane, but it wasn't long until he pulled into the strip mall lot. He pulled in next to a BMW SUV, and began transferring her diaper bag, purse, and jewelry case from one vehicle to the other while she pried Rachel out of the car seat.

As if it was a done deal. Arrogant dick.

He jerked open her door and held out his arms for Rachel. Tam shrank back, clutching the limp child to her chest. "Actually, this is the part where Rachel and I thank you for your help, and wish you a very nice life," she said. "Good-bye, Janos. Please don't keep in touch."

The steel in his dark eyes was utterly at odds with his goofy disguise. "You need help," he said.

"And you think you're helping me?" she flared. "By messing with my babysitter? Turning the cops on me, slandering me to Rachel's adoption agency? Trashing my passports?"

"I did my best for you and your daughter back in that shuttle," he said. "Draw your conclusions, but draw them fast. If you want to fight me, you will lose. You are strong, but I am stronger. You have your poison trinkets, I have knives and guns. You have a child who needs rest, perhaps medical care. Think, Steele. If I wanted you dead, you would be dead. Don't be a fool. Get in the fucking car, and stop giving me trouble."

She assessed her options in a split second. She could call the Mc-Clouds for backup, but if these men had gotten so close to her, chances were they already knew about her connection with the Mc-Clouds, which meant that Rachel wouldn't be safe with any of them.

Nor would any family be who was looking after her.

But she could not deal with this alone and unarmed. With a toddler in her arms, she was toast. If she'd needed any further demonstration of that, she'd gotten it this morning.

She was just so tired, so rattled. She needed so badly for Janos's offer of help to be real, she could not trust her own instincts. After all, Georg Luksch had paid him to drag her in, for God's sake. And the man had a hidden agenda the size of Hong Kong. She could feel it like a subterranean earthquake, rumbling in the depths. And whatever the hell his agenda might be, it could not possibly be good news for her.

But God, she was tired. Inside and out. Tired of being alone, relying only on her own strength, her own energy. And already well into an adrenaline crash, as if some part of her had decided that the danger was past and she was safe to have her meltdown here and now. Hah.

She looked around. It was the crack of dawn, it was really cold, they were in a desolate, deserted strip mall where nothing would be open for hours. Rachel was shivering in her arms.

Janos waited, challenging her with his eyes to look inside him and find a lie. She blinked at the stinging fog of tears and looked, hard.

She did not see one. Fuck it. He'd saved their lives, even if he'd messed with them first. She let out a jerky breath and handed Rachel to him. "All right," she whispered.

Chapter
10

Val slouched in a chair by the bed, grateful for the warmth and silence of the hotel room. Steele cuddled her child under the blankets.

He was immensely relieved that he had not been compelled to use force. He did not want to hurt her, and she was so quick and strong, it would have been inevitable if she had resisted. With the child already so traumatized, it would have been unpleasant, to say the least.

Steele was not doing well. Her lips were bluish, her eyes shadowed, her face an ashy gray. She hugged the child tightly to her body, stroking and murmuring. Rachel's closed eyes looked sunken in her pinched white face.

He, on the other hand, was keeping his long coat on, oozing blood splotch and all, to camouflage his erection. An inconvenient physiological reaction to combat stress. He was sure that Steele would not be surprised by it, but also not amused in her present mood. He had no desire to hear what she would say. Imagining it was enough.

"How is she?" he asked.

"Better. She's calmed down and breathing more deeply now. And she's almost asleep, so shut up," was Steele's caustic reply.

Val sighed and flung his head back. His face itched from the glue, his scalp from the wig. The cotton batting stuffed inside his nose, lips, and cheeks irritated him beyond belief. He wished he could shower to get the cloying stench of marijuana and patchouli out of his nose, but getting naked under a deafening stream of hot water was unwise. If she slipped away now, he no longer had the RF tag on her jewelry case to follow. The first thing she'd done when she'd gotten to the hotel room was to pry the thing out of the case and flush it down the toilet.

He got up and headed to the bathroom, leaving its door wide open so he could see the path to the room door. How had the other team found her? He peeled off fake facial hair and soaped his face as he pondered it. As yet, Novak had no reason to think that he would not comply with the terms of their bargain. It had to be Hegel, PSS.

He pried and spat the cotton out of his mouth into the toilet, flushing it, not about to leave that much DNA where anyone could find it. He rinsed and spat again, thinking. No one but him had the codes and RF frequencies he had tagged Steele's stroller and vehicle with. Hegel knew where she lived, but how could he have known about her trip to the airport in time to get a local team in place? The Taurus she drove had never been tagged. And she would have noticed if anyone was following her on a lonely highway at night.

The only explanation was that Hegel had marked him, not her. That the B team had located her by following him. But how? He'd taken care of the usual things before he left Budapest. New laptop, new phone, new organizer. He had changed every piece of luggage, footwear, clothing.

He'd used every trick he knew to shake followers, checking repeatedly to make sure he was clean. To the point of outright paranoia.

Val stared into the mirror, trying to form a matrix, but he was too exhausted. He looked haggard, his face carved out and shadowed with stubble. He hadn't slept since before he went to Budapest. It showed.

It was hot in the room. Steele had turned up the heat to the maximum to get the baby warm. He popped a sweat under the coat.

Fuck the erection. It wasn't as if she'd never seen one before.

He had to deal with the wound. The bullet had ripped through the fabric of his coat and torn a bloody furrow across the meat of his upper arm. It stung, but he'd taken far worse.

He shrugged off the coat and the bloody shirt, and hissed through clenched teeth as he washed the shoulder with soap and hot water. The sink was spotted with pink, but the wound barely oozed at this point.

He went out and retrieved the medical kit from his bag. Steele and the child were both asleep, at least apparently. They needed it.

He dressed his arm, and sank into the chair again, not bothering to put another shirt on with that heat blasting. He held his gun in his hand, resting on his leg, and watched them sleep.

Steele moved restlessly. Once, she muttered something in a language he could not place. From the tone, it sounded like a plea. He had no intention of dozing off, but the blackout blinds were down and the excessive heat could make him sleepy. His arm throbbed dully.

Tiny hands on his knees jolted him awake. The little girl, huge-eyed, was reaching out to grab the barrel of his Glock.

Cazzo! He jerked the thing up out of her reach. Just what he needed, another brutal shock to his nervous system. "God, no," he whispered. "Don't touch it, *piccola*. Dangerous."

Rachel thought it was a game, of course, and leaped to grab it, gurgling with glee. The nap had evidently restored her. She looked fine.

The laughter woke Steele. She jolted upright and took in the situation in an instant, diving from the bed and grabbing the child around the waist. "Rachel, Jesus! Don't you ever, *ever* touch one of those, baby. Not ever, hear me? God, Janos, what the hell were you thinking, leaving that thing lying around?"

"I did not leave it," he said grimly. "It was in my hand."

"Just keep it the hell out of her reach!" Steele hissed.

Startled and upset, Rachel began to cry. Tam hugged her tightly, looking resigned. "I guess this means she's not in shock."

A shrill and stressful half hour passed before the child was happy again, distracted by an array of tiny toys, random colorful objects and books that Steele produced from the black bag. Val put on a clean shirt and strapped on his shoulder holster in the meantime. He would keep the gun fastened tight and high on his body from now on.

The little girl soon decided that he was more interesting than her toys. She toddled over, holding two small dolls. She held one out.

He took it. And now? Should he animate it? Make admiring comments? He'd never been around children, just Giulietta's baby, when he was young, and that had ended so horribly. He still had queasy dreams about it now and again.

Rachel resolved his dilemma by holding up her other doll and pressing it, chest to chest, against the one he held. She adjusted its stiff, hard little plastic arms until it embraced his.

"Hug," she explained solemnly.

A hot sensation swelled in his chest, tight and uncomfortable. He breathed the strange feeling down and adjusted the arms of his doll until it returned the other's embrace. As best it could, of course, hampered by unyielding plastic and stiff mechanical ball joints. "Hug," he echoed obediently.

Rachel rewarded him with a smile that startled him with its beauty. She pressed the dolls face-to-face. "Kiss?" she inquired.

He laughed at her earnest request. "Let's not rush things," he said. "I am shy. And we barely know each other."

Rachel frowned and knocked the dolls' plastic faces together. "Kiss," she insisted.

"Rachel, don't bother Mr. Janos," Steele said, in a warning tone.

"She is not a bother," Val said, realizing with surprise that it was true. He held up the doll to face hers. "Kiss," he said, resigned.

Rachel rewarded him with another radiant smile. Her doll kissed his with enough intensity for him to start feeling a little strange about it. And Steele was giving him a distinctly unfriendly look.

"What?" he demanded. "I did nothing except get my doll kissed. Passively. My doll did not even kiss back."

Steele shook her head, looking uneasy. "It's strange. How she goes for you. Usually she screams bloody murder around strange men."

"Maybe her instincts are better than yours," he offered.

Tam made a derisive sound. "No, she just has a lot to learn. Learning to watch out for men with handsome faces and big guns comes after basic language skills, how to use a fork, and potty training. Come on, baby, come play with your dolls with Mommy."

Rachel ignored her and held up another small doll to be admired. "Sveti give dollies," she informed Val with great gravity.

"Oh, *si*?" he responded politely. "Who is Sveti?"

"We see Sveti wedding!" She jumped. "Red dress! For me! Pretty!"

"Wedding?" He glanced at Steele. "You're going to a wedding?"

"Today wedding! Today wedding! See Sveti! Mommy promise," Rachel said, glancing fiercely at Steele for corroboration. "Promise!"

A frown marred Steele's pale brow. "Honey, don't babble," she said tightly.

"Want red dress! Want Sveti! Promise!"

Steele massaged her forehead with her fingertips. "I don't have your red dress now, baby," she said wearily. "I left it at home. And Sveti's not here. I'm sorry."

Rachel's face crumpled. Val braced himself for her ambulance siren imitation. *Today wedding.* He didn't place much weight in a three-year-old's sense of time, but Steele's discomfort with Rachel's revelation suggested that there had been plans to go to some event today, before he maneuvered her into running away.

"Is one of your McCloud friends getting married?" he asked.

"None of your damn business, and how did you know about the McClouds anyhow?"

"Want Sveti!" Rachel wailed. "Want wedding!"

"Is there someone at this wedding who you could trust to keep Rachel safe for you for a while?"

"That's none of your damn business either." She got up. "And it's time for us to go. Thanks again for the—"

"Sit down." He put all his force behind the words. "I am trying to save your child's life."

His tone made even Rachel's wails trail off in uncertain whimpers. Steele sat slowly on the edge of the bed again, her full mouth pinched.

"The wedding is today?" he asked. "In Seattle?"

A sullen shrug was her response.

"You were planning to go?" he persisted.

"Before I tried to flee the country, yes," she said bitterly. "Last night's events put a crimp in my social calendar. This morning's adventure didn't help much either."

"We should go," he informed her. "It's the perfect timing."

Her eyes widened. "What's this 'we' crap? We're not going anywhere with you, Janos. I'm not exposing my friends to you and your weirdo homicidal pals. And besides, we have nothing to wear."

"So order something online," he said. "Have it delivered."

She shook her head. "Listen to me, Val Janos, or whoever the hell you are. You haven't even told me yet what the hell is going on. Until you explain to my satisfaction—"

"I can't." He shot a significant look at Rachel.

Rachel's doll was hugging his doll once again. She tilted her head, and peeked up with a flirtatious smile.

"Honey baby, it's time for you to have a bath," Steele said briskly. "I'll go run it for you." She squinted at him. "And you will talk. Quietly, outside the bathroom door, while she bathes."

A few minutes of preparation got Rachel paddling happily in a shallow bath with an assortment of floating rubber toys, produced from the miraculous black bag. Steele sat in the bathroom doorway where she could keep an eye on the child, and gestured for Val to sit opposite her on the floor.

"Talk," she ordered. "Who were those guys?"

"I had no chance to interrogate them, so I cannot be sure," he said. "But I assume they were a local team put in place by PSS."

"PSS?" She looked perplexed. "Aren't you PSS?"

"I was," he said. "I had a disagreement with the organization. I suspect that after that, my boss no longer trusted me to carry out the mission, so he mobilized another team. They will consider me rogue after what happened this morning."

"A disagreement? Over what?" she demanded.

"You," he said baldly. "My boss insisted that I take Rachel and manipulate you with her."

Her face was a pale, impenetrable mask. "And why didn't you?"

He thought of several answers. Dangerous, inappropriate answers. But he was not yet ready to voice them. And she was definitely not yet ready to hear them.

"I don't like hurting children," he said finally. "It was often a problem for me in this work. When the issue came up again, I said enough, *vaffanculo a tutti*. I did not like the job in any case. Coercing a woman into going with a depraved pig like Luksch by threatening her child, *che schifo*. It is squalid." He shrugged. "My boss said that a man in my position cannot afford such scruples. He was right. So I decided to change my position."

"I see." She examined her fingernails. "So, ah, let me get this straight. You followed me and helped me and Rachel in the shuttle just because you're noble and heroic?"

"Ah . . ." He floundered, taken aback.

"I take it this is the part in the story where I'm supposed to be deeply impressed by how honorable you are? And melt like chocolate?"

He took the three steps back in his mind and waited until his anger at her sarcasm faded. "It is not a story," he replied. "It is the truth."

"Hmm." She gazed at her daughter, splashing and humming in the tub. "So they took over all the data on me that you gathered for them and had this B team act on it?"

"No," he said. "This is the part that troubles me. They knew the location of your home because I could not hide it from the satellite. But I do not know how they found you at the airport this morning. I did not share the frequencies that I tagged you with."

She looked thoughtful. "They found me, but you don't know how. Hmmph. I smell a ramped-up version of Good Cop, Bad Cop."

His teeth began to grind. "The good cop does not usually kill the bad cops when that game is played," he said.

"It depends on the stakes," she said. "How hard the game is being played, how ruthless the players, how big the payoff. The psychological effects would be intense with murder thrown in."

He stared at her. "I did not do that," he said.

Her eyes slid away. "Hmm," she murmured. "How noble. And very moving, Janos, but it doesn't explain what you're doing here with us. You should be lying on a beach on another continent, sipping an umbrella drink, putting all the unpleasantness behind you. If what you say is true, nobody is paying you a salary to cramp our style any longer. So why are we here?"

The woman was mercilessly focused. He had hoped to ease around the danger zone for a while, to warm her up, gain her trust. But no. She shoved him straight toward the perilous moment of truth.

"There is . . . something else," he forced out.

She leaned back with a sigh. "Finally, we're getting somewhere."

He had scripted several persuasive ways of approaching the dangerous bargain he meant to offer her, but all of them evaporated out of his head, leaving him with the blunt, unlovely truth.

"I grew up in Budapest," he said, his voice halting.

She tilted an eyebrow. "And this is relevant exactly why, Janos?"

"My mother . . ." He stopped and swallowed. "She was a prostitute, from Romania. She worked in a brothel there, run by a mafiya boss from Ukraina."

Steele's eyes dilated. "Daddy Novak," she said.

He nodded. "I was very young when she died," he said. "I got swept up into his organization as a child. I worked for him for years."

"I see." Her voice was as hard as glass. "And what does your mafiya past have to do with me?"

He closed his eyes, tried to organize his thoughts. This was not going well. He was not making sense, even to himself. "I am trying to explain the connection," he said wearily. "There was a man . . . who helped me years ago. He was kind to me. Educated me, tried to get me out. He failed with the second, through no fault of his own. I care about this man. Novak knows this. He abducted my friend, and now he threatens to torture him to death if I do not . . . deliver you to him."

He did not dare to look at her. The heavy silence was underscored by the child's burbling and splashing from the bathtub.

Steele's face was ashen. She was so startled, she had no sarcasm to counter him. "Does he know about Rachel?" she whispered.

"From what I could tell, no. He did not mention her."

"He must not find out," she said with hushed intensity. "He would never rest until he got her."

He nodded.

She looked down at her hands. They were trembling visibly. She clenched them into fists. "Why are you telling me this, Janos?" she asked. "It's not an efficient tactic if you want to save your friend. Why not just knock me on the head and do the deal?"

Val shook his head. "I was hoping to find a better solution to the problem," he confessed. "One that would not damn me to hell."

She looked dubious. "You think that a solution exists?"

"I hope so," he said. "I do not want to hurt you. And Imre would not thank me for saving him from death and torture at your expense."

"Hmmph," she snorted. "This Imre must have very high standards if he can reason like that in Novak's clutches."

"Oh, God, yes. That he does," Val agreed fervently. "His high standards have been a pain in my ass for most of my life."

Tam waited for more, and threw up her arms. "So?" she prompted him. "The suspense is killing me. Tell me about this better solution."

"I have not formulated it completely," he admitted. "But I want to offer a trade. You help me with my problem, and I help you with yours."

Her eyes narrowed thoughtfully. "Go on."

"By helping eliminate Novak, you help both yourself and your daughter," he said. "I hire a team, and we will set a trap for Novak. You are the bait, pretending to be fooled into being delivered to him. You will be covered on all sides by manpower and electronic backup."

"Ah." Her bright eyes were unreadable. "And what do you offer me in return?"

"I will take care of Georg for you. He will never bother you again."

"Do you mean kill him?" Her eyebrows shot up. "Ambitious."

He shrugged. "I will manage it."

She shook her head, and his heart sank. "It's a bad bargain," she said. "Not a fair trade."

"Why not?" He could not control the jagged edge of frustration in his voice. "We will solve all your problems at once."

"No. Your problem, Janos," she pointed out. "Which is much bigger than mine."

"Is it?" he demanded. "What happened in that shuttle bus did not look like much of a problem to you? Georg Luksch is not a fucking problem for you?"

She dismissed that with a wave of her hand. "If those guys were PSS and working for Georg, then they wouldn't have killed us," she said with irrefutable logic. "And I am perfectly capable of taking care of the Georg problem myself, if it comes to that."

"Oh, yes? With Rachel to protect?" he snarled. "And even if you should succeed at killing Georg, what kind of mother would you be if you are on the run night and day from Daddy Novak for the rest of your short life? He will not rest now that he knows you are alive. You will never sleep again."

She shook her head. "I never slept much anyhow."

Val clenched his fists. "Very well. Would you consider doing it for payment?"

She blinked a few times. "How much payment?"

"At least three million euro, perhaps closer to four," he said rashly. "Everything I own, minus whatever it will cost me to mount this operation. And it will take a little while to pull it all together, transfer the stock options, sell the apartment in Rome, et cetera."

Her eyes widened. She looked toward Rachel, splashing and singing in the bathtub. "A generous offer, but no," she said quietly.

He wanted to scream, pound the walls, smash the lamps. "But if Novak and Georg both are—"

"My chances of surviving what you propose are too small," she cut in. "I appreciate your honesty, and I'm sorry for your friend, but my first responsibility is to Rachel."

"Which is why you should reconsider," he said desperately. "The quality of both your lives will improve if—"

"I know what's at stake," she snapped. "The answer is still no. There is nothing more for us to talk about. Rachel and I will be on our way as soon as I get her dressed. Unless you intend to abduct or murder us, of course. In any case, excuse me while I go shampoo Rachel's hair."

Val sat on his ass outside the bathroom door, limp and bleak and defeated. He stared at Steele where she knelt by the bathtub, her back straight, her husky voice murmuring nonsense to the child as

Rachel sputtered and shrieked at the insult of shampoo. He stared at her black diaper bag, his hand fiddling with the tiny SafeGuard X-Ray Specs burr beacons he had hidden there, in case he got lucky enough to manage to mark her things again. Her murmuring voice floated out of the bathroom. He was out of her line of vision.

He pulled the smallest beacon out, and slid it into the seam at the bottom of her bag. Done. He would know her location, at least for another twenty-four hours. He was not yet ready to admit defeat. And the end of the world.

He got up and logged on to his computer. A few minutes later, Steele carried the wriggling Rachel out wrapped in a big bath towel and dressed her with some difficulty. When Rachel was on the floor again playing with her dolls, Val slid the laptop across the bed and spun the screen around to face her. "Here."

She frowned down at the screen. "What's this?"

"The online catalog for the department store at the mall," he said.

She looked blank. "And? So? What about it?"

"Clothes for the wedding," he said. "We'll have them delivered to the hotel."

Her mouth tightened. "Have you not been listening to a word I said? You're not going to the wedding, Janos. No is no. *Capisci?*"

He gritted his teeth. "Do you need clothes for this event, or do you not?"

She gave him a thunderous glare, and then, out of nowhere, her face miraculously cleared. "Whatever I need, did you say?"

"Whatever," he stubbornly repeated.

Too late, he registered the catlike satisfaction on her face as she tugged the keyboard closer and began to clickity-click with the deft ease of a seasoned online shopper. *Oh, cazzo.* He was in for it.

She was going to make him pay and pay and pay.

Thank God for cosmetics. Tam dabbed still another layer of coverup under her eyes with the makeup sponge. The bruise-colored shadows down there were gruesome to behold without foundation to camouflage them. She studied the effect, and put on the finishing touches: a final brush of mascara to make already thick lashes thicker, a slick of clear gloss to make the bronze-toned lipstick glisten, color on her cheeks to brighten her shocking pallor.

Not bad. Even on a day from hell.

Janos was in the other room, sunk in silence as he perused the details of her Internet order. Yes, she had been bad, very bad. But he deserved to be punished for his mischief-making. He deserved worse for what he'd done to Rosalia alone, let alone the passports, the adoption agency, the cops. She didn't even want to total up how much money he'd cost her.

Therefore, she was authorized to fully enjoy the horrified look on his face when he saw the totals. Hah. Take that, *testa di cazzo*.

She went out into the hotel room and rummaged through the shopping bags, gathering the elements of her ensemble together. Janos watched her take the new shoes out of their box, and then glanced at the receipt for the reference.

"Manolos," he said, his tone aggrieved. "Eight hundred dollars?"

"A bargain," she purred. "Excellent value."

"And the Tigger potty seat? The Cadillac of strollers? Five hundred and eighty seven dollars for cosmetics alone? One thousand, four hundred for a cocktail dress that looks smaller than a hand towel?"

"Looking good is an investment." She unfolded the iridescent bronze-tinted silk stockings with the retro seams up the back and stroked them with an admiring hand. "You did say whatever we needed, didn't you?" She slanted him a look of mock dismay. "Does it exceed your budget? Oh, no! I'll write you a check! Oh, dear . . . whoops, afraid I can't after all. I'm a murder suspect now, you see. My assets will be frozen any time now, if they aren't already. So sorry!"

He made a disgusted sound and she left him to stew, gathering up stockings, shoes, jewelry case, and the dress before she went into the bathroom to pour herself into her outfit.

The stockings and garter belt were delicious, and the dress nicer even than it had looked in the online catalog. Crumpled, stretchy bronze fabric clung lovingly to every curve and hollow. It was almost off the shoulders with built-in support for her bosom that she barely needed. The skirt came down half the length of her thigh. Boldly short for a woman who scorned panties, but she liked living dangerously.

To a point, she mused, thinking of the morning's events. To a point. She was backing way off on living dangerously.

She braided her hair up into a high, tight coronet and fastened it with a bristling array of Deadly Beauty ornaments, all of them fully armed just in case. Her pendant topaz earrings looked great with the dress, also serving in a pinch as a hypodermic loaded with a quick-acting knock-out drug. She pulled out the necklace, the *pièce de resistance*.

Her eyes looked back from the mirror, bleak and miserable. She had to be ruthless now. Quick, decisive. To act without hesitation.

She had to stop dawdling and procrastinating, goddamnit.

"Rachel, honey?" she called. "Come on in here. We've got to do one last potty stop for you."

Rachel peered around the bathroom door, resplendent in her new red velvet dress trimmed with black ruffles. The flamenco three-year-old.

"No pee," she said darkly.

Tam shoved the new Tigger potty seat on to the toilet, tugged down Rachel's tights and swung the little girl up onto the toilet. "You just concentrate," she said. "I want to hear that tinkling sound, OK?"

With Rachel cooperating, Tam took a deep breath, stuck out her tits, and sauntered out.

Janos glanced up. The receipt dropped to his lap, forgotten.

She struck a pose, and let him look. She turned, very slowly, showing off. "Do you like it?" she asked throatily.

Janos cleared his throat. "*Sì*," he said. "You are magnificent."

He stood up, and she walked toward him, standing close enough so that he could smell all the outrageously expensive perfumed body and face creams she had bought on his dime.

"Thank you for the dress," she said softly. "I love it."

"The investment was worth it," he conceded.

She dropped her lashes demurely. "How sweet. Such a generous thing to say." She held up the clasps of the heavy beaten gold necklace with the big, padlock-shaped, moonstone-studded pendant. "Clasp this for me?"

He took them in his fingertips and bent over her head, inhaling her scent. He leaned closer still, until she could feel the brush of his warm breath. He smelled good. His breath smelled good, too. He was so hot, still faintly smelling of patchouli oil, sweat, and man.

She clenched her teeth. Grabbed the pendant in one hand, slid her fingers down to the third bead of the necklace with the other. She found the textured cluster of moonstones, pressed the pendant against his bare shoulder—and pushed the button.

Janos arched and shuddered with a strangled groan for the entire duration of the nerve-scrambling electric zap that she gave him. It was a long one, not out of spite, but because she badly needed an extra margin to get Rachel and all their stuff into a cab and away before he was capable of pursuing them.

He toppled backward onto the bed. It made an enormous rattling crash as his big body hit. Rachel appeared in the corridor seconds later, her tights wound like soft shackles around her wobbly ankles.

Her face was woefully confused. "Val sick?" she asked anxiously. "Need medicine?"

So he was Val to Rachel already, was he? She gritted her teeth, stuffing the taser necklace back into her jewelry case. "Just taking a nap, honey."

Val groaned and tried to speak. Shit. Her margin of safety was slim. The bastard was a tough one. Tam cursed, and hastened to tug up Rachel's panties and tights and get her into her brand-new red winter ski jacket, also bought on Janos's dime. A flurry of gathering shopping bags and scattered toys, babbling incoherent explanations to Rachel, and finally they were out of there. Tam held the wriggling Rachel with one arm and shoved the new stroller, which was heavily laden with bag, purse, potty seat and a cluster of shopping bags, with the other arm.

It started up when they were finally in the cab. Fat, hot tears, sliding right down through her undereye coverup, the cosmetic she could least afford to do without. Goddamn him for making her feel guilty. She dabbed, sniffed, cursed. Tried again to justify herself.

She couldn't give him what he wanted. She could not trust him for a split second. If what he said was true, he had his nuts in a vise, which made him deadly dangerous.

And if he was lying, he was more dangerous still.

She could not expose her friends to him and his organization while they were drinking and partying and dancing, their babies toddling around their feet. She couldn't let him see who she left her child with. He couldn't expect her to. He would not have done so in her place. No one with a functioning brain would. He'd be stupid to take it personally. And Val Janos was anything but stupid.

Still, those tears kept sliding down, one after the other, bringing a gooey landslide of foundation and mascara along with them.

Chapter

11

The satellite phone in Val's pocket vibrated. He counted the rings, twenty of them, but lay there, inert. Unable to coordinate his muscles. All he could do was twitch and fume and wait, furious with himself for letting her drop him. And with such humiliating ease, too. All it took was the short skirt, the long legs, the gleaming lips, the erect nipples.

He struggled until he managed to get his weak, trembling limbs to obey him, and hoisted himself up into a sitting position. He sat on the edge of the bed, hunched over. The phone rang again.

It took seven rings just to get his slack hand into his pocket and pull the thing out. The display informed him that it was Henry.

He answered promptly. "*Sí?* What have you got?"

Henry didn't answer for a few moments. "Uh, Val? Is that you?"

"Who else would answer this phone?" he snarled.

"Your voice sounds strange." Henry sounded suspicious. "What the fuck is wrong with you? Are you drunk?"

"She tased me," he grimly admitted, "and ran."

"Oh."

Henry said nothing, but Val could see his friend in his mind's eye, trying not to grin. The image did nothing to help his mood.

"So, ah, you lost her then, I take it?" Henry asked.

"No. I put an RF transmitter into her diaper bag," he said. "They are going to a wedding now. I will follow them there. As soon as I can walk."

"Want me to monitor it for you?" Henry's voice was a little too solicitous. "I've got nothing happening this evening, and this chick sounds like a real live wire . . . so to speak." He chortled at his own wit. "Give me the frequencies, and I'll—"

"No," Val said curtly. "Thank you, but I will handle it myself."

"I don't doubt it," Henry said. "So, did you want to know what I've got on Zetrinja? Or is this, you know, a bad time?"

Excitement welled up, energizing him. "Tell me," he said.

"August 24, 1992," Henry said. "Colonel Drago Stengl of the JNA and his secret police squad rounded up the Muslim men and boys in Zetrinja and shot them. Thirty-seven dead. The women and girls were loaded into trucks and taken to the concentration camp at Sremska Mitrovica."

It was a familiar enough story. Val had heard countless versions of it. "Did you check the—"

"Yes, of course. I made the calls to the city hall, I checked the census records," Henry assured him. "There were five girls between the ages of ten and twenty who were related to the men and boys who died that day. One of them was the daughter of Petar Zadro, the goldsmith. She was fifteen years old. Her name was—get this—Tamar."

A shiver went up his spine.

"Don't get excited," Henry warned. "I personally think it's just a random coincidence. A woman like her is not likely to use her actual given name, after all the aliases she's used so far. And unless I go there in person and start tracking down school photographs, I can't verify—"

"It is her," Val said. He was dead sure in his balls. He understood perfectly why Steele might risk taking back her own given name. After years of being a blank slate, sometimes a person felt the need to write something on that slate, however simple, and have it stand. And the daughter of a goldsmith might well be drawn to metalworking.

It was enough to convince him. "What happened to Tamar?"

"Her mother and sister died at the concentration camp in the end of September," Henry said. "Your typical heart-tugging Balkans tragedy. No more data on little Tamar after that. She vanishes into thin air."

Henry's cool, cynical tone grated on him. "Who ordered the shooting?" he asked. "Drago Stengl, you said? I have heard the name."

"That's because he hired PSS personnel in the nineties," Henry said. "We did some of his dirty work for him, like as not. Bastard's in hiding now. Charged with a bunch of gruesome war crimes in Croatia. Word is he's dying from some disgusting disease. Appropriate, huh?"

"Do you know where he is?"

"I know where his daughter is," Henry offered. "Found the info in the PSS files on Stengl. Ana Santarini. She lives in Italy on the Amalfi Coast. She married Ignazio Santarini, a rich import-export merchant with ties to the Camorra. Don't you have contacts down there? Weren't you fucking some Camorra mafioso's wife for PSS a few years back? Maybe you can just, ah, insert yourself into that slot again, wangle yourself an introduction to Ana? If it comes to that?"

Val grunted, noncommittal. "Maybe. Could you go to Italy—"

"Already there," Henry said. "I'm in Salerno. I thought you might want me to follow Ana Santarini around, so I took the liberty."

He was speechless. "Thank you," he said. "Please carry on."

"Hey, no problem," Henry said. "I have nothing better to do right now, and Italian girls are hot. I got here this morning. Followed Ms. Ana all day. She's got a nice ass. She went to a private clinic for a couple of hours this afternoon. My guess is Stengl's languishing there. But in any case, you better move your ass before Ms. Live Wire gives you the slip for good. Are you mobile yet?"

"I think so. Later." Val pocketed the phone, glanced in the mirror. He looked like shit, but he had no time for a shower or shave. He dragged on the black tee, buckled on the holster, shrugged on his gray Armani jacket. He had thought about ordering a suit from the department store, but he didn't know how formal the event was. He could not draw attention to himself by being overdressed. In America, it was better to err on the side of overcasual. At least the jeans were black. He was lucky he had not pissed himself when she zapped him.

He packed everything into his SUV, pulled up the frequencies of the beacon he had slipped into Steele's bag, and located them heading south on I-5.

It wasn't difficult to overtake her cab. She had only a twenty-minute head start on him, and he drove fast. An hour on the road found him outside Tacoma, driving through an evergreen forest on a road that led to a resort hotel. Signs identified it as the Huxley Resort and Spa. The icon that indicated her position had stopped there minutes before he arrived. He pulled over at the entrance and waited until he saw a yellow cab pull out before he proceeded into the parking lot. The timing of his entrance was critical. She had to be seated in the hall, exit choked with the wedding party, the ceremony already well begun before she caught sight of him. No chance to protest his intrusion without disrupting the wedding and agitating the child.

He caught sight of Rachel first, dressed as she was in hot red and black; tights, dress, shoes, coat, the crimson hair ribbon in her dark curls. She glowed like a holly berry against the dull grays and browns of the wintry forest, perched on Steele's hip as they walked toward the hotel. Rachel was fussing, arching back, mouth open. He could imagine the rich alto tones of Steele's voice as she wheedled and cajoled.

He kept her in sight, falling casually in with other groups of guests making for the hotel, but he did not let himself stare at her or even think about her. Creatures who were accustomed to being hunted could sense a predator. He kept her in his peripheral vision and emitted a blank white noise screen in his head as he watched the matrix turn.

The gray man. A classic technique for a covert operative, silently projecting, *I am not here. You did not see me. I do not matter.* He was good at it. In fact, it could be overdone. That silent chant could become actually noticeable to those who were trained in such things, like Steele. She would hear him if he chanted too loudly. Even in his mind.

Steele and the child disappeared inside. Val the gray man blended into the crush of people near the entrance and loitered. A glance inside located Steele in the back in a chair far to the side, the child on her lap. Not surprising. He'd overheard enough sessions with the child psychologist to understand Rachel's fear of strangers, particularly men. Steele was creating a safety zone, to limit pre-wedding socializing and have a possible escape route in case of tantrums.

He caught sight of the blond man who had acted as Steele's body-guard at Shibumi near the front of the hall. Davy McCloud looked mildly harrassed, and held a chubby, squirming infant with wild red ringlets in a carrying pouch. Val glanced around for the other body-guard, Nick Ward, but did not see him, until a clot of tuxedoed men in the front of the hall resolved themselves into a semicircle, facing the center aisle.

One of them was Nick. His central position, and the nervous, strangled way that he was tugging at his bow tie indicated that he was the groom. Which meant that his attention was fixed at the back of the hall where his bride would appear.

Gray man, gray man. Val slunk deeper into the shadows behind the door and cursed being so tall, not for the first time. He spotted a chair, snagged it, and sat, putting himself effectively beneath Nick's line of sight. There she was at last. The bride. A rustling murmur arose from the crowd. Heads swiveled. He caught a glimpse of her as she passed through the vestibule. Pretty, a cloud of curly dark hair that reached her shoulders, big green eyes all misty with love and bridal nerves. A lace-covered sheath showed off a memorable figure. She was followed by two very pretty dark-haired girls in rust-colored silk, one of them her younger sister, from the looks of her. The other girl was younger still, only fourteen or so, slender and ethereal.

The string quartet began to play, and everyone stood. Val sighed with relief as the collective point of focus shifted to follow all that dewy feminine beauty on up the aisle and away from him.

Then a buzzing hum in the back of his mind indicated that some-one was staring at him. He had to look around twice before he iden-tified the observer.

It was Rachel. Her arms were clamped around Steele's neck, her face buried against the crumpled iridescent sheen of her mother's scarf. Only her eyes were visible under the mop of dark curls and the floppy crimson bow. Huge, dark owl eyes, staring into his.

She raised her face. Her eyes looked solemn and wise.

He waved at her. Her face dove into the scarf, but in seconds, she peeped up again. This time he ventured a smile. The cycle repeated, but this time when she emerged from the scarf, her eyes were sparkling. The child was smiling at him. Dimpling. Flirting. Her head tilted.

The strangeness of it made him want to laugh. The minister droned on. The sound slid over his ears without penetrating.

Now, he decided. He grabbed his chair, strode over to Steele. He sat down beside her and grinned widely, right into her face. *"Ciao."*

The child dove into the scarf again with a squeak. Steele gasped.

"What the fuck are you doing here?" she hissed in Italian.

He kept the smile nailed firmly on. "Keeping you company," he murmured back in the same language. "Resign yourself. I am your date. You invited me."

"Oh, no. No way are you my date, you—"

"Shhh!" A woman shushed them, frowning. Several others were looking over curiously.

Val leaned closer. "You could scream and yell and throw me out if you want to ruin your friend's wedding," he said softly. "And I'm sure your daughter would help to make the event memorable, too. You could even try to kill me with one of your hair ornaments. That would make a big impression, no? Or you could smile and accept reality. Those are your options. After what you did to me in the hotel room, I will not hesitate to embarrass you."

"Vaffanculo," she hissed. *"Stronzo."*

"I'm a good dancer," he offered.

"Maiale," she hissed. "You are not welcome here. *Va te ne*, before I really do kill you."

Rachel began to whimper. "Mamma?"

Tam shot him one last poisonous look and murmured something soothing to the child. Rachel was emboldened, and soon began to flirt again while her mother stared up at the wedding, mouth clamped. Furious, but neutralized—for now.

Ah, well. He winked at the child. He'd charmed the little one, at least. And the evening was young.

He would take it as progress.

* * *

Manipulative swine. He'd assessed the situation perfectly. If she got agitated, Rachel would freak. If they made a scene, Becca would never forgive her. Becca had doubts about Tam, even though Tam's efforts on behalf of the children kidnapped by the organ pirates had forced her to grudgingly admit that maybe Tam might have some small redeeming qualities—the operative word being "small." Becca was still pissed at the way Tam had kicked her man around during the organ pirate debacle. It wouldn't do to underestimate Becca. After how she'd aquitted herself in that whole Zhoglo night-mare, she'd proved she was not to be fucked with, and Tam re-spected that.

But it was so silly of her to take it personally. That big galoot Nick had deserved every kick in the teeth that Tam had given him, and he was tough enough to take it. Nick himself had no hard feelings.

It didn't matter. Becca was still convinced that Tam was a rude, raving, dangerous hellion. Which, of course, she was. No arguments there. But Nick insisted that they grit their teeth and feign friendli-ness.

So fuck it. Whatever.

The upshot of it all was if Tam wrecked Becca's wedding, no mat-ter how justified she might feel, being jerked around by this gigolo pimp asshole with his big, terrifying agenda, that fragile truce would be dissolved, and the bride would proceed to take Tam apart. Phys-ically. Unpleasant for everyone. Not good for Rachel. To be avoided if at all possible.

Tam cuddled Rachel, glancing down at the little girl's face to see how she was handling . . . holy crap! The kid was smiling at him! Giggling at that smirking pig dog! And he was smiling back, using that knock-you-dead sidelong grin, white teeth flashing, eyes crin-kled. God, what a lethal smile. She wanted to backhand it right off his face.

Bastard. How dare he use Rachel to back her into a corner.

She didn't hear a word of the ceremony. Sveti looked great in her bridesmaid dress, alongside Becca's sister Carrie, but Tam couldn't help notice the sad looks she kept casting at Josh, Becca's brother. Josh was twenty-two years old to Sveti's fourteen. Guaranteed heartbreak. Sveti was already very pretty if a bit too serious, and prone to moping. But Nick and Tam both would beat up Joshie in a heartbeat if he even looked at Sveti cross-eyed, at least for the next four or five years or so. She was far too young, and she'd been through too much horrendous shit already, but still, there it was.

Josh had other fish to fry anyhow. He was dangling at least ten different girlfriends on a string.

She was going to have a talk with that girl. Poor little thing. She wished Sveti could have exactly what she wanted just once in a blue moon. She deserved it, after what she'd gone through with the organ pirates, as well as what she'd done for Rachel. Rachel had only lived through that ordeal because of Sveti's love and care.

Tam would gladly chain up that panting dog of a Joshie in a monastery and keep him pure for Sveti by brute force until she grew up.

But life didn't work that way. People could not be controlled, feelings could not be controlled. She hadn't always believed that, but the last few months of life with Rachel had driven the point home.

People so seldom got what they deserved, for good or for evil, she reflected, casting a sour look at Janos. Rachel was participating enthusiastically in his efforts to undermine her. And everyone had begun to notice that she had company. Tall, dark, handsome company.

Davy recognized Janos and stared at them fixedly as he jiggled little Jeannie in his arms. He looked puzzled and alarmed.

His eyes asked her *is this a problem?*

She made an executive decision in that moment to handle it herself and rolled her eyes to indicate, *no problem, just a pain in the ass.* Hoping it was true. She didn't want to spoil the party for Davy, either, or any of the rest of them. And oh, joy. Now Margot was gawking, too, her eyes like saucers. A little poking and gesticulating, and within seconds, everyone sitting in her orbit was rubbernecking. A wave of stares, grins, whispers followed from Seth, Raine, Liv, Sean.

Connor and Erin, too. Erin smirked knowingly over her son's round blond head. Idiot. Thinking that wild, wonderful sex was finally being had by that snotty bitch in her mountain lair. No doubt reflecting smugly that getting properly nailed would magically render Tam a docile, satisfied pussycat who would be sweet and nice and obliging to everyone henceforth. *Don't hold your breath, babydoll,* she told Erin silently.

Then again, who could blame them for thinking it, after what Davy and Nick witnessed at Shibumi? Everone in the room probably knew the details, the way that crowd gossiped among themselves.

It took a few minutes to identify the prickling heat in her face, it was so unfamiliar. Mother of God. She was blushing. She was shocked at herself. If she needed any further proof of her impending nervous breakdown, this was it. Maybe she was having a hot flash. Premature menopause would be easier to embrace than blushing.

Still. At thirty-one, menopause seemed a bit too much to hope. Flu maybe? A sudden fever? Except that she never got sick.

And since when did she give a shit what anyone thought of her?

She was so absorbed in her own thoughts, the explosion of hoots, howls, and applause made her jump. Nick grabbed his new wife and bent her over in a juicy, triumphant kiss. Tam nuzzled Rachel's warm curls as the organ began to blare, bracing herself for the obligatory physical contact, the mandatory boring chitchat. Torture, every time.

Why did she go to these events, anyway? For Rachel's sake, she supposed, but not entirely. She hated them, yes, but she was honest enough to acknowledge that a piece of her, for some reason, wished she was a person who did not hate them.

Part of her wished very badly that she didn't have to hate everything so goddamn much.

That didn't help her now, though. Not in the midst of being simultaneously bored, encroached upon, invaded, and annoyed by everyone. She muscled a big smile onto her face, clenched her teeth, and put Rachel on the floor as the deluge approached.

Erin was the first to bear down on her, flushed with triumphant delight. "Hey, Tam. You look great. Gorgeous dress, and Rachel is a doll in lipstick red. What a nice surprise to see you here, Mr. Janos!"

"A delight for me, too." He bowed over Erin's hand and gave Tam a sidelong wink before he kissed it, à la Count Dracula.

He would die for that wink, Tam silently vowed. She met Connor's eyes, grimly amused to note that Connor was as unimpressed as she at Janos's slick, Transylvanian gallantry. Erin seemed to be enjoying it, though, and baby Kev as well. Babies liked the guy. Go figure.

It made no sense, but she had no time to wonder about it. Everyone was crowding around to see the latest sideshow—Tam with a date, whoo-hoo—and she was trapped in a dance of embracing arms and social kisses and loud exclamations.

Rachel grabbed her thigh, protesting at being lost in a forest of legs, but before she could extricate herself, the child was swept up and almost out of her field of vision, skinny red legs waving wildly.

She spun around with a gasp. Janos was putting Rachel on his shoulders. She shrieked with delight, eyes wide, cheeks rosy.

"Put her down," she spat at him. "*Figlio di puttana.*"

He blinked innocently. Rachel chortled, wrapping an arm around his forehead. "But why? She loves it."

Tam reached up to grab her. Rachel began to wind up into her ambulance shriek. Tam sighed and let her arms drop.

"She's not completely potty trained, you know," she said. "She often loses it in moments of great excitement. But we're living dangerously today. Taking big risks. No pull-up pants. Just big girl panties. Made out of thin cotton knit."

Janos gazed back, apparently unintimidated. "Your point is?"

She shrugged. "I have fresh underwear and tights in my bag for Rachel if she pees or poops herself, but I have no spare Armani jacket for you when the inevitable happens," she said. "Nor will I have the least sympathy for you. On the contrary. It will make my day."

Janos's white teeth flashed. "You are less likely to stab with a poisoned blade or tase me with a necklace while I have Rachel on my shoulders," he said. "I am safer like this. I will risk it."

"Be it on your head, then. Or your shoulders, and running down your back, as the case may be." Tam noticed the fascinated audience clustered around them. "Oh, for Christ's sake," she snapped. "Don't you folks all have people to kiss? Go on, fuss over the bride before she gets annoyed at me for drawing too much attention to myself! Go!"

The crowd dispersed, smirking at each other. Janos followed her as she hoisted the diaper bag over her shoulder and made her way to the ballroom where the reception was being held. He suffered Rachel's sticky, clutching hands grabbing his ears, his nose, yanking his hair, all with calm good humor.

She spotted a table to the side that was flanked by a long bench, where bulging diaper bags already sat. She recognized them as Margot and Erin's. High chairs were interspersed with the place settings.

She headed for it and found her name. Janos sat down on the other side of Rachel's high chair, lifting her onto his lap and bouncing her. The kid giggled madly, delighted. So dangerous, to let oneself be charmed by so little, she thought darkly. "That's Erin's chair," she informed him.

"There's room for another person," Janos said. "She was happy to see me with you. She'll make space for me."

"Her husband won't be thrilled to have an uninvited stranger with no security clearance plant his arrogant ass right next to his wife and son," Tam said.

"You're my security clearance," he said.

She passed a roll from the breadbasket to Rachel. "Do you want to live to see the dawn? You do understand the futility of following me around, don't you, Janos? I will never do what you have asked. Never. Is that absolutely clear?"

"As crystal," he said.

She watched sourly as Janos was a good sport about having the roll crumbled and smeared all over his Armani. God, how her jaw ached. Social events in general made her tense, and the day's bizarre events and assorted shocking revelations had ratcheted the tension up higher, nudging her toward homicidal on her own scale. Tam had no talent for parties at the best of times. But Becca wouldn't like an impromptu amputation with a steak knife or someone losing an eye to an escargot fork at her nuptial bash. *Behave. Down, girl. Breathe.*

She reached for the cabernet that sat breathing in the middle of the table and sloshed some into her glass. People were already drifting toward her table like gawkers toward a car wreck. She closed her eyes against the pulse of a stress headache.

It was going to get worse before it got better.

Chapter 12

Val fed data into the matrix as he smiled, shook hands, chatted politely. The husband of Erin glowered at him, just as Tam had foreseen, but did not oust him from the table, at least not yet. The other men all regarded him with the barely concealed suspicion he would expect of a group of seasoned security professionals. The women tried without success to hide their curiosity. Tam gazed off into space, her jaw tense. She looked deathly pale beneath her skillfully applied makeup.

She gave him an unfriendly look when he poured her another glass of wine. "Relax," he murmured.

"Sure," she whispered back. "When you stop fucking with my life. And speaking of fucking with lives, have you called the cops off Rosalia's boys yet?"

He was nonplussed. "Ah . . ."

"Do it. This very second. Or else I will announce, in a loud voice, exactly who you are and what you want to this whole table. The aftermath won't be pretty, I promise you that."

"*Sì, sì*. One moment." He pulled out his Palm Pilot, tapped in a quick SMS, and smiled at her. "Done. To confirm my good intentions."

"In a pig's eye." She frowned, unconvinced. "Just like that?"

"Give it twenty minutes," he advised. "Let it trickle down."

"Not one second more," she warned.

He sipped his wine, let his eyes smile at her from over the rim of the glass. She muttered something rude and tore her gaze away.

The younger of the bridesmaids came by, leaning over to kiss Tam and murmur to her in a language that Val was startled to realize was Ukrainian. He'd learned it by necessity in his youth, since a great deal of Novak's business had been connected to the Ukraine.

"Sveti! Sveti!" Rachel crowed with delight, forgetting all about him, and held up her arms, launching herself into midair.

The girl caught her and hugged her, murmuring endearments and covering Rachel's face with kisses.

"You're from Ukraina?" he asked in that language. "Rachel, too?"

She gave him a shy smile that struck him as very sad. "Rachel and I were cellmates in prison," was her unexpected reply. She swung the child onto her hip. "Can I take her over to play with the other kids?" she asked Tamara, in heavily accented English.

"Fine," Tamara said. "Bring her back when they start serving something you think she might eat or whenever you want a break. Thanks, Sveti. You're an angel."

Sveti walked away, her head bent over the toddler's to listen to the child's excited babble.

He gave Tam a questioning look. "Cellmates?"

She shrugged. "Just like she told you. They were locked up by organ pirates for months in a stinking basement room. Sveti's the closest thing Rachel has to real family after that. I fly her over to visit as often as she can come. Excuse me. Since Sveti is watching Rachel, I'll take this opportunity to run to the ladies' room."

Val followed her with his eyes until she vanished. He disliked taking his eyes off her, but Rachel was still visible from here, and he was sure that she would not run without the child.

He turned back to the people at the table. "Organ pirates?" he asked the table at large.

"You mean she hasn't told you how she got Rachel?" asked the sultry redheaded beauty who sat next to Davy McCloud, wide-eyed. "It's an incredible story."

He shook his head. The women tripped over themselves to tell him the tale of the rescue of the orphans. Steele's rush into the jaws of death dressed only in silver spandex. How she had pretended to be a stripper who had lost her way to a bachelor party to create a diversion while the rest of the team sneaked into the compound. How she had neutralized four guards by herself before they could sound the alarm, making it possible for Nick and the rest to charge in and stop the villains just as they were about to cut Sveti's heart out.

He knew the story, but listening to these women tell it gave him a whole new level of information. These people admired Steele. They liked her too. Even trusted her—in a careful way.

"Impressive," he murmured.

"Yeah, that she is," said a blond man who Val's surveillance had pegged as Sean McCloud. "Tam's special. Not to be messed with."

Val acknowledged the blunt warning with a nod. "I would not dream of it," he said blandly. "Particularly not when she is surrounded by such a fierce band of loyal friends."

There was a tense silence. The people at the table exchanged significant glances. Val smiled at them and sipped his wine.

"Mr. Janos is interested in marketing Deadly Beauty in Europe," Erin explained, effectively breaking it.

That touched off a far less emotionally charged conversation that Val could handle smoothly with a tenth of his brain while the rest of it occupied itself with frantic planning.

As soon as the conversation shifted away from him, he excused himself and left the ballroom. He had to find a place to stage the scene that would take place this evening. The minicam was taped discreetly under his arm. It had to happen now, or else Imre would be . . .

No. He could not think of Imre at all. He had to be suave, relaxed. Not desperate. That woman would smell desperation from miles away.

He had to hide it under a layer of impenetrable charm. And still, the word pulsed in his head, like a strobe light. *Now, now, now.*

A long corridor of dimly lit administrative offices was a likely possibility. He strode down the hall, trying all the doors. One of them was open, a utilitarian staff kitchen. Sink, coffeemaker, microwave, cupboard, and small refrigerator for storing staff lunches.

This was it. His only option, he decided, lacking in atmosphere though it was. There was no time to look for someplace better.

A dismantled drip coffeemaker on top of the refrigerator gave him an idea. He stuck the vidcam into the glass pot, and added handfuls of miscellaneous objects from the drawers to hide it: sugar packets and Sweet'n Low, tea bags. He directed the lens so its field of vision was unobscured. He'd programmed it to be light-activated.

God help him. Imre's only hope, at the mercy of a tense, nervous, frightened woman's whim. What bizarre conditions under which to seduce the most beautiful woman he had ever seen. A blues tune began to play, pulsing from afar. The dancing had begun. That might help.

He ran into her outside the bathrooms on his way back. She looked pale. "Are you well?" he asked.

"Great. Perfectly wonderful, thanks to you."

"Let's dance." He slid his arm around her waist as they went into the ballroom and swung her around into his arms.

She went rigid. "Let go of me, you tricky son of a bitch," she said, through a smiling grimace. "Or I'll open your jugular with my hairpin."

"Do not be that way," he wheedled. "We were doing so well. You do not want to upset all your friends, do you? Look at them, so happy for you, thinking that you are finally enjoying yourself. About time, no?"

She harrumphed, stiff as a wooden plank, shoving against his chest to put more space between them. "Little do they know."

He jerked her closer as she stumbled. "Relax, for God's sake."

"Like it's so easy," she muttered. "As if I ever knew how. I don't like being watched, gawked at or speculated about."

Val glanced around. Several of the dancing couples were casting furtive, sidelong glances at them. "Your friends told me the tale of the grand rescue from the organ pirates," he said. "They evidently think that you are a superwoman."

"Hmmph." She rolled her eyes. "They like to dramatize."

"Strange how they trust you," he said. "Especially the women."

She looked offended. "Why would that strike you as strange?"

"Because of their men," he said. "Women tend to be suspicious of other women who are as beautiful as you. It is a brutal fact of nature. You are an inherent threat to them."

She grunted. "Bullshit. Besides, they're all beautiful women themselves. Not one of them has any reason to worry."

"No?" He yanked her into a possessive clinch. "You mean to say you have never taken any of the men in this room as your lover?"

She went motionless, mouth open. "Who, me? If any of those guys cheated on their wives, I would personally remove their testicles."

He was taken aback. "That is vehement," he commented.

"Those men are well taken care of," she went on heatedly. "They have nothing to complain about. And if they did, they wouldn't dream of messing with me. I've put the fear of God into every last one of them."

He willed her to relax against the heat of his body. "Such high standards to hold them to," he teased. "After all, they are only men."

"They can damn well live up to those standards. They have quality women who trust them more than any man deserves to be trusted. If they ever, for one second, demonstrate any lack of appreciation for their good fortune, I will be there standing by. Garden shears in hand."

He cleared his throat, trying not to smile. "They all seem . . . er, more or less intact. I take it that so far they have behaved well?"

She nodded. "Pussywhipped to the last man," she said, with cool satisfaction. "And now kids are coming right and left. I doubt they have the energy to misbehave at this point. Not that it stops most men. Ass-sniffing, leg-humping dogs on the furniture that they are."

He let that caustic attack upon his sex pass without comment, and spun her into a deep, sensual dip. "That reveals so much," he said.

She almost tripped over his foot as he tugged her back up again. "Reveals what? What are you talking about?"

He grinned. "You are secretly a romantic."

That startled a burst of laughter out of her. "Me? Hah!"

"You." He put his mouth to her ear. "Your need for your friends to stay faithful to each other as living proof that true love is possible," he whispered. "Because you keep hoping that it is, no? Even though you are sure in the depths of your heart that it is not, you continue to hope that you might be wrong. It is another one of those bleeding contradictions. You are full of them, Tamara Steele."

"I . . . do not . . ." She squinted at him. "That's such crap. Let's not start the armchair psychology game again. And don't even try to pin a softer side onto me. It won't stick."

"Say what you like. I draw my own conclusions."

"Whatever," she growled. "The truth is still the truth. I'm going to check on Rachel, so get your big groping paws the hell off me."

She wrenched out of his arms, and stalked toward the corner where Sveti entertained Rachel, heels clicking smartly over the gleaming ballroom floor. Fury radiated from her tense, slender figure.

Their dining table was momentarily deserted, all of the other couples either dancing or dealing with their children. The chance he had been waiting for. He strolled back to the table, pulled out his cell, and feigned texting a message while he detached the quarter tablet of tasteless, odorless R-55-Triplex he'd taped inside his pocket.

He let it plop into Steele's wineglass as he reached for his own.

Done. He took a deep swallow, tempted to eat the other three-quarters of the tablet himself, just for a break from this unbearable tension. But he could not. The image of his mother on the bathroom floor was etched indelibly in his mind. Drugs could never be a refuge for him. Nor would he dare risk losing his edge, tonight of all nights.

A quarter dose was the smallest effective dose he could give her in solid form. He'd reasoned that he would have no good opportunity to administer drops unobserved in public. R-55-Triplex was formulated by PSS's lab techs for situations just like this. In larger doses, it had been favorably compared to Ecstasy—just more subtle, with no hangover, headache or thirst. A quarter dose should render her euphoric, mellow, more receptive sexually. Alcohol intensified the effect, food reduced it. But she ate so little. If he could get some more wine into her . . . if she didn't realize that she'd been altered . . . *maybe*.

He took another swallow of wine and smiled and nodded as Davy and Margot McCloud swayed by, entwined. Davy's eyes lingered on him thoughtfully, and then something his wife said drew his attention back to her. Davy smiled and kissed her. The kiss caught fire, right on the dance floor. When they surfaced, the redhead was flushed, heavy-eyed.

Touching, he thought glumly. How nice for them. Sex with no problems, no lies, no betrayal. How pleasant.

He had tried, for a time, to find weak spots to exploit in the Mc-Clouds in the process of reseaching various ways to manipulate Steele. But when it came to McClouds, there were no weak spots, no fault lines. Nothing to exploit. The entire clan was rigidly upright in their business dealings. It was evidently a family trait. Their bank accounts, stock portfolios, and tax returns baffled him. That kind of honesty and transparency in Italy would run a business into the ground in minutes. But to all appearances, they seemed prosperous. A mystery.

He had lost sight of Steele. Panic yawned wide in his belly. He searched the crowd anxiously for that bronze fabric, the flash of her pale face and arms, the gleam of coiled mahogany hair.

Only when he spotted her could he breathe again.

Tam reached across the table and ran her hand through the soft red ringlets of little Jeannie, Davy and Margot's baby daughter, thinking how pretty the baby was with those huge slate-blue eyes, that crazy open-mouthed grin, the four little pearls of teeth popping out, two above and two below, from her pink gums.

Margot's mouth fell open. Tam barely stopped herself from giggling at the other woman's expression. True, she was feeling oddly mellow—for her. She'd downed quite a bit of chianti on an empty stomach, but it was finally relaxing her, thank God. She'd felt like she was made of steel cables strained to the snapping point. Tension that severe had to find some release. It was a physical law, like gravity. If you didn't respect it, bad things happened.

Finally, that headache was backing off, and she could appreciate how nice the McCloud Crowd looked in their wedding finery. Easy on the eyes, as Nick was fond of saying. She leaned her chin on her clasped fingers, appreciating the tender way that Seth was cupping Raine's pregnant belly, whispering something into her ear that made her blush.

Sweet. And it was. Really. She wasn't even being snide. She smiled her approval. Seth caught it and did a startled double take.

Maybe Janos was right about her being a secret romantic.

"I did a background check on Janos," Davy said to her quietly.

Duh, so did I, moron, as soon as I learned of his existence. For some odd reason she refrained from saying it out loud. "And?" she asked graciously.

"He looks good," Davy said heavily. "In fact, he looks too good. Way too good for my tastes."

Tam swiveled to look at the man in question. He was waiting in line at the crowded buffet where he'd gone to fill her plate. She observed his broad shoulders, the elegant shape of his head, the fine cut of his jacket, the excellent shape of his ass.

"Doesn't he, though?" she said. "Mouthwatering."

Margot choked on a burst of laughter. Davy's puzzlement turned to visible alarm. "Are you feeling OK, Tam?"

"I'm fine," she said airily. "Maybe just a tiny little bit drunk."

"You, uh, want to go lie down, or something?"

She was touched by his concern, silly though it was. "No."

She turned away and caught Erin's eye. Erin was discreetly nursing her son under her scarf. For the first time, the sensual intimacy of the madonna-and-child routine did not grate upon Tam's nerves.

"Sveti told me you flew her out for the wedding," Erin said.

Tam nodded. "Maybe she'll come and do a year of American high school, if she can persuade her mother to agree. She'll stay with us."

"I'd have a hard time with that if I were her mom," Erin said fervently. "I'd keep that girl handcuffed to a radiator."

The women contemplated the nightmare Sveti's mother had gone through last year, after her daughter's abduction at Zhoglo's hands and her husband's murder. Months of agonizing uncertainty.

"Speaking of motherhood," Tam said. "I . . . I have a favor to ask."

Erin's eyes widened. "Ask away."

"It's about Rachel." Tam dragged in some air, and forced herself to push on. "If anything happened to me—would you and Connor—"

"Yes," Erin broke in. "God, yes. You don't even have to ask."

Relief she hadn't expected to feel made Tam sag in her chair.

"There's money for her in my will, but I don't have custody yet," she admitted. "The adoption hasn't gone through. There are some problems. If anything should happen to me before I fix them, you'd have to fight for her."

"We would fight for her," Erin said. "Count on it."

The steel in Erin's voice comforted Tam. Tears prickled in her eyes. "Thanks," she said thickly. "That's, ah, good, then."

Janos appeared at her elbow, and placed a plate with several appetizing dabs of food before her. He poured her another glass of wine, flashed her a devastating smile. Amazing. The grooves that flanked his mouth carving into the hollow of his cheek, the shadow of his beard stubble, that fan of eye crinkles . . . add the glint of danger, the lure of the unknown, his ironclad persistence, and voilà. A marvel of nature.

Novak. Georg. She dutifully reminded herself of her enemies, but the alarm bells in her mind were distant and muffled. True, Valery Janos was a liar, a spy and a killer—but such a gorgeous one.

Everything seemed strangely beautiful tonight. The way the light from the tall white candles on the table glimmered in the curved surfaces of the wine and water glasses pleased her. So did the luscious glow of the silver buckets that held the white wine and the champagne. Mellow golden candlelight sparkled and reflected and refracted, softening everything and everyone she looked upon. What a pleasure to draw air into her lungs and feel her ribcage willingly expand to accommodate them. No iron plates clamping down, no need to struggle for air, to fight her way out of a cage of steel. No need to maintain a tight, aching smiling mask on her face.

What a pleasure, just to let herself be happy.

God, she could almost eat. She looked down at the plate and forked up a bite of butterfly pasta with smoked salmon and cream. It felt good in her mouth. She chewed and swallowed, heedless of carbs, saturated fat, calories. What the hell. It was a party, after all. She had some more and washed it down with more wine.

Heat was branded into her cheeks. An alcohol flush, she supposed. She should skip the wine. But she felt so soft, so relaxed. She took a last, farewell swallow. Then another.

"Dance with me?" Janos asked softly.

The reasons why she should not get close to this man scrolled automatically in her head, but she ignored them. She was enjoying this strange, soft glow so intensely. Knowing it couldn't possibly last made it all the more precious.

She hadn't felt like this in . . . well, ever. She'd been too young and innocent before. Back behind that blood-spattered, concrete wall in her mind, crowned with barbed wire, broken glass.

The wall that separated Then from Now.

Tension rose up, clutching at her. *Leave it. Don't go there, even for a second, or you'll kill this feeling and never get it back.*

She took another gulp of wine and pushed her chair back.

Just a dance. He couldn't do anything nasty to her on a public dance floor. She wanted to move to the music with a big, pretty man to hold onto. None of the other men in this room had the courage to touch her.

Janos wasn't afraid of her. That was as dangerous as it was irresistible. She gazed at him, weighing the danger, the temptation.

"Let me check Rachel," she said.

She wafted through the room, Janos padding quietly behind her like some sinuous jungle predator. His enormous presence made her body prickle and tingle, asking a wordless question and waiting breathlessly for his answer—though she knew what it would be.

Men were predictable that way. But for some reason, that fact didn't annoy the hell out of her tonight.

She found Rachel in a high chair, swathed in multiple brocade napkins, face smeared with red sauce, mouth full of pasta. Sveti was coaxing bites into her, while darting intermittent gazes heavy with longing out onto the dance floor.

Tam leaned down to kiss the little girl. "She ate?"

"Pasta with tomato sauce and cheese, french fries, vegetables, and chicken strips," Sveti said triumphantly. "And fresh fruit!"

Good. Rachel lifted goopy hands to grab her, and Tam leaned down, heedless of pasta sauce to accept the hug. The fierce, almost angry rush of love she felt for the little girl was no different from the love she always felt—except that tonight, there was no painful cramp of fear and caution inhibiting her. It felt so good to be grabbed by those little arms. She loved the kid so much it hurt. Like a knife going in and twisting. But tonight, the pain was all right. In fact, the pain felt almost good. It was hardly pain at all. It was something else altogether.

But she was too gone to bother analyzing it. She was no expert on tender emotions. They were too new to her.

She caught another longing glance from Sveti as she straightened up, aimed at Josh Cattrell, dancing with the girlfriend *du jour*. Laughing as he grabbed the girl's ass. Moron.

She leaned over Sveti, murmured in Ukrainian into the girl's ear. "He's not worthy," she said forcefully. "He'll be no good to any woman for years yet. You're ten times more intelligent, beautiful and strong than that heifer he's groping, and in a few years, you'll be more. If he's grown up enough by then to be worth your time, fine. If not, men will be lined up, panting. On their knees. You'll take your pick of them."

Sveti tried to smile. On impulse, Tam kissed her cheek and smoothed the girl's hair off her forehead. Then she backed away, startled by her own emotions.

Janos pulled her gently but insistently onto the dance floor. She relaxed into his arms, letting her head drop back to look up at the garish chandelier in the center of the ceiling. It seemed to spin like a galaxy, a vortex of light. It was delicious to let go, lie back, rely entirely on his strength. She reveled in the sensation, though she knew it was just a passing fantasy. But ah, what a fantasy. Sweet surrender—and way too much wine, no doubt.

It was criminally irresponsible of her to have gotten this tipsy with Rachel to protect after what had happened this morning, but the scolding thought had no sting. She was blissing out on the woodsy, cedary sweetness mixed with salt, rain, moss and summer sunshine that was Val Janos's intoxicating scent. His shoulders were so broad, his arms so solid and thick. Those hard, sinewy muscles beneath her fingers made her want to explore every cut and dip and curve, every marvelous masculine detail. She wanted to drape herself across him. To stretch and preen, like a lioness on a sun-warmed rock.

She felt so relaxed. The closest she'd ever come to this feeling was after a grueling physical workout and a hot shower. But this was different, better. Magic. She floated in his arms, flushed with heat and color. Like a sunset-tinted cloud.

She wanted more than just a dance. Her body yearned, a sharp hunger she was usually too taut and compressed to let herself feel.

Remember who he is. What he wants. Remember Novak and Georg.

She thought about them deliberately, like pressing on a bruise. A desperate ploy to bring her back to her senses, but it didn't take. She was in another place, far from that toxic wasteland. Tempted to give in to his silent invitation. To just use him like a big, beautiful sex toy. Why not? What difference would it make?

No. She wanted it too much. Anytime she wanted something this much, she set herself up for a catastrophe. Sex with Janos would be worse than stupid. It would be nothing less than suicidal.

And speaking of suicidal, look at this. They had swayed right out the ballroom door and into the hall outside. She hadn't even noticed being piloted through the room. She twisted in his arms as he hustled her through the lobby, past the curious stares of other guests.

"Hey!" she whispered fiercely. "Where do you think you're going?"

"Someplace private," he said. "To finish this."

She felt inhibited from trying flashy kung fu moves in public, hoping as she was to keep this thing under the radar. "Finish what?"

He shot her a look that made her feel both foolish for playing dumb and angry at his presumption.

"I agreed to dance with you, Janos. Not fuck you," she said tartly.

"Then we will dance. In private." He swung her around and into a deserted corridor.

She grabbed his wrist, wrenched it down to torque his tendons into screaming agony and drop him to the ground. He flowed like water through her hands, anticipating her every move, and flipped her effortlessly around. She fetched up hard against the wall.

He held her there with his big body. Her feet dangled off the ground. His lips were close to hers; they almost touched. Every molecule in her body vibrated at the contact, generating a wild energy that lit her up like a torch. And she liked it. Goddamn him.

She wrenched her mind into line. "What is it with you, Janos? Was getting tased not enough for you?"

He grinned. "By no means. I find challenge . . . electrifying."

She groaned. "Spare me your razor wit. You're a slow learner."

"No." He nuzzled her ear, his hot breath tickling her. "But I am a good listener. I hear all of the things that you are afraid to say."

"Nothing is more pathetic than a man who projects his gutter fantasies onto women that he lusts after," she snapped.

He laughed. "Gutter fantasies? Is that all sex is to you?"

She writhed in his hard grip. Friction just sweetened the pulsing glow at every point of contact to an unbearable pitch.

"I'll tell you what sex is," she said shakily. "Sex is just a unit of economic exchange. Or else it's a dirty power game."

A small frown creased his brow. "That is all?"

"That is all," she said. "No one has ever convinced me otherwise."

His dark eyes were thoughtful. He broke eye contact, and kissed her bare shoulder, his tender lips moving slowly up her shivering neck.

"I am sorry for you," he said quietly.

She was stung. "Don't be. I'm fine with it since I learned to stop being the victim. I can outplay anyone at that game." *Except for you, you sneaky bastard.*

"I do not doubt it." He cupped her ass, holding her up as he pressed hot kisses to the skin between her breasts. The caress made her nipples tighten, and he rubbed his face voluptuously against her breasts. "Your looks and your body alone guarantee it."

She let out a sharp laugh. "Hah. My looks and body were what got me into trouble in the first place."

She was horrified with herself for saying it. It sounded almost like a whining plea for pity or sympathy. But when he lifted his face, there was no contempt in his eyes. Just a desire that made her breathless.

"Please," he whispered. "Let me prove you wrong."

Her feet touched the ground. He slid his hand up over her hips, her belly, his thumbs flicking tenderly over her nipples. Her sensitized body responded, just as she realized that he had released her hands.

She had not even noticed. She'd been too busy shivering and sighing. This was terrible. So far outside her conscious control, it was like going mad. Her reality shaking loose, breaking down.

But she couldn't give in. She would go down kicking and scratching and shrieking, goddamnit.

She sucked in a breath, gritted her teeth, and fended it off. "Don't feed me your slick gigolo lines, Janos. They won't work on me."

"No?" His hand slid down over her ass, cupping the undercurve with a tender brush of his hand. "Why not?"

"I'm not interested in playing that game with you."

"Are you not?" His hand slid down, then up beneath her dress, curving around her bare buttock, gripping her. Fingertips circling tenderly. Sliding lower.

She steadied her voice, with conscious effort. "I have nothing to gain from winning it. So why bother?"

He hoisted her effortlessly up so that her crotch straddled his. Letting her feel his length, his hardness, his heat. "You do not convince me." He swayed back, holding her against the wall, and looked pointedly down at his thigh. His jeans had a gleaming wet spot.

Her face flamed. This feeling was for the man, not for her. Helpless, desperate, flopping like a fish on a hook, ripe for whatever agenda he might have. She shook her head, but she couldn't stop clenching her thighs around him. Shivers rippled down her legs.

"You want to see how a professional liar and scam artist fakes an orgasm, Janos?" she asked. "While we're at it, I've always wondered how male professionals manage that trick. The technical aspects of it baffle me. Am I about to find out? Shall we trade professional secrets?"

His arms tightened around her. His hand slid up, his fingertip gliding tenderly down the cleft of her buttocks until it found her tight folds, hot and slick and yielding. He stroked her, penetrating her.

To his credit, he did not laugh at her to find her so hot and soft and drenched. His smile was oddly gentle. "*Va bene*," he whispered, his lips brushing hers. "Pretend all you like, *bella*. And I will do the same. Pretend to the best of your ability."

She jerked away from his kiss. "Don't you dare make fun of me."

"Never." He cupped her head and kissed her again, almost angrily. His mouth coaxed hers open just as his finger slid deeper, stroking the whole length of her cunt and then delving deep.

She came instantly, almost painfully, convulsing around his hand. Sobs choked out of her with each deep, wrenching spasm.

He waited, immobile. Listening, feeling. Stroking at her lips tenderly with his own, then a delicate, careful touch of his tongue, the brush of her nipples against his chest, the tip of his tongue sliding into her mouth. No hurry, no fear. Complete mastery. She tried to breathe, tried to speak. There was nothing to say. He had bested her.

His lips caressed her cheekbone, kissing her eyelids, her brow. "The most realistic faked orgasm I ever felt," he whispered. "A tip, *bella*. A faked orgasm is more realistic if you make me work for it. At least a little bit, no? Wait longer next time. I did not even touch your clit."

She licked her dry, trembling lips. "Fuck you." She mouthed the words, but was too breathless to voice them.

A brief smile illuminated his face. "That is what I intend to do," he said. "But first, another fake orgasm. This time, try to wait, no? I will help you."

She twisted against him in protest, only succeeding in lodging his fingers deeper inside her slick channel. She squeezed her thighs around his big hand as he stroked and swirled, following all her nerve pathways as if he were inside her mind.

This time, he did make her wait. He teased and beckoned, but every time she started to crest, he drew back, time after time, until she wanted to scream, writhe, beg. He drove her deeper and deeper into that altered state, mind to mind, shockingly intimate. She struggled around his caressing, invading hand. She was made of lightning, heat, steam, making desperate sounds she barely heard over the pounding of her heart, the roaring in her head. And finally, he brought her off.

The orgasm cracked her wide open.

Behind that wall was something she hadn't known existed. A part of herself she'd thought was long dead. Something wordless and tender and unknown. It shone, dazzling her with its purity.

She must have fainted. She could not tell and did not care. Janos scooped her up into his arms long before she recovered and strode down the hall. He tried every door he passed until one of them opened. He slapped the door open, flipped on the light. It was a staff kitchen.

He set her on her feet, shoved the door to and stared into her eyes as he flipped the door knob with a deliberate "click."

She laughed shakily. "I didn't say you could—"

"I am not asking your permission. You would kick me in the teeth and spit on me as you walk over me with the spiked heels, no?"

She almost betrayed herself by giggling. "Bullshit."

He grinned wickedly. "I know what you like," he said. "A spineless dickhead with no balls who asked nicely would not arouse you, Tamara Steele. We have established this fact beyond all doubt."

Don't presume to know me. She wanted to say it, but her mouth was too busy frantically kissing him.

The kiss was wild, rough. A mutual devouring, and she set the tone. His grip tightened as his lips dragged down her jaw, teeth grazing the tendons of her throat as he wound his hands into her hair, pulling out clips, pins, clasps. He tossed the ornaments carelessly down onto the kitchen counter. He was not afraid of them, despite what she had done to him in the hotel. And he seemed to be sure she would not hurt him.

At least not until she'd gotten what she needed.

He unraveled her hair, spreading out braid-crimped locks and draping them over her shoulders. She felt younger with her hair loose, vulnerable. He pressed his face to her nape, wrapping thick skeins around his fists. Even her hair felt pleasure, tingling in her scalp, swirling through her at each stroking touch down its length.

He tugged her stretchy bodice down over her shoulders, her breasts. His hungry mouth followed the path of his hands, trailing slow, dragging kisses over her collarbone, her chest. His hands slid up her thighs, over the stockings to the smooth, bare skin.

Her legs threatened to give way when Janos stepped back and undid his belt. Delicious anticipation fluttered across the surface of her skin at subtle sounds of leather creaking, buttons popping.

She reached down, impatient, and fumbled to free him from the black denim, the snug black briefs. She grabbed his cock.

His hand covered hers and squeezed. Stroked.

Yes. She made an involuntary sound like a satisfied cat. He was long, heavy, rock hard. Scalding hot, velvety smooth. Every beat of his heart throbbed hard against her palm. She swirled his thick, blunt, cockhead in her palm. It was flushed a fierce, hot red. Very large.

Excellent. She'd never given a damn about size before, but she liked it that Janos's cock was big. She liked excess, she liked overkill.

She'd been hungry for so long. Bring it on. Loads of it.

He shuddered, his fingers fumbling with the condom from his pocket. She wanted to bat the latex out of his hands, hungry for naked contact with his hot skin, but a last, lingering shred of sanity stayed her hand. She'd abandoned the pill after the Novak debacle, figuring contraception would never be an issue in her life again. She doubted she was particularly fertile even without it, but life was full of inconvenient surprises. And there were diseases to consider.

Not that she was in any condition to consider anything. That and all other rational thought melted away to nothing at the sweet shock of contact. Janos slid the head of his thick shaft slowly up and down her cleft, seeking out the strokes, the angles that made her gasp.

He surged deep inside, filling her. Impossibly thick and deep. She didn't recognize the way her body felt. She had no frame of reference at all for this experience. Her body was entirely new, shivering around that secret place inside that had flushed with heat, burst into bloom.

Each surging, rhythmic twist and thrust of his body into hers was a discovery. She lifted herself for more, gasping at the intensity, building, swelling with each deep, slick stroke, sliding over and over a marvelous hot spot inside her that got hotter, hotter. Dear God, there was no end to it, no controlling it. She could feign an utterly convincing orgasm, but she had no clue how to survive real pleasure, to stay on top of it like a canoe in the rapids, to not drown in it, faint from it, go mad from it. He pumped his big, powerful body slowly into hers, his hips swiveling, stirring her into a writhing, moaning frenzy.

The climax drove her still deeper into that magic inner place that she had glimpsed before. He came with her, the force of it reverberating through her body, harmonics blending with hers into a deep chord, unbearably long and sweet and lingering. He was there with her inside that secret place. Souls brushing, melding.

Tam floated in that magical dream for a moment of timeless bliss ... until reality began to intrude. Her mind, always independently crunching the data, and presenting its cool, considered conclusions. Whether she wanted them or not.

She didn't want them, but there was no escaping them. The realization of what he had done stung like a poisoned needle. She'd hidden the truth from herself because temporary relief from that agonizing tension had been so irresistibly pleasurable. But the truth had been right there. That glow, the floating, the gaga mellowness that couldn't be explained by a few glasses of wine.

Staring her in the face. So fucking obvious.

Drugs. The whole thing had been chemically induced. He'd slipped her something subtle, sophisticated, to mellow her ever so slowly and delicately, and then wrangled her into a state of sexual surrender. She'd thought she was good, but he left her in the dust.

She was incapable of speech for minutes. They were poised together, braced against the door. Still joined. The hot, animal smell of sex rose between them. His arms circled her, trembling with strain. His cock was wedged so deep inside her, it pressed up against her womb. Pleasure jolted stubbornly through her limbs. Her body had no pride. It didn't care if it had been grossly deceived, drugged, tricked. Pleasure was pleasure, and her long-suffering body got precious little of it.

Her voice shook with self-loathing. "What exactly did you drug me with, you lying son of a bitch?"

The flash in his eyes, the tension in his mouth confirmed it. Somewhere in her mind, she had still been hoping she was wrong. That this was just her standard paranoid freak routine.

She cringed inside. Hated herself for hoping, hated herself for falling for it, hated him for doing it, hated herself for hating it.

Janos cleared his throat. "I'm . . . sorry." He pried the words out like rusty nails.

Sorry? Holy shit. She was dumbstruck at the raw nerve of him.

"Sorry?" she repeated. "You're *sorry*? You prick. Get away from me. Get out of me." She shoved at the expanse of his chest. She felt trapped, immobilized by the sheer mass of his body, that huge, throbbing member jammed up inside her. She felt invaded.

He withdrew. The slide of his thick shaft still felt shamefully wonderful. Tiny muscles inside her clutched him, unwilling to let go. Her helpless response was humiliating.

He stopped, a question in his eyes, caressing her with the thick bulb of his cock. Ready to give her more, although he'd just come, and explosively, too. The man was a world-class fucking machine.

But what had she expected? He was a professional, after all.

She spat in his face and dissolved into tears.

Chapter
13

Val wiped spit off his face and pulled out of the silken clutch of her body, staring down at the shining pink folds distended around his cock. She left a slick sheen of gleaming lube on the latex.

She hid the tears behind her hand. He tried not to look. He didn't want to see them any more than she wanted them to be seen. She was proud, haughty. Not the kind of woman who used tears as a weapon. God knows, she had plenty of other weapons in her arsenal.

This outcome exceeded his wildest hopes, and yet he felt shattered. He had obtained the means to keep Imre alive for a few more days, but he felt no triumph, not even relief. Just a sickening sense that he was sliding ever deeper into a pit that had no bottom.

It shook him that he had actually lost himself in the experience. He had forgotten Novak, Imre. He had forgotten about the hidden camera. He had forgotten every agenda but that of his own pounding body.

And he could fuck her again, right now. Gladly. All night long.

He disposed of the condom and arranged his erect penis inside his jeans as best he was able. The silent weeping was driving him mad.

"Stop it," he broke out harshly in Italian. "Stop crying, for the love of God. I cannot stand it."

"*Vaffanculo*," she shot back. "I can't control it, and it's your own goddamn fault that I'm stoned. So deal with it, dickhead." She tugged her skirt down. One of her stockings had slipped loose of the garter and rolled halfway down her thigh. He sank to his knees in front of her and rolled it up. The skin of her upper thigh was exquisitely hot and smooth. Lily petal soft. So fucking perfect. Her legs shook. She wobbled on her flimsy, eight-hundred-dollar spike heels.

His legs would shake, too, were he standing.

He did not want her to see the look on his face, so he leaned forward and pressed it against her mound, kissing her. A wordless apology that he knew she would reject violently, but he could not help himself. Could not resist breathing in more of her hot female scent and then more. Letting his secret tears soak into her skirt.

She made a catlike hissing sound and slapped at his face, but without much force. He looked up from that supplicating position at her face, flushed and wet, eye makeup blurred into a mask that just made her brimming eyes look brighter.

So beautiful, it made his chest clench.

He wanted to shove her skirt up and beg for her forgiveness with his tongue, but she would kill him for his pains, and he would not blame her. Even so, he wrapped his arms around her waist and clung to her, like a child. It was a stupid move, a vulnerable position. She could kill him in a hundred ways with the arsenal he'd plucked out of her hair or with her bare hands alone, for that matter.

He did not care. If she wanted to kill him, she was welcome to do so. He deserved it. He braced himself, waited.

No crushing death blow came down, though. No needle's burning sting. Her hands slid into his hair, gripping handfuls of it and yanking, hard. Her nails dug into his scalp.

"You've fucked a lot of people you didn't necessarily want to sleep with in your career, Janos, right?"

He tensed, sensing a tarpit. "Yes," he admitted cautiously.

"Was it difficult?" Her voice was hard. "To drug me up, make me come? Did it hurt? Did you have to grit your teeth, hold your breath?"

It took a minute to gather the courage to answer her, with the stark truth—even though he knew that she would not believe him.

"No." His voice hoarse, raw. "This is the part that hurts. The rest of it was incredible. I've never wanted anything the way I wanted you."

She laughed through her tears. "Me? No, it's not me you wanted. You wanted a piece of me. That's all anyone wants. The pretty part, the smart part, the mean part. The part between my legs. The rest is a pile of broken pieces. No use to anyone."

He tightened his hands on her hips, fingers digging into her curves, feeling the smooth heat of her, the play of sleek, strong muscle.

"The rest of you is beautiful," he whispered. "Broken to pieces or not. All of it is beautiful."

She covered her face, shoulders shaking with bitter laughter. "Oh, shut up," she muttered. "There's no point in bullshit sweet talk. It hurts to listen to it, OK? Let me be, Janos. I will never do what you want me to do. Nothing will convince me, understand? So stop torturing me. Just disappear. I am begging you."

He took his hands off her body, and stood up. "You will not be better off without me. You will have no more peace, Steele. If it is not me shoving you around, it will be someone else." He laid it out for her, his voice flat. "Someone much worse."

"Worse than you?" Her eyes shimmered with furious tears. She dabbed beneath them to wipe up her mascara. "Not possible."

"It is very possible," he said stonily. "When PSS catches up with you, they will take Rachel and lock her in a room somewhere to control you, as they ordered me to do. And you do not want to imagine what will happen when Novak catches up with you . . . and Rachel."

She flinched, and tried to twist up her thick, glossy hair with trembling hands. "And you think that calling the cops on me, messing with Rosalia, fucking with the adoption agency, isn't controlling me with Rachel?"

He dismissed that with a wave of his hand. "Don't be stupid," he snapped. "There is no comparison. I have done my best to protect her."

"Oh, my. I am overwhelmed." She stopped trying to put her hair up, and gathered the bristling array of hair ornaments into her hands as she shook it loose. She unlocked the door, yanked it open, and flung her parting shot at him. "What a fucking hero you are."

He grabbed her wrist. "There's one more reason why you should reconsider," he said. "I have one final thing to offer you."

"Oh, really?" She flung her head back, tear-blurred eyes blazing up at him. "Spit it out."

"Drago Stengl," he said.

The handful of hair ornaments clattered to the ground, bouncing and scattering. Her face was white to the lips.

"No one knows that. How . . . ?" Her voice was a dry whisper.

The change in her eyes unnerved him. He felt as if he had just driven a knife into her chest.

"There was a photograph of you in Novak's files," he admitted. "It was taken at the memorial service some years ago, for the massacre in Zetrinja. I did some research and found out who gave the orders. I thought that you might be interested in, ah . . . news of him."

"News? Of the man who murdered my father? I want more than news." Her voice was colorless, dead. "I want his heart's blood. I want him stretched on the rack. I want him screaming in hell."

He had won, he realized. He had hooked her, but the realization gave him no satisfaction. On the contrary. It made him feel like a piece of shit to use her in this way. Turning a knife in old wounds.

"Where is he?" she asked.

"I don't have his location yet, but I have a solid lead," he hedged. "I will help you follow it. In exchange for your support on my project."

She laughed. "Project? What a word for it. What do you mean by a lead? If you are fucking with me, I swear to God I will kill you."

"I know where his daughter is," he said.

Her soft white throat worked. "Ana," she whispered.

"Yes, Ana. She lives in Italy. She is married to an Italian businessman with connections to the Camorra. I have someone following her right now. A client of mine can introduce us, the wife of a Camorra boss. I can exploit the connection. If you like."

"If . . . I . . . like," she echoed, her voice hollow. She stared at him, or through him. She had forgotten that he was there. She was looking back through the years at something he could not see and did not want to. From her haunted eyes, he understood that it was as vivid as if it were happening here and now.

He understood that. There were moments in his life as well that had burned their indelible afterimage onto every day that followed.

He steeled himself. "So?" he prodded her. "Do we have a bargain?"

She made a choked sound, put her hand over her mouth, and lurched out the door. Her rapid, clicking footsteps receded down the hall.

Val gripped the door frame with his fist. Was that a yes? Nothing was ever obvious with that woman.

Three steps back, he reminded himself, but it was no use. The emotions he'd learned to step back from had never been like these. They had no place, no right to exist. Inconvenient desire and guilt. And grief.

Imre. He gathered up the hair ornaments, retrieved the video camera, and headed out a door at the end of the corridor that led out onto the grounds. He cut through the forest on his way to the parking lot. It was freezing cold. He had not bothered to retrieve his coat, but he was still in a near molten state, from the encounter with Tamara Steele.

He could melt the polar ice caps in this condition.

He loped through frozen leaves and twigs crunching beneath his slippery dress shoes and slid into the car. Hoping desperately that there would be wireless coverage. He did not want to have to drive away from her and Rachel. He hated to let them out of his sight at all.

He booted up the laptop. Ah, joy. There was coverage. He established a connection, activated the tiny videocamera embedded in the screen. Downloaded the digital video footage.

Editing it made his heart pound. The footage was too good, the angle paradoxically perfect, showing every detail of Steele's flushed face, eyes closed, head thrown back, her perfect thighs clamped around his.

His chest ached. This experience was private, precious. And he had to throw it to that fiend, Novak. A chunk of meat to quiet the beast.

He edited out her tears, their conversation. A meaningless attempt to protect what he could of her privacy. He encrypted it, attached it. His finger lingered for minutes over the button. He closed his eyes and thought of Imre's hands.

He clicked "send."

He sat in the dark with his hands clamped over his face for over ten minutes until he could trust himself to link up to the video-phone.

András's grinning face flickered into view. "Ah, there you are. We were enjoying your show. Lucky pig."

"I want to see Imre," Val said stonily.

"Wait." András disappeared. Val waited, staring at the blank screen, the antique chair's carved back. Several minutes passed.

Novak seated himself in front of the computer, grinning. He had licked his purplish lips until they gleamed.

"Well done, Vajda," he said. "Forgive me for making you wait, but I was riveted to the screen. Your performance with La Steele was magnificent. I have not been so stirred in years. I shall set up video screens in the room where I conduct her punishment and loop the footage the entire time. Those will be the last images she ever sees, before I gouge out her eyes. Perfect, eh?"

Val instantly manufactured white noise in his brain to block out the image. It did not work. "I want to speak to Imre," he repeated dully.

"Of course, of course. I had him brought down the minute your video appeared in my inbox. He was privileged to watch it with us. Let me give the chair to him. I wish to go back and watch it again."

Novak dissolved into a swirl of pixels. Another blurred, moving image as Imre was muscled onto the seat that Novak had just left.

The murky blur resolved into Imre's face.

Val stared, his jaw aching. Imre looked shrunken and grayish and small. His eyes were sunk deep into their cavernous sockets. His cheeks looked caved in. He had aged fifteen years in four days.

Val's hands clenched into fists. "Are they treating you well?" He hated himself for saying it. How stupid, how incredibly fucking inane the question was under the circumstances.

Imre's eyebrow gave its habitual ironic upward quirk. "They have not beaten or cut me, if that is what you mean."

"Are you eating?" Val persisted. "You have to eat."

An irritated frown flashed over Imre's face. "Don't be a fool, boy."

An agonizing, helpless silence followed. Val finally broke it, in desperation. "I will get you out of there," he said.

"By betraying that poor woman? Delivering her up to torture and murder? Do not make me party to this, Vajda."

Impotent rage swelled up in Val's throat. "Do . . . not . . . judge . . . me," he ground out.

Imre glanced over to his left. Loud, raucous bursts of laughter and lewd comments were audible. "This man is a demon," he said quietly. "He will drag as many people to hell with him as he possibly can, and he wants you in particular to keep him company. Take care you don't go with him."

"I am doing the best I can!" The words exploded out of him.

"Indeed." Finally, it was the dry, ironic tone that Val knew so well. "Was that your best? May God have mercy on us all. That performance was a bit much for an aged widower, boy."

Val's jaw tightened at the disapproval in Imre's tone. "I cannot believe it," he said. "Here I am, scrambling like a fucking monkey to keep you from dismemberment and death, and you are lecturing me?"

Imre's lips twitched mirthlessly. "Fucking monkey is exactly the term for what I just saw, boy. And yes, I am lecturing you. Old habits die hard. I think you will have to do somewhat better than your best to get out of this predicament. Go with God, Vajda."

The screen flickered, and the picture was lost. Val leaned over and knocked his pulsing forehead against the steering wheel.

Stuck-up, old bastard. Better than his best, his ass. What else could he do? Val was tying his balls in a knot as it was. Fuck Novak, fuck Imre, fuck them all. He wished he could find the nearest cliff to drive off. Let them sort it out however the fuck they wanted.

But he could not. Not an option. Not for him.

One more detail. It had been a wild gamble, assuming that Stengl was located near his daughter, assuming that Donatella could contrive an introduction. Assuming that the vain, capricious Donatella would even speak to him after years of neglecting the connection. She had wearied him to death, but now that he needed her, he regretted having been so lazy. He glanced at his watch. Six AM, an indecent hour to call her, in Italy, but he could not bear to wait.

He would explode.

He fished his cell phone out of his pocket, and closed his eyes to pluck Donatella's number out of his long-term memory. It had been five years since the time he'd spent in San Vito, infiltrating that ring of smugglers, and the woman had a complicated, secret, personal life, aside from the rigors of being a Camorra mafia don's wife. She might well have changed her cell number. She would scratch his eyes out for waking her. But he had never had any difficulty sweetening her.

His jaw clenched at the thought of having to fuck Donatella again. She was a beautiful woman, but she was selfish and spoiled and loud, and she had a streak of random cruelty that chilled him.

Imre. He forced out a harsh breath and dialed.

The phone rang three times. She picked up. *"Chi cazzo sei?"* she snarled. Who the fuck is this?

"Donatella. It's me, Valery." He caressed her with his voice.

"Valerio! *Amore*. I thought you had forgotten me."

"As if I could, *bellissima*," he said. "Forgive me for neglecting you. My life has been complicated lately."

"Hmmph," she grunted. "I can well imagine. What are you thinking, calling at this hour? Imagine if I had been in bed with Ettore. How would I explain myself?"

"You would never take a phone with this SIM card into bed with your husband," he said. "I take it you are in bed with someone else?"

"Do you care, Valerio?" Her voice was falsely sweet.

"Not as long as you love me best," he murmured tenderly.

"How sweet. Always, *carissimo*. Although it would not do to neglect my succulent young Giuseppe, here." She giggled, murmured something inaudible. "Perhaps you can join us some evening. The bed is wide enough for three. And Guiseppe looks . . . mmm, oh, *sì* . . . most enthusiastic at the idea."

"Anything to please you," he murmured promptly. "But first, I have something to ask you. Do you remember the earrings I gave to you, the ones with the poison beads?"

"Of course, *amore*. I treasure them. A fearless gift for a man like you to give to his lover. Did it never occur to you that I might kill you with them in a jealous rage?"

"It occurred to me, yes, but I do not fear death," he said. "The designer of those earrings will be in Italy day after tomorrow, and she has an entire line of beautiful pieces containing all manner of concealed weaponry, poisons, drugs, explosives. Of course, I thought of you. Appropriate adornments for a dangerous beauty like yourself."

"Ah, Valerio. *Tesoro,*" she cooed. "Am I so dangerous? Is that why you stayed away for so long?"

"Only for my peace of mind," he assured her, his voice smooth. "But to give you a treat like this, I will risk coming out of hiding. Would you like to meet this woman, and see her wares?"

"Of course. I wish to see them all."

"I thought so," he said silkily. "I have a favor to ask in return."

"You know that I can deny you nothing, *tesoro*. Ask."

"Do you know a woman named Ana Santarini?"

"Ignazio Santarini's boring wife? What on earth do you want with that stupid cow? You cannot possibly intend to fuck her!"

"No, not at all," he assured her. "But I need an introduction to her for this jewelry designer. Could you arrange it for me? Preferably at her own residence."

He heard the machinery grinding in Donatella's mind. "I might be persuaded . . . if I could have the pleasure of your company once again."

He sighed silently and rolled his eyes. "Of course, *piccola*. Could you arrange for the day after tomorrow, when I bring this designer?"

"So soon? You are crazy! I don't even know if she is in town!"

"Invite her to see the jewelry," he urged. "It would appeal to her."

"And have that Santarini slut know all of the secrets of the pieces that I buy? She will tell everyone! What is the point of it?"

He clenched his fists. "*Ti prego,*" he said softly. "Please. For me."

She made an irritated huffing sound. "I am going to Paris for a week to shop," she announced. "You will join me there?"

"I cannot wait," he said through clenched teeth.

"The entire week? Prepare yourself. It will be strenuous."

"Have no fear," he assured her. "Send me a text message with the meeting time and location with Santarini, *va bene?*"

Donatella paused and made a little clicking sound with her tongue. "Anxious, Valerio?" she purred. "What's going on? Are you in trouble? Tell Donatella all about it, *bambino mio*. Maybe I can help."

A muscle in his jaw started to twitch. He was in a bad way if even an empty-headed *vacca* like Donatella was tuning in to his nervous tension. "You already are helping me," he said softly. "My angel."

"February seventh, in Paris," she reminded. "Mark it on your calendar." There was a thread of steel in Donatella's voice.

"Certainly. *A dopo, dolcezza.*"

A tedious back-and-forth of stupid endearments, and finally he managed to close the telephone. He released a long, controlled sigh.

Three steps back. A week of stud service in a luxury hotel in Paris was not too much to pay for Imre's life. He would do it if he had to. But a sour, wrong feeling clung to him. It made him want to take a bath.

Ah, well, what the fuck. He might be dead by February seventh anyway. That was the best he could do to cheer himself up.

He headed back to the hotel, preparing himself for disaster. Steele had probably fled in the time it had taken to do this infernal errand.

But when he peered into the ballroom, she was there, wrestling a whimpering, protesting Rachel into her coat, bulging black diaper bag dangling on her other shoulder. She was deep in conversation with Erin McCloud. Now the other woman talked earnestly, looking worried. Tam shook her head in response. The McCloud woman patted Steele's shoulder. Tam nodded, hoisted the child onto her hip, and headed toward the exit. Her pale face was set in stark lines, her eyes haunted. She looked so different with her hair down, shining and loose, brushing her perfect ass. Everyone stared as she passed.

She ignored the swathe of speculative murmuring in her wake.

He backed into the lobby and positioned himself carefully, waiting only until the direction she was going to turn was clear before he melted around the corner and into a stairwell.

Relief made his knees weak. She was not going out the front, to the parking lot. She was going out the back toward the breezeway that led to the guest houses. She was not running from him. Not tonight.

He was grateful. He did not have the strength to chase her again. He had no more cards to play, no more tricks. He was all out of ideas. If Steele ran now, his choices were brutally simple.

Steele or Imre. One of them would have to die, badly.

He followed at a safe distance, took note of the door she and

Rachel disappeared into, and then strolled along the herringbone path.

A wrought iron bench sat in the shadows of a huge tree roughly opposite her guest room door. He sat down, bone weary. A thousand years old. The cold of the hard metal bench penetrated his clothes, burning into his flesh. He would have to get his coat if he meant to sit here any length of time, he thought, but he did not move.

He could not take his eyes off that door.

He didn't like being compelled by anything, whether the forces originated from inside himself or out. Being manipulated by Novak, Hegel, even Donatella, was bad enough. Being jerked around by the shadow parts of his own fucked-up psyche was intolerable.

Yet there he sat, rooted to the bench, his ass turning to ice. Guarding her door but not to prevent her from escaping. On the contrary, he wanted to fend off the dangers that lay in wait for her.

He was cast in the wrong role in this fucking Greek tragedy.

People passed by without noticing him lurking motionless in the dark. Then a couple came ambling by. The tall, fair-haired man's face was revealed in a beam of light slicing through the tree boughs. Sean McCloud and his wife, Liv. Sean spotted him and turned off the path. He guided his wife across the frosted grass until they stood before him.

The man's piercing eyes made Val squirm. The picture he made revealed too much. Him sitting like an asshole with no coat outside a woman's closed door. Hands filled with a bristling array of Steele's deadly hair ornaments. A whining, hungry dog hoping to be let in.

Begging for scraps.

"What are you doing out here in the cold?" McCloud demanded.

Val's long exhalation made a vaporous cloud in front of his face. "Standing guard," he said.

His wife, a luscious, buxom brunette, gave him a polite but suspicious look. "If there's any woman on earth who can look out for herself, it's Tam," she said.

Val acknowledged that with a shrug. "Overkill."

McCloud grunted. "Well, then. You've got your work cut out for you." He hesitated, looking puzzled. "Good luck," he added. "I think."

Val inclined his head. The couple turned and walked on. McCloud

He laid the pill on the blanket that covered Imre's cot and stood.

"Take it," he said magnanimously. "I can be reasonable, if you are reasonable with me. I am alone, as you are. We could have such interesting conversations if you would lower yourself to speak to me. We are just two old men, after all, facing the same ultimate fate. I am so curious about you. Vajda got his culture and sophistication from you, no? In fact, thanks to you, he became too good to work for the likes of me." He laughed and patted Imre's shoulder.

Imre flinched.

"I do hope that Vajda succeeds in bringing the woman to me," Novak mused. "I will conduct the punishment upon you, if I must, but to be quite truthful . . . torturing a wretched old man who is already wracked with pain is much less satisfying. Pain is so familiar to you already, you see. The experience falls a bit flat. But do not fear. I am sure my András could wring a lively response, even out of a dying wreck like you. He is so talented. You will see, you will see."

Imre squeezed his eyes shut. Tears slipped down against his will.

One of Novak's men opened the door, the other folded up the chair. They waited until the boss shuffled out.

"Enjoy the pill, Imre." Novak's taunting voice floated through the door as he retreated down the hall.

The door clanged shut, the lock rattled. He was alone again.

The rictus melted. A long, violent palsy of terror shook him.

When the worst of it had passed, he took the pill and slipped it under the mattress. He might well need it more later than he needed it now.

His fingers brushed against the metal frame of the broken eyeglasses.

He pulled them out. Then he loosened the largest unbroken shard of the shattered lens, and pried it carefully from the frame. The glasses were old, made of real glass, not plastic, and the shard was thick, a rough triangle that came to a jagged, sharp point. He pressed it to the pad of his thumb.

A dark drop of blood welled up.

Imre sat motionless for hours, staring fixedly at that shard of glass until the lights snapped off, leaving him in inky darkness.

threw a troubled glance back over his shoulder. The low murmur of their voices faded into the darkness.

He was good at telling lies. The trick was to enter so completely into whatever role he was playing, he practically believed them himself even as he told them. But what he had said to Steele was not a lie. He had blurted out the raw truth to her. More truth than he'd ever told to anyone, even Imre. Braided together with half-truths, yes, but even so.

I've never wanted anything the way I want you. The truth of those words reverberated through him, an explosion from within. It blasted his whole relationship to the world out of alignment. A dangerous secret.

Dangerous secrets are beautiful, don't you agree? He had taken Steele's words in Shibumi as meaningless banter, but now, they rang in his head, as a fundamental truth. Imre had always been his dangerous secret. A treasure that he had to hide just so it could survive.

Most people had to hide their ugliness, their shame. With him, the situation was inverted. He had to keep the beautiful things secret.

Or else risk finding them dead on the bathroom floor.

Ironic. A man like him compelled by an irrational longing to protect Steele, instead of exploiting her. A dangerous secret, indeed. Like her jewel-studded pendant earring bombs. Her taser necklace. It was an urge he would have to keep secret even from her.

He sensed very strongly that she would not welcome it.

The key rattled in the heavy metal door, jolting Imre out of his deep contemplation. He had been mentally walking through the rooms of the Uffizi Gallery, looking at all the pictures he could call to mind. Which was to say, all of them, though his favorites were the clearest.

The mental construct disintegrated. Waves of faintness and dread washed over him.

Another visit. It pleased Gabor Novak to check upon Imre's progress, or degeneration, to put it more clearly. The man liked to prod and pry for weaknessess, to inflict all the psychological torment that he was able. He was fiendishly talented at it.

Imre's defenses were limited to silence, but it was a poor defense. Already, he was cringing as if he was to be beaten or burned.

The metal door swung wide, clanging with an ear-bruising bang against the concrete blocks. Two large men walked in, one training an automatic pistol at Imre, the other carrying a folding chair.

Novak shuffled into the room and seated himself. Beaming.

Imre focused somewhere beyond the man's shoulder, clasping and unclasping his hands and fighting the urge to sit upon them to hide his frightened fingers.

He'd told himself not to be afraid. He was dying anyway, no? Soon he would lose everything he had to lose. If some parts, like fingers, for instance, died sooner, what of it? The pain would soon be behind him.

His efforts were futile. He could not talk himself out of the fear.

Imre was grateful, at least, that he was not wearing his spectacles. Only one lens was still intact. The other had been shattered in the second beating. Having one corrected eye and the other blurred gave him a blinding headache. Since the last thing he needed was more pain from any quarter, he had given up on the glasses altogether, and hidden them under his mattress. Thus, he could not see the hideous details of Novak's face, the feverish glow of those jaundiced, bulbous eyes, only a malevolent blur.

Although he smelled the stench of the man's breath all too well.

"I have been thinking about you a great deal, Imre." Novak had the air of a man conferring an honor. "I believe you and I have something in common." The man's voice was pleasant, chatty.

God forbid, Imre thought, dropping his gaze to his twitching fingers. He willed them to lie still, to not draw attention to themselves.

"I can see by your color, your thinness, that you are being consumed by some wasting disease," Novak said. "Cancer?"

Surprise betrayed Imre into looking up and meeting Novak's eyes. He dropped his gaze just as quickly, but Novak chuckled, pleased.

"I thought so. Liver, stomach, brain? Not long for you now, is it? I can feel it on you, Imre. How ironic for Vajda, is it not? Working so valiantly to save the life of a dying man. How long did they give you?"

Imre tried to swallow, but his throat was too dry. He began to cough, and once he started, he could not stop.

"Not long, no?" Novak laughed again. "Three months? They like to say three months. It's their standard phrase. That's what they told me seven months ago, but I live on, see? Rotting from within, true, but here I am. The pleasure I will take in this woman's death will grant me another month, at least. These punishments charge me like a battery. Would you like to participate? It might have the same effect upon you."

Imre looked up at him once again. "No," he said hoarsely.

Novak blinked and smiled, pleased to have dragged another response out of him. "Then you can be a spectator when the time comes. It won't be long. Vajda works fast. He has always been efficient."

Imre grasped the edge of the bed. Horror darkened his vision. Faintness threatened. He teetered, on the brink of that long, dark fall.

"Poor man," Novak crooned. "I feel for you, being old and infirm myself. The pain is terrible, no?" He dug in his pocket and took out a vial of capsules. He rattled them, then opened the bottle and shook one of them out into his hand. "Powerful slow-release opiates. Shall I give you one? I won't leave you the whole bottle, because you would gobble them all at once, naughty fellow. But I will give you this pill, if you would just explain one thing that continues to puzzle me."

He waited for Imre to reach for the pill, to beg, to ask what the one thing that puzzled him was. But Imre could not have spoken if he wanted to. He was frozen. Fear had turned him into a pillar of salt.

Novak's eyes squinted to bright, wrinkled slits. "I wish to know how your catamite remained so devoted to you. When I was young, a man made me his pet in exchange for food and shelter, just as you did for Vajda. Do you know what I did to him when I was older?"

Please. No. Do not tell me. Imre closed his eyes, summoned up a deafening mental rendition of Bach's first Brandenburg Concerto to drown the words out.

Novak's voice cut through the music like a hot knife through butter. "I removed his skin strip by strip," he said, almost tenderly. "Perhaps I shall do that to the woman. Let us make a tally, Imre. From now on, for every question that you disdain to answer, I tear off a shred of her skin. While you watch."

Chapter 14

Tam sat on the edge of the bed, staring at the blank wall, eyes frozen wide. It made no difference if they were open or closed. She could not block out the images from inside her head. Nor the sounds. She had tried, but rifle fire kept cracking endlessly in the distance. Harrowing screams kept floating up from the dreaded basement cells of Sremska Mitrovica. The cells where the torturers did their work.

She wanted to clap her hands over her ears, but that was problematic, since the sound issued from inside her own head. She kept her hands wound tight, white-knuckled, into the bed covers. Hanging on to her present reality. This expensive, clean, safe hotel room. She was at the Huxley, with her daughter, surrounded by friends. She was not jammed in a moaning crowd of sweating bodies. The misery, the stench, the lice. Packed together too tightly even to lie down on the floor.

Rachel slept, finally, in the bed behind her. Coaxing the over-stimulated little girl to go down after she'd played with Sveti and the other little kids all evening and then overdosed on the chocolate wedding cake had been the usual three-ring circus. Even so, tonight, Tam was not grateful to be left alone with the contents of her own mind.

Amazingly, tonight she would have gladly traded the quiet for noise and distraction. Even a howling tantrum. Just to block it out.

Tough shit for her. Rachel needed the sleep, and Tam was on her own, eyes burning, stomach cramping. Watching the shovelfuls of dirt showering down on Mamma and Irina's wide open eyes.

The memories gave her a crazy sense of double vision. Two realities, superimposed upon each other, one hardly more or less real than the other. The room was warm, but goosebumps prickled over her skin from the cold of that other room, in Titograd, sixteen years ago.

She'd sat on the sagging bed, the faded brocade counterpane cold against her bottom. Wearing only a whorish red silk chemise. All she needed, for his purposes, Stengl had said. She had nothing else to wear. No shoes, no coat. Her breath misted before her rhythmically. The frigid air froze the inside of her nose with each breath.

She wished she knew how to stop breathing. She had tried.

The window of the hotel room was wide open. She'd opened it herself. Snow blew in.

Seconds ticked by on the gold-plated travel clock by the bed. The room was locked, the windows covered by wrought iron bars she could not dislodge. Her fingertips were raw from trying. Snowflakes fluttered and swirled down onto the carpet. They did not melt. Tick, tick, tick.

She sat, and shuddered, waiting for Stengl to come back and want . . . what he always wanted.

Wondering if she'd have time to freeze to death first.

Tam pulled herself forcibly back into awareness of her present surroundings, shaking with remembered cold. Vaguely angry at herself for falling so deep into the bottomless pit of memory. Irresponsible and stupid, whether it was involuntary or not. She got up, padded over to the thermostat and turned it up. Fuck the cold.

Tam lay down and pulled the blanket over herself. She laid her hand on Rachel's bony little back, feeling the soft rise and fall of breathing.

Comforted by the heat, the life vibrating from the little girl.

She was not looking forward to explaining to Rachel that she had to go away for a few days. Thank God for Erin, who had agreed to look after her, and Sveti, too, who had offered to stick around and help, bless her. But it was going to be a bad scene no matter what.

She was exhausted, but still buzzing. Probably the fallout from that drug.

Janos's final offer had rattled her. How did he pull it off? Her most closely guarded, painful secrets, and hey, presto—he just plucked them right out of her head and dangled them in her face. So casually.

Scenes from the past had been playing in her head ever since Janos had pronounced Stengl's name. Complete with full sensory detail.

She was fifteen again, a grief-stricken victim. A helpless toy for anyone who wanted to play with her. And they had. Oh, they had, back in the bad old days. Before she'd learned to turn the tables on them.

She'd had feelers out over the globe, searching for Stengl, that sociopathic son of a bitch, for years. She wanted to snag him before he reached the relative safe haven of the war crimes tribunal.

Oh, yes. She wanted to kill him herself, by hand, at close range. One last attempt to appease the restless ghosts that haunted her sleep.

Revenge. The one lure she absolutely could not resist.

She wondered where Janos was. She'd deliberately refrained from looking to the right or left as she left the ballroom. She didn't want to risk catching his eye and start blushing like an idiot. Or worse yet, sobbing, or screaming. The messed-up hair, the wild stare, the smeared makeup, that was enough fuel for gossip among her friends as it was.

He had not left. Of that, she was sure. He was near, watching her.

On impulse, she slid out of bed and padded barefoot over to the door. She left her hand on the handle for minutes, trying to identify this bright, buzzing feeling. Fear . . . or anticipation.

She opened the door, and was unsurprised to see him there. A sorcerer like him could see right through the walls. He'd seen through the ones in her mind, after all. And they were thicker.

They stared at each other. She was incapable of speech.

He broke the silence. "It's cold," he said, glancing past her to the tiny lump Rachel made on the king sized bed. "Let me come in. You can close the door, to keep the room warm for the child. We must talk."

Tam suppressed the impulse to say something cutting. She let him in, closed the door after him and positioned herself with her back to the narrow blade of light that came out the bathroom door to study his face and still remain an enigmatic silhouette herself.

The attempt was useless. She couldn't read him. His face was a hard, chiseled mask highlighted by sharp-cut shadows.

She gestured for him to follow her into the bathroom. "Keep your voice down," she whispered. "Rachel's a light sleeper. She's exhausted from staying up hours past her bedtime, but she's capable of screaming for an hour if she wakes up. And I just can't face it right now."

He nodded, and followed her into the small, luxurious black marble bathroom. They stared at each other, immobile, but the energy between them was dynamic, swirling. Like the wary circling of duelers.

She could smell his scent. Feel his heat.

"You'll go with me," he said. It was not a question.

She shut her eyes, swallowed. "Congratulations, Janos," she said. "You found the right string to yank. I'll go on one condition, though."

"Name it."

"We take care of Stengl first," she said.

She saw the *no* in his eyes, and shook her head. "This point is not negotiable, Janos. We do Stengl first, or you can try hauling me in to Novak to do the trade directly. I promise I'll put up a good fight."

He shook his head grimly. "No. We can hunt down Stengl at any time, but the timing is crucial for Imre. I am already desperate. Novak established a schedule for when he cuts off—"

"I'm very sorry for Imre, and for you, but that is not my problem." Tam cut through him. Her voice was not loud, but crystal sharp. "My chances of dying in your crazy scheme are too high. I can face that if Stengl is dead. But I do not intend to leave this world before he does. No fucking way, and that is final. Understand?"

A muscle twitched in his jaw. His nostrils flared as he let out a long, audible sigh. He muttered what sounded like an obscenity, in a language she didn't know, and nodded. "Done."

She turned and stared into the mirror, into his eyes. It was easier to meet their reflection than look into them directly. One tiny level of removal from his charisma. Just enough so she could breathe.

She thought of what had happened in the kitchen. The searing pleasure. He was powerful enough, intense enough to anchor her in the here and now, at least while he was fucking her. She could lose herself in him. She wouldn't see that decaying hotel room, the shabby red chemise. Or Stengl leering down at her. Licking his lips.

Her stomach did a nasty, squirming roll. She squeezed her eyes shut, leaned on the sink. Splashed her face with icy water.

When she came up for air, her face numb with cold, he held out one of the fluffy hand towels for her. She patted her face dry, still leaving smears of mascara, despite how often she'd wiped the stuff off.

She looked at herself in the mirror. Her face was ashen but for that hot blush branded across both cheekbones. He loomed behind her, unsmiling. Anger, frustration, desire pulsing off him in great waves.

He wanted her. The intensity of his dark gaze scorched her skin. She could feel the heat, the burn, the pull. That part, at least, was not feigned, no matter what else he wanted from her. The lust was real.

She was used to that vibe from men, but not from a man so completely in command of himself—and so unafraid of her.

His inner power was vast, unfathomable. It pulled, lured her.

He had abandoned the seductive, teasing charm. It was irrelevant. The time for banter was past. She dragged in a shaky breath, listening to the thudding of her own heart in her ears and her own shrill internal monologue. *You can't afford it. You couldn't before. You still can't, idiot.*

But something hungry and jazzed inside her wanted to just grab him. Shove him around. Provoke him, fight with him, kick him, hit him. Engage with him in a very specific, heated way.

The sex in the air between them had gotten so heavy and hot, she could feel it pressing against her skin, like a palpable force. She felt breathless, panicky at its inexorable rise.

"Don't get any ideas," she flung at him. "The drug's worn off."

"Of course," he said. "I am glad."

"Are you? But I imagine you had the duration of its effects calculated down to a fraction of a second," she said.

"No, not that precisely," he admitted. "There were too many variables. I had more like a fifteen-minute window. But you ate more food than I expected. That flattened out the effect."

"That's probably why it took me so long to figure it out," she said.

"Probably."

His easy agreement pissed her off. Was he trying to make her feel better about having been so easily managed? Condescending bastard.

She looked down at her fisted hands. "You're here because you want some more, right? You think you've won? You've found my weak point, and that entitles you to fuck me into submission?"

His expression did not change. "I'm here because you want me here," he said. "Even though you hate yourself for it. Otherwise you would never let me near you."

That blunt, uninflected statement said both too much and too little. Her face heated with humiliation. "You flatter yourself."

"No," he said. "I do not need to."

"You think you can make my fantasies come true even without the benefit of drugs? Good luck, buddy boy. I'm on to your dirty tricks."

"I did it at the club," he reminded her. "The circumstances were difficult. You were flat on the ground, you had just held a poisoned knife to my throat. You had bodyguards outside the door poised to kill for you. And I never even got your clothes off."

She sniffed. "Listen to you congratulating yourself. Bastard."

He shrugged. "If you say so."

His laconic refusal to be baited was driving her mad. She had to shut up. Pride dictated that she not drop her gaze, and maintaining that much contact was challenge enough.

His dark eyes saw so much. She felt transparent.

"You cannot bear the way you feel right now," he said very softly. "I could make you forget. For a little while, at least."

"With what?" she demanded. "Do you have some other pharmaceutical nightstick in your pocket?"

"You know with what."

Her jaw dropped, at the hugeness of his vanity. "Oh! Here comes Janos, and his wonder dick! You mean to grant me a moment of blessed oblivion as a reward for helping with your crazy plan? How generous of you. A mercy fuck. Wow, what a prince. I am overwhelmed."

He was shaking his head before she finished. "You know how much I want you," he reproved her. "I couldn't hide it if I wanted to."

"Bullshit. You can hide and show anything you choose to," she said. "Don't try to persuade me otherwise. I can, too. I've had the same training you have."

"I won't try to persuade you," he said. "The truth is the truth."

"Don't talk about truth," she snapped. "It's a big turnoff coming from a professional liar."

He inclined his head. "Fair enough. If you do not want to hear it."

She wrenched her gaze away from his, feeling fluttery and stupid, and felt them dragged back to his by force. Damn him. That had never happened to her before.

"I want you," he said quietly. "You want me. Why is it so shameful to you to acknowledge this? Why must you always fight it so hard?"

Her hands flew up to cover her hot cheeks, a hatefully femmy gesture that she regretted instantly. "Because you're using me," she said, her voice raw. "It's shameful to let myself be used."

He did not deny it. He was silent for a very long moment. "I am sorry," he said finally. His voice was muted. "I wish that I was not."

Well. Miracle of miracles. At least he was honest about that.

She couldn't say anything snide about it, though. Her voice was stuck behind a stone wall in her throat. Her lips shook. Heat rose in her face. He moved closer, so slowly it was almost imperceptible, but all at once he was right behind her. She craved the heat his body generated.

Needed it, to warm the bone-deep cold inside her. Against the icy room, the red chemise. The snowflakes fluttering down onto the carpet.

She choreographed the words carefully. "Do not . . . wake up . . . Rachel. Understand?"

A brief smile touched his lips. "Try not to make so much noise this time, then."

He shrugged off his jacket, hung it on the door behind him. Stripped off the tight black T-shirt underneath.

She would not let herself gasp or ogle. He thought well enough of himself as it was. But oh, God, it was difficult not to. Wow.

His body was startling. Big, broad, but every muscle sinewy and cut. From hard practical use, not from pumping iron. She'd felt coiled power vibrating when she touched him, she'd experienced the incredible reflexes when he wrestled her in Shibumi. Intelligent muscles, flexible and ready. They knew what to do without being asked twice.

She liked muscles like that. She liked power like that.

A triangle of dark hair on his chest arrowed toward his groin, lost in the low waistband of his jeans. He stood patiently, giving her time to check him out at her leisure. The thick, uptilted slash of his eyebrows, the sharp hollow of his cheekbones. The olive tinge of his skin, the thick bulge of his shoulders. Tendons snaked over his sinewy forearms. Blue veins formed subtle, pleasing patterns beneath his golden skin. She wanted to trace them with her fingertips. Memorize them.

And scars, more than she had imagined. He'd seen some rough use, and recently, too. He had scabs, scrapes. Green and yellow bruises. The bloodstained bandage on his upper arm. A reminder of the injury he'd sustained that morning, fighting to save them. His face was stark in the harsh glare from the lamp embedded in the bathroom mirror. It showed every mark. In this profound silence, the masks had fallen: the smooth businessman, the slick gigolo. He was all warrior now, hard and battered and deadly dangerous.

His eyes were black, his mouth a flat line. No dimples, no grin. He appeared to be taking this seriously. As well he should, considering what he risked, being intimate with someone like her.

He gathered her hair into a thick bunch, lifting it up to bury his nose in it. He kissed the back of her neck. His lips were so hot. So soft.

The contact made her flinch and shudder. Too much.

He hesitated and pressed his scorching heat against her to melt the ice. She had to squeeze her eyes shut, breathe slowly. Deliberately relaxing, accepting his energy into herself.

He did not move, his breath hot against her shoulder, his hands clasped around her upper arms. Minutes crawled by. Time was measured by her frantic heartbeats.

Then he hooked the shoulders of her dress and tugged the stretchy fabric downward, until the edge snagged against the jut of her nipples. He stared at that intently for a long moment, and wrenched the thing down. It dropped around her ankles.

She was naked but for the whorish garter belt and stockings. She was not a short woman, but she looked so small, so delicate, in front of him. She hated feeling delicate. Ghost pale, too, and too young, somehow with all that tangled hair hanging down. A big-eyed innocent. Tarted up in slutty, inappropriate lingerie.

His hands slid up to cup her breasts, and her body rippled in his hands. She stifled a whimper. Her skin almost hurt, it was so sensitive to every tiny touch. Vulnerable.

"Why did you do that to me?" she asked, her voice muted.

He nuzzled her shoulder, toying with her nipples with his thumbs. "Do what? The drug, you mean?"

She twisted in his grasp to meet his eyes. "What else?"

He lifted an eyebrow. "You dare to be indignant, after what you did to me in the hotel room?"

She waved her hand, irritated. "That's different. I asked nicely for you to fuck off. Then I asked not nicely. You didn't respond, so I had to put you down. Too bad. Very simple. Nothing personal. But drugging me to seduce me is completely different. That's extremely personal."

His hands dropped from her breasts and gripped her waist, stroking the curve of her belly. His eyes slid away from hers.

"I needed to get close to you," he admitted. "And your defenses are so strong. It is practically impossible to get through them. I think that I could have done so, given time—"

"You think very well of yourself," she cut in, stung.

"Given time," he repeated firmly, "I could have done so. I did, at Shibumi. But Imre does not have time, and I do not have time."

"So it was all about Imre, then? Just as I thought." She felt an irrational urge to weep, scream, shove him away. "Not about me."

"No." His face contracted. His arms circled her, wrapping around her and dragging her close against his chest. She felt the bulge of his erection, prodding her buttocks. "God, no. I want you. Do not doubt it."

She squeezed her eyes shut. Of course, he had to say that. She would be a boneheaded bimbo to let herself believe it. But still, she stood there, wrapped in his warmth, her mind melting down.

He felt so good. Every cell of her body was thirstily sucking up his hot energy. There was so much of it. So much of him. He was delicious.

"It still doesn't track," she said stubbornly. "What does sex have to do with Imre? We won't be fucking our way into Novak's stronghold."

He dropped his face to her shoulder and started kissing her again. "You found me out," he said. "I wanted you, I could not melt you, and I could not bear to wait. Forgive me. I am a filthy *porcone*. The truth is out."

"Stop using that word," she snapped.

He lifted his head, eyes narrowed. "What word?"

"Truth," she clarified, her voice cutting. "It bugs me."

His face went somber. "Of course it does. It is the thing you need, above all else, no? The thing you long for, whether you know it or not."

She snorted. "And how do you know this secret longing?"

"Because I need it as well," he said. "We are two of a kind."

The low, gentle vibration of his voice was the magic touch that slid through her defenses. She stopped fighting him, and herself. Her body ached for contact. Her nails dug into his forearms and her breath hitched with each slow, skillful stroke over her skin.

He slid his hand down between her legs, stroking the damp seam of her labia with a fingertip, in no hurry to penetrate. It was just an invitation, a gentle call to all her nerves to get ready, to work themselves into tingling awareness. He rubbed her clit, a lazy, undemanding swirl around . . . around. Reminding her that he was thinking about it, that he had big plans for it . . . and *oh* . . .

God. A shudder arced through her body. The accumulated tension of years, violently unwound by his light touch, throbbing through her.

Tears shimmered in her eyes. She squeezed them shut.

"I barely touch you, and you come apart," he murmured. "Beautiful."

But it didn't make her feel beautiful. It made her feel like she had no skin. Foolish and needy. And so goddamn *stupid*.

She couldn't bear to play the fool again so soon. She couldn't push him away, either.

So she chose another path.

Instinctively, she threw a switch inside her brain. A technique she'd learned when she was very young, and it had served her well. Her seductive siren persona, the part of her that could drive men mad with pleasure while mentally composing a grocery list. A part of herself she had never intended to use again after the Novak debacle. It was ready to do its job, though, and it was a blessed relief to feel that power rise, bolstered by her confidence in her own beauty, her practiced skill at giving pleasure.

It had never failed her, except with Kurt Novak. And he'd been a special case, being something both less and more than human.

But Janos was wonderfully human. It would flatten him to the ground, just as he had done to her. *Yes.* She couldn't wait.

She turned and shoved him back against the wall. He looked startled by her sudden aggression. She splayed her hands over his hot, hard chest. Her palms crackled with the hot polarity between them.

His eyes narrowed at the change in her. She sought out every tiny detail of him with her fingertips, then her lips. She trailed hot, moist kisses down his chest, feeling him shiver and gasp as she kissed and tongued the tight, dark nubs of his nipples, perched on the flat, hard shelf of his pecs. Tasting his sharp salt flavor. She slid her hands down over the rippled belly muscles, the silken grain of dark hair arrowing down to his waistband. She wrenched the buttons of his jeans open, yanked them down his thighs, combed that arrow of hair with her fingertips down to where it swelled again to a springy tuft at his groin.

And his cock. So thick and broad, filling her hand. The slit at the tip was gleaming with slippery pre-come. She anointed her hand with it and stroked, pulled, gripped, milked him. His eyes closed, and he flung his head back. His breath rasped harshly.

Ah, yes. This was much better. She was in control. Disposed to make his wildest dreams come true, to be his nympho siren, blow his mind, rock his world. She sank to her knees with theatrical slowness, breathing in the salt tang of his skin, the hot musk of his groin.

His cock jutted out so far she had to scoot back to accommodate him. She stroked the whole throbbing, empurpled length of his broad, veined stalk with her tongue, swirling it all around the crimson head. She took him into her mouth, creating the wet, silken suction that all men dreamed of with her lips and her tongue, varying it with luscious lapping, teasing flutters, deep and bold and hungry. She caressed the dips and swells and hollows of his naked hips.

She deepened the strokes, pulling him as far as she could into her throat, suckling hard, fluttering her fingers under his heavy balls. He wound his fingers into her hair, urging her on with pleading tugs, now and again holding her still and drawing back to climax without ejaculating. Three times. The man had astonishing self-control.

She would make him lose his control, goddamnit. She would punish him for demolishing her life, for making her want him so badly. For being so strong, so difficult, so persistent. She would make him explode and weep and beg. She would show him who was boss.

He cupped her face in his hands and pulled it gently away from his body. "No," he said unsteadily.

She looked up, confused, and wiped her mouth. "No, what? No, not yet? No, not in my mouth? Be specific."

"Not with a sex toy," he said. "I prefer the real woman."

The rejection was a slap. Soul deep. Entirely unexpected. She stared, shocked to immobility, then rose and backed as far away as the small room would allow. "If you hate it, just fuck off."

He winced. "No. I did not hate it. You misunderstand me."

She laughed bitterly. "That's for sure. Ungrateful prick. I've never had any complaints before."

"I am sure that you have not." His eyes sharpened to that penetrating look she was beginning to dread. It made her feel too fragile. "You went to your comfort zone, no? I do not want to go there, where you have entertained all your other lovers."

She gasped, at his outrageous nerve. "All my other . . . oh! Am I not good enough for you?"

"Do not be ridiculous," he said. "It is only that I prefer you as you are."

Yeah. As vulnerable and raw as the grief-stricken girl she had been. *No.*

"I can't." She was horrified to hear her voice breaking.

He reached out, brushed her hair off her face. "You can trust me," he urged gently. "I will not hurt you."

She flinched away from his touch and covered her shaking mouth. "You have," she said. "If you don't want me, then go."

He blew out a fierce, frustrated breath. "I knew you would be like this. Sooner or later, something inside you would run away and hide, and I would be left with a beautiful doll in my arms."

"Whore, you mean, not doll," she hissed. "Go ahead, say it. It's how you make me feel."

He lifted a lock of her hair and pressed his lips to it, stroking it against his cheek. "I would be the last one to judge a whore," he said quietly. "I know what it means to do what you must to survive."

She jerked her hair back out of his grasp. "How could you know? Do you know how it feels to be used like a thing and tossed aside afterward like garbage? What you have to turn yourself into, just to survive?"

"Yes," he said.

She stopped, mesmerized by his aura of tightly leashed power and his battered, inscrutably beautiful face. "You?" Her voice cracked. "Oh, please. Give me a fucking break. Your job experience as a professional gigolo is irrelevant, Janos. Look at you. You're a man, you're six foot four, you're at least two hundred and fifty pounds. No one could use you and toss you. You have no clue."

"You are wrong." He glanced down at his own body, and gave her an odd, lopsided smile that struck her as heartbreakingly sad. "You hate men too much to imagine that they could ever be vulnerable, no? I was not always this big."

She closed her mouth and chewed her lip. "Oh," she murmured.

"I was young when I . . . when it happened," he said. "But it is not something that you forget."

An awkward silence lengthened between them. He had cut her anger off neatly at the knees. He had a frightening talent for that.

It could be a lie. But something about the spareness of his words, the look on his face made her think that perhaps it was the truth.

Truth. There it was again. That volatile, changeable, dangerous word. Dogging her at every turn. At the center of everything.

"So . . . now you're fine?" she asked. "You're all over it?"

He shrugged. "You find ways to take your power back."

"Yes, that's exactly it. Taking my power back," she muttered. "That's exactly what I was trying to do."

He frowned. "I don't want to play games with you."

"So what the fuck *do* you want? I was giving you the benefit of everything I have to give a man, everything I know, and you reject it, you ungrateful son of a bitch. So what do you want? Spell it out for me!"

He opened his hands, looking bewildered. "It is . . . a feeling. I do not know how to explain it. I never felt it before. It is like seeing without eyes. Something beyond the senses. But it was amazing."

The desire to believe every word he said, to fall into this honey-baited trap, was so strong, it almost swept her away. But he was too damn smart. Sharp enough to read her mind, to know exactly what would tempt her, what would melt her.

She wiped angry tears away. Gave him a hollow laugh. "You want something that doesn't exist, Janos. Or something that's long dead."

His face turned obstinate. "I felt it before you took me in your mouth. You were there with me, and suddenly you were not, and I was being fellated by a beautiful *cortigiana*, her mind and heart a million miles away from me. I am sorry. I did not mean to hurt your feelings. But it made me feel lonely." He gave her a rueful shrug.

Tam rolled her eyes. "Oh, crap. I'm doing the one man in the whole world who gets depressed and lonely when a woman blows him."

"Yes, yes. I know. There are worse things," he cut in impatiently. "I have no reason to complain. You almost killed me with pleasure. But it is not enough, after feeling the other."

"Keep in mind, the last time you screwed me, I was high, remember? I won't let you do that to me again. What you felt was not real. It was just a chemical fantasy."

"I did not take the drug, so the drug could not have created it," he said stubbornly. "It only removed your barrier to it."

"Same difference," she informed him. "My barrier is up and it's staying up. So put your clothes back on and get your high standards and your tight ass out of my hotel room before I—"

"No," he said.

"What do you mean, no?"

"Me putting on my clothes and leaving you alone tonight is not one of the options you have right now," he announced. "In fact, you have no options. There is only one outcome possible. Resign yourself."

His implacable tone infuriated her. "Don't you dare throw your weight around, Janos. I know you're strong, but no one compels me. Trust me, it's not worth the price I would make you pay."

His eyes gleamed. "Is it not?"

"Want to die?" she asked. "I am not speaking figuratively, Janos."

His face brightened. "Excellent!" he encouraged. "I prefer you murderous and for real to smiling and false."

"Oh, you are nuts." She lunged for the door. He yanked her up off her feet from behind, his hard arm clamped under her ribcage, holding her against his hot body. She tried hooking his ankles, elbowing his ribs, twisting like an eel, but his strength was enormous. "Goddamn you," she whispered furiously. "Put me down."

"Shhh," he murmured. "You'll wake the child."

She started to feel panicked. "Put me down! This is where you get back at me for the necklace, right?"

"Shhh. Not at all," he soothed. "I do not hold a grudge. That was my fault for letting down my guard. I will not make that mistake again."

His cool, controlled tone drove her mad. "Oh, no," she said, breathlessly. "You're not angry. While you won't let me go and threaten me with forced sex. Not angry at all. Right."

He kissed the side of her neck. "Don't be foolish," he said. "You need me to be strong for you. Gently now. Or you'll hurt yourself."

"No," she snarled, writhing. "I'll hurt *you*."

"I will not allow you to hurt me," he said calmly. "You got the better of me today with your necklace, but I have you now and I will not let you go until I get what I want."

Tears of pure frustration pricked and burned in her eyes. "I told you already, *stronzo*. What you want doesn't exist!"

"No?" He turned her until they both looked into the mirror. "Look at you," he said. "Finally, color in your face. Your eyes are shining. You are on fire."

"Of course," she snapped. "I'm furious with you!"

"Good, then. It works," he said. "I know what you want. You like strength. You must have been so disappointed in me this afternoon, going down so easily, like a slaughtered pig. But I will make it up to you. I will not let you win again. You are safe this time. Trust me."

Trust him. Hah. What a joke. He bent her forward, so her trapped arms rested on the cold marble countertop. Her eyes met his in the mirror. Her breath was shortened by rage—and excitement.

He knocked her legs wider with his knee.

She bit her lip as his hand slid between her legs, touching the lips of her pussy. Slipping between them, a slow, tender glide. Up and down, and up . . . and tenderly around her clit. Over and over. Her breath caught. "You're with me now," he said roughly. "That is the feeling I want."

"Sure, I am. I'm helpless and immobilized, you prick," she said sharply. "Is that how you like it?"

"Helpless? You?" He bit her earlobe. "You are the furthest thing from helpless I have ever met. You are a man-eating female tiger in the jungle. Perhaps you will rip out my throat afterward, but it will be worth it." He dragged his teeth tenderly down the side of her neck, as he prodded two fingers between her slick folds and thrust them slowly, deeply inside.

She gasped silently and clenched around the intrusion.

"I would love to lick your clit, make you come with my mouth," he murmured against her skin. "But you are so tense, so electric. I would have to restrain you hand and foot to do it properly. Someday I will do it. If we ever have the privacy. If we ever have a chance to use a bed."

One hand. Oh my.

His delving fingers found a marvelous, melting hot spot inside her, shocking a whimper out of her. He leaned into it as soon as he perceived it and lavished it with attention, stroking the pad of his finger over it and over it, until the deep, throbbing flush of pleasure rose, sharpened and then pulsed heavily through every nerve.

She relaxed over his strong arm, panting. Thighs wet, tangled hair falling in thick swirls to the marble sink. She licked sweat off her upper lip and felt him ripping open the condom with his teeth.

Was this her chance, while he was busy with that? She could probably do some surprise damage—

She didn't. She was shaking. And famished for what she knew would come next.

She shut her eyes and almost keened with delight when she felt it. The thick, blunt head of his cock nudging and prodding. Insisting. And then the long, impossibly tight slide of total penetration.

She shoved back against him, clamping every muscle around the huge, throbbing presence inside her. She felt so hot, so taut. So full.

Just a few slow strokes to find the rhythm they needed, and they were off on a wild, violent ride. Their eyes were locked in the mirror, their bodies locked into a jarring, headlong rhythm. His arms circled her, his hands clasping with hers on the cold marble, a straining tangle of white-knuckled fingers. Her breasts jiggled with each thrust.

They gasped for air. Choked back the noises. She bit her lip until she tasted blood to keep from gasping, moaning. The impossible things he had said were true. They had gone over to the edge to someplace new. Someplace beautiful.

The danger zone.

She'd never let anyone so close. He could destroy her so easily from in there. But in his strong grip, she felt safe enough to let go and let the pleasure drive her toward that thundering oblivion that awaited them. Maybe it was a mistake. A lie, an illusion, a deadly trap.

She didn't care. She gave in, let go, and he followed her.

They exploded together.

They stared at each other afterward for panting, speechless minutes. Finally, he withdrew from her body and disposed of the condom. He lifted her until she stood upright and smoothed the hair away from her damp face.

She stood there, arms at her sides, head flung back onto his shoulder. She stared at her naked self, at the flush over her chest, her neck, her face. Her lips were crimson. When his arms circled her, a ripple of acceptance welcomed the wonderful heat of him. Her body welcomed the warm, tender kisses he dropped on her shoulder, her back. Craved the slow, hot stroke of his big hands caressing her waist, her belly. No resistance. Such an odd sensation.

She could get used to this. Come to need it, even. Long for it. Dream of it when she didn't have it.

Which would be soon enough.

"So? Am I condemned to death for my insolence?" he asked.

She licked her lips and considered her reply. "Your sentence is remanded for now," she said lazily. "I'm too tired to kill you tonight. But I can't speak for later. So stay sharp."

His grin flashed. He kissed her throat. "Shower with me?"

She shook her head. "Not a chance, with Rachel asleep outside. I go first, and you stand by the door and let me know if she wakes up. And do not, under any circumstances, go out there naked, got it? She's still asleep but just in case—she doesn't need a lesson in human anatomy at the tender age of three."

He nodded, docile enough. Tam stepped into the shower, knotting her hair on top of her head, and soaped herself up.

Her body felt unrecognizable. Her skin was still so sensitive, her private parts throbbing. Sore, from hard use. Flushed with continuing pleasure. All she had to do was contract her thigh muscles, and mini-orgasms throbbed down her thighs, through her knees and calves, tingling right down to the tips of her toes.

Janos stood at the ready with a big, fluffy towel when she got out. She allowed him to dry her, lifting her limbs and turning with the regal grace of a queen accepting the ministrations of her body servant. He'd be in for a rude surprise if he expected her to return the favor, though.

She left him in the bathroom and went out, rummaging through the shopping bags until she found the nightshirt she'd ordered on his credit card. She ripped off the tags and slipped it on. Nice. Then she slid into bed next to Rachel, and reached out, keeping a little distance, but wanting to feel the comforting rise and fall of Rachel's little back.

Soundly sleeping. Good.

A few minutes later, the bathroom door opened. Val's magnificent body was silhouetted in the door frame. Steam billowed out. He'd put his jeans back on and was carefully taping a fresh bandage onto the wound on his shoulder.

He switched off the bathroom light, and became just a denser, deeper shadow amongst shadows.

"I want to stay here tonight," he said. "To guard you."

Of course. To make sure she didn't panic and bolt was more like it. It irritated her to have another life-or-death decision to make when she was so damned tired. But what was the point in splitting hairs? He'd already breached every barrier she had, physical or psychological.

It wasn't in his best interests to hurt them as far as she could tell. If it was, he would have taken care of it already.

What the hell. She didn't have the juice to throw him out.

"Sleep on the floor if you like," she offered coolly. "There's a pillow and more blankets in the closet, I believe. Help yourself."

She could barely make out his silent shadow in the dark, but she had a feeling he was smiling. She rose up onto her elbow. "Don't even think about the bed," she said in a forceful whisper. "I may have let you into my body, but I just met you a day ago, and I watched you do in three men today. And you are, by God, not sleeping next to my baby girl."

"Of course not." His deep voice vibrated with suppressed amusement. "It is already an honor that you let me stay in the same room with her. I am moved."

She snorted. "Pfft. Don't overdo it, Janos."

He glided to the closet, took out blankets and pillows, and lay one of them down across the doorway. He tossed the pillow on it, swathed the other blanket around himself, and stretched out without a word.

She had expected to slide directly into sleep, but her overloaded nerves had pushed her beyond sleep into another place. Thoughts and worries jostled in her head. She was too rattled to sort them out.

But one thing kept circling back. Nudging at her and making her queasy and wakeful. One random, irrelevant detail.

"Janos?" she whispered.

He yawned. "We've been through so much together," he said sleepily. "And we've made love twice. Can you not call me Val?"

"That wasn't love that we made, and if I knew your real name, I'd use it."

He was quiet for a moment. "Val is as real as any other name, Tamar Zadro."

Her childhood name sent a cold shiver through her. "Call me Tam Steele, please," she said tightly. "Tell me something, Janos."

"If I can," he said. "But only if you will call me Val."

"How old were you?" she asked. "When it happened to you?"

He didn't feign incomprehension, but he was silent for so long she finally concluded he wasn't going to answer at all.

"The first time?" he said, at last. "Eleven."

She winced in the dark. "Oh."

Silent minutes went by. Finally, Janos sat up, huffing out a sharp, irritated breath. "Stop thinking about it," he said gruffly.

She was startled. "Huh? What do you mean?"

"I can hear you thinking about it. Please stop. I think about it myself as little as possible."

Her chest jerked with involuntary laughter. "I'll try not to."

After a moment, he spoke again. "And you? How old were you?"

"Fifteen," she admitted.

"Ah."

A few more moments of that, and she was the one to snap at him. "Would you stop thinking about it, goddamnit?"

He laughed softly. "Hypocritical bitch."

"Yes, that would be me," she said crabbily. "And now, would you kindly stop your chattering and let me get some goddamn sleep?"

"You started it," he pointed out logically enough.

"Shut up, Janos."

"Call me Val, for the love of God," he said wearily, and rolled over so that his back was to her.

She stared into the dark for a very long time, trying not to think about anything.

Chapter
15

Sleep was impossible despite how exhausted he was. He felt buzzed, wired. Proximity to that woman acted on his brain like a powerful chemical stimulant.

If he kept her close enough, he might never need to sleep again.

Tamar and Rachel were still asleep. Tamar cuddled Rachel, the child's back tight to her belly, her arms wrapped tightly around her. Rachel's curly black head was tucked under her chin and Tamar looked like a little girl clutching a doll that she feared would be taken from her.

Not by him, he vowed silently. Not by him. He would die first.

His phone vibrated in his pocket. He plucked it out, and opened the text message from Donatella. It was terse and to the point.

**meeting with la santarini 10:30 Tuesday
dreaming of Paris baci e abbraci, D**

Relief almost brought tears into his eyes. He drew in a huge breath. One point of agonizing dread and tension eased, though there were plenty more of them vibrating inside him to choose from.

He noticed Rachel's pink fuzzy blanket draped over the chair. It gave him an idea. He fished in his jacket for the case of miniature spyware he'd been carrying everywhere he went, picking the same type he'd put into Tamar's jewelry case, but he fished out the slightly larger size, for the sake of the longer battery life.

Three days, guaranteed, the catalog had boasted. Maybe more.

They weren't the PSS-sanctioned transmitters that he usually used. When he'd researched the McClouds and Seth Mackey, he'd been intrigued with the merchandise in the SafeGuard online catalog. He had ordered an array of products to test and been agreeably surprised. Their software was better than that of PSS, and he liked the sleek, easy-to-use designs. The beacon burrs, as the catalog called them, were miniature X-Ray Specs GPS tracers, the smallest of them as slender as a wild grass seed. A pointed needle tip made for easy placement, no unstitching necessary. The tiny electronic parts and supercondensed battery were packed into a narrow plastic capsule. One slid it into a hem or fabric lining, and the thing was done.

He stared at Tamar for a moment to see if she was still asleep. She would read his gesture as threatening if she saw it, but if they should ever need the tracers, she would be grateful for them.

Swift, discreet action. He inserted one into Rachel's stuffed bear, another into the upholstery of her new stroller, a third into her ski jacket. Overkill, but he didn't care. He was the one who had put this child at risk. He wanted options should anything happen to her while they were in Europe. He only wished the batteries lasted longer.

He resumed the kung fu he'd been practicing for several silent hours. He'd tried meditating on the matrix, but he was buzzing at too high a frequency to have any hopes of centering himself.

He had to keep his wits about him—not so much against the enemies massed against them, but against Tamar herself. It took constant, careful attention to have anything to do with the woman. She was so sharp, so prickly and contentious. And so fucking beautiful.

She scrambled his circuits like an electrical storm.

He felt her eyes on the back of his neck as he sank down into a tiger crouch. His gaze flicked over her as he spun. Tamar was propped on her elbow, looking at him with squint-eyed, sleepy suspicion.

He continued without acknowledging her and silently finished the movement.

When he was done, she was on her feet with her back to him, punching a number into her cell phone. She spoke in a hushed voice, in Portuguese. "Rosalia? Yes, it's Tam . . . yes, I just called to find out how your . . . oh, really? Wonderful, Rosalia, thank God. I'm so glad you got it all straightened out so quickly . . . no, actually Rachel and I are out of town right now . . . yes, for a few days, yet. I'm not sure how many. You just take a vacation and relax, and I'll call you when I get back. OK. Thanks to you, too. Take care, Rosalia. Good-bye."

She clicked her phone shut, and glared at him. He gave her an I-told-you-so shrug.

"Well, and so what?" she snapped. "Don't give me that smug look. It was a shitty thing to do in the first place. You scared the poor woman to death. To say nothing of how her sons felt. You should pay them monetary damages for lost sleep and mental anguish. Embarrassing them at their place of work just to mess with me. It was unforgivable."

He shrugged. "I will pay them damages, if you like, when all this is over. But it's fine, now. I have arranged for an introduction to Ana Santarini. We have an appointment with her in two days."

She frowned. "So long from now? Do we have to waste an entire—"

"She is in Italy," he reminded her patiently. "We lose a day traveling, and when we arrive in Rome, we still have hours of driving to do. Do you have enough jewelry with you to show to a client without going home to get more? I suspect going back would be dangerous."

"I have everything I showed you at Shibumi, and then some," she said. "All unarmed, of course, but I have the means to arm some packed in my case."

"Good. We should get on our way," he said.

"Val," she said sweetly. "You've forgotten one small but very important detail. You killed my passport. I have others, but I expect you've killed them, too. Am I right?"

"I have a passport for you," he said, neatly sidestepping her landmine of a question. "Today, you are Anita Borg. Belgian."

"I don't want to use anything that PSS has in their files," she said.

"They do not know about this one," he told her. "I had one made secretly, weeks ago, at my expense. I like to have options. Always."

Her mouth tightened as she glanced back at Rachel's sleeping form on the bed. "We can't go anywhere near Sea-Tac."

"This is true. We will leave from Portland, which means we have a two hour drive ahead of us, minimum, to add to our travel time. Therefore, we must move. Soon." He glanced pointedly at Rachel.

Tamar's face darkened. "She needs her sleep," she said rebelliously. "She went to bed late last night. She's wiped out."

Val felt his jaw twitch. "I'll go get my laptop from the car and book the flights," he said grimly. "When I return, you must be ready."

"For breakfast," Tam specified. "With Erin and Connor and Kev and Sveti to soften the blow. I can't just dump the kid and disappear with no buildup, Janos, so take that into account when you book your flights."

"Call me Val," he said through clenched teeth. She didn't.

He sprinted through the bracing cold in the forest, soaring on that wild, jagged high. His feet barely touched the ground. He could not identify the source of the euphoria. The aftereffects of that intense sexual encounter, no doubt. He had not filmed it, not this last time. That, at least, was theirs. Secret and private. He should have filmed it to be sure he had another installment for Imre, but he couldn't bear to.

Another time. Because there would be another time, and another, and another. If he was anywhere near that woman, he would be trying to seduce her. The urge to assail her defenses was out of his control.

Oddly enough, he was getting used to being out of control.

It was inadvisable to get so excited. The woman would drug, stun, or shoot him at the slightest provocation, after all. But what they had done last night was burned into his sense memory. Every word, every gesture. Every succulent, dangerous, deadly detail of her.

He slid into the cold SUV, forcing warmth and circulation into numb fingers, logged on, and found an afternoon flight for Rome via Atlanta. Though the way she was dragging her feet, so reluctant to leave her child, it was doubtful they would actually catch it. He stowed his pistol in the case beneath the seat. He regretted leaving it behind, but even in checked baggage, a pistol attracted attention.

He was gratified when he got back to see that Tamar had moved briskly once he was not there to see it. Rachel was bathed, dressed, and stuffed into her coat, and Tamar was gathering the odds and ends of yesterday's spending spree, shoving items into shopping bags. She was casually dressed: designer jeans, a loose, nubbly beige sweater.

"I can't climb on a plane with my lingerie and toiletries falling out of a paper shopping bag," she bitched.

"I anticipated this problem, which is why I ordered you a suitcase yesterday," was his smooth rejoinder.

"Hmmph." She tossed her things into the suitcase he had hauled back from the SUV without any thanks and shrugged on her coat.

She scooped Rachel up, but the little girl leaned out of her arms and reached for Val. He swept her up, placed her on his shoulders, and set a brisk pace toward the main hotel, Tamar trailing sullenly behind.

Breakfast was a tense affair, though they had a lot of company. Val sipped coffee and stared grimly at the minutes ticking by on his watch. Sveti tried to persuade Rachel to consume scrambled eggs and pancakes, but the little girl had realized that her mother's departure was imminent, and she was cranky. Tamar's friends, gathered at the table, were all giving him cold-eyed looks that seemed to say, although Tamar had not told them exactly where she was going or why, they suspected it—and him.

Tamar, on the other hand, was overwhelming Erin and her husband with a long list scrawled on hotel stationery of the pediatrician's recommendations for Rachel's diet, allergies, and food intolerances. Then the nightly physical therapy exercises, the massages for ankles and hip, the asthma medications, cortisone drops for croup, ear drops, and so on. Minutes ticked by. Twenty. Thirty.

Connor McCloud's eyes glazed over halfway through, and Erin had long since passed her own child over to one of her sisters-in-law, frowning anxiously as she took careful little notes on the margin of the list. Words poured out of Tamar like water from a fire hose. Her fists were clenched, jaw tight, eyes red.

She cared, terribly. It hurt her to leave. He hated hurting her.

He pushed guilt away with a series of rationalizations. If they succeeded, the quality of Rachel and Tamar's life would be immensely improved. His offer was probably their only hope of continued survival.

If Hegel had come in Val's stead or sent any other operative, Tamar would already be in Georg's hands, and Rachel would be locked up alone, in a terrifying limbo. And if Novak should come to know of the child . . .

His mind shied away from the thought.

Then again, if Tamar and Rachel had managed to flee the day before, they might have had a fighting chance alone, somewhere in the world, under a new name. Anyone's guess.

And Imre would have been doomed to a slow and horrible death.

He took a swallow of the strong, black coffee. Bitter as poison. There was no point thinking about it. He had made his choice and set it all in motion. What was done was done.

"Three drops, did you write that down? Two milliliters of distilled water in the aerosol machine, and make sure she's watching Elmo or Pooh while you do it, or nothing doing. Did you get that?"

Rachel began to wail.

"Got that," Erin said distractedly, scribbling. "Three drops, two milliliters—Elmo, Pooh."

"I'll give you some cash for the medicines." Tamar dug into her purse. Her voice vibrated with tension, pitched loudly enough to be heard over Rachel's wailing.

Erin rolled her eyes. "Get real."

"I mean it," Tamar insisted. "This stuff costs big bucks at the pharmacy. I can't let you—"

"Screw you, Tam," Connor said brusquely. "Don't insult us. Now go and hug that kid, for God's sake, before we all get thrown out of this place for disturbing the peace. Don't you have a plane to catch?"

Tamar made a harsh, wordless sound and grabbed the screaming child, pulling her onto her lap. She buried her face against Rachel's hair and murmured to her between ear-splitting shrieks.

Val strategically fled the dining hall at this point, as many others were choosing to do with him, but he couldn't get away from the anguished sounds without leaving the building entirely. It was terrible.

Final good-byes, loading of cars, transferring of car seats, final admonitions, and still more final good-byes ensued. A teeth-grinding interval later, they were finally pulling onto the interstate in blessed silence. Tamar's hands were clenched, her back stiff. Her stony silence had an accusing weight that got heavier with each mile that passed.

By the time they were halfway to Portland, he could stand it no longer. "Would you stop it?" he blurted. "I am sorry your daughter is unhappy, but it is not forever. We have to work fast so—"

"If we survive at all," Tamar pointed out. "Or if I survive, rather. Let's be honest. I'm the one whose head is on the block."

He blew out a harsh breath. "I have tried in every way to make this risk worth your while," he said urgently. "For Rachel, too. She will survive without you for a few—"

"Look, you don't know how it feels, OK? So why don't you just fuck off and let me sulk?"

He turned away, stung into silence. It was true enough. He did not know how it felt. Nor would he ever want to learn.

They speeded down the highway in a hostile silence for over an hour. By the time they reached signs for Highway 205 and the Portland Airport, he was contemplating an odd, unexpected thought.

He glanced over at her set face, her red eyes. Whatever Tamar might lack in manners or maternal softness, one thing was certain. A child of hers would never have to wonder if her mother cared.

Tam cared so much, it looked like she was about to explode.

Whatever she had done in the past, she was ready to defend her young with fang and claw. He thought of his own childhood. His conclusion was glaringly obvious.

Rachel was fortunate. And the child knew it. With her experience, she knew in her bones that the monsters under the bed were all too real. The mother she'd handpicked was perfect for battling monsters.

He waited for a few more miles and blurted it out.

"You are a good mother," he said.

Tamar gave him an incredulous look. "And how could someone like you make a judgment like that?"

He was affronted. "What do you mean, someone like me? Why not me? I am entitled to my opinions, like anyone else."

She made a derisive sound. "You're not like anyone else, Janos," she said. "And besides, the poor kid could have been kidnapped or murdered yesterday, remember? Thanks to you, I might add."

He bristled. "Ah, *sì*? Forgive me for trying to keep you from getting abducted or slaughtered—"

"Adopting Rachel at all was an irresponsible act, considering who and what I am," she continued grimly. "It's just like you said in Shibumi. I'm using her. I'm a crazy, selfish bitch." She paused and swallowed. "And this stunt I'm pulling now has got to be the craziest, most selfish thing I've ever done. Forget the slick reasons why. Let's be brutally honest, OK? I'm in this for the revenge. No other reason." She looked out her window. "If I get snuffed, she'll probably be better off with Erin and Connor anyhow."

Against his will, memories flashed into Val's mind. The day he'd found his mother dead on the bathroom floor. Giulietta, the Italian girl from Palermo, another whore in Kustler's stable, who had shared their apartment for a while. Her baby girl had died in her crib one icy cold winter day, right next to an open window, while Giulietta floated on the bed nearby in a heroin daze.

He could still see Giulietta in his mind's eye, when she came down from her high. Staring into the crib with her hands on her face. Eyes staring out of her head. Screaming.

She'd screamed for hours, or so it had seemed to him at the time. Those screams still echoed distantly through his mind. He pushed the memory away. It still made his gut feel hollow.

"You are wrong," he said stubbornly. "She would not be better off without you. You're a good mother. And I know. Trust me. I have seen some bad ones."

She shot him a piercing glance, opened her mouth to speak . . . and shut it again. Something in his voice or face had blocked whatever cutting thing she'd been poised to say. Just as well. His nerves were more raw than usual today. He stared straight out the windshield and concentrated on driving. Willing her not to ask questions.

Reminiscences from his grim childhood were not calculated to lighten anybody's mood.

Things went with blessed smoothness at the airport. In short order, they were stretched out in big, soft reclining seats in the first-class section of the jumbo airliner, both of them pretending to sleep.

He couldn't stop stealing glances at her hand, where it rested on her shapely, jeans-clad thigh. It looked so strong and capable, and yet delicate, the slenderness of her fingers accentuated by the heavy, savage-looking thumb ring she wore, made of contrasting bands of colored gold. He wondered what defense applications the ring had, and decided that an airplane would be an indiscreet place to ask.

He liked her French manicure. He liked the fading, gummy shadow of a child's fake tattoo on her slender wrist, some cartoon character that populated an American three-year-old's fantasy world. A tender, secret detail that made him smile. He liked the way her sweater cuff draped over her forearm. So graceful, every curve, every line of her.

She infuriated him; she fascinated him. He was obsessed. He accepted that fact, let it sink in without resisting it. Made it part of the matrix so that he would take it into account while making decisions.

He was going to seduce her again at the first opportunity. This fact had the weight and inevitability of natural law, the kind that governed the turning of the planets, the movement of the stars.

Not just to save Imre, though. Not anymore. God help him, he had just tripled his problems and responsibilities. Imre, Tamar, Rachel.

At this point, the only way to save himself was by somehow saving them all.

Never again. Tam established it in her head, a constant drone beneath the frantic chatter of all the other thoughts and fears and feelings. The man was inside her head, invading her thoughts, her senses. Compromising her powers of reasoning. She could not afford to be so distracted on the eve of the riskiest stunt of her entire career.

If it was just about sex, that would have been bad enough, but it wasn't. These flashes of emotional connection shook her, disarmed her, left her speechless and stammering. Buzzing with feelings.

She was curious about him, fascinated by him, interested in him, like a teenage girl crushed out on a rock star. Robot Bitch had gone to pieces. Rachel had started the disintegration process, and Val Janos was the killing blow. Life was so much simpler back in the good old days when Robot Bitch ruled.

She was unsteady all the time. Bowled over by his scent. How did a guy with the massive dose of male hormones necessary to render him that potent and dangerous still manage to smell so good? It was against the basic laws of nature.

She kept sneaking peeks at him. Checking out the length of his legs, the broad, hard shape of his chest, the outrageous breadth of his shoulders. Mmmm, how she liked big, thick, cut shoulders that she couldn't quite get her fingers around. And his somber, beautiful face. His beard stubble was starting to get soft, not scratchy. She had no whisker burn, even after last night's mad nuzzling.

She wanted to explore him, to set off into the uncharted wilderness of his fascinating self and never come back. She wanted to open his pants and play with his big, beautiful cock like a toy. To study the patterns his body hair made on his skin. To memorize every scar. To hear all of the scar stories. And tell him hers, too. If he was interested.

She wanted to shock him, rock him, make him crazy with lust.

And laugh with him. Of all things. Stupid fantasy. Dream on.

Her only recourse was to keep her mouth shut, her eyes averted, and ignore him as much as possible. She kept her eyes fixed on the moonlit clouds outside the oval window. They had dimmed the lights in the forward cabin, and the curtain was pulled for privacy.

It would have been far better if it wasn't. That drawn curtain gave her some very, very dangerous ideas.

She unfolded the blanket the airline had provided and swathed herself from neck to toe, determined to feign sleep. She had no intention at all of giving into it with so much to occupy her mind, but her tired body betrayed her.

She tipped straight into an uneasy dream.

She was wearing the red chemise Stengl had dressed her in, and searching desperately for something to wear, anything but that hateful scrap of limp red silk. She could find nothing. Even being naked would be better, but the chemise wouldn't come off. The red silk stuck to her like a stain. She tore at her body until it was bleeding, and then suddenly, her body was no longer a woman's body—it was a doll, brittle and fragile. Crack, she held a stiff leg with no joint, a high-heeled foot with painted red toenails like a storefront mannequin. Then the other leg broke off. She shattered from within, exploding in a shower of dusty shards.

Even broken into pieces, you are beautiful.

She knew that velvet voice. She recognized the strong hand sifting through broken shards, shreds of red silk until he found it. Her heart.

It looked like a cheap toy or a pincushion. Made of puffy red satin stuffed with fluff, trimmed with lace and tiny bows. He dusted it off and cradled it in his big hand. It transformed, glowing. Light shone right through his hands. It beat, it shone, it blazed through his fingers. Alive.

Heat glowed in her body, a deep, yearning throb, and she came back to consciousness very slowly and carefully, as if something inside her knew she'd be cheated of her prize if she rushed it. She drifted with majestic slowness, letting waves of pleasure intensify, rocking her higher until the crest broke and pulsed in long breaking waves.

Her eyes opened, amazed, to see the darkened cabin of the plane, the drawn curtain, the blanket under her chin. And Val, leaning over her, his eyes gleaming in the dimness. His hand, down the front of her jeans.

Oh. She'd bought the next jeans size up, since Rachel's you-take-a-bite-and-then-I-take-a-bite game had put a little extra layer of meat on her ass, but she hadn't filled out the new size entirely. There was plenty of room for his hand. His fingers rested on either side of her throbbing clit, catching it in a gentle, patient clasp . . . waiting to see what she thought of the situation now that she was awake.

She licked her lips, cleared her throat. What the hell did she think of it? She knew how her body felt about it, but that was not relevant. Her body had no vote in this. Her head had to prevail. She gathered her strength to be bitchy, shove him away. It was a tremendous effort.

"You sneaky bastard," she whispered. "Is this your usual move? Wait until the woman is drugged or asleep, and then you make your move? You should be ashamed."

He looked completely unembarrassed. "No, Tamar. Only with you. I must use every dirty trick I can devise, or I will get nowhere."

"You're a snake." Her voice quivered, like her thighs.

"*Sì, certo.* I would do anything to feel you come again. Any desperate, wrong, immoral thing and feel no shame at all. Be warned."

The low rasp of his voice caressed her, his coffee-scented breath tickled her ear. Her face glowed, hot as a coal. It made her think of the heart in her dream. Magically transformed.

The decision was making itself, the yearning heat in her body drowning out the fear, the doubts, the *never again.*

Oh, fuck it. Why never? Why not? Life was hard and short, and getting harder and shorter every day. And she wasn't very talented at yielding to pleasure anyway, even if she was inclined to seek it out, which she wasn't. It was now, or it was probably never again.

After all, she was trapped in a plane. She had nothing better to do. It wasn't as if she was wasting precious time she could be using to solve her and Rachel's problems. So why not?

Let the man multitask. He was so talented at it.

He teased her mound, caressing her with his fingertips without penetrating her. "If we had privacy and a bed, I'd strip off those jeans and put you on top of me," he muttered into her ear. "I'd pull you down very slowly, letting your pussy accept me, a long, slow, tight glide, like a glove on my *cazzo.* Then I'd grab your hips and fuck you from below while I stared up at your breasts, bouncing above. Every inch of you flushed and hot with desire. Making all the noise you like."

She licked her dry lips. "Were you aware that position is for the woman to control? That's the whole point of it. Guess it never occurred to a prehistoric lunk like you."

"You want control, Tamar?" His smile flashed in the dim light. "Fight me for it. I love the way you come around me when you lose."

She had to struggle hard to muster her defenses. Particularly with his clever finger stroking tenderly just above the hood of her clit. A touch she could barely feel, and yet . . . *oh*. She could feel nothing else.

"I hate you," she said distractedly. "You need a lesson."

"You will be too tired to give me one when I am finished," he said. "You'll be so exhausted, you won't even struggle when I tie you down, to lick your clit and tongue-fuck you into another orgasm. Then I'll take you again. Watching every detail. The way my *cazzo* slides into you, those slick pink pussy lips kissing my whole length as I pull out . . . and push in, again and again, ah. The way you take all of me, every last centimeter, until the head of my *cazzo* is rammed up inside you, against the core of you, so tight, rocking and throbbing—"

"Stop it," she whispered. "No more talk."

"No?"

She held his gaze as she popped open the buttons on her jeans, and wiggled lower in the seat to give him more scope. She parted her legs, letting him deeper, and shoved his hand inside her jeans. "Get to work," she said. "And make it good. Or you'll pay for your teasing."

He took her up on the invitation, sliding two fingers into her cleft. She was so, so juicy and swollen. She moved against him almost frantically, it felt so good, clamping her thighs around him.

Val curved his fingers into a gentle hook, circling tenderly over the glowing places inside her that were flushed with expectant pleasure while his thumb took care of her clit, doing a perfect little tremolo . . . ah, God, talk about multitasking.

He slapped the seat divider up and covered her mouth with his.

He was as talented with his mouth as he was with his hands, but it wasn't his skill that stirred her. It was the look in his eyes. Not triumphant, or smug, or pleased with himself. Just quietly desperate.

She closed her eyes, and saw that dream heart glowing in the gentle cradle of his hand. Light shining through his fingers.

Don't get squishy about dreams. Dreams will betray you, said a scolding inner voice.

Don't ruin this for me, she told it. *A little pleasure, for God's sake. A little bit of pleasure, once in a blue moon.*

She knew the choreography of kisses, just as she knew every

other sexual technique, but she'd never felt the raw, driving desire behind a kiss before. The whole point of a kiss. As if there was a precious elixir to be had from the mouth of the other, something they would both die without and only pleading passion could bring it forth.

She squeezed and writhed, breathless in the dark. He was so good. Perfect. The only thing she would have gladly changed about this moment was that she wanted the thrusting prong of his fingers to be that thick, meaty cock. She wanted to twine her naked legs around him and take him to the hilt, to feel his strength jarring into her with that wild, pounding rhythm that took her breath. She wanted all the room and softness of a big bed to do justice to his outrageous bounty.

No time to be dissatisfied, though. She was coming apart, tightening around him with every tiny muscle inside herself. Sensations, emotions, welling up together.

They overflowed, swirling, rushing. Carrying her gently away.

He lifted his head slowly afterward. There was no need to say anything. The tension in his hand still clamped over her mound, the bulge in his jeans, his dark, burning eyes said it all.

He fell heavily back into his chair as she got his jeans open. There was a glow of pink on the bottom of the window shade, signifying that dawn was at hand—which meant that a flight attendant could pull aside the curtain and offer them coffee and pastry at any moment.

She did not care. She wrenched down the stretchy black fabric of his briefs and took his thick, throbbing shaft into her hand with a sigh. Beautiful. Stone hard and broad and swollen, longer than any cock had practical reason to be, thick enough to be a bit of a problem. Overkill.

She squeezed her thighs around the juicy glow of lingering pleasure as she licked up glistening drops of pre-come. He gasped for air.

She sucked him into her mouth, relishing the salty taste, the hardness of his flesh, the silky skin, the deep throb of his heartbeat pulsing against her tongue.

Last night, she'd wanted to assault him with her skill. Now, she just wanted to be so close his pleasure would be her own, every stroke, every moan. She craved that closeness. She'd been alone so long.

She needed both hands to perform a proper blow job on this man. It was hard just to get his cockhead into her mouth, let alone the rest of it, but with the skillful addition of bold, twisting handwork and a generous amount of slippery spit, that was no problem at all.

It was perfect, feeling his response, the trembling dig of his fingers into her scalp, the hot, rich male smell of him, the tension in his muscular frame as he bent over her as he built up to it—and a volcanic explosion in her mouth. He spurted an outrageous amount of come into her mouth in complete and utter silence. Such self-control.

She kept him nestled inside the warm well of her mouth until the rhythmic spurts finally slowed down and eased off. She pulled her head away and admired the gleaming length of him, milking the last few creamy drops of come and licking them up, with tender, teasing flicks of her tongue. The sound he made was almost a whimper. His hands tightened in her hair. They were both damp with sweat.

She sat up, wiggling back down into her own seat and buttoning her jeans. She pulled her sweater down and her blanket back up. Val tucked his cock into his pants, adjusted his clothes, and fished a bottle of mineral water out of the seat pocket. He presented it to her.

Nice touch. The least he could do. She drank deeply and pulled her blanket back up to her chin. As if it were any kind of protection from his seductive power.

"Proud of yourself?" She forced some sharpness into her tone.

He shook his head. "Humbled," he said softly. "And destroyed."

She was getting embarrassed now, which always made her irritable. "I need a bath in the worst way," she whispered. "And we have hours of travel time to go. Nor do I have clean clothes to spare."

"Sorry, Tamar." The sympathy on his face was fake. "When we get to Italy, we will buy you more clothing. And the hotel room I have booked in San Vito has a magnificent bathroom. A deep tub, with hydromassage. A beautiful marble shower, for two."

"Why are you calling me that?" she demanded. "Nobody calls me that. It's Tam, if you please."

"I like it that nobody calls you that," he said quietly. "And I like it that it is your real name."

"Real." She snorted. "What's real?"

He reached out, slowly drew his fingertip over her upper lip. Then the tender inner part of it. Her mouth trembled in response. His finger smelled of her.

"This was real," he said softly. "No comfort zone. I loved it."

She blushed idiotically. "Hmph. Whatever. I want that shower. Your gooey gigolo sweet talk won't help me with that. The bathroom in San Vito is still five thousand kilometers away. And you still trust me with your credit card?"

"Fuck, no," he said, with feeling. "This time, I choose what you buy."

She startled herself by giggling. He took advantage of the unshielded moment to grab her hand.

She stiffened. Her first instinct was to yank it back, as if she'd been burned. She stopped herself, by force of will, her nerves on edge.

Their hands were both a bit sticky, but it wasn't as if either one of them had cause to complain. She had never actually held a man's hand in her life. Other parts of a man, yes. But not hands.

It was uncomfortably, weirdly intimate. Almost, well . . . nice. In a way that was dangerously different from sex.

But then again, what did it matter if she indulged in a silly lovey-dovey fantasy? Even if it blew up in her face. Who would it hurt?

You, she told herself. *It'll hurt you. You're letting the man literally fuck your brains out, and the end result will not be pretty.*

She acknowledged that brutal truth, she accepted it, she swallowed it down . . . but she did not let go of his hand.

Chapter 16

If Val had not been so worried about Imre, so conscious of time, he would have actually been having fun with Tamar. He enjoyed her caustic wit, her sharp honesty. She stimulated him on every level.

They checked into the beautiful, baroque-era hotel in San Vito, and he hurried her up the grand staircase and down the high-ceilinged corridor to their room with unconcealed impatience. He had paid a ridiculous sum to reserve this particular room. It had a loggia, with three arches on the terrace, a spectacular view of the town rising steeply out of the azure sea and clinging to the mountain slopes, and of La Roccia, the huge rock formation that cut the town into two parts.

Not that he gave her time to look at it. He slammed the door shut and fell upon her, like a beast. True to form, she shoved him back, with a strength that still surprised him from such a slender woman.

"Do not take me for granted!"

He advanced on her. "I'm not," he said. "I'm taking you, period."

"The cave man game only goes so far, Val," she warned.

Ah, *sì*. She was calling him Val, at last. Something inside him capered for joy. "Far enough for my purposes." He grabbed her, heedless of her swatting hands, and flung her down onto the bed.

She struggled, but if she hadn't been having a good time, he would be on his back, fighting for his very life. As it was, her eyes glowed, her color was high, she shoved, flailed, and slapped at him with high energy, but no lethal intentions. His body knew the difference.

He risked letting go of her wrists for long enough to unbutton her jeans, and got a couple of sharp slaps for his trouble. He snatched her hands and flung himself on top of her, his face red and tingling pleasantly from the blows. The bed rocked and bounced. He pinned her wrists and grinned into her furious face.

"Finally, a bed," he said. "I thought it would never happen."

"What makes you think it will happen now, *porco?*" she shot back. "After twenty-four hours of travel and no bath? Dream on!"

"Twenty-four hours of foreplay," he countered, pulling down her jeans. "Fuck the bath. Bathe later. Trust me, you will need a bath later."

They wrestled and writhed and struggled. He was on the verge of coming in his jeans, before he finally got her naked beneath him. He got a painful, two-fingered jab to his throat when he spared a hand to open his pants. The blow could have been lethal, had she cared to make it so. He wouldn't take such a harmless version of it personally.

"We have a problem," he told her. "I need my hands to get a condom on, but if I let go of you, you'll rip out my throat."

"Hah. Sounds like it's your problem, not mine," she informed him.

"Not at all. My solution to the problem is simple." He grabbed his aching, throbbing cock, and nudged it inside her.

She was slick, swollen, and taut, with no latex to dull the amazing heat of her. He drove forward in one long, lunging thrust, and could have died from delight from this moment. It was worth every blow, every slap, every scratch. Every last insult.

She gasped and went still. "Wait! That's no solution!"

"I have no diseases," he assured her. "I am always careful, and I am tested regularly."

"Me, too, but that's not the problem," she said. "I'm not using contraception."

He was startled. "Ah. I see."

"So get out of me. I do not want a baby from you."

He tried to withdraw, but his body played tricks on him. He just found himself gliding deeper, rubbing, rocking. Just once . . . and then once more. "I won't come inside you," he promised. "Just a few strokes . . . in . . . and out, like this." He lunged deep, twisting his rod.

Tamar caught her breath and arched, shoving her hips back to take more of him. She bit her flushed red lips and clutched his chest, her nails digging deep. "All it takes is one! And I don't trust a man to have that kind of self-control. I don't trust men for anything. So get out of me!"

He tilted his eyebrow. "You may be amazed to hear it, but I have noticed this lack of trust," he said wryly.

"And? So?" Her bright eyes challenged him.

"So? I must prove you wrong. I will do as you ask." He pulled out, regretting every clinging, caressing millimeter of sweet connection he was losing. "You cannot imagine what this *galanterie* is costing me."

"Poor baby." She sat up, coiling herself into a siren's pose.

He rummaged for the condom, whipped the thing on and advanced on her, his erection jutting urgently before him.

"Do not tell me I must start from zero once again," he begged.

The smile she gave him was razor sharp. "What makes you think you've racked up any points at all?"

Savage frustration flared inside him. He breathed it down with great difficulty "You will not give in to me for one single instant, no? No matter how much you want to."

Her taunting smile faded, and for a brief, naked instant, he saw something in her eyes, something frantic and lost, like a trapped animal. "I can't," she said starkly. "I just . . . can't."

He was taken aback. The confession moved him, though it maddened him, too. He sensed her need, her frustration. The aching tension. Steel cables strung so tight they hummed from the strain.

He'd never wanted so badly to be tender to a woman, and he had never met a woman so desperately in need of tenderness. But it was unbearable to her. She simply could not tolerate it. Yet.

Until she could, he would just close his eyes, take a deep breath, and follow his instincts.

"Then don't," he said. He lunged for the bed.

She spun, trying to scramble away. She let out a startled grunt as he landed on top of her. All his weight. There would be no escape from the pleasure he meant to inflict upon her.

His hand slid down, caressing her trembling ass cheeks, sliding lower. Playing with her tender folds. Silken smooth, hairless, perfect. He tongued and kissed the back of her neck, her trembling spine as he pinned her flat, immobile, and played with her clit, her juicy cunt.

When her first climax wrenched through her, he savored the powerful, clutching pulses, her hitching, gasping breath, and then waited for the insults, the verbal slaps.

They did not come. She buried her face in the bedclothes, and shook. Wordless.

He forced his cock inside while tremors still rippled through her. When she caught her breath and raised her head, he was seated deep within, rocking slowly in that tight, gliding sheath. Waiting for a cue.

"Someday, you will let me be gentle with you," he said.

Her hair swung as she shook her head in negation. "Don't hold your breath," she said jerkily. "I can't even be gentle with myself."

"I am patient," he told her. "I can wait."

"Shut up. Get to work, Val," she snapped. "You talk too much."

There was his signal. She rocked back to take in more of him.

He meant to give her everything he had to give, all the power and control, the technique, but something snapped, and they spun out of control together, heaving and bucking against each other, dripping with sweat. He held her in a grip that would leave bruises. She clutched handfuls of sheets with white-knuckled fingers. She did not fight him.

The danger zone, terrifying and wild and wonderful.

She looked over her shoulder. "Turn me over," she demanded, panting. "I want to see your face. I want to see if you're for real."

"Of course I am." He didn't even question the truth of those words before they burst out. He pulled out, flipped her over, folding her legs wide to stare at the perfect pink flower of her pussy. She was so flexible, elastic as a dancer. Her skin, soft as a fine new leaf unfurling. Every curve and hollow astonished his eyes.

He mounted her again before she could change her mind, and they found their rhythm face to face. She stared into his eyes, undulating frantically, nails digging as the energy of her climax began to crest.

She panicked then and started slapping him, in a disordered, haphazard way, her eyes bright with furious tears. "Damn you," she hissed. "Damn you, you son of a bitch."

He tried to catch her hands, but she wrenched them away with a snarl. He just let go, let her pummel at him while their bodies slammed frantically together. She needed that violent struggle for dominance, and he sensed that she needed him to win it for her sake. But nothing she could do to him could hurt him now. He was riding a thundering crest of colossal pleasure.

Some time later, who knew how long, he found himself on his side, facing her. They were bathed in sweat, their arms still around each other, clutching. Her legs wound around his hips.

He tried to loosen his grip, but his shaking muscles would not immediately obey him. Their hearts thudded against each other.

He willed his arms to relax. Their bodies unglued with a little wet sound. He pulled his gleaming, softening cock out of her. They fell back onto their backs, shivering in the cool room as their sweat dried.

Someone knocked on the other side of the wall. "*Ehi. Auguri, amico,*" their neighbor called in a dry, amused voice. Hey. Congratulations, pal.

Neither of them had the energy even to react.

When he dared to look at her, she flinched away from his gaze and dragged herself up to the edge of the bed. He laid his hand against the elegant curve of her shoulder blade. She started away as if his hand had burned her and got to her feet. She stumbled, her legs buckling beneath her, and caught herself against the wall.

He jerked up, alarmed. "Are you—"

"Fine." She spat the words out. "I'm *fine.*"

He stetched out a pleading hand. "Tamar—"

"Don't," she said. "Just don't. I'm going to take a shower. I'll be a while. Don't bug me."

He stared at her retreating back, flinched at the slam of the door.

The brass key clicked and ground in the antique lock. The shower began to hiss against the marble. His heart still drummed. And beneath it, his belly was cold and heavy with guilt for what came next.

Now, damn it. This was his only chance. Still, he sat on the bed like a lump of lead. Miserable.

Imre. Novak's game would continue, and tomorrow a fresh piece of erotic footage was due, to keep Imre in one piece. Val couldn't be queasy and hesitant about getting it. After all, he was not literally hurting or betraying her by doing this. God knows, he was putting his whole heart into fucking her. He had never been so honest and forthright with any woman in his life—except about this. This one little detail.

The rationalizations didn't work. He had to do what he'd learned to do as a boy, when Kustler sent him to certain apartments, certain houses. Special clients. Or when he had no appointments, and was sent out to work the streets. The cars would stop for him, and he would put the mechanism to work. Break off a piece of himself. Let it get into the car and do the job while his mind floated somewhere apart and safe. Numb.

He had survived it. It had gotten easier with time. But this, for some reason, did not.

He unfastened the cellophane that covered the plant he'd ordered via the Internet from a local florist. A voluminous fern. He rigged the little camera in the shadow of two gracefully draped fronds. Adjusted the angle to make sure he got the bed. Adjusted the leafy fronds, to conceal the camera but not block the view. He would make it right with her somehow. God grant, she never had to know at all.

A great deal to hope, the way his luck was going.

After an hour in the shower, Tam began to feel ridiculous, cowering in the billows of steam. She was appalled to be feeling this way. Emotions sprawled over her face. Truths she never meant to say, or even knew were true, bursting out with no warning. She couldn't trust herself to act in her own best interests. And there was the humiliating phenomenon of morphing into a mindless, scratching cat in heat whenever he looked at her with those smoldering eyes.

And she would do it again. Right now. She would just march right out there buck naked and leap on him with all four paws. At the slightest provocation.

She shut off the water, toweled dry. The mirror was obscured by condensation, which was good, because she didn't want to look at her own face. Not when she was this angry at herself.

Working a comb through her hair killed another twenty or so minutes. It was getting stupidly long, but she hadn't wanted to bother with dying or styling it for so long, it had evolved into its own new super straight look that suited her austere mood these days. She considered slicking it back with styling gel into a tight, wet braid, and then rejected the idea. Let it dry, and hang wherever the hell it wanted. She was sick and tired of trying to control every last fucking tiny detail. Enough.

Same with her eyes. She stared into her travel-reddened topaz eyes in the mirror, hating the idea of inflicting colored contacts on them again, without even the benefit of a night's sleep. What did she care if Val knew the real color? He knew every other significant fact about her. Why balk at this?

To hell with useless barriers. They were draining her energy.

She wrapped a huge bath towel around herself and flung open the door. Val sat naked on the bed, waiting for her. Or rather, waiting for his turn in the bathroom. The guy probably had to piss like a racehorse after all their traveling. She had no sympathy in the least. Served the presumptuous fucker right for not booking her a room of her own.

But the bitchy mental chatter faded as she took in that huge, sculpted golden body, his intense, somber face. His thick penis was impressive even when it was soft, dangling against a springy twist of curling hair. Her fingers curled with the urge to grab him and pet it.

He sensed the thought and his penis twitched, lengthened.

She turned away deliberately and went to rummage through the suitcase he'd ordered for her. She dabbed herself with expensive face cream, deodorized her pits with the ridiculously pricey bottle of deodorant. What a blast of naughty, fleeting fun she'd had with that online catalog. The criteria by which she'd chosen each item had been exquisitely simple. She'd just gone for whatever cost most.

It wasn't as if he didn't already know that she was a vengeful bitch. She'd made no effort to keep it a secret.

"I will take a shower, and we will get some dinner," he said.

Right. Like it was a good idea for her peace of mind to have a romantic candlelit dinner with this man in San Vito, of all places. Pound the final nail into her coffin, why didn't he.

"I'm not hungry," she said. "You go on. I want to rest."

"*Stronzate*." His voice was curt. "You ate nothing at breakfast at the Huxley, nothing at the Portland airport, nothing on the plane but coffee and water, nothing at the Rome airport, nothing in the Auto-grill. The last food that you ate were four bites of pasta at the wedding buffet. I counted them. You cannot continue to function like this. You are acting irresponsibly and unprofessionally. You will come with me, and get some fucking dinner."

She bristled. "Do not order me."

He sighed, and tilted his head to the side, as if praying for patience and inspiration. "Tamar. *Bellissima*," he said wearily. "Please. Be reasonable. This is Italy. You need have no fear of the food here."

"That's not it," she snapped.

He raised an eyebrow. "Ah. Fear of me, then?"

"Fuck, no!"

"Well, then? An eating disorder? A bid for control over your life? How sad. Let us discuss your feelings now, get to the bottom of this problem, so that you can eat before you collapse, no?"

She laughed at the thought in spite of herself. "Picture it. Thrashing through my emotional issues on the couch with Dr. Val. I can just imagine what you would prescribe as treatment."

His eyes gleamed. The corners of his lips curled up. His penis lifted eagerly.

Tam rolled her eyes, and threw up her hands. "All right, fine," she said. "Dinner. If it makes you happy."

"It makes me ecstatic. Five minutes," he said.

She yanked on her sweater, the jeans he'd bought for her at a boutique on the main drag of one of the little towns they'd passed through on the winding coastal highway of Amalfi. She slipped on the black suede half-boots from yesterday's catalog adventure, her default earrings, the ones with the hypodermic and the soporific, and the multiblade ring, the one she had named for Liv Endicott, Sean's wife.

It wasn't much in terms of weaponry, but it was better than nothing. She decided not to bother with makeup. She didn't have the energy to create illusions. Tonight was all about the truth. Being real.

Then she sat down facing the loggia that framed the sunset over the Mar Tirreno and put in a call on her cell phone to Connor and Erin.

Erin picked up. "Hello?"

Tam winced. Rachel was making noise—a lot of noise—in the background. "Hey, Erin, it's me. We just arrived. How's it going?"

Erin sounded resigned. "It's going," she said. "She's a tough cookie, but she has to give in sometime."

Hmmph. Tam had her doubts about that, knowing Rachel the way she did, but there was no point in saying so. Let Erin hope for the best. "Did she sleep? Or eat, at all?"

"No, and no. She's on strike. Hold on, let me see if she'll talk to you. She's on a speech strike, too. Hey, sweetheart, calm down. You want to talk to Mamma?"

Rachel was startled into silence, and then gave a cry of heartbreaking rage and abandonment.

Aw, shit. Tam slumped, and put her face into her hands. She felt sorry for Rachel, for herself, and mostly for Erin and Con and Sveti, who had to be bug-eyed by now. No one knew better than Tam how stressful a wigged-out Rachel could be.

Erin came back on the line. "Looks like she's not up for a chat." She sounded exhausted. "We have had some good moments, though. She's a sweet kid. But she misses you."

"Erin, I'm sorry." Tam felt helpless and guilty. She missed Rachel like crazy. It was hitting her hard.

"It's not your fault. I understand, and we will all live."

Conversation was impossible under the circumstances, so they signed off. Tam rested her face in her hands and wondered how long this depraved drama was going to take. And if Rachel could weather it.

She had to, she told herself. She had to.

Val touched her shoulder. She jumped. "Shit, you startled me!"

"*Perdonami*," he murmured. "Bad news?"

She shrugged, feeling overwhelmed. "Rachel's miserable," she said bluntly. "So's everyone around her. Big surprise."

He was silent for a moment. "I'm sorry."

She got up, and turned her back to him. "And thrilled to be thousands of miles away from it, right?"

He wisely left her alone to think and got dressed. She did not watch him clothe his spectacular nakedness. The bathed, shaved, combed, scented, designer-clothing-draped, mind-blowing finished product was enough for her nerves to take. Naked, he blew her circuits.

He took her to a restaurant that he knew well, judging from the authoritative way that he led her through the steep, twisting streets, and from the deferential way that they were treated once they arrived. The place was small and out of the way, but quietly beautiful. The food and wine were superb, although Val regarded her choice of green salad, roasted vegetables and grilled fish with dark disapproval.

"Not enough," he growled. He tried to load her up with some of his *tagliolini alla boscaiola*, and a slice of his enormous, bloody *tagliata di manzo*.

Nice try, she thought, staring at the snarl of oily, garlicky fresh pasta and the hot pink slab of tender meat he had dumped on her plate. He couldn't make her eat it, though. He had better luck with the wine, making it his business to keep her glass very full.

"Are you trying to get me drunk?" she asked.

He shrugged. "I am hoping to relax you. Would it work?"

"No," she informed him. "I never relax. And by the way. I might as well tell you right now so you can wrap your mind around the concept. There will be no more sex tonight. Zero sex. So forget it. OK? Don't even give me that look. I don't want to see it on your face."

But he didn't obey. That sexy, devastating smile showed no signs of fading. He sawed off a chunk of his *tagliata*, chewed it as he studied her thoughtfully from beneath those hooded eyes, and wiped his mouth with the napkin. "Ah. No?"

"No," she repeated firmly, fending off the urge to repeat herself. Bleating like a fluffy lamb, losing credibility with each repetition.

He sipped his wine. "You seemed to like it," he observed.

"Whether I liked it or not is beside the point. I'm exhausted. I can't face another blitzkrieg. I want sleep. Peace, quiet, and privacy."

"It does not have to be that way," he remarked, his voice bland. "I can be gentle. I can be playful. I can do it any way you want it."

"That's what I'm afraid of," she blurted.

He gazed at her. "You're afraid to find out what you really want?"

That suave, superior air irritated her. "Stop with the fucking psychoanalysis, Val. You're a hit man. Not a shrink."

"I am not a hit man," he said mildly. "But all this talk of sex reminds me of something that I meant to ask you."

She braced herself. "Ask," she said.

"Why no contraception? I would have thought a woman like you would be prepared for anything."

Her hackles rose. "A woman like me?" she repeated slowly. "And just what is that supposed to mean?"

He waved his arm in that eloquent way that only Latin men could without seeming effeminate. "Professional, pragmatic. A risk taker."

She dangled her wineglass between her fingers and considered the novel concept of telling him the flat, unbeautiful truth. She was too tired, too wired, too jet-lagged to sidestep the question.

"I've been celibate for years," she said. "I had every intention of staying that way for the rest of my life. And as such, I didn't see the point in loading my body up with useless artificial hormones."

He looked discreetly shocked. "Really? You? What a waste. It is criminal, the very idea. Why, for the love of God?"

She was about to tell him to piss off and mind his own goddamn business. The words stopped somewhere along the pipeline and petered out into a long silence. "Did you know Kurt Novak?" she asked.

His mouth tightened in disgust. "Unfortunately, yes," he said. "He was vile."

"Yes, he was. And Georg?"

"No better," he said. "Kurt's slobbering lap dog."

"Exactly. I should never have gotten mixed up with them, but I did. I was trying to get revenge for someone Kurt had killed. It blew up in my face."

"I see," he murmured."

She was unable to meet his eyes. "Those two clinched it for me. I was done with men. I thought they were both dead that day that Kurt got killed. I wish I'd checked Georg more closely. I would have been happy to do the honors myself after what he . . . well. Whatever."

"I'm sorry." Val's voice was careful and neutral. "It is terrible."

She stared down at the blank white tablecloth and forced herself to endure silence. If he had oozed practiced sympathy, she'd have thrown it back in his face, but his plain, matter-of-fact comprehension was bearable. She breathed and bore it. For a minute or so. Then the intense, significant silence started driving her mad.

Time to break it and introduce an extreme change of subject.

"My turn to ask the invasive questions," she said crisply. "So tell me, Val. How did you get to be the way you are? I'm dying of curiosity."

He slanted her an amused look. "And how am I?"

"Slick, urbane, charming, well spoken," she said. "The languages, the crazy mind control. Your background doesn't explain any of that. You don't fit the profile of a punch drunk mafiya thug at all."

He twirled *tagliolini* around his fork, his eyes averted. "I was given intensive training from PSS," he said finally. "They invested a fortune in me. But the important things . . . that was all Imre's doing."

She was the one this time to use the silence to refill his glass and prod him to continue. "Your friend? The one who . . ." She stopped, unwilling to invoke the monster and let him take over the conversation.

"Yes," Val said. "The one that I want to save. He welcomed me into his home. *Che Cristo*, he must have had nerves of steel. An illiterate, violent, thieving, louse-ridden, twelve-year-old rent boy. He fed me, played me music, let me sleep in his apartment. I would never risk it myself."

"He must be an unusual person," she said.

"Yes." A faraway smile flashed over his face. "He taught me to use my mind. And about the world outside. He taught me that I might have some value, other than just a . . ." He stopped, shook his head sharply. "Something besides picking pockets, selling cigarettes, dealing drugs. Or sucking cocks in the backseat of a car under a bridge."

Tam was startled. That was the first glimpse of bitterness about the past that he had ever let her see, but that one glimpse hinted at a hidden ocean of it. "So he was the reason that you didn't go under."

"Yes." He stared intently into the bulb of his wineglass as if it were a crystal ball. "He was my refuge. He was . . ." His face contracted. He looked away from her, Adam's apple bobbing.

Tam dropped her gaze to give him privacy. She gazed at the wobbling candle flame and waited for him to break the silence himself.

"I was fortunate to have Imre." His voice sounded halting and forced, as if he was convincing himself. "But for all his efforts, I drag it behind me, like a ten-ton anchor. If he dies, because of me . . ."

And me, Tam thought, but she shoved the thought away. She could not carry Imre on her shoulders, too. She had enough burdens.

"I know what you mean about the anchor," she said.

Val's hand had been inches from hers on the snowy tablecloth, but it had drifted closer. The tip of his finger made contact with hers, the faintest touch possible, yet a shock ran through her. Without any conscious volition on her part, one finger after another made contact with his corresponding ones, lifting until they were palm to palm.

The delicate connection shimmered and glowed. Neither of them acknowledged it with word or glance. It was a tiny miracle that would hide its face in embarrassment if looked at too closely.

"And you?" His eyes met hers, full of somber challenge. "I could ask the same question of you, knowing what I know about your past. About Zetrinja. What made you the way you are?"

She laughed and echoed his own words back to him. "What am I? Besides being a monster pain in the ass, you mean?"

He ignored her teasing. "Brilliant, creative, rich, successful. And powerful. You didn't go under, either."

Not yet, she thought bleakly, thinking of Novak, Georg, Stengl. She shoved the thoughts away and gave his question the consideration it deserved after his own naked honesty.

"I got my strength from what I had before," she said. "My family. Not perfect but . . . wonderful. I knew I had value because they had thought so, even if they were all gone. So I clung to that. And I survived."

They weren't looking at each other at all, now. It was too much. But his fingers slid down between hers and closed, clasping hers. A rush of heat. Exquisite, understated intimacy.

"You are fortunate," he said.

She realized that it was true. Amazingly. Everything was relative. She'd once had something precious. Something he had never known.

"As for the rest of it . . ." She shook her head. "It was random. I didn't care about the scams I ran, the banks I robbed, the men I slept with. I didn't care about getting rich. It just happened. It was like a video game. Robot Bitch, looking for a thrill. So I'm bored? Fine. Depose a dictator or steal twenty million euro, just for laughs. It gets old, though. I got really bored. I just . . . didn't care."

"What do you care about?" he asked.

She thought about it. "Rachel," she said. "My friends. My freedom. My privacy. And my work. I care very much about my work."

"The jewelry? A strange craft for you to choose."

"Not really," she replied. "My father was a metalsmith. I was his apprentice. He was an artist. He should have been a world-renowned designer for the talent he had, but he didn't care about being famous. He just loved the craft. He didn't even care about being paid. Which drove my mother crazy." She smiled at the memory.

"Beauty for beauty's sake alone?" Val offered gently.

"I suppose so," she said.

Val leaned over their clasped hands and dropped a kiss on her knuckle. "Your family was Muslim, then?"

She shrugged. "A mixed marriage. My mother was an Orthodox Christian from Ukraina. She was the one who cared about religion. We celebrated Easter, Christmas. My father just worshipped beauty. And his wife. He adored her."

He kissed her hand again and waited patiently for more.

"They met in Paris." She found herself continuing, for some unknown reason. "He was an adventurer, a wandering rebel. She was an illegal immigrant, working in a garment sweatshop, dreaming of studying someday at the Sorbonne. He was twenty-two, she was nineteen. He was beautiful, she was beautiful—"

"I do not wonder at it," he said.

"They fell madly in love," she continued. "I was born. They had no money. Then my grandfather got sick and called my father home. We went to Zetrinja to see him, and we never left the place. Until Colonel Drago Stengl of the JNA and his secret death squad came marching in."

His hand tightened over hers. She clung to it.

"It was so ironic," she whispered. "He was the gentlest man I ever knew. I hardly ever heard him raise his voice, for my whole childhood. And they executed him. Just stood him up and shot him for being a paramilitary. Can you believe it? Him, a fucking paramilitary. God."

Her heart started to race, stomach rolling as she stared down at the oil on her plate, the flecks of chopped parsley. The red, juicy chunk of Val's steak. Her blood pressure was dropping.

Enough. She had already told him more than she'd ever told any other living person.

She jerked her hand out from under his, breaking the spell. "I don't want to talk about it anymore," she said tightly. "Let's get back to business. Do you know where we can get some decent firepower around here? I don't like being on the same continent with that filthy scum without a gun. Or two, or three."

"I agree completely. A friend of mine is in Salerno, arranging it for us," he said. "We will meet with him tomorrow."

"Good. Get me a Glock 9mm or a SIG .357, with a good supply of ammo and spare cartridges. I want a Ruger for backup. A shoulder holster, an ankle holster and a hip strap, if he can find one. I also want some plastique for the bomblets. I don't need much."

He nodded, sipping his wine. "I will see what I can do."

"You do that." Their conversation about the past had killed what appetite she'd had. She pushed her half-finished plate away. "I'm done."

They were silent as they walked back to the hotel. Tam prepared herself psychologically should he try to take her hand again. She couldn't quite tell if she was relieved or disappointed when he did not.

Back at the room, she wasted no time getting ready for sleep, and slid beneath the rumpled covers. "What's the plan for tomorrow?"

"We have an appointment with Donatella Amato and Ana Santarini, at ten thirty tomorrow morning," he told her. "At Ana's house near Positano. Then, we make our plan, based on what Henry tells us tomorrow, and our own observations."

A shiver racked her, the chill touch of the past. Like an animated corpse's finger on the back of her neck. Then he began to strip off his clothing, and every coherent thought fled from her head.

"Hey!" she said. "Janos!"

He wrenched off his shirt, peeling the sleeves off his thick muscled arms. "Call me Val, for the love of God. *Sì?*"

"I want to sleep alone," she said pointedly. "I told you that."

He looked around the room in mock dismay. "But there is only one bed."

"Whose fault is that? I didn't book the room, bozo."

He stripped off his pants, leaving only black briefs that outlined his manly package. She wrenched her gaze away.

"But I wanted this room. I wanted the beautiful view and the loggia for you." He gave her a brazen, deal-with-it grin and slid into bed with her. "Rest easy. I will not come on to you." He stretched out his long body, folding his arms back behind his head. "Relax and sleep," he urged. "Tomorrow you must be sharp to meet this Santarini woman."

Tam hunched up against the headboard, hugging her knees to her chest. "I already have met her."

Val sat bolt upright. "Met her?" He sounded outraged. "*Che cazzo dici?* This is terrible! You did not tell me that!"

"You didn't ask," Tam said.

"But will she recognize you?" he demanded. "We cannot risk—"

"No. She won't recognize me. It was sixteen years ago. I had puppy fat, shorter hair, a different nose. I've had cosmetic surgery, more than once. My eye color will be different. My energy is different. And Ana is so self-absorbed, she'll never make the connection."

He leaned back, mollified. "Hmmph. How do you know her?"

This subject was on her short list of the last things on earth that she wanted to talk about, but it seemed stupid to refuse. She'd already shared details from the past in the restaurant, without breaking down, or triggering a stress flashback. Thank God.

She composed herself. She could do this. Cool, methodical. A list of events as they occurred, no digressing, no expanding.

"I was Stengl's mistress for a few months," she said.

Val went rigid. He slowly turned, staring down at her. Shocked.

"His mistress?" he said. "After what he—after your family—"

"My father was shot with the rest of the men and boys that day." She recited the facts in a leaden voice. "My mother and little sister and I were taken to Sremska Mitrovica. The concentration camp. It was a filthy shithole. Irina died first. A flu of some kind. The diarrhea carried her off. Then my mother, though I'm not sure it was flu that killed her. I think she'd just had enough."

"Ah, Tamar," he whispered. "I did not know. I am sorry."

"I caught his eye, somehow," Tam continued grimly. "I don't know how I could have attracted anyone, as filthy as I was. They never let us bathe in that place. But he noticed me. He pulled me out, took me to Titograd. Installed me in a hotel room to play with in his off-hours. There was no one left to notice or care what happened to me. They were all dead." She stared down at her hands, twisting the sheet. "I was locked in that room for weeks. Months, maybe. In limbo. I lost track of time."

Val rolled back onto his side, propping his head on his hand. "Go on," he prompted quietly.

"When he was done with what he'd come to accomplish, he still wasn't quite done with me," she said. "He brought me back to his house in Belgrade. Ana was living there. She was nineteen. She loathed me. She acted like a jealous wife. I think he'd probably had his sick fun with her, too. She had the vibe of a girl who had been used in that way. His wife had been dead for years, and he was just that kind of man."

"*Che schifo,*" Val murmured.

She looked away. "I was all right. In fact, I have Ana to thank for the concept of wearable weaponry. She put the idea into my head."

The look on his face was almost dread. "Oh? How is that?"

"She cooked up a stupid plot to get rid of me," Tam said. "Persuaded one of her boyfriends to come in and have sex with me while she took pictures. She wanted to show them to her father, to show him what a nasty tart I was, I suppose. Lame, in terms of a plan. She wasn't what I would call creative. But it backfired on her."

He shifted on the bed, his eyes intent and fascinated. "*Sì?* How?"

"I had a pin brooch that had belonged to my mother," she said. "A cheap thing, cubic zirconium. When I was locked in, I would just sit and hold it in my hand. I was holding it when Ana and her friend came in. When he tried to rape me, I fought back. I got in a lucky jab. Pierced his scrotum. You cannot even imagine the sounds that he made."

Val's horrified flinch could be felt through the bed frame.

"He got blood poisoning," Tam said, with dark satisfaction.

Val hissed through his teeth. "Did he . . . lose his . . . ?"

"I never found out. I hope so," Tam said. "He deserved to. Ana didn't bother me again. And Stengl got tired of me soon after that."

"What happened then?"

"Aren't you just full of questions?" she grumbled. "Shut up and let me sleep, why don't you? We've got a big day tomorrow."

"Please tell me, Tamar," he said softly.

She sighed. "He passed me on to one of his subordinates. It was all sort of a blur to me. Up to that point. That was when I started to sharpen up. I realized that I had to start choosing my lovers. Trading up, instead of down. Or I'd get passed lower and lower in the pecking order every time until I lost all my status as a sex object. That's bad. That's when you get used up and tossed onto the scrap heap."

He nodded, with perfect understanding. "So you did? Start choosing?"

"Of course. It's all in the attitude. I learned fast. Men are simple, basic creatures. Not that hard to manage." She paused, eyed him for a moment and amended her statement. "For the most part, anyway. Now shut up. My throat hurts from talking so much."

She clicked off her bedside lamp. A moment of silence in the dark, and Val scooted toward her. To her horror, he gathered her into his arms. She stiffened, in spite of how good he felt. How hot and strong.

"Damnit, Janos," she growled. "You're pushing me. I told you—"

"You did," he agreed. "And call me Val."

"I do not want to—"

"I know. I heard you the first time. I am not trying to seduce you. I just want to embrace you after what you told me. I cannot help it."

"Thanks for the thought, but I'm not comfortable with—"

"Give it a chance," he coaxed. "I know you can. I've seen you do it. Just pretend that I am Rachel."

That made her laugh. "Ah, Val? There are a couple of really noticeable differences between you and Rachel. They're hard to miss."

"Perhaps, but the basic principles are the same." He tugged her closer, massaging her shoulder. "Just hold me," he wheedled, his voice a teasing caress. "Put my head under your chin, rub my back. Say sweet tender things to me when I wake in the night and feel frightened."

Her laughter was nervous this time. "You wish. I've had a long day, and my sense of humor wasn't great to begin with. Being mauled by a naked spy who smells like a French whore is not my idea of—"

"Shhh. Just let me hold you. Think about Rachel. It is not so hard to hold her, no?"

"That's different," she snapped. "I love her."

A hole yawned in her insides. As if her sudden revelation could somehow endanger Rachel. She winced inwardly. Ah, God. She was so fucked up, it was embarrassing.

"That's the trick, then," he encouraged her. "Just pretend that you love me."

Those words hit her someplace deep, like an ice pick sinking in. She stiffened, bracing against the awful pain of it.

"Fuck, no," she whispered. "No tricks. No pretending. That's worse than nothing, and you ought to goddamn well know it, you flip son of a bitch." Her voice quavered off. It was happening again.

She buried her face in the pillow and tried in vain to stop it. It was like trying to stop a landslide.

Val curled himself around her like a big, warm animal, patting her back and kissing her nape as she gave in to the storm of silent sobbing. "Forgive me," he murmured. "I spoke without thinking. I am sorry. For all of it."

"I'm not crying because of that," she snarled, but the soggy words became garbled. She was dismayed to realize that she was. She really was. And that was not good news. That was a lot of unshed tears. Way more than they had time to cope with. They had too much work to do.

Ah, hell. Maybe it would scare him out of her bed, she thought with a spark of vindictive amusement. Served him right for dragging up the past. Getting her all whipped up into a frenzy. Invasive jerk.

But he did not leave. He just cuddled her. He tucked her head under his chin, stroked her back, and murmured sweet, senseless, tender things in a jumbled soup of languages.

When the deluge finally moved through her and passed on, it left her beaten to the ground. Too exhausted to object to the fact that even after all the tears, the drama, the sneaky bastard still dared to pretend that he loved her.

Chapter
17

Tam's eyes fluttered open to a scene of perfect beauty. She blinked, disoriented. She was in a baroque painting. Arches, sky. Clouds glowing a delicate pink, lit by the sunrise. The morning star glittering in the vault of pale blue and gold. All that was missing were the cherubs cavorting.

Her body felt so soft, so warm . . . ah. That would explain it. Beneath the thick wool blankets, she was wrapped in Val's arms.

It was the first time in her life that she had awakened in a man's arms without stiffening and trying to establish her personal space again as soon as possible.

This morning, she was in absolutely no hurry. She could happily stay just like this. A little moment of stolen peace. She wanted it to last and last.

She gazed at his sleeping face. Slumber soothed the rough edges, the lines of stress and strain. He looked vulnerable.

She didn't want him to be vulnerable. She had enough problems. Let him be tough as razor wire, steel spikes, boot leather. Let him look out for himself, for God's sake.

But her hand hovered over the contours of his face, taking in every detail. Each scar, the shape of his bones, the strength of his jaw. Each line and hair. Her finger almost touched his cheek, close enough to stroke its fuzzy nap without touching him, feeling his vital heat.

His sleeping face looked so young. She thought of his bleak childhood. It clutched her heart, how strong he was, how uncomplaining. How fragile.

I wasn't always this big.

It made her jaw clench painfully to think of anyone hurting the vulnerable boy that he had been.

She cuddled closer. Her skin was so sensitive every brush of contact was a kiss, a deliberate caress. There was a throbbing glow in her belly and heart, a quivering tightness in her throat. Hot eyes. Her face wore an expression she'd never felt before. She wondered if she'd recognize herself in the mirror. She was afraid to look.

She didn't want to call it happiness. That implied too much idiocy on her part. It was more like a kind of madness. But so lovely. So soft.

She should squash it. She knew how to suppress painful emotions. It had to be easier to kill beautiful ones. They were more delicate. The urge was almost automatic—but she suspended it, breathing deep to catch it, like the vanishing smell of a violet. So easily banished or lost.

Her fingertips gave in to temptation. She finally did touch his cheek, enjoying the supple heat of his skin. She studied the hollow of his throat, the tendons in his neck. The dramatic sweep of his eyebrows, each dark hair a pen stroke that emphasized his masculine beauty.

There was an ugly, recent scar twisting across the thick front part of his shoulder. A bullet wound, not the one he'd suffered on the bus. Her fingers hovered over it and moved away. Scar tissue could be extremely sensitive.

His eyes had opened. She felt a jolt of alarm, as if she'd been caught doing something for which she would be punished.

But his eyes did not mock her. They mirrored her own. Full of wonder.

He drew in a breath. Without meaning to, she touched her finger to his lips to silence him. Whatever he might say could ruin it. The moment was as fragile as a snowflake or a curling whorl of smoke. One of a kind, never again. Utterly improbable.

Let it breathe, unfold. Let it just exist for a while before they cheapened it with blunt words and hard realities. Please. Just a little pink and gold dawn fantasy. It wasn't so much to ask, she told herself rebelliously. She might never feel this way again in her life. In fact, she might not even have a life. No, it was not so goddamn much to ask.

She made do with so little. She never let herself complain.

His lips were so soft against her hand. The warm rose blush of them against her finger was a miracle of nature. He clasped her palm, cradling it inside his own, and kissed her fingers. He turned it and kissed her palm. Reverently. As if her hand were a precious, holy reliquary. As if kissing it could grant power and redemption.

Their lips brushed. A glancing touch, so soft, it was more like a thought. The kiss bloomed sweetly, slowly. Their bodies melded.

Fear clawed inside her, and lost. She wanted to get inside him, she wanted him to be inside her. She wanted to see and know him, to be seen and known. All of her, all of him. The bitter and the sweet.

She climbed on top of him, flinging off the nightshirt. She welcomed the dawn chill against her hot skin. Her skin just perceived the coolness as another caress, and Val had heat to spare, blazing beneath her. So big and powerful. She straddled him, positioning his stiff penis carefully, adjusting the angle, then closed her eyes and flung her head back with a sigh of delight as she sank down, enveloping his beautiful, enormous cock into herself. She felt so tight and full, she could barely move at first, but she melted into him and found a way.

There was no awkwardness, no anger. They clasped each other's hands for balance, seeking the perfect angles, the perfect rhythm of sliding, surging dance. Pleasure licked up her every nerve, flames leaping and dancing for joy. She touched his face, exploring with her fingers. He reached up and touched her face. Their eyes locked.

Amazed at the startling grace of it. The unexpected gift.

She climaxed several long, lovely, melting times before she realized that he would not come himself. She had not put latex on him.

He would just serve her with his big, hot, beautiful male body, for as long as she pleased, however long it took. She loved his control. She slid off his rigid shaft, wiggling down his stunning body to take him in her mouth, and give back some measure of what he had given her.

He didn't take long. He was primed. His climax jerked through him, and he spurted into her mouth. She held him there until all the wrenching pleasure had coursed through him and left him trembling and limp.

She crawled back up to sprawl on top of him, chest to chest.

He opened his mouth. "Tamar, I—"

"No." She stopped him instinctively.

He looked frustrated. "But I did not expect for—"

"Me neither. But we can't talk about it. There's nothing to talk about yet, Val. We can't make any promises or any plans. You can't make any melodramatic declarations. We have a job to do. So don't even say it. Don't even start."

His mouth tightened. He looked mutinous. "But we—"

"No." She put her finger on his mouth, and was so pleased by the way his lips felt, she kept it there, caressing the softness and the warmth. She went on. "I will tell you what happens now. We put this thing between us, exactly as it is, into a strongbox with an encrypted lock. We hide the box and keep it safe while we go out there and do our jobs. If we both survive, we come back after and see if something is still alive inside that box. And we deal with it then."

He frowned. "Things don't live in locked boxes."

"Strong things might linger for a while." She tilted her head to the side and gave him a sly smile. "It also gives you some wiggle room. Think about what you really want. Me, Rachel. We're a pair, and you know us by now. We're complicated chicks. A huge pain in the ass, times two. Difficult. Expensive. High maintenance. Lots of big, hairy issues. Think about it long and hard, loverboy. Long and hard."

His dark eyes narrowed with that look that pierced through all her walls. "You cannot intimidate me," he said. "Do not try. It bores me."

God forbid. She made a scoffing noise, but she was smiling inside. Secretly loving it that she could not intimidate him.

She slid off his body, and off the bed. "Anyhow, it's time to get ready," she said, turning away. "The box is closed. So's the subject."

She pawed through her limited wardrobe choices, seeking just the right look to encounter that spoiled bitch Ana. At least Tam assumed she was still a spoiled bitch after sixteen years. Time did not tend to improve people. Particularly the bad ones.

She concluded that her best bet would be chic, armored, but not particularly sexy. The sleek gray tailored suit with the nipped-in jacket and the flaring trouser legs over a black silk blouse. Bounty from her pirate's raid. A good, understated foil for the poison horn necklace, the multiblade Liv ring and her sleep-shooting earrings. There was room for a gun, too, beneath the jacket, should she ever get lucky enough to score one. Contacts, to turn her eyes a smoky gray. A dab of powder to accentuate her pallor, a smudged lining of black eyeliner and mascara, for that harsh, dangerous air, good for the jewelry presentation. The cute black half boots, and she'd done the best she could with the materials she had to work with.

She'd pretended to ignore Val as he got ready, not even allowing herself to watch him shave, though he'd left the bathroom door open and done it in the nude. Shameless exhibitionist.

She waited to ogle him until he was safely dressed in his habitual uniform; black over black, a charcoal dress shirt, black jeans, black jacket, gleaming boots. As usual, he smelled amazing. His strong, sculpted jaw looked baby smooth. She had to force herself not to yank his face down to stroke and sniff. She'd probably end up tossing him on the bed again, and they didn't have time to play.

They stopped in the dining room on Val's insistence. Tam sipped an espresso while he inhaled cornetti, salami and cheese sandwiches, hard-boiled eggs, coffee cake, and God alone knew what all else. She rolled her eyes through the inevitable lecture about her not eating enough, cut mercifully short by a chime from his cell phone. He clicked on the message.

"Henry will meet us at a *stazione di servizio* on the Autostrada," he told her. "Thirty kilometers from here."

They were very quiet on the Autostrada, speaking in short, terse phrases of practical things. Acting like colleagues, not lovers. His tone was polite and distant, his teasing charm gone. She missed it.

She had only herself to blame, though. She was the one who had mandated that they lock all tender emotions in a box. But not to kill them. Oh, God, no. To protect them, rather. To keep them off the gunnery range for as long as possible. To give them a fighting chance.

They might die anyway, she reflected bleakly. Things so often did.

Henry Berne, Val's friend, was waiting for them in the dining room of the Autogrill restaurant, sipping a cappucino. He rose to his feet when they approached, eyes widening appreciatively as he checked her out. He was a handsome man, huge and muscular, square jawed, barrel chested and blue eyed, the classic American football player type. Inches taller than Val, even. They shook hands. His accent as they murmured introductions marked him as American, from the Midwest, although accents could deceive. Her own often did.

They sat down at the table. Berne's eyes lingered on her in the silence that settled over them before getting down to business. He cast a speculative glance at her, then at Val.

"I could have met you at your hotel, for breakfast," Berne said, his voice neutral. "Getting nervous, Val? You don't even want your friends to know where you're sleeping? What, dontcha trust me?"

Val shrugged, unoffended. "Just being careful. You must not take it personally. Surely you are not getting your feelings hurt."

"Me? Fuck, no."

"Good," Val said in a businesslike tone. "What have you got for me?"

"Not a lot. Two days isn't long enough to do surveillance. But I already heard the rumors about Stengl rotting away in a luxury clinic, so it makes sense that it's near his daughter. And this place here looks promising." Berne pulled a file out of a battered briefcase and pushed it across the table. He opened it, and tapped an address scribbled on a scrap paper-clipped to some photos.

"Yesterday and the day before, she went to this address outside

Nocera at around five o'clock," he said. "It's a private clinic. High security, no advertisement, no information available on the Internet." He plucked out a photo, and tapped it. "There's the entrance. Biometric security. I've seen a retina scan machine and a full palm and five fingerprint lock. There's no going in without Ana herself, unless you want to bring one of her eyes and one of her hands with you."

"Messy," Val observed.

"Yeah, a little. She stayed for more than an hour both times."

Tam stared at the photo. At this distance, it was hard to be sure that the woman with her back to the camera was Ana, presenting her hand to the palm lock. But Tam couldn't rule it out, either.

There it was, a direct link to the worst nightmares of her past. And she felt nothing as she stared at that frozen image. How odd.

She dragged her attention back to the men's conversation.

"Take care," Berne was saying quietly. "Word is out that you are persona non grata. There's money to be had in telling them where you are or even where you've been. Don't stay in one place for long."

Val's face was shuttered. "Just long enough to do what needs to be done."

Berne passed another scrap of paper across the table to Val. "Come to this address in Salerno today. I've arranged for some goodies for you. Hope you have a big budget. This guy's not cheap."

"Not a problem." Val tucked it into his jacket. "Thank you. As soon as we conclude this matter, I will be contacting you for the details, of our next adventure."

"I can hardly wait." Berne turned his gaze to her and gave her a knowing smile that bugged her. Who the hell did he think he was, anyway? What did he think he knew about her just from ogling? She gave him a dazzling smile and watched his face go blank.

She didn't like him, but that meant very little, since she tended not to like men at all as a rule. Except for the McCloud Crowd. Though 'like' was the wrong word, considering how intensely they annoyed her. She trusted them, rather. Which she supposed implied liking.

And she really liked Val. Which she supposed implied trust.

God help her. She was actually starting to trust the man. It gave her the shivers. This emotional stuff was way too complicated for a cold bitch like herself.

". . . to go? It is time we moved, Tamar."

She wrenched her attention back to the two men, who were looking at her oddly. Berne rose to his feet and slapped Val's shoulder, jerking his chin toward her. "Watch yourself, buddy," he muttered.

Watch yourself, her ass. Watch out for what? Tam observed the guy walk out with unfriendly eyes.

"You trust him?" she murmured to Val.

He slanted her a wry glance. "Yes. He's saved my life more than once. And I have returned the favor. We have been friends for years."

"But you didn't tell him what hotel we were in."

"It is no reflection upon him." Val shrugged. "Caution is a habit. And I like to keep things as simple as possible. It makes the process of elimination easier. It is a protection for him, too. PSS is his life."

"But not yours?" she inquired.

He gazed straight back at her, unsmiling. "Not mine."

It was a perfect day for a drive up the twists and turns of the Amalfi coast. Tam felt a funny tug inside herself, an odd longing to take a step out of time, a vacation from reality. Just to give her a chance to take a deep breath and enjoy this man, this place. There was a glowing sparkle to the air, even in winter. The place seemed soaked with light: the craggy, pale rocks, the scrubby silver-green foliage that clung to them, the verdant stairsteps of terraced gardens, the ancient white villages hanging precipitously over the sea.

But time raced relentlessly forward. In too short a time, they had reached the home of Ana Santarini. It was an exquisitely restored Renaissance-era *masseria* perched on the crest of a hill overlooking the sea. A wrought iron gate hummed aside to let them in, and they drove down a road bounded by ancient stonework. On one side, there was a sheer drop to the brilliant blue sea; on the other, an orchard of olive trees centuries old, each one like a gnarled goblin statue.

That bitch Ana had done well for herself, Tam reflected. Although one needed a look at the mafioso husband to be sure it was worth it.

A big, grim-faced man stopped them at the end of the driveway, looked them over, and showed them where to park. They were led into the house and left in a large, lovely salon with vaulted ceilings painted with original frescos, and decorated with priceless antiques. An enormous veranda looked out over the sea.

A woman stood by the window, dramatically posed, ass jutting out. She turned at their entrance and flashed a calculating glance at Tam before wrapping a dazzling smile of welcome across her face. Not Ana. This was a striking thirty-something. Fake redhead. Lots of makeup, fake tits, and big, rolling green eyes. Must be Donatella.

Tam hated her on sight. She sensed that the feeling was mutual.

The creature flung herself at Val. "Valerio! *Amore*. At last," she purred. "You look wonderful, *tesoro*." Her eyes flicked to Tam and then back to Val. "And you smell . . . as good as ever. Mmm, *delizioso*."

Tam watched Donatella do the Italian two-kiss choreography, then cup Val's face in her hands, gaze adoringly into his eyes, fling her head back, and give him three more. Smack, smack, smack.

Tam's hackles rose. My, how very, very friendly Val and Donatella were. Old pals. Touching. It would have irritated the living shit out of her, had she not been distracted by the second woman, who appeared in the doorway at that moment. Tam's stomach lurched, abruptly.

Oh, yes. It was Ana, all right. Looking better than Tam might have hoped. Black hair swept into an elegant roll, her buxom figure shown off by a simple black sheath dress. Her ass was a bit on the large side, but the shelf of her surgically enhanced bosom balanced it out. She'd had some work done on her forehead and neck that made her look weirdly smooth and taut under her makeup, like a television personality.

Ana ignored Tam completely as she watched Donatella crawling all over Val. It was clear from her face that she was accustomed to being the center of attention. As such, Donatella was not her favorite person.

Huh. Tam could relate. Donatella's spike-clawed nails dragged possessively over Val's chest, palpating. Tam's own nails dug into her palms.

Well, well. Val hadn't said anything about having fucked this Donatella woman. Not that Tam had any right or reason to be annoyed if he had, but still. Her lip curled involuntarily. That petulant, pinheaded, plastic slut? How had he gotten through it without fainting from boredom?

Men were such indiscriminate pigs. She did the introduction routine, shaking both women's cool, manicured, diamond-laden hands, and kept her smiling mask riveted in place. Ignoring the *die, bitch* vibes that were ricocheting wildly all over the room.

". . . permit me to introduce you to Ms. Steele, the artist behind the designs," Val was saying, smiling and making no effort to extricate himself from Donatella's tentacles.

Donatella and Ana swiveled their perfectly coiffed heads in unison and cast identical cool glances over Tam.

"Oh, yes, of course," Ana said. "Donatella has been telling me about your jewelry. Very intriguing. You're not at all what I expected."

Tam smiled sweetly, eyes big, and refrained from asking what Ana had expected. She was entirely uninterested in what went on in Ana's empty head.

Then Ana surprised her by frowning and taking a closer look.

"Have we met?" she asked.

Val's smile froze. His eyes flicked to hers, alarmed.

Tam shook her head. "I'm sure I would remember," she said.

Ana preened. "I imagine you would," she said, dismissing the matter with a wave of her crimson claws.

But Donatella had now been languishing for too many seconds off of center stage. "Valerio, you are an angel for arranging this for me," she broke in. "And a private showing, too. I've been dying to lay my hands on some of these pieces."

"Actually, it's not the wearer who is supposed to die," Tam pointed out helpfully. "If all goes well, that is. There is an element of risk that has to be considered."

Donatella's blank look turned into a fuck-you smile. "Of course."

"Is there a table where I can lay them out for you?" Tam asked.

Things proceeded smoothly from that point. For all Ana's glaring shortcomings as a human being, and all Donatella's stomach-turning grabs at Val, the women were dream customers. Deep pockets, limitless self-indulgence, an absolute sense of entitlement plus a pinch of competition all added up to big, big sales. The not so subtle one-upmanship probably prodded the two women to buy three times as many pieces as each one would have on her own. It was a possible sales technique that she'd never considered.

Not that she'd ever use it. Women like these annoyed her too much. Forced to spend time with them, she would feel like killing them. Problematic, killing your customers. Word got around. Bad for business.

That was one of the reasons she esteemed the McCloud Crowd women. Not one of them were cat bitches, pretty though they all were.

Tam wondered if the sales would go through. It depended on the timing. She could make two hundred thousand bucks, and in these complicated days, she could use the cash. But hey, she had a date with destiny to kill this woman's father. It wouldn't do to get greedy.

"Usually, I just leave instructions on how to arm the pieces on a password-protected Internet bulletin board," Tam explained. "But for special customers like you, I'll make an exception. I still need to obtain the explosives and the poisons. I'll come back another day and show you personally how to arm them."

"How soon?" Ana's eyes glittered with eagerness, and suddenly, Tam wondered about the woman's relationship with her husband.

"Tomorrow?" Val suggested. "At four o'clock?"

Ana frowned. "Four o'clock is not good for me," she said. "I have an appointment at five. Can you come earlier?"

"Three?" Tam offered.

"Very well. I will expect you tomorrow at three." Ana gave her a sugary smile. "I assume you prefer cash?"

"If possible. And you might consider dismissing the domestic staff for the day," Tam said. "So we can have privacy to speak freely."

"I'll see to it," Ana assured her.

They exchanged bright, glittering fuck-you smiles once again.

Donatella broke in. "And when can we meet to arm mine?" she

demanded petulantly. "I need my jewelry armed soon." Her voice dropped, and her eyes flicked toward Val. "I will need them, to keep a certain tall, dark, and handsome lover in his proper place. In Paris."

Paris? What the fuck was that about?

Tam made an appointment with the woman for the following week, but such was her feeling of unreality, she did not even note the time or date they agreed upon. The information just came out of her mouth and then floated out of her head. Who knew if the appointment would take place? She could die a horrible death by that day.

But who knew from one minute to the next when death would pounce? It was always a rude surprise. Who could have imagined that hot August morning that her family had gotten up. A morning like any other. Breakfast like any other. Laughing and teasing and squabbling.

But that had been it. The last day. The last morning. The last breakfast. Who knew?

The high-pitched, empty-headed chatter of the two women faded in her mind. The sound of hens clucking. Faraway dogs barking. The distance between herself and the rest of the world widened into a vast buffer of awful silence. She was utterly alone, sealed inside it.

Tomorrow she was going to find out once and for all if revenge could make any difference. Ghosts clustered around her: Mamma, her father, and Irina standing next to her, clutching Tam's knee with her chubby, dimpled ghost hand. Her liquid dark eyes so uncannily like Rachel's eyes. She'd been barely two when—

No. Not now. No fits. Not in front of Ana and Donatella.

Tam shut her eyes and saw the dirt scattering into their wide-open eyes. Her ears were starting to roar, her heart to pound.

She tried to tune into the hens clucking, dogs barking, just to grab onto something else. Focus on anything else. Anything at all.

". . . so we can eat late," Donatella was cooing into Val's ear, in a tone Tam was not meant to overhear. "The cook at La Cantinola will be happy to cook for us, even after eleven o'clock. I'm a special client. And there's a lovely room above La Cantinola, with a sea view . . ."

Listen to that. Brazen slut. Trying to coax Val into meeting her for dinner and a quickie.

Val, to his credit, was wiggling like an eel, vacillating between lavish compliments and careful excuses. But the bitch's hands were all over him. And he was not pushing them off.

The anger helped. It made that sick, sinking feeling back off.

Good. Anger worked, so she embraced it. Bastard. Dog. *Porcone.* He would pay for that, later. In blood.

The atmosphere in the car for the drive back to San Vito was sub-zero. Tam did not even look at him, she just stared straight ahead, radiating a bone-chilling cold with more vicious intensity than he'd ever felt from a woman. Or at least, that he'd ever bothered to notice.

"Would you tell me my crime?" he demanded finally, when they were approaching the San Vito exit.

"No crime," she said, her voice cool, toneless. "I just can't imagine how you actually managed to go through with it, that's all."

"With what?" he demanded. Although he knew.

She shot him a glance that indicated that she knew that he knew and did not appreciate his dissembling.

He sighed and offered it up. "It was some years ago. I was undercover. Investigating a smuggling ring. Her husband was involved. She was angry at him. I needed info. It was unavoidable."

"Oh, really? I suppose you fought, tooth and claw," she said.

"No. I did my job," he said stiffly. "Just as you have always done."

"Oh, so now we're throwing whore darts, are we?"

He shook his head. "It was not particularly memorable," he said flatly. "Nor was it altogether unpleasant. I have no burning desire to repeat the experience. It did facilitate my job."

"Works with me, too, eh? Smooth, Val. Fucking your targets into boneless submission. What a trick."

"Bullshit," he spat out. "After this morning, you know that is not true."

"How do I know that? With a man as slick and smooth and pretty as you, how could I possibly know that for sure? Gigolo Janos. So you have a date to meet her in Paris, hmm? If you want to go meet her for dinner and cunnilingus tonight at La Cantinola, please feel free."

He pulled into the hotel parking, muttering obscenities, and grabbed her jewelry case. "Come," he snarled. "I will walk you to the hotel, and then I must go to Salerno." He had planned to keep her close to him, but not in this mood. They would end up killing each other.

She jerked the jewelry case out of his hand. "You remember my shopping list?"

"Of course."

"Then there's no need to escort me through a crowded parking lot." She slammed out of the car. "I can escort myself."

He loped after her and jerked her shoulder around. "Do not be an idiot."

"Why not? Seems like it hasn't put you off before."

He seized her shoulders. "You are playing games, Tamar. Stop it."

"Don't maul me, you oaf—"

"It is stupid and out of character for you to be so angry about my past professional dealings with a woman like that. You are using this as an excuse, no? You would rather be angry at me and jealous about Donatella than feel whatever it is you are really feeling. No? About your past, your family? Ana or Stengl?"

The fight went out of her, and the color drained out of her face. "No," she whispered. "Don't try to psychoanalyze me."

"Then do not cry out for a fucking diagnosis. You are acting like a child. If you need distraction from the way you are feeling, I will come to the room with you now and give you one that you will never forget."

She stumbled away, grabbing the stonework railing that led up to the hotel entrance. "No," she said unsteadily. "We have work to do."

"Then go do it," he said harshly. "I will distract you when I get back. At great length. Count upon it."

She scurried up the stairs, disappearing into the lobby of the hotel. Val stared after her, his face hot. He was half tempted to follow her up and make good on his promise, here and now. She would protest and fight and scratch and bite, like always . . . but then . . . ah, *Dio.*

He went back to the car, clenching and unclenching his hands to unload the tension. And the guilt.

He had to edit and send another piece of footage, the one from that morning, to Novak. This was killing him. It got worse every day.

He got into the car, booted up, attached the thin cable. Downloaded the footage. He watched it and relived it. The way she moved, the light shining off her body. Her hands, touching his hair, his face. Her back to the camera, slender and straight as a blade, the perfect curve of her hips swelling out as she straddled him.

His own face to the camera, his feelings revealed. Transfixed by her beauty.

He cut out as much of it as he could and still satisfy the filthy old satyr, and was trying to connect to the Web when the split second realization came to him. Air moved in the car that should not move. Tiny movements, plays of light and shadow, out of place. He froze.

A small sound. *No.* He reached for a gun that was not there.

Too late. A cold circle of metal pressed against the nape of his neck.

"Hello, Janos," Hegel said.

Chapter
18

Tam stood by the door, people swirling around her, and watched Val's tall, broad shouldered form stride briskly back to the parking lot.

Anxiety clawed at her. A presentiment of doom. She wanted to run after him, grab his hand, beg him to stay close.

Grow the fuck up. He'd been right to call her on that silly tantrum about Donatella. He'd nailed her right to the wall. His specialty.

God knows, what he'd done with Donatella was nothing she hadn't done herself. Get-it-over-with sex to further whatever other agenda she might have. Like staying alive, for instance.

But she had to pull herself together, get back to work. She needed to organize her poison and drug supplies for tomorrow's charade with Ana. Devise a plan for getting into the clinic and decide what she would do once she got there. She had to be smart, focused, ruthless.

She ran up the stairs. When she turned out of the staircase into the corridor, two men waited. Guns appeared suddenly in their hands.

"Don't move," one of them said.

They flanked her, seized her by both arms. A pistol jabbed, brutally hard, into the small of her back. She refused to gasp at the pain. The faces of the two men were unreadable. "Who—"

"Quiet," one of them hissed.

They dragged her to the end of the corridor and into the emergency stairwell, then up two flights. They stopped outside the first door in the hall. One of them rapped on it.

"Come in," said a familiar voice. The door opened.

Georg sat on the bed facing her, his legs wide, his hands on his knees. His ruined teeth had been capped. Their bright, unnatural whiteness gave his predatory grin a surreal effect.

Georg barked out orders in Hungarian for his men to leave. Tam was left standing before him, clutching her briefcase and purse. Forcing herself to smile. She hid her fear with the ease of long, hard practice.

He looked better than he had four years ago. He'd been a bald, scarred monstrosity during her nightmare sojourn with Kurt Novak. Since then, the scars on his face had been smoothed out with surgery and time. Instead of the twisting, ropy red worms crawling over his face, the scars were thin, silvery irregularities in his pallid skin. He looked like a man whose face had been taken apart and put back together not quite straight. One side of his mouth pulled up in a permanent smirk; one of his eye sockets was smaller than the other, the eyelid pulled too tight. His hair was buzz cut very short. He was thin, his prominent cheekbones blade sharp. His electric blue eyes glowed hot in deep eye sockets, like the headlights of a car in the dark.

A car that was about to run her down.

She sensed the vicious strength of his madness. She saw it in his eyes, his smile. It had started before she met him, and it had ripened to fullness since then. Her skin crawled. Her mouth was dry.

"Georg," she said warmly. "What an unexpected pleasure. I had no idea you were still alive."

Right. Such a delightful surprise. As if she hadn't been dragged at gunpoint to his door. Whatever.

"I almost wasn't," he said. "I was confined to a prison hospital for almost a year. Old Novak got me out."

"That was good of him," she said. "And I never knew."

His smile widened. "You couldn't have known. You would have

found a way to come to me. After what we shared, I was sure of that."

She funneled her shudder of disgust expertly into another burst of projected warmth. "And how did you know that?"

"Because of what you did for me." He said the words as if it should be obvious.

Hmm. This was a puzzle. As far as Tam knew, she had tried with every effort at her disposal to kill his scrawny, milk white ass. Under the circumstances, however, it seemed unwise to say so. Bursting his mad fantasy bubble would seal her doom. She was in no rush for that.

"And what exactly did I do?" She ventured a secret smile, as if they were playing a flirtatious game.

Georg smiled back. "You did for me what I was too weak to do for myself. Kurt was so strong, I could not see past his strength to realize my own. But you saw it. You saw my potential."

"Yes," she said obediently. "Yes, I did."

"It was meant for me!" Georg waved his arm around. "The money, the power, the whole empire! But I would never have been anything but Kurt's servant if you had not freed me."

A deep breath. She took the plunge. "It was a huge risk," she said slowly. "But in the end, it was worth it. Look what you have become."

"I am grateful," he said solemnly. "I nearly died for it, but thanks to you, it was Kurt that died. And you are like his widow. You were born to rule at the emperor's side, but instead of being Kurt's consort, you were meant to be mine, Tamara. Do you see? Do you feel it?"

She widened her eyes, as if in wondering realization. Her destiny revealed. "Ah. Yes. Now I understand."

He got up and walked slowly toward her, circling her. "You did not know, but I have been protecting you for years," he said.

Her knees weakened as she thought of Rachel. "Me? Really?"

"I told old Novak you died. That I had seen your bleeding body."

She let her jaw drop in theatrical amazement. That would explain why she had survived for so long. It had always seemed improbable to her. Too good to be true that the old man had ignored her for so long.

"I didn't know," she whispered. "I thought no one knew where I was. But I might have known I could never hide from you."

"I hear you have an adopted child," he said. "This is of some concern to me. I hope you understand what a commitment of time and energy it will be to stand at my side and help run the global organization that I have in hand. To say nothing of how much it is about to expand."

Tam gave him a supremely casual shrug. "Don't worry about my priorities," she assured him. "I'll make arrangements for the child. There will be no conflicts at all."

Georg's smile widened. "I knew you would understand. And now, Tamara . . . give me what I have been waiting for . . . for years now."

"And, ah, what is that?" She braced herself.

His pale lips thinned over those big fake teeth. "You."

Her stomach twisted unpleasantly. She put down her briefcase, smiling, shining, glowing at him while a rapid-fire situation analysis crunched in her mind. She was alone with him, and that was a plus, but he was certainly armed to the teeth. He was a lethally quick fighter. Thin though he was, he had to outweigh her by over a third, and he had a much longer reach. He was a tall man, over six two. Insane, perhaps, but not stupid. He would be on his guard.

Her best bet were the earrings, but not until he was writhing on top of her, distracted by sexual pleasure. Then, once he was safely knocked out, she could kill him at her leisure in any of a dozen ways.

The trick would be to keep from vomiting or passing out while being intimate with him. She had lost her professional cool, and she had Val Janos and his manly mojo to thank for it. It was much easier to calmly contemplate the pits of hell when one didn't have a shining paradise to compare it to. Damn him.

She shoved the thoughts away. This was all about survival now. She would deal with the mess later.

Georg held out his hand imperiously. "Well? Come here."

She lurched toward him as if she'd been shoved from behind. His hand clamped her wrist. It was damp. Clammy and horribly strong, like the strangling coils of a snake.

"What, ah, do you want?" she asked faintly.

He grinned like a carnivorous dinosaur. "Take off your clothes."

"Interesting footage you've got there." Hegel let out an oily chuckle. "I see why you've been dragging your heels. Didn't want to stop fucking her, hmm? And immortalizing the experience, too. Run back that last bit. I love the shape of her ass when she bends over you. And I go wild for a shaved pussy. Silky soft. Mmm. Run it back."

"Fuck you," Val said.

The gun dug harder into his neck. "Run it back," Hegel repeated.

Val snapped the screen closed. "No," he said.

Hegel leaned forward until Val could feel the moist heat of the man's breath. "Don't fuck with me, Janos. Do you know how bad your behavior made me look? Do you have the faintest idea how pissed I am with you? Because you're just about to find out."

Val started to turn. The gun dug deeper. "One false move, Janos," Hegel muttered. "Pulling this trigger would be a pleasure."

Three steps back. Val set the mechanism in operation, let the matrix start to turn in his mind, and floated apart from it. Or rather, he tried to, but the anxious question flew out of him without his permission. "Where is she? What is happening to her?"

"I expect she's at the hotel with Georg. Although that twisted freak needs lots of help to get it on. You know, I bet she'll thank me in the end for forcing the issue."

Val could imagine exactly what Tamar would say if she heard those words. "You think so?" he said distantly.

"Oh, yes. There are worse things than being pounded by one of the richest guys in the world, even if he is out of his fucking gourd. And that kind of woman is sure to realize it real fast. You've done all right for yourself, Janos, but you can't compete with hundreds of millions in drug, prostitution, and gun-running money. And if the moves he's about to make pan out, his empire is going to expand. I'll do everything I can to see that happen. This is the ass to kiss, Janos. Too bad you dipped your wick in the sacred well, you bad boy. Georg won't like that. In spite of his sexual quirks."

He hated to give Hegel the satisfaction, but fear prevailed, and the question burst out. "What sexual quirks?"

"Oh, nothing really that dirty," Hegel said lightly. "He likes being watched, that's all. No matter what he does, even if it's just a blow job, someone has to be standing there watching, or else his dick goes south. I don't mind watching myself. Particularly when he gets generous afterward. Me, I don't mind a buttered bun now and then."

Sexual confidences from Hegel—ugh. Val's stomach churned. He changed the subject. "Who were those men at the Sea-Tac airport?"

"Oh, the ones you slaughtered? That was just an insurance policy. A local team based out of Olympia. I mobilized them when it looked like I couldn't count on you. They were incompetent fucks, but wonder of wonders, you ended up doing your job anyway, Janos. Convenient, getting her over the pond without us having to deal with her kid. That would have been a big pain in the ass, having to keep a three-year-old's ass wiped. Start the car."

"How did you find me?"

"I have my ways," Hegel said. "You're not as smart as you think you are, Janos. And we need to get something straight right now. I've got no problem killing you where you sit. You know how I always told you how dangerous it is to get attached? I practice what I preach."

"I do not doubt it," Val muttered.

"I am not attached to you. Yes, we invested tens of millions in training you, but that's OK. We got more than our money's worth by now. And even the most expensive machine eventually breaks down. Repairs cost more and more, you reach the point of diminishing returns, and it's off to the wrecking yard. Start the car up, shitbird, or the bullet goes into the base of your skull. Nobody's watching. Nobody cares. We've got the woman now. Congratulations, asshole. You are now officially irrelevant."

Val revved up all his senses, hyperalert for a split second chance to do something, anything, as he put the car into reverse and backed out of the lot.

Hegel directed him through the town and out onto a winding, potholed road that wound up the mountainside. They reached a wide spot in the road, with a decayed, crumbling stonework wall. An overlook point at a steep cliff. There was a deep, rocky gully from rain washout behind.

It was the kind of remote, forgotten place where lovers came to park and junkies came to shoot up. In point of fact, the ground was liberally scattered with condoms and syringes.

"Stop here," Hegel said. "Hold out your right hand."

Val hesitated. Hegel intended to send him over the cliff, attached to the car. He had to play for time. Good thing the car was a stick shift. "How will I change gears?"

"Shut the fuck up and hold out your right hand. Keep your left on the steering wheel where I can see it or I'll blow out your brains."

Val held it up. Hegel snapped a cuff onto it with one hand, grinding the muzzle of his gun into Val's neck with the other.

A cell phone beeped. A text message arriving. Not his.

Hegel laughed. "The guy works fast."

Val's gut crawled with apprehension. "Meaning?"

"Meaning Georg's hot to fuck her now. Jealous?" Hegel chuckled. "Fucking asshole. He just texted me his room number. He wants his audience and I'm the lucky winner. My treat, for hunting you two down. Maybe he'll even give me a ride when he's done. He likes watching as much as he likes being watched, and he'll be in a generous mood once he blows his wad. And man, I would like to make that hellcat squeal—"

Val whipped the empty handcuff back into Hegel's face, lightning quick, with an explosion of energy from far beyond his conscious mind. He jerked himself sideways without thinking, just as the gun went off.

It barely missed him. The windshield crumbled. Val wrenched the car into reverse, accelerating hard toward the deep, rocky ditch behind them. Time dilated. Hegel bellowed. Val flinched as the gun blasted again. A hole appeared in the dashboard. Stuffing exploded out of the seat next to Val's shoulder. They rattled, bumped, sped backward—

They tipped. *Crash*, the car landed on its ass in the gully. It toppled onto its side, bouncing, tipping. Glass blew out, metal shrieked. The bones in Val's skeleton tried to shake loose of each other.

As soon as he was sure he was still alive, Val shoved open the warped driver's side door and scrambled out, vaulting over rocks. His legs were weak and shaking. He dropped behind a large boulder, braced for the bullets to start flying from the broken, crumpled car windows. Hot blood trickled down his face.

Silence.

The laptop. The footage. Imre. Ah, fuck, *no*.

Val crept closer to the car. No movement, no sound. He peered inside. Hegel was crumpled up inside, unconscious. Blood streamed down his face and neck from an impact wound on his temple.

Val sagged. Pure relief surged through him for a bare second, before he kicked himself into action again. Tamar. He had to save Tamar.

He climbed on top of the car and lowered himself down into the open door. He collected the laptop first. It looked intact, thank God. Then he slithered into the backseat and groped around for Hegel's H&K and cell phone. Both were slippery with Hegel's blood. He fished in the man's pockets until he found a full ammo cartridge. He stuck the H&K into the back of his pants, and flipped the phone open, looking for the text message.

348. A room number, unless it was a code. In which case, he would rip each door of the hotel off its hinges until he found them.

He looked at Hegel's bleeding face, and pressed his finger to the man's thick throat. His pulse was strong. He would have killed Hegel without a qualm in a straight fight, but he balked at the idea of executing an unconscious man.

Fuck it. He would just leave it up to chance. Imre would say he was digging his conscience out from under the two-ton rock where he had hidden it. He levered himself up, vaulted out of the ruined car. It wobbled and swayed. He stared at it, panting. Clutching the laptop.

He needed clean transportation.

As if in answer to the thought, a pimpled youth on a scooter came buzzing around the corner. He took in the crumpled car, blood-streaked Val staggering in the road, and skidded to a stop.

"Hai bisogno di aiuto?" he gasped, eyes huge.

He sure as hell did need help. *"Sì.* Your scooter," Val told him. "Get off."

The kid blinked at him stupidly. *"Come? Scusa?"*

"The Vespino. Here." Val yanked a wad of cash out of his pocket, easily five times the value of the thing. "Take this, call it a rental fee. Wait 'til tomorrow, and report it stolen. You'll get it back."

"But I—but—"

Val shoved the money into the breast pocket of the boy's shirt, and briskly knocked him off the scooter and onto his ass. He shoved his laptop into the battered *portapacchi* strapped to the back, and took off.

The boy ran after him, yelling. The tiny motor groaned in protest. He gunned it as much as he could. Which was not much.

That dickhead Georg needed an audience to perform? Excellent.

He was about to get a spectator that he would never forget.

Chapter
19

G eorg hung his shoulder holster over the antique mirror, and approached her. "Turn around. Slowly," he directed.

Tam affixed a seductive smile on her face and did so, spinning
sensually in a graceful pirouette.

Georg reached for her. His clammy hands fastened on her bare
skin, groping her breasts, squeezing her ass. They made her nau-
seous.

"Change your hair back," Georg said, frowning. "I liked it better
before. Shorter, and curlier, and red. I liked the red."

"Of course," she murmured. "Anything you like."

Georg whipped off his shirt, displaying a wiry, muscled chest,
milk white and mottled with twisting scars. "Touch me," he ordered.

She moved closer, sliding her fingers over his ribs. She tried to
make the gesture sensual, but her shaking fingers stuck to his damp
skin. *Think metal, stone, gems,* she told herself. *Cold and hard. Think of
needles, poisons. Earrings.*

As always, it was split second timing that would make or break
the success of her plan. He clutched her naked body to his sweaty
chest, his breath smothering against her face. A streak of foamy spittle hung on his tight, quivering lips. She tried not to focus on it. And
to think this man had once been considered handsome.

He kicked off his shoes, undid his belt, shoved down his pants.

He was half hard, his pink penis twitching. He reached down, massaged it almost to three-quarters, but it soon dropped back to its previous state.

Interesting. That could save her maidenly virtue, such as it was, or it could get her killed, depending on how the wind blew. She swallowed, hardened her belly muscles and faced reality. She knew exactly what a good whore was expected to do in these circumstances.

She began to sink to her knees, smiling seductively even as her gorge rose. "Shall I . . . ?"

"No." He yanked her back up. "No, it's always like this with me. I need someone to watch. So we'll just wait until he gets back."

"Watch? He? Who?"

"Hegel." Georg grabbed his pants and fished a cell phone out of the pocket. He tapped a brief message into it. "The PSS agent. The handler for that rogue agent who's causing all the trouble, Janos. He wanted to watch today. It's his reward, for locating you and Janos."

She was alarmed. "Watch what?"

"Us," he said impatiently, as if she was playing dumb to annoy him. "I need that to make it work. I like to be watched, the way Kurt watched us. We just have to wait a minute or two. Be patient. If he takes longer than that, I'll call some of my other men to do it."

Tam was appalled. She glanced discreetly at his groin and quickly away. He'd lost his arousal completely. His penis was shrinking nervously back against a tuft of blond pubic hair. Part of her wanted to cheer. *Yes, go ahead and cower, little guy,* she wanted to crow. *Hide from me. You're right. I'm very dangerous.*

But men acted weird when their dicks didn't work. It made them much more difficult to manage, to flatter, to predict. "Are you sure you don't want me to—"

"Shut up," he said.

She sank down onto the bed and arranged herself in a sexy pose. Her mind was spinning its wheels, dismayed. This was bad. No moment of sexual bliss when he was distracted to stick him with the earring, at least not until a fully armed PSS operative was looming over the bed, watching every move, gun in hand. Ah, shit.

She had her limits. She had to kill him right now. No choice.

"By the way, you will fuck him afterward." Georg's eyes had gone beady and hard. "He deserves a treat. For having found you."

All the blood in her body suddenly congealed. "But I . . . only want to be with you," she said, her eyes big and beseeching. "Do I have to—"

"You must do as I tell you." Georg's tone was falsely gentle. "You will rule at my side, Tamara, but never forget who is in charge. I like to watch. And you are the one I like to watch." His lips twisted into a thin, lopsided smile with a strange flash of hatred in it. "I know you love it. I'll make sure you're satisfied every day. After you satisfy me, of course."

Her smile tightened into a grimace of disgust. And she thought things had been bad with Kurt. There was always further to fall.

She had to kill him before Hegel arrived.

She forced herself to smile and held out her hand. "You understand me so well," she said throatily. "Most men would be intimidated by that, but not you. It takes complete mastery of self for a man not to be afraid of a woman's true desires."

Georg's chest puffed. His eyes glowed with self-satisfied vanity. "Yes. I have mastered myself, Tamara. And I will master you."

She held out her hand and fluttered her eyelashes. "Y-y-yes," she whispered. "Come to bed. I've been waiting so long." She held her arms up, pleading. Longing to be mastered.

His eyelids quivered. A primal part of his brain sensed a trap, but his vanity and madness were stronger.

He sat down on the bed. Tam wrapped herself around him, legs straddling him, and leaned her head upon his shoulder, arms clasped around his neck. He had an alien, bitter scent to his fishy-textured skin. Her hair stuck unpleasantly to his damp flesh.

"You are fortunate that I found you when I did," he said.

"I wish it had happened sooner," she murmured softly. "I've been alone so long."

"I searched harder when old man Novak found out you were alive. He was irritated with me. Sent my emissary back to me in a cardboard box. Some of him, anyway."

"How horrible," she whispered.

"Not a problem," he assured her. "It just speeded up an inevitable development."

She lifted her head to look curiously into his face and grasp the earring beneath her concealing fall of hair. "What development?" she said automatically, just to keep him talking while she unsnapped the stem and got the hypodermic into position to stab into his throat . . .

"He's a walking corpse," Georg said, with satisfaction. "Rotted with cancer, but he refuses to die. It doesn't matter. I have plans."

Her fingers froze, the mini-hypodermic poised oh-so-close to the skin of his throat. "Oh?" she asked casually. "What plans?"

Georg laughed. "I could just wait for the inevitable, but my claim to his business interests would be clearer if I assassinate him first. And now he threatens my woman. It's time to show the world who is the new boss."

Imre. The thought was accompanied by a stab of despair for what this meant for herself. Imre's chance. "When? Soon?"

His lips twisted in an indulgent smile. "Why so curious?"

She looked up at him archly through her lashes. "The man wants me dead."

Georg stroked her hair, grabbed a handful, and wound it tightly around his fist, pulling until tears started into her eyes. "You have nothing to fear from him now," Georg assured her. "Not now that you're with me. Nothing can touch you. Nothing will get near you. You are mine."

"Of course I am, but please. Indulge me," she coaxed. "Can it be soon? Can I come? Can I help? Please tell me you're going to include me in these adventures. I'm not the stay-at-home type."

He laughed. "It's one of the things I love about you, my bloodthirsty vampire queen. Soon. I can make it soon, if you prefer it."

"Oh, yes," she breathed, all excited. "I prefer it."

Something inside her screamed in protest at what she was about to do to herself. She let the hand with the hypodermic drop, sliding the tiny device between her middle and ring finger.

No, no, no, the fifteen-year-old girl inside her sobbed. *Don't make me do this. Not again.*

But she had to. This was the perfect scenario. A gift of fate—for Val and Imre, if not for her. But having a hateful, foul-breath goblin jerking and heaving on top of her while another watched, salivating for his turn—that had not been part of the bargain.

Oh, God, no. She couldn't face that. Not again. Not now.

It's only temporary, she told herself, not for the first time.

Hah. Temporary was a fictitious concept. Time was not linear, and she was not made of metal or gemstones, much as she wished that she were. Kurt, Georg, Drago Stengl, they had all been temporary, and even so, they had warped her almost beyond redemption.

For love? Could she? She thought of the look on Val's face when he talked of Imre.

Love? Like he'll love you after this, if he ever really did. He's just a man. You can't. There's only so much a woman can bear.

But it was the only way. If Rachel was going to have any sort of mother—even one like her—this was her best chance to survive. To be inside the attacking force, provide information to Val from within, create a diversion during a rescue attempt—it was streamlined, it was perfect. It made sense. It beckoned to her as the intelligent, practical solution. And if she managed to kill Georg in the process, so much the better.

Her arms tightened around him. "Why's he taking so long?" she complained.

"He'll be here soon. He's dealing with that agent. Maybe Janos is taking longer to eliminate than Hegel anticip—"

Crash. The door burst open. Val took in the tableau on the bed, and dove toward Georg. His grimace of rage made his face almost unrecognizable.

Georg flung her away from himself with a hoarse shout. Tam rolled off the bed and thudded to the floor.

Val leaped on top of him. *Crack*, a pistol in Val's hand connected with Georg's face. Blood spattered and flew, along with a couple of teeth, arcing across the coverlet. Georg's leg whipped out, his foot connecting with Val's jaw. Val spun away, bounced off the wall, and came right back at him with a roar, crashing into him. The two men toppled off the bed and grappled on the floor, Val on top.

A smashing blow to the nose, and Georg lay limp, eyes closed, blood streaming over his mouth and chin. Val raised his hand to chop down—

"No!" Tam lunged, grabbed his arm to block the killing blow. "Stop! You idiot!"

He stared at her. "What do you mean, stop? Is this not what we agreed? Was this not the plan?"

"No! He's going to kill Novak!" she whispered fiercely. "Soon! In days! This is our chance, Val! To save Imre! Listen to me, goddamnit!"

Val stared at her, panting. Struggling with the powerful instinct to conclude his kill. His eyes were tormented with confusion.

"Do not kill him." She enunciated the words very clearly. "Not yet. Use him first, you fucking idiot! Why do you think he's not already dead by now? Why do you think I was naked in a bed with that freak in the first place? What, do you think I pull stunts like this for my health?"

Val stared at the unconscious man, his huge fists shook. "Novak?" He repeated the name helplessly. It was all his mind could take in.

"Georg has a plan to kill Novak. Soon! We could use it," she said. "I'll stay with Georg, and let you know when he—"

"No." His hand clamped over her forearm. "You're not staying."

"Calm down, Val," she soothed. "Be professional. Take advantage of the situation. Don't be a baby. This way, I can feed information—"

"*No.* Shut up, and put on your fucking clothes."

The fury in his voice rocked her back. She stared into his hard face, feeling slapped. She knew that look. That judging look that pushed her away from him, and said *whore.*

She hadn't even had sex with that hideous turd, but she would pay the price anyway, just for having been willing to do so. And for Imre's sake, too. She was such a fool. Such a goddamn fool.

Well, and so. Fuck him, too, then. Fuck them all.

She got up, deliberately flaunting her naked body, and pulled on the clothes Georg had made her remove. She grabbed Georg's automatic pistol and holster from the dresser, checked the cartridge. Full—fifteen shots. Better than nothing. She stuck it in her purse.

As soon as she was decent, briefcase and purse in hand, he dragged her out of the room. Three men were sprawled in the hall outside. All of them unconscious. Val hauled them into the room and left them there in a bleeding heap.

He dragged her into the stairwell, and they sped down, barely staying on their feet. The ground floor had a door that led out to a side street. A little blue Vespino waited. Val swung his leg over it, waited for her to climb on behind. His eyes dared her to make a snide comment.

She had to struggle not to laugh. After all the blood, all the drama, a sky blue Vespino? It was an anticlimax, buzzing around the hills of San Vito on a mini-scooter, like a couple of thirteen-year-old *innamorati* looking for a place to smooch.

But Val's thunderous face discouraged laughter.

András bent over the hotel room door, the lock pick hidden by his big hand. The antique locks of the old hotel were laughably easy to pick.

He had just arrived in San Vito. Old Novak had gotten nervous, not surprisingly, and sent András to secure the situation. This job would begin with a candid conversation with Ferenc, their spy in Georg's organization. The man's usefulness was beginning to erode, despite the generous sums they paid him. Jakab's bloody delivery in the cardboard box had rattled him. The time was fast approaching when Ferenc would need to be recycled into some fresh use. But not quite yet.

The man sprawled on the bed with an ice pack on his face sprang into the air when the door swung open. His face was grotesquely bruised and swollen. His reddened eyes widened.

"Oh, fuck," he moaned. "No. You."

"Me," András agreed, strolling into the room.

"You're insane to come here!" Ferenc whispered hoarsely. "I might not have been alone! The others could come back any time! Do you have any idea what would happen to me if Luksch realized that I am the—"

"But he hasn't yet." As if he gave a shit.

"You don't understand," Ferenc said urgently. "Luksch is suspicious of all of us ever since Jakab was killed! Ever since Novak found out about PSS and the woman, he knows that one of us is—"

"And did you not take this into account when you cashed the check?" András reminded him gently. "All of the many, many checks?"

"But . . . but he will kill me," Ferenc whined. "He will—"

"Shut up." András grabbed a chair from the desk, and rested his bulk on its spindly legs. "From the condition of your face, I assume you have met Janos?"

Ferenc's face darkened. He struggled to his feet off the bed.

"He took us by surprise," he said sullenly. "You should see the other men. Iwan's ribs and collarbone are broken, Miklós is in the hospital with head and neck injuries. Hegel, too. Hegel's lucky to be alive at all."

"Hegel is in the hospital?" András was startled. That was remarkable enough to stop him from shutting off the man's prattle with his fist. He knew the man, from Novak's own dealings with PSS. It would take a great deal to get the better of Hegel. "What hospital?"

Ferenc's face furrowed as he struggled to remember. "I Santi Medici," he said after a doubtful pause. "I think."

"His room number?"

"How the fuck would I know?" Ferenc grumbled. "I didn't send the man flowers. And you should leave. Immediately, before Luksch—"

"What name is he using?"

Ferenc gaped stupidly. "Who?"

"Hegel, you dickbrained idiot," András said, with saintly patience.

Ferenc hid behind the ice pack. "It was an American passport. Mike something. Fowler, I think. Mike Fowler."

András filed it all away, his foot tapping thoughtfully on the carpet. "And how did he locate the woman and the PSS agent?"

"He had a GPS tracer on one of them. Don't know which one. Christ, this hurts. That bastard broke my nose. I saw Hegel running the program on his laptop a couple times, monitoring them."

"Where is his hotel room?" András got up, took a step toward the bed.

"It's a floor above this one," Ferenc said sulkily, hanging his head. "He had to be next to the stairwell. You have to go, before Luksch—"

Crack. András punched the man's already broken nose knocking him to the floor. Ferenc huddled, whimpering and gasping for air. András stared down at him thoughtfully, massaging his knuckles. Ferenc held his nose, choking. Blood streamed through his fingers.

"If I hear you whine again, I will call Luksch myself and tell him who our spy is," András said calmly. "Be grateful I did not kill you."

He let the door swing shut behind him, and headed to the stairwell, to search Hegel's room, hoping that the man would not be comatose once he got to the hospital to speak to him. He needed Hegel conscious, at least for a few minutes. That was all that was necessary, for his purposes. After that, well . . . why not? Since Hegel had shown the poor taste and judgment to throw in his lot with Georg . . .

András just might indulge himself. It had been a very long time.

The one good thing about the Vespino was that it made conversation impossible. Anything he could have said to Tamar now would only make things worse.

Knowing that it wasn't her fault, that she'd been compelled—ah, God. It did not help. He wanted to kill Georg for doing that to her.

And not only Georg. It was not enough. Others should die, too, for everything that had led up to it. Years of cruelty and misfortune, of doing what she had to do to survive.

And in spite of it all, she was so strong. Shining and beautiful.

The headwind blew tears of rage out of the corners of his eyes. He wanted to slaughter them all himself, all the way back to Stengl. That psychotic prick that had murdered her family, used her for a toy, and abandoned her to fend for herself when she was just a grieving child.

Just like him.

Cristo. He'd always congratulated himself for having left his own past behind so completely, for letting it affect him so little. But in the days that he had spent with Tamar, the scab had been torn away, revealing a festering sore he had not even known was there.

He had never really felt the pain of it, but he felt it now. Oh, yes, he felt it now. For her sake, not for his own, but it hardly mattered.

It was all the same fucking pain.

Sex with her was like nothing he'd even known. He was a master of technique, an artisan of pleasure, but Tamar revealed his technique for exactly what it was. Empty tricks, sleight of hand. Forgotten, evaporated in the blaze of white-hot, screaming intensity that she provoked in him.

The very thought of it stirred him. His dick was hard. Her long hair swirled and stung their faces as they sped into the headwind. Drops of rain stung, too. Her arms held his torso gingerly like she was afraid to touch him.

She leaned forward and called into his ear. "Where are we going?"

He shrugged. "How the fuck should I know?" he shouted back, the wind whipping the words away from his mouth. "I am open to any brilliant suggestions you might have."

That shut her up. Menacing clouds scudded heavily across the sky. It was starting to rain harder

They spotted the rusty metal sign at the same time, full of what appeared to be small bullet holes. It advertised an *agriturismo*, a farm that sold local foodstuffs, some of which also rented rooms. *Le Cinque Querce*. Five Oaks. 5.2 km. Tam pointed at the sign.

He nodded, and slewed the Vespino around onto a narrow dirt road that had a canopy of overhanging trees and shrubs above and a deep, thorn-choked ravine below.

They bumped and thudded along the road, following crooked hand-lettered signs each time it forked into various orchards until they turned onto what could be called a driveway only in the loosest sense of the word: a winding kilometer and a half of rocky dirt track through an orchard of olives dotted with the occasional fig, lemon, or orange tree.

The place itself was an ancient *casale* of a mottled salmon pink streaked with yellow and and gray from hundreds of years of weather. Around it sprawled a humble fattoria and a powerful aroma of animal shit. Sheep, goats, and chickens wandered at will, and the sweet smell of raindrops pattering down onto the dust tickled his nose. He smelled pine, the aromatic herbs that clung to the crumbling drywall that lined the road. The flagstoned space in front of the *casale* was crowded with agricultural equipment, puddled oil spots, rusted-out cars.

It did not look promising as a hotel.

They shot each other doubtful looks as a door creaked open. A woman came out, as wide as a refrigerator, with thick, swollen legs like posts. She was a figure from another century, with a stringy salt-and-pepper bun, moles on her cheeks sprouting tufts of coarse hair, a black ankle-length dress with a blood-smeared apron, a heavy crucifix. A dead chicken swung by the neck from her hand.

"*Sì?*" she asked, in tones of deep suspicion.

"Is this the Five Oaks Agriturismo?" Val glanced around, looking for the oaks. None were in evidence. Rain splattered down more heavily every second, plastering their jackets to their shoulders, their hair to their faces.

"*Sì*," the woman said slowly. Her scowling gaze lingered on the handcuff dangling from his bloodied hand.

"Do you have a room for two available?" Val persisted.

The woman grunted, eyes sunk deep in squinting wrinkles. "I would have to clean it," she informed them, chin thrust out. "It is years that no one sleeps there. You must wait until it is cleaned."

Val glanced up at the driving rain. "How long would that take?"

She shrugged. "A few hours."

Hours? God help them."We don't mind if it has not been cleaned," he wheedled. "Please, Signora, do not trouble yourself."

She grunted again, rolling her eyes, and jerked her bearded chin for them to follow her.

They circled around the *casale*. Luxuriant weeds grew around the flagstones, and the path was carpeted by drifts of slimy dead leaves and lined with rotting canvas bags of unidentified detritus. Around the back of the sparsely windowed structure was a chicken run, a fallow garden full of heaps of dead brush, and a warped, ancient wooden door that hung upon heavy, rusty hinges that looked medieval. The door was as high as Val's shoulder.

The signora wiped chicken blood from her hand onto her apron and yanked. The small door opened with a shriek of rusty hinges and warped wood. A shower of splinters and flakes of ancient white-wash pattered to the ground. There were no locks, just latches, sliding bolts.

She preceded them into a vaulted room and opened two shutters. The smell of mildew was overwhelming. Tiny transparent scorpions, alarmed by the sudden influx of light, chased each other across the windowsills in a panic. A shutter hung askew on a broken hinge.

There was a sagging wrought iron bed in the corner, a four-poster with a lugubrious rendition of the *Madonna Addolorata* painted on the iron headboard. The Madonna's face was pallid and miserable, shadowy bags under her weeping eyes. She was swathed in black lace as she gazed into the sky and mourned her crucified son. The other three walls of the room were lined with a bizarre assortment of mismatched marble-topped dressers and termite-gnawed credenzas. There was an ancient, rickety table, two mismatched wooden folding chairs. No TV or phone, of course. Val pulled out Hegel's cell. No coverage.

"Questo e' tutto," the woman said heavily. This is it.

Val looked at Tamar. She shrugged. "I've slept in worse places."

He turned back to the signora. *"Va bene,"* he said. "Can we get some dinner?"

"You can eat with the family at eight," the signora announced.

Val caught the flash of naked fear in Tamar's eyes, and manufactured a charming smile. "Could we just have something in our room? Something simple is fine. Bread and cheese and wine?"

The signora cleared her throat, a phlegmy hack of disapproval. "I'll bring something." She indicated with the chicken in the direction of an ancient armoire, with enough force to make the dead bird molt pinfeathers onto the cracked tile floor. "There are more pillows and blankets in there. I will bring food later. I am the Signora Concetta."

With that information, she stumped out, leaving the door open.

Gusts of rain and the smell of sheep shit blew in, a welcome burst of freshness and moist moving air in the moldy dimness of the room.

They looked at each other for a long moment.

"Well," Tamar said briskly. "I doubt that anyone will look for us here." She set her purse and the Deadly Beauty briefcase down and pulled open a small door, peering into what proved to be a tiny bathroom with brown-streaked porcelain fixtures that had to be more than a century old. "At least there are towels in here," she remarked. "Who needs toilet paper?"

Tamar's attempt at lightness made things worse. Val sat down on the bed, releasing a puff of dust that danced in the light from the door. He stared at her. She stared back. The light from the tiny windows was tinted by the foliage outside to a dim, unearthly green.

Gusts of strong wind whined around the *casale*, banging the little wooden door open against the outside wall. The rain finally let go in a rushing deluge. Its sweet, heady perfume deepened with every minute.

Tamar stepped forward, crossing her arms. "Go ahead," she said. "Say it. I see it in your face, anyhow."

"What do you see?" he asked. "What do you expect me to say?"

"Whore," she said.

Val stared down at his own bloodied fists and fingered the dangling handcuff still attached to his wrists, and listened to the rain for a long moment. "I did not think that. And I will not say it."

"Don't make it worse by lying." Her tilted eyes glittered with unshed tears.

"You ask a great deal of me," he said. "I find my woman naked in the arms of a mafiya drug lord, and you scold me for being unhappy?"

She laughed. "Your woman? Hah! I belong to myself, Janos. I had two options. Kill him or fuck him. My first choice was to kill him. I was a nanosecond away from doing that when he told me his plans."

Val swallowed bile. He forced the words out through a constricted throat. "And?"

"I realized that by killing him, I would be killing Imre," she said, her voice hushed. "Or at least, killing your best chance to save him."

His irrational anger grew with every word she said. "Ah. So you were naked in his arms for my sake?"

She nodded. "Yes. Your sake," she said. "And Imre's."

His fists clenched, his jaw. His heart thudded. "And you expect me to thank you for that?"

Her eyes glowed hotly. "Yes! I do! I expect you to fall to your knees and kiss my ass for that! Why else, Val? Why else on earth would I willingly do that to myself? I had nothing to gain. Nothing! I could have killed him myself without your help, gone to take care of Stengl on my own, and never bothered with you and your complicated, dangerous problems ever again. But I didn't. God help me, I didn't."

"And his billions?" he asked. "Is that not worth fucking him?"

She jerked back, her eyes huge with startled hurt. "Would you fuck Georg Luksch for a billion dollars?" she asked. "Or five billion?"

He shook his head.

"Then what makes you think I would?"

He shook his head, denying everything they were saying, everything that was happening, but she went on, her voice tight.

"You have no idea what was in store for me. He would have passed me around to his men every day for his own entertainment. And to punish me for being female, of course."

He put his face into his hands. "Please be quiet. Just stop."

"Can you believe it? A selfish bitch like me, struck down by a self-sacrificing heroine complex. I actually thought that saving your friend from death by torture would be worth . . . that. I actually thought that you would understand. That it was a gift."

"Tamar—"

"It's a mistake I won't make again." She slung her purse over her shoulder and grabbed her jewelry case. "As of this moment, our arrangement is dissolved. Save your friend on your own. You don't deserve my help. Good-bye."

He was on his feet with his arms around her before she reached the door.

"Don't you dare." She wrenched, spinning in his arms, and he suddenly found a gun shoved under his chin. Georg's gun.

"Tamar. No. Do not do this." He forced the dry sound past the pressure of the gun against his throat.

"Try to stop me, and I will kill you. Let go of me, Janos."

He let his arms slide lower, embracing her. She was as stiff as a wooden statue. "No."

The gun dug deeper. "I mean it." Her voice shook.

"So shoot me," he said. "Go on. End it."

She narrowed her eyes. "You used this trick on me before."

"It worked before," he said.

"I'm wise to you now," she said. "It won't work again."

"Yes, it will," he said quietly. "Because this time it is not a trick. I know you now, Tamar. You will not shoot me. Put the gun away."

Seconds dragged, oppressive with waiting. Rain rushed, an enormous, diffused sound all around them. Far-off thunder cracked and rumbled.

Crystalline tears welled up in her eyes, glittering in the gathering darkness. "Damn you," she whispered.

He pushed the barrel of the gun away from his chin, took the thing out of her unresisting hand, and put it back in her purse.

He placed the bag gently on the ground and reached for her.

Chapter
20

She struggled, of course. She could not help herself. It was a given, an automatic response. But the fight was a frantic search for some place to put that desperate energy raging inside her. She fought how hard she wanted him, how much she was beginning to need him. She fought that sad, yearning ache that scared her out of her wits.

Not just for his beauty, his intensity, his fabulous cock. She wanted the life-giving elixir of his kisses, she wanted to wander through the boundless wilderness of him, to get lost in him. She wanted to devour him, soak him up, drink him in. She wanted to be devoured.

Stubborn bastard. She was furious at him for being a stubborn dickhead about Georg, and at the same time, pathetically grateful that he had stopped her from drinking that toxic brew.

He had saved her. From Georg, from herself. How dare he.

Val pushed her against the wall, wrenching her arms behind her, and for some reason, his smoldering barbarian energy did not piss her off. She'd encountered that conquering warrior vibe in her lovers before, and had been secretly amused by it. Never tempted. Never stirred. It was just another weakness to be exploited, another blind spot to turn to her advantage. She'd toyed with men's vanity, their illusions about themselves. She'd made them dance to her tune when she bothered with them at all. Puppets. Clowns. Big bore.

But Val was no clown. He had no illusions, no vanity. Val danced to no tune but his own. And she was anything but bored.

He was going to throw her down on the bed and fuck her, and she could not wait. She was going to explode, combust. She needed Val's delicious hot scent to drive away the memory of Georg's bitter odor, Georg's sour breath, the damp, bruising clutch of Georg's hands. After today's nightmare, she was crazy for it, but she just couldn't . . . stop . . . struggling. Her muscles trembled with the electric compulsion.

He immobilized her in his huge embrace and leaned, pinning her body against the wall. "Tell me that you want me," he said.

She squinted, disoriented. "What?"

"Tell me that you want me," he repeated impatiently. "I don't trust myself to read you."

She wrenched at her trapped wrists. "Why the hell not?"

He made a frustrated sound. "I want it too much," he burst out. "I need it too much. I do not want to . . . how did you put it? Project my gutter fantasies onto you?"

She shook with breathless, hysterical laughter, every inch of her tensed against his body. "Why this sudden insecurity?"

His face was tense, a mask of rigid self-control in the shadowy room. "I do not want to be like him," he said starkly.

Tam gasped in astonishment. The idea was so incongruous, she almost couldn't process it. "Him? Georg? Hah!" Her voice cracked. "You are nothing like him! As if!" She shoved him hard to punctuate her statement. "You are his polar opposite!"

His grin flashed. "Ah. Good, then. This heartens me."

She made a frantic growling sound, lunged forward, and sank her teeth into his neck, hard enough to hurt. "Goddamn it, Val," she hissed when she let go. "Don't be sweet. Not right now. You're ruining the barbarian conqueror vibe. Keep waffling like this, and I'm going to have to put you down."

He laughed, a free, delighted sound. Plaster dust and flakes of paint pattered down on the antique tile floor as he pushed her back against the wall. He wrenched her jacket down over her shoulders and off, then attacked the buttons of her blouse.

She gave him a shove that rocked him back a bare couple of inches. "Hey. If you rip the only clothing I have to put on my body, I swear to God, I will kill you. Slowly and painfully."

He slowly uncurled his fisted fingers and let go of the handful of silk, but he did not step back. "Take it off," he commanded.

She unbuttoned the blouse, and that was as far as his patience would stretch. He wrenched the sleeves down, flung the blouse away.

He stared at her breasts, his gaze hot and intent as he slid his sensitive fingertips slowly around her nipples. Tender, lazy strokes that left glowing streaks of light and heat in their wake, every nerve wanting him back. Hungering for more. Her nipples tingled. He bent low, and she gasped at the faintest contact, the scratchy brush of his stubbled cheeks, the softness of his lips. His swirling tongue, the wet suckling pull of his hot mouth. He kept her like that, topless and trembling against the wall while he made love to her breasts, until her tension melted, softened.

He gathered her up into his arms and tossed her on the bed. His huge shoulders were silhouetted against the dim light filtering in the door as he loomed over her, his face in menacing shadow. He tugged off her boots, her pants. Flung them behind him. His own clothes followed.

He was naked. So strong and powerful and hot against her skin. The empty shackle of the handcuff dangled, a kinky fashion accessory swinging and glinting on his wrist.

Something to push against, that was what he'd offered her the night they met. That was exactly what she needed, to keep pushing and pushing, until she finally pushed through that wall into someplace where she could stand to be. Someplace where her nerves weren't firing in crazy panic. Someplace where she could let herself relax and feel it.

Val could give her that. He was tough enough. Brave enough.

He climbed on top of her, folding her legs high, draping them over his shoulders. Stroking his hands down the fine, sensitive skin of her inner thigh. He covered her with his body, caressing her pussy, and found her slick and wet.

But not wet enough for his first deep, relentless thrust.

She cried out and scratched his chest, drawing blood. He just stared down, pinning her beneath him against the swaying bed.

"Do not ever do that to me again," he said.

She swatted at him, hard. "Do not think your big dick gives you the right to give me orders, loverboy." She spat the words at him.

He seized her hands, pinned them on either side of her head. "Never . . . again," he repeated hoarsely, punctuating each word with a deep, jarring lunge of his body.

She writhed and wiggled, squeezing and clenching around his thick shaft. "You still don't get it, do you? It was the only way!"

He went still on top of her, his fingers tightening painfully around hers. "I will never get it," he said. "It is too much. Do not ask it of me."

She wound her legs around his hips, squeezing the little muscles of her pussy around his cock with all her strength. Lifting herself against him, to feel that sweet, hot, gliding thickness caressing her deep inside. "I'm not asking anything of you but this," she said fiercely. "So why don't you just shut the fuck up and give it to me?"

He did. Deep and hard, every thrust jolted her wonderfully closer to the place she needed to be. With each thrust she grew slicker, hotter, more eager for the next, more desperate for the licking flames, the unbearable sweetness, brightening, sharpening. Piercing bliss.

The bed squeaked and groaned. Val's breath was hard, panting. She gasped for breath. Small sounds against the vast, diffused backdrop of lashing rain outside the open door, distant thunder, wind whipping the foliage outside, the fragrant, rain-scented chill. Their twined bodies churned, clenched around a molten core of sensation.

It exploded into bloom. Melting sweetness throbbed through her, endlessly. She floated through that infinite realm. Filled with grace.

He took longer to finish, gathering handfuls of her hair and burying his face against his shoulder. His climax tore through him violently. His hips pounded hard against her body.

They lay together, limp and damp afterward. Their twined bodies generated sensual, enfolding heat, despite the cold of the room. Day had faded completely. They rested, formless as clouds in the blue half light, in an otherworld apart from all the pain and confusion and danger.

She wished they could stay there together forever. She never wanted to break this fragile bubble of calm—but she had to.

She turned his face, tilting his chin up so that he looked up into her eyes. There was something he had to know.

"I did not fuck him," she said. "I would have, true, but I didn't. You know that, don't you?"

He nodded. "Yes," he said. "I know that."

"He couldn't have performed, anyway. Not without an audience. It's his thing."

"I know. Hegel told me." Val said.

"He got that from Kurt," she said. "Kurt liked that. So, of course, Georg fixated on it. Kurt was God for him. I think what Georg truly wanted was just, well, Kurt. That was his way to get . . . closer."

Val flinched, dragging himself out of her body. "Please. No more details. I cannot stand it."

That infuriated her for some reason. She felt thrown back upon herself. "Why? Can't you handle it, Val? Do I disgust you?"

His head swiveled around. "Shut up," he said fiercely.

His harshness startled her. She curled up, wrapping her arms around her knees. "Fine," she said distantly. "So we won't talk."

Val seized her by the shoulders and gave her a short, hard shake.

"I cannot stand the thought of anyone hurting you," he said. "Not now, not in the past, and not in the future. Is that so fucking offensive to you, Tamar?" His eyes bored into hers, daring her to object.

She gaped at him, disarmed. "Um. I see." She cleared her throat, and said the first thing that popped into her head. "Val? Could you get that handcuff off your wrist? It's bugging me. Sort of like, ah, as if you were walking around with your fly open."

He made a frustrated sound and got up, puttering around in the dimness to search in his discarded jacket on the floor. He pulled a tiny kit out of the pocket, smaller than a cigarette case, full of small tools.

He came back to the bed and switched on the flickering fluorescent light by the bed, and scowled with concentration as he picked the lock mechanism.

She rolled closer to him and stroked the dips and curves of his muscular thigh with her fingertips. It took him only a minute before he leaned over and snapped one of the open cuffs onto a wrought iron loop that decorated the painted metal headboard.

"It looks perverse, hanging underneath the *Madonna Addolorata*," she said. "Sort of sacrilegious."

He snapped off the light. The darkness seemed much deeper now. "It seems appropriate to me," he said. "Under the circumstances."

She didn't want to touch that with a ten-foot pole. She got up from the bed—and stopped cold, as hot semen trickled down her thigh.

She stiffened in shock. "We didn't . . ." Her voice trailed off.

Val's dark gaze was unapologetic, and unsurprised. "No," he said flatly. "We didn't."

She stood like a statue, her hands flat on her belly. There was nothing to say. She couldn't blame him, despite his aggressiveness. That carelessness was mutual, and they both knew it. If he hadn't jumped her, she would have jumped him. Without a thought of protecting herself.

Fear swept through her like an icy wind, weakening her limbs. The dark got abruptly darker, the air swirling through the door colder against her sweat-chilled skin.

She felt so fucking vulnerable.

"Is it a dangerous time?" he asked in a carefully neutral voice.

She harrumphed. "Who the hell knows? This is me, Val. This is Tam. Do I look like a woman with a predictable cycle? Could anything about me be characterized as regular? Get real."

His chest jerked with dry laughter. "Ah, *sì*? And what does a regular woman look like?"

Her shoulders lifted, dropped. "Not like me, that's for sure," she muttered. "I don't even eat. I go for months with no period. Nothing about me is normal."

"Yes, this is so," he agreed, a little too readily.

She slanted him a cool glance and hurried into the bathroom.

The water from the bidet was icy cold, and there was no soap, but it didn't matter. She washed until her private parts burned from the cold, all too aware of the futility of the gesture. She dried off, wrapped the threadbare towel around herself. When she came out, Val was motionless on the bed.

"Promise me something," he said.

"I don't make promises," she said. "To anyone."

"I demand it." His voice hardened.

"Demand all you want," she replied. "Feel free. It changes nothing."

But he persisted. "Never do that to me again, Tamar."

"Do what?" She injected a fake lightness into her tone. "I've done a lot of unforgivable things lately. Help me keep them straight."

"Do not use your body as currency."

Anger boiled up inside her like lava. How dare he. He, of all people, should know better. "Do you think I ever wanted to, in my life?" she demanded, incredulous. "Did you ever want to, Val? What are you telling me? That you can protect me from the greed and lust and cruelty of all men forever? Do you think I can be sure I won't be in a situation where I have to trade sex for the chance to live for another fucking ten minutes? Like today, for instance? Don't be stupid! It makes me angry!"

"Just . . . promise it." He bit the words out slowly.

"No," she said.

He wrenched the towel off her body. His cock was lengthening. His eyes gleamed in the dark with undimmed intensity. Oh, God. Men. As if his huge, waving erection had anything to do with anything.

She clenched her jaw. "I will not lie to you," she said.

"I'm not asking for a lie." His voice vibrated with intensity. "I'm asking for you to change the truth."

She shook, a tremor of laughter that was closer to tears. "Oh? Like it's so easy? The truth is the truth, Val. You can't change it. You can't control a damn thing. There is no limit to how bad things can get. If you accept that, you'll be stronger. Maybe you'll survive. That's the best a person can hope for."

"I love your strength," he said quietly. "Your strength excites me. Your cruelty exhausts me."

She shook her head. "It would be so easy to lie to you." Her voice trembled despite her best efforts to steady it. "I could have said, oh, sure, baby, you bet. I promise, cross my heart. But I didn't. Not to you, Val. I've given you what I've never given any man in my life, you thick-skulled, ungrateful prick. What I never imagined giving anyone. And you call it cruelty."

He grabbed her hips as she began to turn away, and jerked her close, pressing his face against her mound. His mouth moved, hot and hungrily against her clit, his strong, clever tongue probing, seeking.

The feeling was knee-weakening, shockingly wonderful, but she was too electric, too emotional to bear it. She swatted at his face. "No."

His expression was now impossible to read in the darkness. "Your 'no' is meaningless." His voice was low, as soft as silk. Full of his own secret knowledge of her. His mysterious power.

She shivered at its promise. "Too bad for you. Let go."

"No, I will not." He flung her down onto the bed, and yanked her arm toward the headboard.

Too late, she realized what he planned, and by then, the cuff was snapped closed over her wrist. She flailed and slapped with her free hand, but he slid down the length of her and pulled her body on the bed so that she was stretched out, long and taut. All she could reach were handfuls of his hair, which she grabbed, yanked. In vain.

He put his mouth to her, and loved her with it, eagerly, desperately. He suckled, licked and swirled her into a state of slick, creamy desperation. Jerking, shivering. Trying not to whimper and beg.

The handcuffs helped, perversely. Even though she yanked and rattled, even though the metal hurt, the cuff gave her a fixed point of reference that she could cling to. It left the rest of her free . . . to feel it.

Really feel it, as she never had before. She'd always had to pretend to like cunnilingus, for those lovers who had insisted upon it. Too intimate, too exposed. It had been hard to pretend.

She wasn't pretending now. She writhed at the tender tremolo fluttering across her clit, the slide up and down the furled folds of her labia, the plunge of his tongue into her pussy. He found her sweet spots, and exploited them, exalted them.

Time stretched and warped. She came apart, over and over, until she stopped struggling and lay there, damp and sprawled and vibrating.

He turned on the hideous bedside lamp, and picked the lock again, then petted and kissed the angry red marks on her wrist.

She glanced at the huge erection waving right at eye level, and cleared her throat. "Ah, do you plan to do anything with that?"

"If you want it," he said quietly. "I get tired of hearing only no."

"You won't hear it this time." She caressed his cock with one hand and cupped his balls with the other, swirling her fingers tenderly around the hot, heavy globes. She pulled him down on top of her, guided him between her legs. Nudging, wiggling, pressing him inside.

Tears welled into her eyes at the perfection of it when he pushed himself deeper. They settled into a lazy rocking against the squeaking bed, clutching and sighing, riding the soft, surging waves. In no hurry. It was all pleasure. It was all perfect. He was perfect.

And if she were not so exhausted, that would have terrified her.

When they were too tired to move, he rolled over onto her and stared down, as if he could see her face in the dark. "Someday you will make that promise to me," he said.

She put her hands on his cheeks, stroking the angular shape of his bones, the faint, scratchy sting of his beard. "I will not make false promises," she said softly. "Not to you, Val."

He turned his head, kissed her palm, with those soft, hot, supple lips. "No," he said, his voice stubborn. "The promise will be real."

She shook her head. "You're wildly romantic, Val, did you know that?"

"I suppose," he said. "Since I met you, I have become so."

"I hate to break this to you, but I'm the most unromantic person on the planet," she told him. "Which doesn't mean that I don't care.

I did what I did because I care. I wish I could make you understand that."

"I do understand it." He grabbed her hand, rubbed it against his cheek. "But I reject it. I will not ask that of the woman I love. I would not ask it of myself. The subject is closed."

Love. The word made shivers of marvelous terror course through her. Along with something else, something nameless, sweet and dangerous, that fluttered through her, rustling her, like wind shaking a tree.

She shoved it away instinctively. "Toughen up, Val."

"Leave the subject alone," he growled. "It is irrelevant now. We have burned that bridge, and thank God for it."

"Not at all," Tam said crisply. "As far as he knows, you burst in and abducted me. I could contact him, feed his vanity—"

"No!"

She sighed. "Damn it, Val. Do you want to save Imre, or not?"

"Don't put it in those terms. It is an intolerable thought. Just let me protect you. Please. For once."

She was startled, and moved. "I don't need protecting," she told him.

"Of course you do not," he said wearily. "I do not give a fuck whether you do or not. I want to protect you anyway."

She shook her head.

He grabbed her shoulder, squeezed it, shook it. "Tamar. My love." His voice sounded exhausted. "If someone offered to protect me, I would not spit in her eye. I would be flattered. Perhaps even . . . touched."

"Oh, I think we've got the touching part all covered," she murmured, smiling in the dark. "Do you need protecting, Val?"

"No. But it would be nice to have someone care enough to try."

She pressed her face against his shoulder and licked, savoring the deep, salty flavor of his dried sweat. Relaxing against his heat, his strength. She inhaled and realized that her chest had relaxed.

She was breathing so deeply. The breaths so unforced.

It was true, what he said. It would be tragically futile, to try and protect someone like her.

But it was so nice that he cared enough to try.

* * *

The overhead light switched on, without warning. Val and Tam both sprang up, Tam lunging for the purse, with the gun . . .

Ah. Never mind. It was just Signora Concetta, her hand on the lightswitch, her eyes huge and shocked. She crossed herself.

Tam grabbed for the towel that lay on the floor and wrapped it around herself. Val had no such recourse. He got up, picked up his trousers, and started putting them on. Lazy and unhurried.

The signora took a long look at Val's body, and cleared her throat, with a great, phleghmy, gurgling cough. She looked as if she were trying not to smile, though the expression looked a bit rusty.

"*Scusatemi*. You wanted dinner," she said stiffly.

"So I did," Val said calmly. "I still do. Especially now."

The good lady had taken Val's suggestion of wine, bread and cheese as a challenge to inflict death by food. The assault started with a jug of homemade wine and two thick crockery cups to drink it out of. Then a crusty loaf of bread, a wedge of cheese with a filthy green rind that looked like it had been rolled in dead grass, and a creamy, yellow-white interior that smelled powerfully of sheep. A huge, phallic chunk of homemade salami followed.

"*Cinghiale*," the signora said proudly. "Wild boar. My sons killed it."

Then she went out onto the patio and bent over what they then realized was an enormous wheelbarrow. She began bringing in earthenware oven crocks, each wrapped in its own artfully knotted dish towel, each filled with a fragrant hot baked or stewed dish.

She covered the rickety table with them and went out again. Her next armful of jars held vegetables preserved in vinegar, oil and garlic; sun-dried tomatos, eggplants, peppers, olives. A basket of freshly picked oranges was the crowning touch, or so they thought until the signora reached into her apron pocket and pulled out a slender-necked corked bottle filled with a pale yellow liquor.

"Limoncello," she announced proudly. "My own lemons. Very good."

Val grabbed the lady's hand, which fortunately no longer appeared to be covered with chicken blood, and kissed it fervently.

"Signora, you are an angel sent from heaven," he declared. "Thank you from the bottom of my heart."

The signora yanked her hand back with a smirk and took a long, appreciative look at Val's naked chest and half-fastened pants. She grunted her approval. "You will need it," she said. *"Buon appetito."*

"God, yes," he said in heartfelt tones.

The signora frowned at Tam and pinched her upper arm. "Eat some of my *braciole*," she admonished. "You're too skinny. That man will squash you."

After the signora had gone, they perched on the rickety, termite-riddled chairs on each side of the loaded table, and dug into the feast.

Tam discovered, to her astonishment, that food just kept on going right into her and space kept opening up for more. It was so different from her usual feeling when eating or trying to—that the food was bumping up against a blank stone wall that would let nothing through.

Not tonight. Tonight, she was open, yawning wide, eager.

Usually, strong tastes repelled her. Tonight, they were strangely marvelous. She ate three times as much as she usually managed to choke down, and Val inhaled over ten times that much on his own.

When she finally stopped, stuffed, she sat back and just watched in awe as he continued to eat, and eat, and eat.

"You're risking your life with that stuff, you know," she informed him. He layered sun-dried tomatoes with the wild boar salami, cheese, and fleshy red festoons of peppers on a huge chunk of dripping, oil-soaked bread. "Salmonella, botulism, and ten other lethal bacteria that I could name."

"Don't name them." His white teeth bit down, eyes closing in delight as he chewed. "And this from a woman who travels with at least twenty different types of deadly poison in her beauty case?"

Tam grabbed an orange and began to peel. At least its contents would be more or less sterile. "That's different. Those compounds were cooked in a lab under controlled conditions by people who hold advanced degrees in chemistry from MIT and Stanford."

He ripped off another chunk of bread and fearlessly prepared another heap. "But they do not taste as good," he pointed out.

She took a bite of orange. The explosive, tangy sweetness made her gasp. "The chicken blood alone might carry you away," she warned.

Val stabbed his fork into the crock that held thinly sliced dark meat wrapped around flavorful cheese, hot pepper, parsley and garlic, floating in a rich lake of spiced tomato sauce. He chewed fearlessly and stared her in the face, a suggestive gleam in his eyes.

"Don't think for one second that you're going to kiss me after you eat all that garlic," she warned him.

"Don't think for one second that you can deny me," he retorted coolly. "I'm much bigger than you are. Faster, too."

"Ah, but I'm more treacherous," she teased him.

His face sobered. He looked at the food in his hand as if he'd forgotten what to do with it. "I would not want to put that to the test."

She missed that fleeting moment of lightness. It was so rare in her life to laugh and joke, kick around a man and have him come back for more. To have fun. Typical Tam. Trust her to kill it by accident.

She tended to kill things, as a rule. She abruptly hated herself for it. "I won't betray you if I can help it," she said, a lame attempt to save the moment.

"Me neither," he replied quietly. "I swear it."

She lost her appetite for the uneaten orange, delicious though it was. She held it out. "Freshen your breath with this," she commanded. "And then come back to bed."

That worked, but sex always did with men. His face brightened.

He devoured the orange, stripped off his pants to reveal his already lengthening cock, and slid between the sheets, holding the covers up for her. Oddly, his doggish male predictability bothered her less than usual tonight. She eased between the covers, curling up against his heat.

He was, of course, at full salute. It was ridiculous, but she felt too mellow to say anything about it, even when he rolled on top of her.

She was wet and soft from the last time, and very sensitive. He pushed his big phallus slowly inside her. Tam looped her arms around his shoulders and wiggled, seeking the perfect angle.

"Do not come inside me again," she warned.

"I will not come at all," he assured her. "I've come enough."

She made a dubious sound. He took her face in his hands and looked earnestly into her eyes. "Trust me," he said. "Please."

The snide comeback was ready on her lips, but somehow she

stopped it. It was the look in his eyes, the intensity behind the words.

He wasn't feeding her a line, jerking her around. It was a plea from someplace deep within him. He wasn't even talking about sex.

She swallowed, clamping down on her mortal dread of being made a fool of. She could risk this. Maybe just this much, for once.

"I will . . . try to," she said, haltingly.

He bent his head down and kissed her reverently on the forehead.

"Thank you," he said. "I will try to be worthy of your trust."

That was too much for her. "Oh, stop it, you melodramatic fool," she snapped. "Don't get swishy on me, Val. I can't handle it."

He proceeded to wrap her in a breathlessly tight, hot, marvelous embrace and express himself nonverbally, most eloquently . . . and to her utter satisfaction.

András strolled down the darkened corridor of I Santi Medici. The security of the place was lax. He'd slipped in a door that someone had left conveniently propped open; he'd sauntered through dim, deserted halls and stairwells, and he'd been obliged to kill no one so far. The nurses and doctors on call at this indecent hour had all been elsewhere, chatting in the nurse's station, or dozing on unused beds. No one noticed him sliding by like a big, quiet ghost.

He knew exactly where to go, having sent flowers earlier that afternoon. The stringy youth who he'd paid to deliver them had ascertained the room number for him. Ah, yes, there it was, a big bouquet of calla lilies and birds-of-paradise. The nurses had placed it with the other flowers clustered around the white and blue ceramic statue of the Madonna who presided at the end of the corridor, her electric crown glowing eerily in the darkness.

A grim-faced old man in pajamas and a green bathrobe sat outside his room door with an IV in his arm, the rack clutched in his fist. No doubt trying to evade the groaning or flatulence of his roomates. He blinked at András with clouded eyes. A witness. Pity. András took note of the room number. Unfortunate for the old man, but he was well into his eighties and clearly not enjoying his life overmuch. András would probably be doing him a favor by holding his nose shut for a few minutes after he finished with Hegel.

Hegel was not alone in his room either, András was irritated to note. He hadn't wanted to conduct a full scale massacre tonight. At least the other man was sleeping. A stringy, grayish creature with a chicken neck and a mouth that gaped wide and toothless.

Hegel's eyes were closed. His head was bandaged and one arm was in a cast. András grasped the nurse call button, which dangled on the end of a plastic cord, and looped it up high over the IV rack next to the bed. Well out of the man's reach. He grabbed a chair and sat down.

Hegel's eyes popped open at the scrape of the chair, widening with alarm when he saw who sat before him. András was ready with the rubber ball, which he shoved into Hegel's mouth. He wrapped a gag of rubber around the man's mouth to hold it in, knotting it behind his head. He fastened Hegel's good hand to the metal bedstead with a cable tie, pulling it tight enough to cut off the circulation.

Then he laid a heavy hand over the other man's throat, putting a relentless pressure on his larynx. "We need to talk," he said. "My original plan was to cut or burn you for a few minutes before we started to demonstrate my commitment, but you must be loaded with pain medications right now. My skills would be wasted on you. But I could puncture your eyeball, for instance, with this." He held up a long, gleaming needle. "Or saw off one of your ears with this." He held up a serrated blade, one of the offerings of his multiblade pocketknife.

Hegel's eyes protruded. He made a gurgling sound in his throat.

"Or we could skip that part of the conversation and speak of Tamara Steele and Val Janos," András suggested.

Hegel nodded frantically.

"I will take off the gag," András told him. "If you speak above a whisper, I will put it back in, saw off one ear, and deflate one eye. Do we understand each other?"

Another frantic nod. András reached back, loosened the rubber gag, and plucked out the ball, wiping the spit off on Hegel's sheets.

Hegel coughed, staring wide-eyed at the other man. His jowled face glistened with pain and fear sweat.

András reached into his briefcase and took out the laptop which he had taken from Hegel's hotel room after speaking with Ferenc. He opened it, perched it on the man's chest, and unfastened the tourniquet that held his arm to the bed. "The password, please."

András observed carefully as the man's stubby, trembling finger punched a sequence of letters, numbers and symbols into the computer. He committed the password to memory.

"And now, explain to me how you have been monitoring Janos and Steele," he said.

Hegel cleared his throat. "Janos has an RF trace implanted in his body." His voice was thick and hoarse. "He doesn't know."

András chuckled. "How despicable of you, Hegel. That's cheating. Tell me about the frequency, and how the tracking software works."

Hegel swallowed, licked his lips. "But I can't—"

Pop, the ball was wedged into his mouth again, and András's big hand ground the man's teeth into his lips on top of it. "I do not want to hear those words again," he said. "First your eyes, and then your ears. Is that turd Luksch worth that kind of loyalty?"

Hegel squeezed his eyes shut and shook his head.

András lifted his hand, and let the other man push the ball out with his tongue, coughing desperately. András gestured toward the laptop. "Tell me everything," he said softly.

It took twenty minutes to pry the technical information out of the man: the frequency of the trace, the use of the software, how to access archived data, how to monitor in real time. Relatively simple for András, who had used similar technology many times before.

He stared at the screen, committing to memory the exact spot where the man was lurking this very night. Some obscure point in the mountains, several kilometers from the main coastal highway. Thinking he was safe and hidden. It gave András a pleasurable feeling of power.

Good. It was all good. This was becoming so easy, it might not even be a worthy challenge, he reflected with faint amusement. But he would gladly exchange challenge for speed. It reflected well upon him in any case. And his work here was done.

He took the laptop, stowed it, and stood. He looked down at

Hegel, trying to think if there was any reason on earth, any reason at all, not to kill him. The man saw death in his eyes and held up his hand to ward it off. András had seen that classic gesture many times.

"There's more," he said hastily.

András fondled the knife in one pocket. "More? What more?"

"Don't kill me. Help me get away from here, from Georg, and I'll tell you everything I—"

"Don't try to bargain with me, fool," András said. "You will tell me everything you know now, or I will cut off your dick and choke you to death with it. What more do you have?"

Hegel swallowed repeatedly. "The child," he said hoarsely.

András frowned down at him. "What child?"

"She has a child. Steele. She adopted a girl. Three years old."

András began to grin. Ah, yes. This would make the old man very happy. "Where is she?"

"I don't know exactly. She appeared on the airport security cameras in Sea-Tac International three days ago. I had three men following Janos in an attempt to locate Steele and the child. He killed the men, took Steele and the girl, and from that point, all I know is that he climbed on a plane in Portland with Steele alone. Somewhere between Sea-Tac and Portland International Airport, they left the child with someone. I do have some archived footage from the night between those events, and I know he spent them at a luxury resort between Tacoma and Seattle," Hegel babbled on. "A place called the Huxley. I assume they left the kid with someone during that interval, but I didn't investigate any further because Luksch just wanted Steele. Nothing else."

András sat down on the chair, chewing the inside of his lip.

"She has, ah, dark curly hair," Hegel added, a note of desperation in his voice, the sound of a man with no bargaining chips left. "She's small, very thin for her age. And she's extremely—"

Thhtp. The silenced Glock drilled a bullet between Hegel's eyes. The man flopped back onto his pillow and gazed blankly into the air.

"Thank you," András said softly.

He gazed at his handiwork for a moment. The slumped body on the bed lacked dramatic impact. He really ought to put a bit more artistry into it. He didn't have time to get truly creative, but the boss always appreciated that personal touch.

András shrugged off his jacket to save the bloodstains, clicked open his case and took out a small saw and a pair of industrial strength rubber gloves. A few minutes later, he was relatively pleased by the artistic effect of Hegel's head, nestled in the center of the blood-soaked coverlet, severed hands clasped piously beneath his chin. He snapped a picture on his cell phone, encrypted it, sent it to the boss. The old man needed a pick-me-up. Waiting made him frantic.

András heard an unintelligible sound, turned, found that the man in the other bed was awake and staring at him, eyes bugged out.

Automatically, András aimed the gun at the man's forehead—and then paused, taking note of the lopsided mouth, the fellow's garbled attempts at speech. Stroke. András's grandfather had suffered from a stroke when András was a child. He still remembered the horrified fascination he'd felt at the old man's distorted face, his helpless frustration. His vain attempts to communicate.

It made him almost nostalgic. Poor old Grandfather.

No need to risk another shot. Each time the silencer was slightly less effective, and this poor old man would never be able to describe him. András tucked the gun into his jacket, leaned over the man's bed and put his finger to his smiling lips.

"Shhh," he murmured. "Not one word, eh? Our little secret."

The man's eyes and mouth kept stretching wider. A red mote in his eye began to grow and grow. His eyelid filled with blood. It welled over and trickled down his pale cheeks, like a miraculous blood-weeping statue of the Virgin. He was having another catastrophic stroke before András's eyes.

András could not help but smile at the irony of it. It was one of those days. He was riding great cresting waves of death. Exhilarating.

Ah, yes. Which reminded him. Green Bathrobe. Details, details.

He slid into room 14. Green Bathrobe was asleep, as were his two roomates. András took a pillow from the unoccupied bed and pressed it over the man's face, counting with slow, deadly patience while his mind churned, compiling a list of professionals in the Seattle area.

Someone who could locate and discreetly extract Tamar's child. The boss would want her, the way a greedy brat wanted toys and chocolate.

Admittedly, he didn't have much time left to play.

And András would be the one to deliver this treat. A turn of the knife to show the old man his error in having favored Georg over András as successor after Kurt's death after years of loyal service.

Some silent moments later, the other inhabitants of the room still slept, and Green Bathrobe's pulse was absent.

András slid back down the hall like a shadow again, his hand on the butt of his gun. Daring fate. Let someone come out of the nurse's station and force him to shoot again and again. To leave a pile—no, a towering mountain of bleeding bodies in his wake.

Once he started riding that wave, he never wanted to stop.

Chapter 21

Harry Whelan was having a stressful day. Assistant managing the Huxley on a busy day with two weddings and a banquet made him brusque. When Nancy, one of the check-in clerks, asked him to deal with a cop who had questions about a guest, he was short with her.

"Tell him we don't give out information about our guests," he snapped. "It's Huxley security policy. As you know."

"I did, but he kept insisting—"

"Does he have a warrant? Tell him to get a warrant."

"Please, Harry, I did, but he won't listen to me. Will you come talk to him? He'll listen to you."

Harry groaned, but Nancy was so cute with big blue eyes and substantial breasts that strained her green uniform vest to the limit of what was professionally appropriate. He was actually contemplating breaking his no-dating-in-the-workplace rule and asking her out. He hustled down the hall to the front desk, puffing out his chest.

A burly man with a beard waited. He smiled at Harry, who did not smile back. Not when his time was being wasted. "Can I help you?"

The man held out his hand, and Harry shook it. "Raymond Clive, FBI," he said. "Are you the manager, Mr. Whelan?"

His nametag read AM, which should be clear enough, Harry thought. "Assistant Manager," he specified.

"May I speak with you in private?" Clive asked.

"I might as well tell you right now that it's the Huxley's security policy not to share information about our guests with any—"

"Please, Mr. Whelan. Can we speak privately?" The man leaned over the counter and pitched his voice lower. "It's a delicate matter."

Harry sighed. This delicate matter had to be today? With six rooms overbooked, a banquet chef gone missing, and an embarrassing sewer crisis in the back six units of the guest houses? "Come on," he snapped.

In his office, he sat behind his desk and indicated for Clive to sit on the other side. The man grabbed another chair and dragged it around to Harry's side of the desk. He scooted closer so that his knee touched Harry's. Harry shrank back. "It's a little tight back here," he said stiffly. "Could you sit in the chair on the other side of the—"

"We have a problem, and time is of the essence, Mr. Whelan. A small child is in jeopardy. She's been kidnapped," Clive said. "In situations like these, a man can be excused for bending the rules—even the security rules of the Huxley."

"Do you have a warrant? If you don't, I just can't—"

"I can get one, but I would waste precious time. In missing child cases, every minute counts," Clive said.

The only good thing about still being assistant manager was that he could pass the buck. His boss would not appreciate being bothered, but they did not pay Harry enough to take on this kind of responsibility. "I'll talk to my supervisor," Harry said. He reached for the intercom. "Did you guys issue an Amber Alert? Doesn't that come first—"

To his alarm, Clive reached out and grabbed Harry's hand. Tightly. So tightly, in fact, that the bones of his fingers felt like they were grinding against each other. "Wait, Mr. Whelan," he said. "Just wait."

Harry yanked, and the man's big, hairy fingers tightened further. Harry gasped. "Uh, please. That, uh . . . hurts."

"Of course." A tug, and Harry's chair shot forward. He bumped into Clive's knees. To his horror, the other man was gripping his crotch. With a brutal, powerful hand. It was a level of pain Harry had never imagined. His balls had to be ruptured.

"Don't make a sound or I will twist them off." The man's teeth flashed in his dark beard. "Keep your hands out where I can see them."

A knife appeared in his hand, a wicked-looking black thing with a serrated portion near the handle. A razor sharp tip.

"Listen carefully, Mr. Whelan," Clive said softly. "If your attitude does not change quickly, I will open your pants with this knife and castrate you as you sit, right here. A neat incision in your scrotum, I detach your testicles with surgical precision, flick, flick, and voilà, there they'll be, on the floor, with a minimum of bloodshed. I hate mess."

"No," Harry gasped. "No, no, no."

"No? All right, then. We do have alternatives, fortunately. Let's discuss the security policy of the Huxley once again."

Harry stared at him, wheezing for breath. The pain was making him faint. "You're not FBI," he gasped.

"It's none of your concern what I am. Not a sound, Mr. Whelan. Be brave." The knife dug into the side of Harry's testicles. A strangled sound issued from his throat, like the whine of a balloon letting out air. "A three-year-old girl with curly dark hair spent time in this building the day before yesterday," Clive went on. "Find out who she left with."

Harry tried to breathe. His lungs would not expand. His ribs were frozen. His hands clutched the desk, as if he were drowning. "I—I—"

"Think, Mr. Whelan," Clive encouraged him. "Think."

"D-d-day before yesterday, there was an afternoon wedding," he forced out. "Big party, lots of overnight guests."

"Well, then. The guest list would be an excellent place to start. Turn to the computer screen, put your hand on the mouse. Show me who checked in that afternoon. Show me a list of all the rooms that had notations regarding infants or small children."

Harry pulled them up. The man leaned forward to peer at the screen, jabbing the knife deeper in the process. He tried not to shriek.

"Shut up, Mr. Whelan," Clive said absently. "Hmm. Four single women with children, six couples. Did you see any of them?"

"N-n-no," Harry gasped. "I wasn't out on the front desk. I don't work the desk. I work back here."

"Oh. How unfortunate for you." The knife dug deeper. "Perhaps one of your colleagues? If I took this knife away for a moment, you could consult with one of them. Could you behave, if I did that, Mr. Whelan? Would you be a good boy? Can I count on you?"

Harry nodded, violently.

"Because if you give me any trouble, you will regret it. And so will your colleague. Is this clear?"

"Yes," Harry gasped. "Yes, please. I'll call one of them. Please."

Clive removed the crushing pressure of his fingers. Tears of relief streamed down Harry's face, clogging his nose. He wiped them on his sleeve, and tried to remember who had been on the desk that day. Nancy, for sure. He stabbed her button. "Nancy? Could you come back here for a minute?" His voice was watery and high.

"Sure, Harry. Just a sec, got to finish up this guest."

She was there in two interminable minutes, eyes big and puzzled. Harry made a huge effort to control his face, his voice, his bowels. Clive's knife hovered in front of his crotch, beneath the desk, menacing him. "Nancy, do you remember that wedding party two days ago?"

"Sure," she said. "Becca Cattrell and Nick Ward. Harry? Are you OK? You look kind of strange." She looked curiously at the bearded man.

The knife dug into Harry's balls again. Harry sucked air, and forced a weak smile onto his face. "I'm fine. Little headache. Do you remember a three-year-old girl in that wedding reception? Dark curly hair?"

Nancy's big eyes rolled. "Oh, my God, yes. That kid screamed the place down the morning after, in the dining room. I've never heard anything like it in my life, and I've heard some doozies when I worked day care. Talk about living birth control."

"Do you remember her parents' names?"

Nancy frowned thoughtfully. "She was with her mom, I remember that. A glamorpuss type, like a top model. I didn't check her in. Charlie did, but she's out sick today. The glamorpuss left with the gorgeous foreign guy. That was why the kid flipped out, because her mom had to go somewhere without her."

"What guy? What was his name?" Harry begged.

Nancy shrugged. "I don't know. I don't think he had his own room booked. One of us would've remembered. The guy was, like, movie star good-looking. It was unreal, the two of them together."

Harry could not think straight enough to form a response to that, trying as he was not to vomit from the white-hot pressure of the knife tip.

Clive asked, "And who did the child leave with?"

Her face cleared. "That's easy. It was with one of those McCloud guys. I remember the name because there were three of them, and all the girls at the desk were checking them out. Drop dead gorgeous, all three of them. Brothers, I guess. Like, be still my heart."

"Which one?" Harry burst out. "Just tell me which one it was!"

Nancy blinked at his tone, startled. "One of the ones with a baby," she offered timidly. "Two of them had babies. Cute as can be. I don't remember which one, though. Look, do you want some Advil or Tylenol? Or at least some coffee? You do not look good at all."

"No. I'm fine," Harry said.

Clive drew the knife away, and it was all Harry could do not to collapse into sobs. "Is that enough?" He turned imploring eyes on Clive.

The man smiled genially and nodded. "That's fine."

"Thanks for your help, Nancy," Harry said. "You can go."

Nancy left, throwing a worried glance back over her shoulder. "You let me know if you change your mind about that Advil," she said.

The door clicked closed. Harry began to sob silently.

"Don't fall apart yet, Mr. Whelan," Clive chided him. "I need printouts of the credit cards you billed for those two rooms, please."

Somehow Harry managed to perform that task. Clive tucked the sheets into his pocket, and spun the knife, a twinkling show of dexterity, like a baton twirler. "Thank you, Mr. Whelan. You've been very helpful. And in case you're tempted to discuss what just happened with anyone . . . your supervisor, for instance, or the police, or the McClouds—"

"I won't," Harry assured him, his voice breaking. "I promise."

"Or your mother," Clive continued. "Or even that pretty colleague, the one who's so worried about you. My associates and I informed ourselves before I came here. Your address, for instance. Where you live with your mother in that Victorian home in Tacoma. Pretty, but those old houses are firetraps. It would be tragic to come home from work and find that your mother had been burned to death in a house fire, hmm? Batteries run down in the smoke alarms. Tsk tsk. Terrible shame."

"I promise, I—"

"And then there is Nancy, that lovely girl who wants to play nurse. Isn't that sweet of her. She lives in that apartment complex on the other side of the park, all alone with her cat, in unit 8D. Violent things can happen at night to young women all alone. Just terrible. You wouldn't want to be responsible for something like that, would you?"

Harry shook his head, and realized to his dismay that he could not stop shaking it. It just kept on twisting, back and forth. *No. No. No.*

Clive smiled and grabbed the top of Harry's head, forcing it to stop turning. "Excellent, then. We understand each other." He held out his hand, as if they had just conducted a normal business meeting.

Harry was horrified to realize that his slavish obedience to the other man actually extended to automatically holding out his trembling hand to shake. Clive shook it and gave it one last, agonizingly painful squeeze. Harry cringed and squealed like a whipped dog.

"Have a great day, Mr. Whelan. Thanks again for all your help."

The door closed. Harry collapsed on his desk. His throat felt like it would implode. His groin throbbed. He felt raped, torn. Bleeding inside. He hadn't known how easy it would be to be mortally hurt.

Then it flashed in his mind, like a pop-up banner on the computer. An appalling thought.

What a man like that might do to a three-year-old girl.

He shoved the thought away as if it electrocuted him. Too much. He couldn't deal with that too. That little girl was not his responsibility. This was not his fault. He had not caused this.

There was a timid knock on the door. He scrambled for a fast food napkin to wipe his eyes and nose. "What is it?" he snapped.

Nancy peeked in the door. "Harry? I just, um, saw that guy go out. I thought I'd check on you. I was wondering . . . what the eff?"

For one crazy instant, he was tempted to tell her everything. What a sweet relief it would be, to let someone else carry some of the weight of the horribleness of the ten minutes that had just passed. Then he thought about her all alone at night with her cat in unit 8D.

No. Don't.

He blew his nose again. "That was a tricky situation," he said, hating the phlegm-clogged, officious tone in his own voice. "Sometimes in this business, you just have to make a judgment call."

"Ah," she said. "Um. OK. Harry, are you sure you're—"

"Yes! I'm fine! It's just this sinus thing I get sometimes. Allergies. It's no big deal. Don't worry about me."

"OK." Her face reddened. The door started to close.

"Nancy?" His voice had a wobbly, pleading tone. He took a deep breath to steady it as she opened the door and peeked back in. "Uh . . . don't mention this to anyone else, OK?" he begged. "I mean, no one."

She looked almost scared. "Whatever," she said softly.

The door closed. There was a strange finality to the sound. As if the door was closing on the person he had fantasized about becoming.

He'd been cut down, trimmed into something that would always be smaller now. Someone who would never get rid of that pot belly and train to run in the local 10K. Never ask Nancy Ware out to the Blues In The Park concert series. Never get his own place and move out of his mother's house. Someone who would never make general manager.

He grabbed the wastebasket, vomited into it until bitter snot hung from his face over the plastic sack. He mopped it off, touched his balls, wondered if they were irreparably damaged.

Wondered if it would be a relief to run his car off the road into the river tonight when he got off work. Just to make this awful feeling stop.

* * *

"Push with your legs," Sveti encouraged her. "Up and down. That way you can go higher all by yourself."

Rachel tried valiantly, but she didn't really have much luck coordinating the frantic movement of her skinny little legs with the rhythm of the swing. Still, she put all her effort into it, flopping like a freshly caught fish in the bucket-style kiddie swing, giggling madly.

It was getting very dark, and the gray sky was fading to night on one side. It was also extremely cold, but they were having so much fun in the park playground, neither wanted to leave quite yet. After all, they could see the lit-up windows of Connor and Erin's house right on the other side of the park, like a beacon of safety. After days of shrieking for Mamma, Rachel was finally calming down. She was not really eating yet and when she talked at all, she stuttered, but things were looking up. Right now she was laughing and smiling. Sveti was grateful to see it. Reluctant to let go of the moment.

The whole afternoon had gone relatively well so far. Rachel seemed to enjoy the story circle at the kids' room in the local library, and the level of English had been perfect for Sveti's comprehension level, too. In fact, she'd used Erin's library card to check out a whole tote bag full of children's books to study. She had to hurry up and learn.

Not just for Josh, either, she told herself sternly. Forget stupid Josh. She wasn't thinking about his green eyes, his big grin.

This was for her. Just her. She wanted to study here, go to college here. Something to do with small children. Teaching, childhood development, psychology, and someday maybe even medical school and pediatrics.

It made her so happy to see how Rachel had grown, how much better she walked. To see that rosy red blush in her cheeks. She glowed like a Christmas light in her puffy red ski jacket and red sparkling cap. No one would ever call her chubby, but she looked so much better than back in the bad old days, when she'd seemed like a wizened little troll.

It all seemed so improbable to Sveti sometimes. The strange flip-flop of reality. Sometimes her life seemed like a dream of heaven. Being free, seeing the sky, the trees, the flowers. Seeing Rachel happy with someone who loved her. Having her own mother again.

But that stinking basement room haunted her. Piss-stained mattresses, hollow-eyed children. Doom hanging over them. Constant fear and dread. She wondered if that was the reality, and this was the dream. She could wake up at any time and find herself there again.

It was a nightmare that wouldn't let her go. Knowing that there were places like that, cruelty like that. Monstrous selfishness like that. Once known, you couldn't unknow it. And it was hard not to think about it.

All she could do was enjoy a little girl giggling on a playground swing in her puffy red coat and try to hold the dark at bay.

These sad, dark thoughts had sobered and chilled her enough to make her want to get herself and Rachel quickly back to the safety to the McCloud house. It was full of people, voices, and laughter tonight. Both of Connor's brothers were there with their wives, for dinner. They were incredibly nice to her, but their loudness, their breezy American exuberance, their torrents of hard-to-understand English, oh. It made her intensely shy.

She would do what she always did. Retreat, make herself useful, play with the babies. She liked it and it made everyone so grateful.

Rachel put up a fuss about leaving, and Sveti compromised. She spun Rachel once more on the merry-go-round, a sedate spin that made the little girl shriek with delight. Then another clamber up the rope net, three more passes down the slide, and twilight had become dark.

Her neck started to prickle.

They set off through the trees. Suddenly Sveti had become anxious. So much that her quickening pace pulled Rachel right off her crooked little ankles. Rachel squawked and began to cry.

Sveti scooped her up into her arms and began to jog toward the far side of the park, keeping those lit-up windows in sight. Running was a mistake, though. It threw a panic switch inside her and she began to run faster and faster. Her feet flew, but they were wobbly with fear.

And when the black sedan pulled up right in front of her, she skidded to a stop with a shout and dropped to her knees, twisting to save Rachel from being squashed. She landed painfully on one wrist. Library books spilled out on the frosty grass.

Both doors opened, men boiled out. Big men in dark ski caps and black jackets, and oh God, they were coming for her—and this was not happening, not happening, this was not possible—not again.

One snatched the shrieking Rachel. Sveti grabbed his booted foot and hung on. He yelled something, stomped his weight onto the boot she was clutching, and kicked her in the ribs with the other.

The pain was huge, jolting her lungs, loosening her grip. The man wrenched his foot away, kicked her again in the leg for good measure. Rachel flailed under his arm, shrilling her high, thin wail of terror. The car doors thumped closed. Sveti stumbled up to her feet and flung herself at the shiny black car, screaming at it in Ukrainian, the ugliest words she knew, words she'd learned from Yuri and Martina, her jailors. Ugly, filthy, angry words she'd sworn she'd never say. The car took off, tires squealing, knocking her around to spin like a top and fall to her bloodied knees once again.

Only then did it occur to her to look at the license plate as the car sped away, but it was thickly spattered with mud and her eyes swam with tears. She dashed them away, peered desperately, but could make out only the first A and the form of Mt. Rainier. Washington plates.

The taillights became two malevolent red eyes, glancing back at her. Mocking, leering at her. Then the car turned the corner, and was gone.

Chapter
22

Val opened his eyes and made his peace with the fact that the erotic grace of yesterday's amazing dawn lovemaking was a fluke. Not a thing to plan for, or even hope for.

Tamara had been up for a while. Quiet as a ghost, if she had managed not to wake him. She was washed, dressed, hair braided back at the nape of her neck. She sat crosslegged on a ragged plaid blanket with her Deadly Beauty paraphernalia laid out before her in the opened briefcase, contemplating vials, powders and potions.

Her beautiful face was calm, in a state of total focused concentration. A lethal alchemist. His dangerous sorceress.

She felt the weight of his eyes upon her and looked up. Amazingly, he got a fleeting, almost shy smile, before the mantle of sarcastic distance settled back over her.

He sighed. Fool that he was, strung out on the wild, potent magic hidden deep inside the most complicated emotional defense mechanism he had ever encountered—outside of madness, that is. Or drugs.

His life would never be simple again. But hey. Fuck simplicity. His had never been simple. Not since his birth. *Evviva le complicazioni.*

There was a heavy knock on the door. "*Ehi, ragazzi.* Your breakfast is outside the door," said Signora Concetta. "The caffé is *bella calda calda*, eh? Don't let it get cold."

"*Grazie mille*," he called back to her. "I'll get it right away."

Tam gave him a mocking grin. "Oh, go on. Get it now. You know you want it. She's lingering out there hoping to get another peek at that manly apparatus of yours, and who can blame her?"

He threw the covers off and stood, letting his manly apparatus wave like a banner before him. "I do not want to scare anyone."

Her lips curved into a quick, appreciative smile before she could stop herself. "Mmm," she murmured coolly. "I'm not scared, big boy. Unfortunately, though, I am busy. Don't bug me with that thing of yours. And the signora's made of stern stuff. Go on, get your breakfast. Make her day. She deserves a treat. She works hard."

He plucked the towel off the bedpost where it hung, making the handcuff rattle, and wrapped it around his waist. It tented comically over his cock like a flagpole. Tam snickered. "Coward."

He ignored her and threw the bolt on the door. He had to crouch to get through the frame without giving himself a concussion.

A blaze of pale winter sunshine and sweet, rainwashed, herb-scented morning air assaulted his eyes and nose. Birds twittered madly in the trees.

The signora had taken away the wheelbarrow with last night's dishes. She was industriously sweeping dead leaves off the patio. She stopped to give him a once-over, and crossed herself as her eyes lit on his crotch. "*Madonna santissima*," she murmured.

He crouched for the tray, and gave her a brass-faced grin. "*Buon giorno*, Signora. Dinner was magnificent. *Grazie di nuovo*."

"You'll like my *pastiera*," the good lady informed him. "I make the best *pastiera* in Campania."

"I love pastiera," he assured her. "*A dopo*, Signora." He ducked back into the privacy of their room with his prize.

The smell of espresso steaming out of the blackened pot on the tray dragged even Tamara to her feet and to the table. A thick, chipped red crockery plate held several big, moist wedges of *pastiera*, an egg and ricotta pie made with candied fruit, boiled wheat and orange-flower water. The sight filled his heart with joy after the sexual energy put forth the night before. He lost no time devouring a wedge.

Tam sipped unsweetened coffee and watched him with her wide, fascinated golden eyes. "You probably just took in a thousand calories with that one piece alone," she informed him, her voice wondering.

He grabbed another piece. "Oh, *sì*," he sighed.

The tray held a tall glass bottle of milk. Tam popped the cork and sniffed. Her eyes lit up, and to his astonishment, she poured some out into a glass and drank it.

"Fresh, real milk," she said. "They have a cow here."

He laughed around a mouthful of pastry. "Unpasteurized milk? You? You're taking your life in your hands."

She gulped some more milk and licked her lips. "We had a cow when I was a child," she confided. "I have never tasted milk like that since then until now. Sweet. With that aroma of flowers."

"So is this," he said. "Sweet, with an aroma of flowers." He broke off a lump of the cake and held it up to her lips.

She regarded it dubiously. "I'm not the flowery type," she warned.

"Eat some of it," he pleaded. "Please, Tamar. If you care for me at all. I love to see you eat."

She was gearing up to refuse, and then she stopped. She processed something in private, deep inside the impenetrable fortress of her mind. She smiled at him, opened her lush lips, and accepted it.

She chewed. "Pretty good," she said cautiously. "Maybe I'll have a very small piece, and then I need to get back to work. So stop flogging me with your manly apparatus. That tactic won't work."

The towel that covered his tentpole erection had fallen off, leaving his penis hopefully brushing against her hip. He sighed. "I will compensate with food," he said wistfully.

"You do that. I'm busy planning my approach with Ana." She ate her small chunk of *pastiera* in a few dainty bites and folded her legs up on the blanket.

"We'll go to her as soon as I get back," he said. "I have to go and rent a car."

She didn't look up from her contemplation of her poisons. "No, we won't," she said quietly. "You aren't going with me, Val. This is something I do on my own."

Something flinty and cold clicked into place inside him.

"Absolutely not," he said. "We are in this together now."

"When it comes to Georg and Novak, certainly," she said. "But not with Stengl or Ana. That's my business, my past, my nightmare. You stay out of it. It makes more sense."

"Not anymore," he said. "And you can't go until I get back with a decent vehicle anyway. You can't ride up to the Santarinis' door on a Vespino. Even Ana has enough of a brain to smell something strange."

"Hmm." She broke eye contact, fussed with her vials.

It made him nervous. She seemed most dangerous in this state of quiet passive retreat, somehow out of his reach. Plotting whatever the fuck she pleased, no matter what he said or thought to the contrary.

It made him frantic.

He clamped down on the urge to drag her with him to San Vito. He could not. There was still that fucking video footage to send off.

"Do not go anywhere without me," he reiterated more sharply. "I still have not figured out how they found us yesterday. Or at the airport in Seattle, either, for that matter. Until I do—"

"Yeah. Do you actually think it's best I sit here on my ass alone and wait for them? A sitting duck?"

"Do you want the car, or not?" he snarled.

"Of course I do." Her voice was cool and remote.

They carefully left it at that, but he was still uneasy when he took off on the Vespino some twenty minutes later. The thing buzzed along, whining like a mosquito at a maddening fifty kilometers an hour, sixty on the downhill slopes. His first stop would be the car rental place in San Vito. He was fast running through available identities, having compromised two of them in the past three days already. It galled him that they had caught them in San Vito. Not even Henry had known the hotel.

He took some time to approach the car rental place, studying the hillside above for parked cars or loiterers. No one seemed to be watching. After a half hour, he gritted his teeth and risked it.

He chose a sleek, low-slung silver Opel Tigra sportscar. Not quite worthy of a femme fatale like Tamara Steele, but more appropriate than the Vespino.

The next project was to send that three-times-cursed footage to Novak. Today was the second deadline day—this evening, to be precise, but since God alone knew what would be happening by this evening, he would do well to get it over with. He found a place to park down on the deserted beach on the north side of La Roccia, the enormous rock formation that divided San Vito into halves, San Vito Nord and San Vito Sud. The rock that housed the smuggler's caves.

It was close enough to the cluster of tourist hotels that clung to the slopes over the beach to have wi-fi. He booted up and established the connection.

He ignored the heaviness in his chest, sent it, and sat there, leaden and cold. Might as well wait for those filthy pigs to have their grunting, snorting fun before he connected to Skype.

He didn't want to listen to them watching it this time.

Imre dangled between the grasping hands of the two men who dragged him down the corridors. He'd learned to his cost that there was no point trying to stay on his feet. The effort seemed to irritate them even more. His toes bumped over the carpet runner, painfully.

They had told him nothing, but he assumed it was time for another videoconference with Vajda, who must have provided more erotic footage to fuel Novak's evil machine. What bizarre coin the poor boy paid, for the meager comfort of seeing his foster father alive. Barely alive. But soon Vajda would be free. To save his soul.

Not that Imre even wanted to think about souls, or the saving or the losing of them. He was not ready to do this desperate thing, in spite of having spent all his dark, quiet hours working himself into a state of readiness, over and over. Only to have doubt assail him afresh every time.

He had picked open the inner seam of his shabby trousers, and pinpointed the exact location of his femoral artery, contemplating the sudden puncture wound that he had to inflict upon himself in order to bleed out fast enough. Fortunately, he was so emaciated, his veins and arteries were easy to find. His skeletal body could function as an anatomy poster for bones and blood vessels, if not for muscle tissue.

He would have one chance to get it right. The femoral artery was the fastest way. Opening it could kill a man in less than two minutes. He was not sure where he had learned this fact—no doubt some foolish detective novel read in a moment of weakness, but his brain had seized on the fact. He hoped to God it was true.

A wave of faintness came over him, making him sag lower in the grip of the two gorillas dragging him. Faint with pain and with fear that this was a sin that might lose him his chance to join Ilona and Tina where they waited with the angels.

Of course, in the bitter darkness of the night in his stinking cell, even the possibility of joining Ilona and Tina had seemed naive and stupid. Heaven could not be so easily reached after death.

But still, in his loneliness, he hoped.

His blood pressure was too low. Not good, for bleeding out quickly. He barely felt like he had anything inside to bleed. He felt like a pithy, dry orange, a desiccated lemon. All stringy pulp, no juice.

Forgive me, Ilona, Tina, he repeated, eyes closed. The shard of glass from the lens of his eyeglasses was tucked inside his cheek. He fiddled at it with his tongue, feeling the sharp edge, tasting blood. *I am not doing this for myself, but for Vajda*, he pleaded, to the demons of doubt, swarming around him like buzzing insects. And after all, he was only anticipating his own inevitable death, no?

Was it really for Vajda? Was it just fear of pain? Could any man be blamed for a mortal sin in such circumstances? In their rambling, one-sided conversations, Novak had detailed his favorite techniques for inflicting maximum agony to Imre. Death was preferable. Nausea gripped him. He could not faint. Must not. One chance. Only one.

They dragged him into Novak's library, over lurid colors cast by the stained glass, through the warm glow of wood paneling. They flung him into a seat in front of the computer with a force that jarred his degenerating bones and made him drag in dry gasps of pain.

Novak was there, waiting for him. He sat down next to Imre, grinning. "We have another juicy treat from your little friend. You would enjoy seeing him in action once again? For old times' sake?

So talented, our Vajda. Watch this, my friend, watch this. Gregor, play it for him."

Gregor clicked with the mouse until the video image filled the large screen.

Imre watched, his jaw set, having learned the futility of trying not to look the last time. He still had hematomas in his arm, from Novak's hideously strong fingers, his thick, yellowed nails.

A bedroom, dimly lit with pale morning light. A man and a woman, moving slowly together on the bed in the classic rhythm of love, her astride. The camera clearly showed the woman's lovely profile, her graceful back, the gentleness in her hands as she cupped Vajda's face.

Vajda's face had a look upon it that Imre had never imagined seeing. He clasped the woman's hands in his, lifted them to his lips.

Imre watched, in growing amazement. This was not pornography.

In truth, the other one had not been either, but this one was still less so. It was imbued with tenderness. Imre saw it in every gesture. A concert pianist, he had trained intensively all his life in the art of imparting real emotion, true tenderness with every gesture, every phrase. He knew the real thing when he saw it. He felt it in his chest, his gut. This was real intimacy. Intimacy that had been kidnapped and held for ransom.

He felt an urge to weep at the awful irony of it. His Vajda loved this woman, of all women. This was Vajda's chance at having what Imre had had, for those few short, wonderful years with Ilona. Seven years of grace, and then a lifetime of gratitude for even that much, despite the loneliness, the silence. The waiting.

He would not let this be taken from his poor boy. Vajda had been robbed of too much already.

Imre's doubts were gone. This thing would be done out of love, not fear.

Tough, tender Vajda. Son of his heart. Tears started from his eyes, crept down his cheeks. He was such a pathetic ruin, his captors might notice. He did not bother to wipe them away.

He looked up, and saw Ilona smiling at him, from the other side of the computer table. An angel, untouched by the filth of that place. She wore her old blue housedress and sweater. Her sweet face shone with pride. His heart leaped at the sight of her. It wouldn't be long now.

He dragged in a deep breath. May God have mercy on his soul.

Novak sat in front of the computer screen, grinning as the pixels tightened into focus.

"You received the footage?" Val asked mechanically.

"Yes, of course. Very moving, most romantic. Although I personally preferred the dynamism of the previous encounter," Novak said. "Perhaps the next time, you could vary the menu a bit?"

Val sat there and stared at him, rendered mute by impotent fury. Novak waited for Val to apologize for not being sexually entertaining enough. He stared stonily into the camera's black eye.

Novak made an impatient sound. "Well, then," he said. "I will let you speak to your friend. He intrigues me, you know. Despite his dislike of conversation. Here, move your chair a bit. I'll get out of your way."

Novak gestured and the computer was shifted so that the angle included Imre, who sat next to him.

He was even more reduced than he had been before. A shriveled wraith. Only his eyes had life. They were luminous with tears.

Answering tears surged up, clogging Val's throat, and blocking the meaningless questions poised on his tongue. *Are you well. Have they hurt you. Can you hold on for a little while longer.*

"Vajda, listen carefully," Imre said softly, in French. "I am about to give you a gift, my son. Take it and be free."

He put his hand to his mouth and pulled out what appeared to be a small shard of glass.

Horrified dread swelled inside Val. "Imre, no! What are you—"

"Good-bye." Imre's hand stabbed down. Someone shouted. People leaped for Imre, and the chair spun back. Blood sprayed high. Imre's hand waved in the air, drenched with shiny red. Novak was bellowing, incoherently. The wall spun into view, spattered with blood.

Someone hit the keyboard with their fist. The image disappeared.

Chapter
23

András sat in the beachside bar, sipping his sixth espresso as he studied the monitor that revealed Janos's position. The man had been wandering around the beach aimlessly after renting himself a car. The local man with the handheld monitor had him under visual surveillance, not far away. Everything was firmly under control.

Unfortunately, he had not brought Tamara on this pleasure jaunt. András had hoped to wrap this matter up this morning and get on his way. He wondered, with a stab of doubt, if Janos had bonded with Steele. Fucking a beautiful woman could have that effect on an unwary man. But Janos was anything but unwary. He was a seasoned professional and Novak's hold over him was strong.

He would order the man to deliver her today, and perhaps the matter would end there. A swift, professional exchange.

If not, however, the situation would probably require protracted, sophisticated torture, and he suspected that Janos would take a great deal of time, effort and soundproof privacy to break. András was more than equal to the task.

His cell vibrated. He glanced at it, and was surprised to see that it was from the big boss himself. He answered promptly. "Yes?"

"Do you have them yet?"

András paused, startled at the urgency in the old man's tone. "I have Janos under my eye physically right now, but not Steele."

"Bring them in," Novak rapped out. "Today. Immediately. Do everything you can to bring them in. There's been a change in plans."

"What change?"

"We've lost our leverage with Janos," Novak said. "The old man killed himself. Slashed his femoral artery, right over my favorite Turkish rug. While on the videophone to Janos."

András leaned back and was grateful that his boss could not see the appreciative smile that curved his mouth. "Don't worry. I'll bring him in. The woman as well. And I have another prize for you."

"And that is?" Novak's voice sounded sulky.

András savored the moment. "Steele's daughter. Three years old. A lovely flower for you to pluck. Already en route from Seattle."

There was an astonished pause, and then a harsh, wheezing crack of laughter. "András, you are a genius."

I know, you selfish old bastard, and so why did you favor that fawning pup Luksch over me? "I live to serve you, boss," he said.

"Call me when you have them," Novak said.

András considered his options. He had no idea when Janos would rejoin the woman. No idea what she might do in the meantime. Too many unknowns. She could take off on her own and fuck them all.

Best to force her whereabouts out of Janos now, reduce the number of variables immediately. He texted the others of his makeshift local team to converge on Janos's beach. If the man decided to be difficult, one of them had to know of a deserted garage or warehouse nearby where András could exercise his special talents to the fullest.

Val put the computer on the passenger seat very carefully. As if it were a wounded person who could not be jarred. His hands felt numb.

On autopilot, he grabbed the car keys and pushed open the car door. He stumbled out onto the rocky beach and kept walking, all the way to where it sloped down to the rocky little coves.

He fell to his knees. He couldn't think, couldn't move. He was cut loose, spinning in space.

Memories played in his mind. Games of chess in the twilight, cups of tea. Philosophy, lectures and arguments and admonishments that made him roll his eyes and scoff, secretly enjoying the attention. Bach and Chopin, Dante and Socrates and Galileo. Van Gogh, Picasso, Rembrandt. The world Imre had shown him. So beautiful, outside that squalid hole he was mired in like a fucking tarpit. Beautiful, even though Val could never quite reach it. Like a mirage in the desert, forever taunting him.

The pebbles roared with each wave that slapped the beach. He realized that he'd come to the place Domenico had brought him when he'd been infiltrating the smuggling ring and fucking Donatella.

The honeycomb of smugglers' caves.

Tourists came from all over the world to stroll the beach, sip cappuccino, and take boat rides inside the glowing, flickering lakes inside those mysterious caves. No idea of the cruelty and violence and greed that always lurked just out of sight behind the mask of beauty.

Imre. He started to cry, covering his face, shoulders jerking. He felt like the twelve-year-old boy he had been when Imre had befriended him, and showed him what trust looked like. How kindness felt.

The first time he had understood what kindness even was. He had never known it before, not really. Val's own mother had not been cruel—but she was broken, weak. Too degraded by drugs and disappointment to trust. Too lost in despair to be kind.

He had loved her anyway, desperately, but he knew even then that she was broken. Kindness required strength and courage. Coherence.

These types of thoughts were so unfamiliar to his mind, it almost hurt to think them. Like eyes opening up for the first time, squinting and awash with tears, unable to bear the brilliant light.

Tamar was the strongest, most courageous woman he had ever known. Strong enough to trust. Strong enough to be kind, too, whether she knew it or not. Kindness from her would be something real. Something he could touch, grab on to. Something he could live in.

He had a dizzy sense of being adrift, swirling, with no oars, no sense of direction. He had to find a course to set, fast. To save the last chance he had for a real life. Him and Tamar and Rachel. They could run together to the ends of the earth. Disappear like smoke.

Anything so that Imre's desperate last move would not be in vain.

Get Tamar. Get away. He was equal to that with the resources he had, if he moved his ass, made his weak knees, his jelly-like thighs move. If he could stop the tears.

There would be time enough for tears later at that haven at the ends of the earth. With his family around him.

His family. His heart felt like it would burst. Ah, Imre.

He rubbed the tears out of his eyes again, and that was when he saw them, gleaming in front of his face. Highly shined, pointy-toed, hand-tooled black Italian leather shoes. Well-tailored pants draped over them. A long black cashmere coat, flapping in the raw sea breeze.

Val's gaze traveled up, saw the big, silenced pistol. Big shoulders. Thick neck. Sealed, hard mouth. Black snake eyes.

András. There were five other men with him. Large, bulky men. Italian, and local, from the looks of them. They shifted into position around him.

"You've been called home," András said. "Where's the woman?"

He started to rise to his feet. The pistol swung up, aimed at his face. He sank back down. In his peripheral vision, tourists wandered on the beach, too far away to blunder by and help or be witnesses. One of András's men held a tracking device.

A tracking device? How had they tagged him? *How?*

Two thoughts blazed in his head. Contradictory thoughts. The first was that finally, he was free to die after Imre's gift. Tamar was smart enough, crafty enough to slip away and save herself on her own.

The second was that they could not kill him outright—yet. Not without prying her position out of him first.

So fuck the guns. He'd trained hard for years in the art of fighting from a crouching or kneeling position. Fighting six men on their feet from that position was problematic, but who cared. He had nothing better to do. He was free to die if he damn well felt like it.

No. He thought of Tamar, and suddenly, he did not feel like it.

His lower body exploded upward, balanced on his hands, boot heel connecting with the chin of the man nearest him, *crunch*. The man pinwheeled backward and fell to the ground, gurgling. Val's other leg whipped around like a lash and hooked the legs of the next man, dragging him down with a vicious jerk.

Action detonated something inside him, the anger and fear and humiliation of the past days abruptly channeled into berserk madness. He got in a vicious punch to the point of the man's nose, which loosened his grip on his gun, which Val wrenched loose and out of his hands. He swung it up, shot the man point blank in the gut.

Another man was diving for him. *Thhtp*, he got one into the thigh, knocking his legs out from under him. The man toppled in Val's direction. Two heavy bodies weighing him down to the jagged rocks.

He struggled, heaving, breaking loose just in time to roll away from a kick from András that would have cracked his spine. He caught it on his hip, let its energy keep him rolling up onto his feet.

He kept the pain at bay as András came on with a growling shout. Parried a slashing blow to the neck, trapped András's wrist in a tendon-twisting hold, spun him around and sent him flying into one of his men, who tripped and fell on his ass.

András sprawled on top of him, roaring with rage.

Go. This was his cue to run and test the hopeful theory that they could not shoot him, not without Tamar. Not fatally, at least.

Two shots rang out. Neither hit him. András howled in his thickly accented Italian. "No, dickhead idiot! Hold your fire! We need him alive!"

He slipped, rolled, slid down the steep rocks to the drop-off to the little cove beach where Domenico had showed him the belly-crawl entrance to the cave—and stopped, teetering on the brink.

That entrance had been accessible at low tide. At high tide, on a cold, blustery winter's day with the sea wildly agitated, that little cove was deep beneath a seething, heaving bowl of frigid foam.

He leaped.

The living room was full of people, but no one seemed to be able to speak. The words had all been said and repeated, over and over.

Now they were locked in a nail-chewing, coffee-sipping, miserable silence.

Sveti stared down into the cup of cold herbal tea, rocking back and forth. Her taped ribs hurt every time she drew breath, her wrist throbbed in the brace, her bandaged knees and hands burned and stung, but she deserved it. Worse, even, for letting that happen to Rachel. Again.

"Did you call her again?" she asked.

Connor shook his head. "I've called her over ten times. She's still unreachable."

Sveti felt her face crumple. She covered it with her hands. "She will hate me so much," she whispered.

"Wrong. Fuck, no," Sean said roughly. "Nobody but nobody blames you, Sveti. Tam won't, either. It was our fault for not being careful. Not taking this thing seriously enough. We've all gotten slack. You were right outside the house, for Christ's sake."

Sveti shook her head. "I didn't even get a car license number."

"Don't sweat it," Davy said flatly. "It would have been bogus and it wouldn't have helped us. Anyone gunning for Tam is a hard-core professional."

"Davy!" his wife snapped. "Isn't Sveti miserable enough already?"

"Sorry," Davy said.

The police had been and gone, an Amber Alert had been issued, but no one had any illusions that they would be able to find whoever had taken Rachel. All the McClouds and their close friends were there, crowded into Connor and Erin's living room. All except for Nick and Becca, off on their honeymoon in Mexico on a beach in the sun. Sveti wished that he were here, too.

She rubbed her swollen eyes and struggled to breathe around the fear and grief. How scared Rachel must be, all alone with those bad men. It hurt to think of it, worse than any physical pain she could imagine. It would be so much easier to cut it off, to not care, but she had never had any luck with that. She'd tried very hard when she was with the organ thieves, but it had never taken. Not really.

So this was the truth she'd been wondering about. The lurking nightmare of cruelty was reality. Freedom and flowers and the blue sky—that part was just the hopeful dream. It was the answer to her dilemma.

Now she knew the truth. And her only refuge was anger.

"They will never do this to me again," she heard herself say.

Everyone in the room looked at her, as if afraid her mind had cracked under the strain. She looked around, wild-eyed. She had to make them understand with the limited English that she had.

"They will not do this to me again. The assholes," she said. "I won't let them. I want to become like Tam. I want to be able to kick the asses of the assholes. Anyone who hurts or scares a little child, I want to . . . to cut off their balls. Put out their eyes. Rip out their guts."

Then they were looking at her, and she knew they were seeing her ninety-pound frame, her skinny wrists, how wispy and weak and insignificant she was. Fury flashed through her. Her fingers clenched into fists as hard as diamonds, for all they were so tiny.

"It doesn't matter that I'm small." Her voice was high, shaking. "I'm not stupid. That's more important. I can get stronger. I can use guns, bombs, rocket launchers. I will make those fuckers pay."

Margot sat down next to her and slid an arm around her waist. "I don't doubt it for a second, sweetheart," she said. "But we have to get this thing sorted out. I understand how angry you are—and how scared. And how young."

The men looked at each other with obvious alarm. Their women glared right back at them. There was a moment of curious tension.

Sean made a noncommittal sound. "Huh. Well, then. I guess it's gonna be law enforcement for you, honey, just like your dad," he said. "Someday."

Connor's head sunk down between his shoulders. "I can't believe this," he said for the tenth time. "Right outside the door. We should have sent Rachel to Stone Island with—"

"Bodyguards and an armored car, and two of us. Suck it up and let it go," Sean said harshly.

"Jesus," Con muttered, "Tam trusted me to protect her kid. And I let her down. I'm a fucking brain-dead idiot *dick*."

"Stop right there, bro," Davy said. "Don't. Not useful."

Connor's head came up, eyes blazing. "It could have been Kev," he said. "Easily. Or Jeannie. He's got as much of a grudge against me and Erin as he does with Tam. If the people in my family ever have a hope in hell of sleeping through the night, those fuckers have got to die."

"Of course," Sean said. "So we'll do it. Let's move on."

"Move where?" Connor's voice was vicious. "We have no leads. Just a couple of badass lowlife fuckers in Eastern Europe with the means and the motive. But where? Which one?"

"Maybe they'll make contact, just to taunt us," Sean said. "Or maybe Tam will have a clue. Something's got to give. Call her again."

Connor picked up the phone, pushed a button, waited. He shook his head and let it drop into his hands. They fell into a silence as cold and heavy as lead.

How the fuck had they found him?

The question burned in Val's mind as he dragged himself up out of the icy water. The jagged rocks tore and sliced at his hands and knees. Fortunately, he was too numb to really feel it.

When he'd last been here with Domenico at low tide, they'd been equipped with scuba suits, neoprene gripper gloves, flashlights attached to their headgear. It had been high summer, five years ago.

He composed his mind as best he could to remember the twists and turns of the place, the loops, the dead ends. Only one access to the caves was large, light and attractive enough to develop for tourists. The rest was a dank, dripping labyrinth, most of which had to be squeezed through to keep from ripping off one's scalp.

How had they found him? Every stitch of clothing he had on had been bought two days before in Sorrento en route from the airport.

The ugly truth sank in, slithering into his mind, starting with his belly and creeping its slow, relentless way into his conscious mind.

Not his clothes. Not his equipment. Him. He himself, Val Janos, his physical body, had an RF transmitter in it somewhere.

That was how Hegel's Seattle team got to Tam and Rachel at the airport—by following him. That was how they'd been nailed the

droned on in English. ". . . butterfly chamber, so called for the
[shap]e of the mineral formation in the center . . ."

["W]ould you look at that, Rhonda?" a fat, middle-aged man called
[i]n English. "In January! Must be a German or a Swede."

[T]he tour guide looked over and gaped. "*Ehi! Tu!*" she shouted
"Swimming is not allowed in La Grotta!"

[It] took several attempts to get the words out of his throat, he was
[shiv]ering so hard. "*Va benissimo,*" he spluttered. "Believe me, *signo-*
[ra]. I was just leaving."

[H]e was grateful when he finally crawled up onto the rocks at the
[ent]rance. He could barely move, but he couldn't crouch there and
[jus]t shiver and quake while passersby watched wide-eyed, and the
[tra]nsmitter betrayed him with RF bursts. He forced himself to trail
[beh]ind a departing group, following them into the crowded port.
[Try]ing not to stagger and lurch like a zombie. Failing, for the most
[par]t.

[San] Vito was a tourist trap even in winter for the English and Ger-
[m]ans and Scandinavians, for whom this nippy air was balmy and this
[w]atery sunshine practically tropical. He picked up his pace as he
[m]oved through the surging crowd, but did not allow himself to run.
[H]e was dead if he acted like prey. Nor could he look over his shoul-
[d]er, up at La Roccia, although the effort not to was killing him. An-
[d]rás or one of his men was almost certainly peering down with
[b]inoculars.

A ferry heading to a cluster of nearby islands was docked and
[l]oading, with a long file of vehicles in the chute to drive on. Val
[d]ucked through the line of cars and staggered alongside it, shoulders hunched, head down. Trying to look as unobtrusive as a dripping, bleeding, beaten up, hypothermic man at the point of going
into shock could be.

Finally, he spotted a diversion. A small, three-wheeled agricultural utility vehicle driven by a grizzled old man. From the stink, it
had held fish that morning. The fisherman had come to the main-
land to sell his catch and was heading back to his island home.

Val dug the bloody capsule out of his pocket, tossed it into the
back of the rickety contraption, and began to walk faster and faster.

day before at the hotel. That must have been how András had gotten him today. Which meant that Hegel must be dead.

He felt humiliated. He lacked the mental flexibility to think an
unthinkable thought. Fucking thick-skulled idiot.

Being deep inside a cave solved the problem in the short term.
There was no way they could trace him now. But unless he intended
to take up residence there and eat eyeless fish who subsisted only
on bat shit, he had to come up with a better idea, and fast. If they
knew where he was, they could very well know where he had been.
That would be András's next move once he got tired of searching for
Val here.

Tam was waiting in one of those places that was almost certainly
archived in their files—unless she had already thumbed her nose at
him and left. Altogether possible, knowing her. Probable enough
even to hope for. He hoped she would be her usual difficult, inde-
pendent self and get the hell out of there.

There was the pebbly underground beach that he remembered.
He felt the smoother surface, the little sliding rocks beneath his
feet. Underwater, of course, but he remembered this spot because it
had not been entirely lightless. A deep crack in La Roccia had created a narrow canyon that let in a gleam of indirect light from the
outside. From some distance beyond, he could hear the waves
crashing, and a dim glow filtered down. What had been three meters
of pebbly wet beach at low tide was now a narrow, half-meter strip of
jagged rock, the weird, stalactite-sprouting ceiling slanting down
low to meet it. Too low to sit.

He shook violently from the cold. His torn knees and hands stung
from the salt water. His face and hip stung and throbbed from blows
he hadn't noticed during the fight, and his shoulder—

His shoulder. He reached up to touch the scar from the bullet
wound last year. He'd been examined and treated by doctors in
PSS's pay, after having infuriated Hegel and several others with his
inconvenient scruples about child killing. Those doctors had been
the ones to sew him up in that secret clinic in Bogotá.

The shoulder had been slightly inflamed ever since. He felt nothing out of the ordinary palpating it, although his fingers were numb.
He'd thought the chronic pain in the scar was normal enough. It

wasn't the only old wound or scar he had that ached and throbbed. He didn't heal as fast as he had ten years before.

So he'd assumed. Not anymore.

He could not leave this cave and go to Tam with that thing inside him. He could lead them away from her, but eventually they would catch up with him and overcome him. His resources were almost tapped out, whereas Novak's were limitless.

And unfortunately for him, he had witnessed what András could do to a man to extract information. He had never forgotten the experience. Val could not hold out forever. Not against that.

The shoulder was his best and only guess. He had to do it here and now. He could think of no place where he would have more light, other than La Grotta's tourist chamber. What a show that would be for the English and German visitors on the pleasure boats.

He would rather not be sitting nipple deep in ice cold saltwater for an operation like this, but there was no alternative. He freed his knife from the sheath Velcro'ed to his ankle. Not easy. His hands barely functioned. Getting off the waterlogged jacket and unbuttoning his shirt was the next challenge. His fingers felt thick, dead. He was lucky the wound was in front of his shoulder.

Luck? Hah. He was the only miserable fool on earth who could call a detail like that luck. The knife point shook over the scarred meat of his shoulder as he breathed deep, gathering the courage. Wasn't this just the story of his fucking life. Forever contemplating the knife he had to stab himself with.

Self-pity would not help him. Nor would he warm up any more, waiting. He would only get colder until he was in shock.

So do it, testa di cazzo. Cut. Now.

His muscles jerked, driving the knife into what he desperately hoped was the right direction—the spot where the most pain was concentrated. He stifled the scream into a strangled moan. Tears streamed down his face. He locked his jaw into a grimace that threatened to loosen his teeth—and thought of Imre. That shard of glass, stabbing downward with such resolve. Imre's courage. His gift.

Again. He prodded. Blood welled up, slippery and hot as it trickled down his arm. Salt burned in the wound. He prodded deeper, making a low, desperate sound in his throat.

Again. He dragged in a sobbing breath, ch[...] blade. Cut again.

This time he could not stifle the shout of p[...] ened. He dug around with the knife tip, willi[...] to stabilize—and felt it. Yes. A tickety-click, of so[...] something that was not muscle, tendon, cartilag[...]

He dug in with his fingers and felt the very t[...] and smooth. Then it slid away from his blunt fi[...] tweezers, he needed light. He tried again, pre[...] ragged, tormented flesh on either side of where i[...] it out.

It popped out and almost dropped into the ink[...] shaking hand grabbed at the air. It bounced four [...] he caught it.

He rocked back and forth, gasping desperately [...] utes before he could bear to open his eyes and exam[...]

A bloody little capsule, no larger than a pill. So[...] plastic or ceramic. He puzzled for a split second al[...] source. His own body's electromagnetic field, perhap[...]

He didn't have the mental energy to wonder, wav[...] away from vomiting or fainting. If he fainted, he woul[...]

More decisions. He could drop the thing into the w[...] be done with it. That would stall the search but not [...] needed to play for time, and the transmitter was the [...] had to play.

He stuck it into his pocket.

He had nothing to bandage the wound with, and he [...] through the caves anyway, so he dragged his sodden shir[...] back on over his shuddering torso, almost screaming at [...] soggy, salty fabric against the wound. He could only hop[...] salt would help disinfect it. He lurched forward into the c[...]

What felt like hours of blundering and suffering followe[...] by pure chance, he saw the flickering glow of the light from[...] caves filtering in from the other side of the huge rock form[...] swam out into the lake, and found himself looking up at one of[...] that brought groups of tourists in to tour the scenic part of th[...] The boat slid by. A row of astonished faces stared down as [...]

Soon he was heading up the steep hill, taking every short cut through the meandering cobblestoned switchbacks. If he could get down to the car without being seen, he had half a chance.

He finally gave in to the nervous urge to lope, despite jolting agony in his shoulder at every step. Everyone was staring at him anyway.

Chapter
24

András was murderously angry, and the long, hard, breathless climb up to the top of La Roccia did not help his temper. That sneaky bastard had disappeared into the sea, and now he was holed up and out of range in the caves. Janos couldn't stay inside for long, of course. He was soaking wet. He had to come out before he died of cold. But he was a tough son of a bitch and that process could be a slow one.

Meanwhile, András's reputation for speed had just been put at risk. And old man Novak waited, chewing his yellowed nails.

None of his worthless local team had been willing to follow Janos into the smugglers' caves, though most of them had been inside them at one time or another. Two had been dispatched to watch other exits from the caves on the north side of La Roccia, one was a lump of gut-shot meat on the beach, and the other was not far behind, bleeding onto the rocks from a thigh wound and attracting unwelcome attention. With luck, he was comatose or at least unconscious.

András had described exactly what would happen to anyone who had the misfortune to be wounded and then talked to the police. He hoped those cretins knew just how sincere he had been.

Which left only himself and that brain-dead ape Angelo to slog their way up and over La Roccia to monitor the other Grotta exit, the tourist one. If he hadn't been down by two men, he would have killed the fuckhead himself, for shooting at Janos after he had been briefed on the necessity of keeping the man alive. Of course, the idiot was the brother of Massimo, the gut-shot man, but even so. That was no fucking excuse for unprofessional behavior. Orders were orders.

Angelo huffed and puffed over the crest of La Roccia, and flung himself down onto a flat rock to wheeze and gasp, silently protesting the pace that András had set. He clutched the handheld monitor that András had gleaned from Hegel's room.

"On your feet," András growled. "He could already be outside the cave. Let's go."

Angelo heaved his muscle-bound bulk up and followed him down the stonework switchback path at a heavy, shambling run. András stopped at a scenic overlook with benches not far from the bottom, and booted up the laptop to scan for the signal. His heart thumped when he saw the icon finally appear, blinking. He clicked, enlarging the map until it was a detailed street map of the San Vito port area.

And there he was, the crafty son of a bitch. Lurking down on the edge of the water, no more than three hundred yards from András's own current position. He should be visible. Saliva rushed into his mouth as he peered down at the busy port swarming with tourists. Then another slight movement on the screen caught his eye.

He glanced down, alarmed, and watched the icon detach itself from the shore, move out over the water. What the fuck . . . ?

András shielded his eyes from the sun and squinted. The ferry whistle shrilled. Oh, shit. No. The prick had climbed onto a boat and was sailing away to some godforsaken rock in the Mediterranean.

"On your feet," he snarled at the ape, who had once again dropped down onto his lazy ass, wheezing. "We need to find someone with a boat immediately to get us to wherever that ferry is going."

To András's surprise, Angelo made himself useful by promptly locating a man with a powerful motorboat, fast enough to get to the island before the ferry did. A smuggler, no doubt. Negotiations were swiftly concluded. András peeled several hundred-euro notes off his money roll, put them onto the man's grimy palm and was climbing on board, one leg on the side of the boat, when suddenly he stopped.

Motionless, he sniffed the air as a shiver ran down his back, half in and half out of the boat. Angelo and his avaricious smuggler friend waited, their peasant faces blank and stupid.

He, after all, had been the one in the goddamn hurry. But the ferry retreating before him did not make saliva pump into his mouth. He was beset with doubts.

A trick?

But the tracer was inside the man's body. How was it possible?

He stepped back onto the dock. "You go on," he said. "Get to the island before that ferry does and watch for him. Follow him with the handheld. Call me immediately if you locate him."

"*Sì, sì, certo,*" Angelo muttered sullenly.

"And if you kill him, I will rip out your liver with my hands and feed it to a stray dog while you watch. Is that clear?"

The smuggler blinked. His eyes darted between András and Angelo. Angelo nodded. "Where are you going?" he asked.

"To make sure he hasn't fucked me by going in the opposite direction," András snapped. "Now go."

A taxi was just letting out a clump of Dutch tourists in front of the nearest beachside hotel. András slid inside it gratefully. "Take me to the beach on the north side of La Roccia," he said. "One hundred more euro if you get there in less than ten minutes."

The man's eyes lit up. The taxi dashed out onto the road and jounced up the cobblestoned streets.

It took the man eleven minutes to get to the other side, but András was not inclined to quibble. They jerked to a stop right next to the ice-cream stand near where Janos's rented Opel Tigra had been parked. The car was gone. So his instinct had been correct—unless, of course, someone had stolen the car, always a possibility in southern Italy. He shoved the hundred euros into the hand of the taxista, and got out.

A slim, dark-eyed girl no more than seventeen presided behind the counter of the ice-cream stand. Pretty breasts, shown off by a low-cut pink leotard under her artfully opened sweater. Taut dark nipples shadowed the pale fabric. She would have seen who took the car. He gave her his nicest smile, but she shrank back.

"Did you see someone get into that Opel that was parked over there a little while ago?" he asked.

She opened and closed her rosy mouth. "*Sì*. A man."

"And what did he look like?" he asked.

Her big, limpid eyes went blink, blink. "I don't remember, really."

"Ah." András reached into his pocket, and pulled out a twenty-euro note. He slid it across the counter.

"Tall," she said helpfully. "Dark."

He waited for more. She shrugged. He pulled out another twenty.

She fluttered her lashes, made it disappear. "Wet," she said. "He looked wet and cold. Like he was bleeding, too. His shoulder. And arm."

So. Confirmed. Janos had gouged out the RF trace and gotten the better of him. But not for long. He had a fix on their nighttime position. Where else could a cold, wet, wounded man go but to ground? And to Steele? On track again. All was well.

He gave the girl a murderous smile. Her face went white. He'd gotten what he needed from her, but the sulky, grasping little bitch hadn't made it easy. He didn't like that. He reached over the counter and gave her nipple a vicious pinch that she would feel for the next ten days.

She shrieked and clutched her chest, staring at him wildly.

"Thank you for your help, *signorina*," he said pleasantly.

He headed for his car, reflecting that the ice-cream whore was lucky he was so pressed for time. Or else he would have made her earn every last cent of that money, ten times over.

On her hands and knees.

"Is this the only thing you have?" Tam asked for the third time.

Pantaleo, Signora Concetta's youngest son, gave her a grunt that she could only interpret as a yes, since it was followed by no other options.

She stared at the rusted 1965 Fiat 500. Inside, the upholstery was rotted to stinking gray dust. Shreds of ceiling fabric hung like cobwebs. The original color was impossible to determine. The exposed foam padding of the seats had discolored to deep orange, degenerating into grainy chunks; the dash coated with greasy dust. The backseat had been ripped out to make room for farm tools. Three windows were taped shut and the windshield was cracked and cloudy. A rearview mirror swung forlornly on a piece of duct tape. There were no side mirrors. She could see the ground through the holes in the floor.

The Vespino would have been better. At least it had a certain breezy, kitschy charm, whereas this thing looked post-apocalyptic, a vehicle of absolute last resort. She was tempted for the umpteenth time to just offer a fifty-euro note and ask someone in the signora's family to drive her to the nearest car rental place, but for the fact that she was reluctant to let them know where she went. It was not healthy for anyone to know her business. In fact, her and Val's presence here was not healthy for these people. It was high time they moved on and found another hiding place.

"Don't worry," Pantaleo said. "*Cammina, cammina.* It runs, it runs. There's even a liter or so of benzina in it. Six hundred euro. For seven, I'll even throw in all the farm tools."

Uh-huh. Right. Like she was going to be harvesting any olive orchards in the near future. She gave him an eloquent look. He responded with a gap-toothed, can't-blame-a-guy-for-trying grin.

She reached for her purse. "Three hundred," she said sternly. "And you are robbing me. Please get all the junk out of it. Now."

Pantaleo's grin widened. He threw open the back door and began hauling out armfuls of junk and dumping it onto the ground. He took the money she held out and dug into his pocket for the key. "We have to go to the notary public, to do the *passaggio di proprietà*," he said.

For this piece of shit? She gave him a coaxing smile. "Could we take care of that another day? Pretend I borrowed it until then, all right?" God knew she was going to abandon the wretched little turd of a car at the first opportunity. The very minute she rented one.

Pantaleo looked doubtful, but made no protest as she plucked the key from his dirty fingers and slipped it into her pocket.

The whole situation made her very twitchy. Renting a car was an unwanted level of exposure. Georg had to have surmised that she and Val needed one, and there were not so many places to obtain them in this immediate area. All undoubtedly being watched.

At least no one would expect her to be driving a 1965 Fiat 500 held together with nothing but rust. But on the flip side, she would attract attention just by looking so ridiculous in it.

Stop dithering and get to it, she lectured herself.

Truth to tell, she actually had been stalling. She was angry and baffled at herself. It was so unlike her.

It had taken a certain amount of time to prepare her plan of attack for Ana, of course, and to arm the appropriate jewelry pieces. Another reasonably long interval had been necessary to bathe, groom, arm, and adorn herself to her satisfaction. She fiddled uncomfortably with the matching tongue studs that she'd chosen for the occasion. She didn't like body piercings much as a fashion statement, but the studs were the only weapon for an intensely personal job like this one.

They belonged to a secret, personal category of Deadly Beauty designs called Ultimate Weapons—but only in her head, since she'd never spoken of them out loud to a living soul. They were ideas she had not developed commercially because they were too dangerous. Besides, many of them had no aesthetic component of any kind.

They were just for herself. Her paranoid, fucked-up self.

She put each weapon she designed through a certain algorithm she had developed to estimate the risk factor to the wearer. Any weapon with an over fifty percent risk factor of accidental death went into the Ultimates category and as such, was not saleable.

The tongue studs had a seventy-five percent risk of death.

She just had to make her tongue relax and stop worrying the things, or she could break the capsules prematurely. That would be disastrous. *Self-control, Steele.*

Yikes. She'd never had such difficulty summoning it.

After she dressed and prepared, she'd taken a few moments to center herself and find that calm, chilly, professional inside her.

Robot Bitch. Right. That was where it all broke down. Because Robot Bitch was nowhere to be found, and without her, Tam was lost and dithering. No other word for it.

Not wanting Val to come back and find her gone. It felt like such a flagrant fuck-you. Not wanting to reject his help, to hurt his feelings, of all crazy things. Not wanting to make him angry. God, since when had she ever given a shit about whether or not she made a man angry?

If said man was not holding a gun to her head or a knife to her throat, that is. There were exceptions.

And this was another exception, God help her. She did care, enough so to box herself in and fritter away precious time hoping he'd get back before she'd gotten around to leaving. So that they could have a proper knock-down, drag-out fight that she could definitively win, forcing him to acknowledge that they'd be better off if she went alone.

Hah. Dream on. That knock-down, drag-out fight was a problematic scenario. Val was bigger, stronger, and quicker than her, though she hated to admit it. Stubbornly unreasonable, too. And very intense about protecting her, which was touching and sweet and manly of him, but oh, dear God, what an inconvenient pain in the ass.

The only way to win an argument with a man strong enough to be worth arguing with was to just slip away and do as she pleased while he was looking elsewhere. Deal with the fallout later. That had always been her policy before. So what had changed?

Never mind. She was afraid to examine that question too closely.

After all, she was calculating cold-blooded murder. If Janos didn't ride shotgun, he had a small measure of plausible deniability with Ana, Donatella, their Camorra husbands, and the Italian authorities.

And the more streamlined her plan of invading the clinic, the better. For him, too. She understood his desire to monitor the situation so that he could keep her in one piece to help him save Imre, but solo, she could handle this more smoothly.

Besides, Val was too damn pretty. He attracted attention from every side. It was like hauling around a jewel-draped pink elephant. People looked, people took note, people remembered. Especially women. He was wildly impractical, as an accessory. To murder, anyway.

She herself was pale and severe today in her somewhat limp and wrinkled suit, hair braided tightly back. No makeup. Unlikely to attract undue attention. Ana would certainly notice that Tam was wearing the same clothes as yesterday, which bugged her, but there was no remedy for that except for shopping, and she had no time for anything so frivolous, or she would miss her window. It was today or it was never.

And? So? *Move it, Steele.* She forced herself to pick up the pace, hustling back to their funky room for a blanket to cover the filthy seat of the Fiat and protect her clothes. She grabbed her briefcase and purse, and off she went to find a decent car to drive and get the job done.

If all went well, she'd be back soon to face down Val's wrath with her usual sass. And then she would go with him to Hungary and keep her end of the bargain.

And his wrath did always translate into spectacular sex. She was pleasantly aching and sore from last night's massive dose.

She practically knocked Val over as she turned the corner of the *casale.* He tottered at the impact, a frightening apparition. Dead pale, blood and bruises on his face, hollow-eyed. He put out his hand to the building for balance, stumbled, and jolted down onto one knee.

It was a body blow to see him like that. It knocked out her air.

"Jesus, Janos! What happened to you?" she demanded.

He shuddered and swayed on his knees, teeth chattering. He smelled like the sea. He'd gone for a dip, for Christ's sake. The raw mountain breeze whipped around them. She reached down and gripped him under his armpits, dragging him to his feet. The fabric of his wet jacket was sticky and dark on one side. Blood. "Oh, *merde,*" she muttered. "You're wounded. What the fuck happened to you?"

"András," he whispered. "Novak."

Great. Just great. The baddies, all converging on them, and it had to be today. "Come on, let me get you out of this wind. You look like ten different kinds of shit, Janos. I should never have let you go out by yourself. I might have known you'd fuck it up. Men."

His pale, shaking lips twitched at that, but he stumbled, thudding against the building with a gasp of pain. She loaded as much of his weight as she could onto her shoulder, on the nonbleeding side. She was not trashing her one outfit if she could help it.

Once inside, she whipped off her own jacket, rolled up her

sleeves, and pushed him down until he sat on the bed. She started in with his shoes, peeled off the sodden pants and briefs. He moaned with pain when she started in on the jacket, so she slowed down, peeling it off what appeared to be the good arm first, and then lifting the blood-soaked sleeve gingerly away. Then the shirt.

She sucked air through her teeth when she saw the ragged, oozing mess of his shoulder and hurried to the bathroom, rummaging for the cleanest towel she could find. She pressed his torso down onto the bed, heaved his long legs up until he was lying flat, then dragged the thickest wool blanket out of the armoire and laid it over him.

"You lie there and warm up," she said. "I'll go get some disinfectant from the signora."

Breathless seconds later, she was eyeing the sleek little Opel parked in the *ulivetto* as she banged the signora's door. Nice. At least he'd gotten some decent wheels before getting himself fucked up.

She burst out her request for disinfectant, bandages, and dry clothes as soon as the door opened, and realized that her voice was thin, high and shaking, like a child. Whoa. *Breathe, Steele. Breathe.*

The signora's face furrowed into a deep scowl. "He is in trouble?"

Tam gave her an expressive shrug. "*E' un tipo fuocoso,*" she confided. He's a fiery type. She hoped the older woman would assume he'd gotten into a stupid, macho fight.

The signora shook her head. "Men," she muttered darkly. She shoved open the door to the kitchen and gestured Tam inside.

The room was huge, spotless, a baroque-era kitchen with appliances that dated from the 1950s. She disappeared into the inner rooms and returned moments later, presenting a bottle of alcohol, rolls and pads of gauze, and, miracle of miracles, surgical bandages—the kind you could buy over the counter in the States. Left behind by other tourists? Who knew? They just might close the wound.

The older woman thrust some men's clothes at her.

"They will be short for him," she warned. "I don't have any pants long enough for that one."

Tam thanked her effusively and scurried back, heart pounding wildly, as if Val might die or disappear if she took her eyes off him.

He was still shivering violently, even under the heavy wool. She turned on the light and hastened to deal with the shoulder wound.

It alarmed her. Deep, jagged and uneven, it looked like it needed internal and external stitches from an ER doc who knew what the fuck she or he was doing, not a seat-of-the-pants emergency medic like herself. She cleaned it as best she could, wincing in sympathy as he sucked in a tortured breath at the sting of the disinfectant.

She bandaged it, following the directions on the box to close the torn flesh until the surgical glue set. It took only seconds. Whether it would hold, she didn't know. The shoulder was the worst, but she worked on his battered hands and knees as well. Then she dove into the poison kit, where she kept her emergency pharmaceuticals. Too bad she didn't have a topical anesthetic, but at least there was a full spectrum intramuscular antibiotic. She loaded the syringe, poised it over his good arm.

"Allergic to antibiotics?" she asked. "Don't even think about going into anaphylactic shock on me, big boy. My nerves are shot as it is."

He shook his head, eyes squeezed shut. She jabbed.

He was still vibrating with cold, and in the absence of a hot bath, she could think of only one solution to that. She stripped off the rest of her clothes, lifted the blanket, and clambered on top of him.

She braced herself for a shock, but oh, God, he was cold. Shuddering, clammy, sticky with sea salt. She wrapped her arms around him, tried to give him all the warmth she had. Wishing there was more. She wanted to cover every inch of him with comfort. Wanted to be bigger, wider, softer. A down comforter of a woman. Not a tight, wound up, stringy female, all bent metal and barbed wire and twine.

The contact seemed to help him anyway, thank God. His shuddering began to ease, and he began taking deeper breaths. She ran her fingers through his salt-stiffened hair, which had dried into a spiky punk do, which she kind of liked. À la Hollywood bad boy.

"What the hell happened to you, anyway?" she asked.

He opened his eyes. To her alarm, they welled full of tears.

"Imre is dead," he whispered brokenly. "He killed himself. I watched it on videophone. He stabbed a piece of glass into his femoral artery." His voice was shaking like a young boy's. "He did it to free me."

She drew in a long, careful breath. "Oh, my poor baby," she whispered. "I'm so sorry."

It was either exactly the right or exactly the wrong thing to have said, because it melted him right down, and that, to her startled horror, melted her down too.

The two of them blubbered, arms wrapped tight and shaking around each other. As if his grief and loss were her own.

And it was, she realized, as she cried against his chest. It was her own, and *he* was her own. He had been for quite a while now, but she hadn't wanted to face it yet. She should have known when he'd made her cry by telling her to pretend she loved him two nights before. She should have known after that dream, after he picked up her stuffed valentine heart out of the dust and rubble of her broken doll self and brought it to life. Miraculously.

When the emotional storm subsided, she wiped her face, propped her chin on her forearms. Both of them embarrassed and shy.

She sniffed back her tears, and went on the offensive as usual. "So? Let's have it, loverboy. The bruises, the shoulder, the dip in the sea?"

"András," he said.

She nodded. She knew the man, and wished that she didn't. It was not safe to be on that guy's radar screen. He was in the same class as Kurt and Georg. "How did András find us?"

"He had a tracer on me. He must have gotten it from Hegel."

That was a nasty shock. "He had a what?" Her voice squeaked.

He jerked his chin in the direction of his shoulder. "There," he said. "It must have been in there since I was treated for that bullet wound last year. Looks like PSS stopped trusting me even then. They wanted to keep me under control. Hegel must be dead, I assume."

"So that's how they found us at the hotel. And the airport, too."

"Yes." His voice was subdued. "By following me. I should have figured it out earlier. I'm sorry."

"It's not your fault," she heard herself say. Though of course, it was. She couldn't help the meaningless words from coming out. Look at her, trying to make the guy feel better about almost getting her and Rachel killed, hah. What a gooey, soft-headed chump she was becoming. Frightening to contemplate.

The story came out of him, terse, halting phrases issued from his chattering teeth. The death-defying dive into the stormy sea, swimming through icy salt water in underground caves, digging transmitters out of his own body in the watery dark with the tip of a pocketknife. Could she have done it?

"Why didn't—"

He shook his head. "I couldn't call you," he said simply. "I couldn't lead him to you. And there was no time for a doctor. András would have had me and that would have been it. Game over."

"Got it," was all she said.

He started to give her his habitual shrug, but froze halfway through, grimacing in pain.

She refused to let herself melt with pity. His machismo was pointless. His pain hurt her. If he suffered needlessly, then so did she. Life had too much suffering in it as it was. Suffering needlessly pissed her off, big-time.

But not all of him hurt. Amazingly, Val's body was stirring beneath her, his cock growing long and hot and hard against her belly. She wriggled against it, hardly believing the evidence of her own senses. Yes, sure enough. Rock hard and ready. Even now.

"Val," she said sternly. "You have got to be kidding."

"Sorry," he said innocently.

"You know that this naked hugging thing is strictly therapeutic in nature, right? I was worried about hypothermia and shock. I was not looking to wank your willie. We don't have time."

"No?" he said. "But you are so beautiful. So hot and strong and full of life." His arms tightened, pulling her closer. "And I love you."

She stiffened. "Don't get flowery on me, Val," she warned. "I can't take that kind of thing. You know that. So just don't do it."

"I love you," he repeated stubbornly. "I almost died today, and I

would have missed my chance to tell you, although I am sure that
you know it. So I will say it if I damn well please, and you will listen.
I love you. I mean every word. I love you, Tamar."

Her eyes leaked, her face was hot. This was so not fair. Not now,
on top of everything. She wanted to tell him she loved him too, but
the words were backed up, bottlenecked behind a burning knot.

She hid her face against his good shoulder. Waited until her throat
opened up and she could trust herself to harrumph.

"Well," she muttered, "you can't be too badly hurt, if you're rubbing your erection against me and carrying on about deathless love.
I suppose that's good news. Now what?"

That flashing, deep-grooved grin was so beautiful, it practically
broke her into pieces. "My tough babe," he murmured. "I hate to
say it, my love, because there is no place on earth I would rather be
than beneath your naked body, but we must run quickly. And far."

"But you cut the tracer out, right?"

"I was in this bed with that thing transmitting for sixteen hours,"
he said. "He will check here. Perhaps he is already on his way. I
hope I bought time with my ferry trick, but I cannot count on it."

She stared into his eyes, her mind working furiously. "You have
the car," she said. "We'll go and find another place where you can
rest up while I deal with Ana and Stengl. I have to get that over
with. Then, I'm all yours. We will run. Anywhere you want."

His face went somber, and he gazed up at her for a long moment.
"Perhaps you have not understood," he said carefully. "Our plans
have changed. We must leave it, Tamar. All of it. Stengl, too."

Everything went cold and distant around her, as it had in Ana's
salone. She felt a door slam shut inside her. A door with her bereaved
fifteen-year-old self behind it. *No.* She took a deep breath.

"No, Val," she said. "I came all this way for this. I'm not leaving
until it is done. Don't try to stop me."

But she could already see that he didn't get it. He couldn't. How
could he? He'd already rearranged his reality, and Stengl was not relevant to his reality. Only to hers. She was alone with the nightmare
of her past and she always would be.

She actually tried, for a few seconds, to imagine letting it go. Just walking away. But she'd gone too far down that road by now. She'd spent too many years imagining Drago Stengl's face when he saw her standing before him and knew death was near.

When he finally understood what he had done to her. To all of them. Knowing that at last the bill had come due.

She couldn't let it go. Or rather, it would not let her go. It had clutched her like a skeletal claw for her whole adult life. Its grip was not easing now. It clamped down, a death grip, crushing her. She couldn't endure any more of that. Not if deliverance was possible.

He cupped her face and stared earnestly into her eyes. "Imre did this to set me free," he said, his voice urgent. "I cannot waste his gift. I cannot risk the last thing on earth that I care about. I want to make a life with you. I never dreamed of such a thing, but you have made me dream of it, and now I must have it."

"And Rachel?" she asked.

He waved an eloquent hand. "Of course we will get Rachel," he said forcefully. "I am not stupid. I know she comes first."

He felt her stiffness, her unresponsiveness, and gave her an impatient shake. "Let it go for Rachel, Tamar. For us. Think of it. You are contemplating murder. The Italian police will pursue you no matter what the man has done. The Camorra will pursue you on Santarini's behalf for killing his father-in-law. Your problems will multiply. Do not try to do this thing. I will stop you. It will fuck our only chance. And I will not risk you now, do you understand? It is no longer an option."

She absorbed that. Everything it meant, everything she had to do. A knife turned slowly inside her chest. "Easy for you to say, Janos," she whispered. "You've been cut loose. I haven't."

His face went tight. He lifted his head off the pillow. "I just watched the one person on earth that I could claim as family bleed to death for me. Do not talk to me of what is easy."

She slid off his body and onto the floor, turning her back and gathered the force to do what she had to do next. "I'm sorry," she said quietly. "I didn't mean to imply that it was an easy morning for you."

He reached for her, stroking her arm. "Tamar. My love. Please."

She turned and looked down at the hand that held her. The one attached to his good shoulder. So strong and beautiful despite the scabbed, ragged knuckles. As skillful and tender as it was lethal.

She grabbed it, pulled it up, kissed it. Silently saying good-bye.

And swiftly snapped the handcuff that hung open from the wrought iron headboard around his wrist. "I'm so sorry," she whispered.

He stared at her, openmouthed, and then exploded upward, erupting in a stream of profanity that sounded like Romanian. He rattled the thing violently, twisted it, jerked. Red bloomed afresh on the white gauze of his shoulder, spotting and spreading. The surgical bandage underneath peeled half off.

"Oh, God, stop that. Don't flail around like that," she begged. "You'll hurt yourself worse."

"What the *fuck* do you think you're doing, you treacherous bitch?"

She flinched. His anger hurt more than she'd ever dreamed, with all her defenses down. "I'm sorry," she repeated, fogging up again, and stumbled clumsily back out of range of his lunging, grasping hand.

"Get back here," he snarled. "Open this fucking thing. Now!"

She shook her head. "I can't," she whispered. "I'm sorry." She darted in to snatch up her clothes and scrambled out of range again to yank them onto her body. "I don't want to hurt you."

"Ah, *sì?*" he said viciously. "And this is why you shackle me naked to a bed? Staked out like a fucking goat for András when he comes? Oh, yes, Tamar. I can see how much you care."

"When I come back—"

"When you come back, my balls will have been sliced off and shoved down my throat," he snarled. "Is that what you wanted all along? Did you not have the courage to do the deed yourself?"

She realized that tears were rolling down her face as she shook her head. "No. I have no intention of leaving you like this for long—"

"Then just open it!" he bellowed. "Give me the pick kit!"

"Please just shut up for a second and listen to me," she begged. "There's a piece of shit Fiat 500 out in the *ulivetto* that belongs to me." She dug the key out of her pocket. "I bought it from Pantaleo, the signora's son. Here are the keys, so you're not grounded—"

"Fuck the car!" he roared. "The cuffs, you crazy *puttana*—"

"I said to shut up and listen!" she flared. She crouched down and plucked the keys to the Opel out of the sodden pants crumpled on the floor.

He made a derisive sound. "Ah. So. You take my car as well?"

"You have the Fiat, so don't bitch." She tossed the key Pantaleo had given her onto the bed. "You have dry clothes right here, and I will leave you my cell phone, too, so you're not—"

"Fuck the cell phone! Let me loose!" The bedframe rattled, thudded, scraped against the floor. He jerked at it, maddened.

She jittered uneasily backward. Time to beat hell out of there. "I will leave your pick set right by your hand," she went on desperately. "And Georg's gun. I don't wish you any harm. On the contrary. Please believe me."

He held out his hand. "Give me the gun."

"Right," she muttered. She let out a long breath and let her arm fly up, darting like a lash to spray the soporific from her barrette into his face. "After for the gun, big boy. I'm not quite that stupid."

It was a tiny blast, the shortest her finger could coordinate. "This won't last long," she told him hastily. "A quarter of an hour at most. Probably less, because you're so big. And then . . . you can get free."

He stared at her, stunned into silence, and the air escaped all at once from his lungs. He sat down heavily on the bed, blinking.

His eyes were bleak. He looked utterly betrayed.

"I'm sorry," she whispered again, her voice breaking oddly. "Just a little head start. That's all I need."

He opened his mouth, tried to speak, seemed puzzled when he could not.

"I'll buy a cell phone when I finish," she told him. "I'll call you after this just to see if you still want to have anything to do with me. If not, just tell me to fuck off then. You have that to look forward to."

He swayed, wavered. She pushed him gently down onto the bed, hating the painfully hyperextended angle of his trapped arm.

She scooped up his legs again, heaving them onto the bed, and tugged at his feet to ease the pull. Then she covered him with the wool blanket, laid the gun by his hand, the cell phone, the tiny lock pick kit.

She kissed his forehead, his cheekbone, his jaw. His lips. Her last chance to touch him without getting killed, probably. He hated her now.

He tasted like the sea. Salty. Like life. It was crushing her heart.

His eyes, amazingly, were still open. Still giving her that fierce, accusing look. Fighting it like crazy. He was so damn strong.

God, how she loved that. How she loved him.

She cupped his face, kissed him hungrily once again. "I love you, too," she said. Amazing how much easier it was to say that when she knew that he could not respond. What a hopelessly twisted, sicko wench she was. "I love you, Val Janos," she repeated more forcefully. "I really do. I hope you can forgive me for this someday."

On impulse, she pried the multiblade ring off her thumb, and slid it onto his ring finger.

She grabbed her stuff, hot tears streaming, and bolted.

Chapter
25

András pulled off the dirt track. His sedan bumped over the rough ground, crunching through heaps of dried brush and cut olive branches. That clump of pines looked just right for hiding his vehicle from the road, before hiking in quietly closer to the archived location he had on file for Janos's icon. The one where the man had spent the night. He regretted not having backup, but Janos was wounded and exhausted, and Steele was, after all, a woman. A capable one, by all accounts, but he could handle any woman.

In fact, he was looking forward to it, ever since he saw that first clip of vid footage that Janos had sent. Watching her stunning body move against Janos had fired up his blood. He wanted some of that.

And once he had Steele, he could finally destroy Janos, which would be most satisfying. The man was annoying the shit out of him.

If they were here, of course. But he was sure that they were. He could feel them, from the way his heart revved, his senses sharpened, his dick tingled. He licked his lips.

He heard the car the minute his own car door thudded shut, and crouched, peering from behind the thick, gnarled trunks of the ancient olives.

The Opel that Janos had rented. Only one person inside. Not until the car was almost past did he make out Steele's delicate, feminine profile. So. He'd gotten here just in time. He watched the car bounce down the rutted track and turn onto the narrow paved road that led back toward the coastal highway.

He hurried back to his car. It would be tricky, to stay far enough back not to be noticed and close enough to see which way she turned once she got to the highway. But he was nothing if not tricky.

Fuck Janos. He would stick to Steele, take her down, and get her back to Novak this very day. And he bet that Novak wouldn't mind if he took a measure of his reward directly out of the woman's hide.

As long as the old man got to watch it. All part of the fun.

"The effect of Amplix 15 is instantaneous, particularly at such a concentrated dose." Tam loaded the miniature hypodermic with ten drops of the solution she had just showed Ana how to weigh and mix. "And very intense. The person administering the poison actually risks injury herself from the target's convulsions. They are violent enough to snap bones. If the target's still alive at that point, hemorrhaging begins. If the heart doesn't stop first. Be prepared for a mess."

"And the antidote?" Ana's eyes were glowing. Impressed, in spite of herself.

Tam gazed at her. "No antidote," she said. "No time. We're talking certain death in forty seconds or less." She situated the needle tip onto the reservoir, clicked it into place, and slid the apparatus into the jewel-studded gold cylinder that formed the body of the earring, then screwed the threading of the weighted jeweled bead into place over the needle.

She passed it to Ana, observing the tiny flinch before the woman accepted it. Pah. Gutless weenie. Not a worthy wearer of Deadly Beauty.

"I believe in arming both earrings," she said. "One never knows which hand will be free. Or even what the rest of the evening will bring."

"How about the dipped blades? Do they kill in the same amount of time?" Ana gingerly picked up a hairclip, pushed the button, and slid out the wickedly sharp two-inch blade. She swooped it around, fantasizing homicide, like a child with a toy sword.

Tam kept her eyes from rolling as she scribbled down the mixing proportions for the Amplix 15. "A bit more slowly," she told the woman. "It's a different compound. TR-8321 takes more like a minute and twenty seconds."

"And the antidote?"

Tam gazed at her for a long moment, then gave her a mysterious smile. "No antidote," she repeated. "It's against my philosophy. No one should have armed Deadly Beauty pieces on her person unless she is absolutely sure of what she is doing. If she feels the need for the antidote because she's afraid she might change her mind at the last moment, then perhaps she should pay someone more professional to do her dirty work for her. And wear something a bit more classic and safe. Like, say, Cartier."

Ana's eyes tightened, showing the tiny dry lines around them, caked with heavy makeup. "I know what I am doing," she snapped.

Tam nodded. "Excellent," she said. "I love to see a confident woman. Here are instructions for arming the grenade pendants. I regret that I was not able to get the materials for you. I know it's not an easy matter to discreetly obtain that kind of item."

"Not a problem for me," Ana preened. "I have my sources."

"Good. Including the materials for arming each piece usually adds an extra fifteen percent onto the total price, but I'm waiving this fee in your case," Tam said, gathering up the sheaf of instructions. "Here are online sources for each ingredient in these recipes, as well as possible pretexts for ordering them, should you find it necessary to rearm any of the pieces. And remember, Mrs. Santarini. No shortcuts, no omissions, no substitutions. The recipes are precise and specific."

"I understand," Ana said impatiently. "And now I'm afraid I have to cut this short, Ms. Steele. I have an appointment this afternoon that I cannot miss, and you arrived so much later than we had agreed yesterday, it's thrown my entire day out of alignment!"

The self-pitying whine in the woman's voice grated on Tam's nerves. She tried to look contrite. "I'm sorry. It was a complicated morning."

"Normally I would offer you coffee, but since I dismissed the domestic staff this morning at your suggestion, there is no one to prepare it," the woman complained. "I didn't even have lunch today."

Awww. Poor hungry, desperate Ana. Maybe her big fluffy ass would diminish slightly as a result. Tam tried to look appropriately horrified. "That's terrible," she murmured. "I'm so sorry that I inconvenienced you."

"Here's your money." Ana opened a drawer, and pulled out several paper-wrapped packs of bills. "One hundred and ten thousand euro, as agreed yesterday. Nonsequential banknotes of fifty and one hundred."

Tam tucked the cash into her purse. A girl couldn't have too much of it. After all, whether she succeeded with this plan or not, she'd still provided a genuine service to the woman, so it was not stealing. And nice thick stacks of money were always handy in a desperate fugitive flight.

With or without Val.

She pushed away a stab of pain. Forced herself to focus.

Ana shrugged into her coat. "Thank goodness I asked GianCarlo to bring the car around before he left," she muttered. "I really am pressed for time, Ms. Steele. Are you ready to leave? Please?"

"Just one last detail." She picked up the golden earring she'd just shown Ana how to arm with Amplix 15, and switched it with the duplicate that she had hidden in her pocket. "Let me show you something. A little caveat."

Ana adjusted the fluffy fur collar of her jacket and made an impatient sound. Her heels clicked across the tiles. "What is it now?"

"Just a moment. This is important." Tam unscrewed the bead, pressed the lever that released the spring that held the needle inside. She pressed until a single drop of fluid trembled on the tip. It shone like a diamond in the afternoon light that slanted through the windows of the *salone.* "A demonstration of how these weapons can be applied."

Ana snorted. "That's not necessary. And I don't appreciate—ay!"

Tam had seized her elbow and pressed the needle to Ana's wrist.

Ana froze in place. "Ah . . . take that needle away from my arm," she said in a strangled voice. "Immediately."

"I'm afraid not," Tam said. "Walk, please. Toward the door. Right foot, then left foot. That's the way. We're taking my car to Nocera."

Ana's eyes dilated. Her face went gray under the mask of cosmetics. "How do you know where I . . . oh, my God. Who are you?"

"If you have to ask, I'm too bored with your self-absorbed stupidity to bother explaining." Tam towed the woman along, letting her feel a faint sting of the needle tip against her skin. "Guess. Dredge through your memory. It will give you something to do as we drive."

Ana began to cry noisily as Tam dragged her toward the Opel. "I don't understand," she whimpered. "Please don't hurt me."

Tam clenched her jaw. The noisy sobbing and wet snuffling sounds were intensely unpleasant to listen to. Robot Bitch, she reminded herself. Get the job done. "Open the car door, and get in."

Ana slid into the car with a thump, her eyes already dripping gothic black streaks down her cheeks.

"Do you have a remote opener for the electronic gate in your purse?" Tam demanded. "I hope for your sake that you do."

Ana nodded, hiccuping pitifully.

"Get it out and toss it onto the driver's seat."

Ana did so. Tam sucked in a sigh of relief, grabbed her hairclip, and squirted the soporific into Ana's face.

Ana's head flopped to the side almost instantly. Snot cascaded from her nose down over her mouth. Tam averted her eyes, grateful for the silence. This would keep her quiet for the twenty or so minutes it would take to get to the clinic. So far, so good.

She slid into the driver's seat. Ana was sagging sideways, which put her body unpleasantly close to Tam's. She shoved the other woman upright on the seat and strapped her slack body in.

The remote really did open the gate, to her relief. Would have been a fine joke on her if it hadn't.

She felt better once she was speeding around the curves on the mountain highway. Driving very fast gave her something to concentrate on other than how monumentally shitty all this was making her feel.

Robot Bitch was not supposed to feel shitty. She wasn't supposed to have feelings, period. She just got the job done, boom boom boom.

Tam reminded herself grimly of what Ana had tried to do to her.

Her ugliness, her spite. She thought of driving that pin into Ana's boyfriend's scrotum. Her first real strike for freedom, for payback.

She'd come a long way since then, but she felt like she was crawling back into a prison and pulling the door shut after herself.

She'd thought this experience would be cleansing. Cathartic. It wasn't. Looking at the unconscious woman's slack, drooling mouth, she didn't feel cleansed. She felt, paradoxically, soiled. And cuffing Val to the bed made her feel that way, too. Only much, much worse.

A vague, formless fear stirred inside her, that she had drifted too far. She was going down a road that had no escape. She was doomed.

She stomped it. None of this doom shit. She did not have the luxury of doubt. It wasn't part of her personal philosophy.

The problem was, that was feeling a little tight lately. Like a pair of outgrown shoes.

The decrepit Fiat shuddered and threatened to fall apart at any speed above forty-five kilometers an hour. Amazingly, the Vespino with its buzzing fifty-cubic-centimeter miniature motor had been quicker. No wonder Tamar had considered the ten minutes or so that he'd been unconscious to be a sufficient head start. The real head start was the velocity of the fucking toy car.

He drove with grim purpose, leaning forward to squint through the cracked, filthy windshield in a desperate attempt to see the road well enough not to kill himself. He pondered how much time he might gain or lose by procuring another car, either by stealing or renting, but came up with no useful ideas. San Vito was the closest place, but he could hardly go back there to rent, and going anywhere else would cost him still more time. And as groggy and addled as he was, he was in no shape to steal a car. He'd probably get caught and get himself beaten to death by an eighty-year-old man. Something ignominious like that.

Besides, his clothing fit the car. The ragged wool sweater with the cigarette burns and the brownish-yellow underarm sweat stains, the pilled, threadbare pants that did not succeed in covering his ankles though they did threaten to slide off his ass. All that could be said for them was they were dry.

The signora must have laughed up her sleeve when she picked them out of her rag bag. He would have been amused at her little joke, if he hadn't been so angry and miserable.

And in pain. Everything hurt. Most of all his shoulder, but there wasn't a centimeter of the rest of him, inside or out, that did not sting, ache or burn in sympathy. His head throbbed like a rotten tooth. Hung over from whatever drug Tamar had zapped him with, no doubt.

He felt humiliated. Betrayed into confessing his love, and she'd fucked him over to reward him for his idiocy. Served him right for being such a fatuous dickhead.

So why was he following her? He could turn his back and go.

He could not answer that question. He couldn't stop himself, either. Burning stubbornness, that was all it was. He hated being bested.

He stared at the ring on his finger. Tamar's ring. What the hell she had meant by leaving it with him, he did not dare to imagine.

But he had not taken it off.

Tamar's cell phone beeped from his pocket, as he finally came into an area of coverage. Val pulled it out and glanced at it.

He glanced again. Twenty *chiamate non risposte*. Twenty unanswered calls. He ran his eye over the numbers visible in the display. All the same number, all with a Seattle area code. Someone in the Seattle area had been desperately trying to call her all night long.

That could not be good news. He thought suddenly of Rachel. The bars of the prison Imre had tried to free him from closed in on him again, along with the chill of fear.

No, please. Not that. Not her baby girl.

He'd just poised his thumb over the callback option when the phone rang. The phone registered an unknown number, and in a moment of wild, irrational hope, he thought it might be Tamar.

He stabbed the button to answer. "*Sì?*"

There was a suspicious pause, and Connor McCloud's voice rasped through the line. "Who the hell is this?"

"It's Val Janos," he said. "What happened?"

"Rachel," Connor said. "They got Rachel."

The creeping dread solidified instantly into horror. He flash froze it and put it aside. No time for it. No time for anything now but action.

"Who?" he asked. "When?"

"How the fuck do we know who? She was playing with Sveti in the park right outside the house. A black sedan with three men in it pulled up. They roughed up Sveti, took Rachel, and took off. It was six PM."

"*Cazzo,*" Val whispered.

"Yeah," Connor agreed. "Where the fuck is Tam? And why doesn't she have her fucking phone?"

Val let out the tension with a sharp, gusty breath. "She's off to assassinate someone," he said grimly. "We disagreed about it. She handcuffed me to a bed and drugged me. I just got free. I'm hoping to catch up with her before she gets arrested. Or killed."

"Ah." There was an uncomfortable pause. "Well, there you go. That's our Tam for you. Are you having fun yet?"

"Fuck you," Val said.

"Sure. Whatever. Moving on. I was hoping you two might know—"

"Novak," he said flatly. "Check the RF tags for Rachel's position."

Connor sucked in a sharp breath. "Holy shit. I can't believe this. You tagged Rachel? With what?"

"SafeGuard beacons," Val said. "One in her bear, one in her stroller, one in her blanket, one in her coat. That red puffy one."

"She might still have the coat with her." Connor's voice vibrated with excitement. "Frequencies?"

"I don't have them on me," Val said. "The paperwork was lost when we had to run from our hotel two days ago, but you can get the frequencies from your own database. I ordered them online two weeks ago under the name Robert Perkins. They were shipped to a Tacoma address. I used the second smallest ones for her. Four of the burr beacons."

"You're a man after my own heart, Janos. I'm calling from the airport. We're booked through to Paris, since it was the first flight we could get to anyplace in Europe, but we didn't know where we needed to go from there."

"Almost certainly Hungary. Call me again if you find a signal for Rachel," Val said. "I'll get Tamar, if I can, and meet you in Budapest."

He hung up, pressed down hard on the accelerator, ignoring the car's freaky whines, shudders and shimmies of protest.

For Rachel's sake, the fucking car could make one last effort.

Her timing was spot on. Ana's eyelids fluttered as Tam parked the Opel in front of the clinic. She circled to the passenger's side, jerked the door open, unbuckled Ana, and swatted her sticky cheeks.

"Wake up," she said crisply. "Showtime."

Ana groaned, her eyes dim and foggy. "What?"

Tam handed her a handful of makeup removal pads and a compact mirror from her purse. "Fix your face."

Ana glanced at herself in the mirror, gasped in horror, and woke right up. She spent the next couple of minutes repairing her mask. When Tam sensed that she was starting to stall, she yanked Ana's elbow and dragged her up and out of the car.

Ana twisted away. "What are you going to—ow!"

The needle pierced the underside of Ana's coat sleeve, digging into her forearm so that Tam could stroll alongside her and hold her arm, oh-so-friendly and companionable. Ana squeaked and flinched.

"Move carefully," Tam told her. "Now listen. I am the Dottoressa Tiziana Gadaleta. A specialist in . . . what disease is he suffering from?"

"N-n-no one is quite s-sure," Ana quavered. "Some kind of tropical parasite, they think. It attacks the nerves. He's immobilized, but he still feels awful pain. It's . . . it's terrible. Please. Don't make it worse. He's already suffering so much."

"All right, I'm a specialist in tropical parasites." How appropriate, she reflected. The worst of both worlds. Paralyzed, but still in pain.

Funny. She'd felt that way herself for sixteen years.

Ana dragged her feet. "Wh-what are you going to do to him?"

"Shut up and move," Tam snapped as they approached the door.

The woman started to whimper. Tam leaned in to her ear. "One wrong move, and the needle goes in," she murmured. "Don't doubt

it. I have nothing to lose." For the first time in her life, Tam realized
that statement was a lie. The realization did not feel good. In fact, it
made her feel horribly vulnerable.

Oh, how she missed Robot Bitch.

Ana staggered beside her like a zombie. The man at the guard
booth slid open a glass panel and leaned down. "*Buona sera*, Signora
Santarini," he said. "What's the name of your visitor?"

"D-dottoressa Tiziana Gadaleta," Ana quavered.

The man didn't look up as he scribbled the name on his register.
Perhaps out of carelessness. Or maybe the clinic's posh visitors were
habitually in this emotional state. Ana peered into the retina scan,
presented her hand for the palm lock. A mechanical door sighed
open.

The clinic was chilly and modern inside. It seemed designed to
make one feel both important and vaguely sedated. White-clad doctors hustled officiously to and fro on their important business. No
one seemed to notice them. Excellent.

Ana hesitated. Tam smiled pleasantly and prompted her with the
needle's point. "Take me to him. Now."

Ana sniffed back her tears with violent effort and led her obediently down a series of corridors and stairways. She stopped outside a
room, tears streaming down her face.

"Papa," she said brokenly. "Oh, please. Don't do this. Please."

Christ, this was torture. *Damn* Robot Bitch, to leave her in the
lurch right now, in her hour of need. "Open the door," Tam urged
through gritted teeth.

Ana pushed open the door. Tam shoved her inside, glanced at the
man on the bed to make sure it was the right person.

It was. She stared at the long form lying on the bed, the dark,
sunken eyes that fastened on hers. They widened ever so slightly.

She shoved the needle in. Ana's jaw dropped in horror as Tam
pressed the plunger.

"Don't worry, I switched the earrings. It's just a sedative," Tam
assured her in Ana's last second of lucidity. She gently broke Ana's
tumble to the floor. Left her in a heap of wool and fur by the door.

She walked to the bed. Stengl stared up at her. His breath was la-
bored. He wore an oxygen mask over his nose and mouth.

Odd. She'd pictured this crucial, life-changing moment so many times. She felt nothing. Blank and cool, as if he were a stranger.

He looked insubstantial. He was a tall man, but skeletally thin now. She remembered a giant. Sweaty, malodorous, crushingly heavy.

His pale skin was like parchment, his lips peeling and colorless.

There was no need to speak. At least he recognized her, unlike Ana. She had that much satisfaction. There was no surprise in his eyes. If anything, she sensed a look of relief. He knew she'd come to kill him. The end of his suffering was at hand.

She came closer, bent over him. Stared into his bloodshot, watery eyes, wondering who was in there. How he could have done it. Rifle fire crackled in her head. Screams from the basement cells. Dirt scattering down into Mama and Irina's eyes. Her nails dug into her palms.

His eyes were avid with eagerness for her to free him.

Images superimposed themselves over the man's face in her mind. Her father, smiling over the jewelry bench as he taught her the craft they both loved. Playing with little Irina. Mamma, fussing over Tam's pronunciation of French, Russian, Italian, Ukrainian. Lecturing her about politics, philosophy, and manners. Telling her daughter how she was going to love studying at the Sorbonne some-day, as she herself had so longed to do.

The life she would have had, the life her little sister Irina would have had. Bones and dust.

She looked at him, and the anger didn't rise up and choke her as it always had before. The place where it had been had changed. She'd broken her heart wide open, made space inside it for Rachel, and then still more space, for Val. She was transformed, transfigured.

She felt as big as the sky in there.

There was no monster here to vanquish. All power to hurt had been drained out of the creature on that bed. He was a burned-out battery. She would obtain nothing by killing him—and she could lose everything. She was no longer a woman with nothing to lose. She had everything that was precious. Everything to protect and cherish.

He was not worth it.

The strangest sensation opened up inside her at that realization, thrumming in the newly open space inside her chest. Like light, like heat, like music. Sweet, high-pitched sound, far-off children singing.

If she killed him, she would be linked to him. She would carry him forever. All the strength that she needed for the people she loved, she would have to give to Drago Stengl until the day that she died.

She'd carried him long enough. Let his own pain crush him out of existence with its own stately, majestic pace. Why rush it?

She could turn away. Leave him behind. She really could.

He sensed his precious deliverance drifting inexorably away from him, and opened his bloodshot eyes wide in alarm. He tried to speak.

She shook her head. "No," she said softly, in Croatian. "Today is not your lucky day." The long unused language felt strange in her mouth.

She turned her back and walked away. She stopped at the door and looked down at Ana. Leaned over, felt the other woman's pulse.

Strong and steady. She'd wake up in a few minutes and be fine.

Tam walked out of the room and down the corridor. Her feet started going faster, 'til she was running. Then practically sprinting.

She forced herself to slow down. *Self-control, please. Get a grip.*

It was hard to keep her pace steady. She wanted to run headlong toward her new life. The chance she would give herself, if it wasn't too late. She wanted to run toward this new self with her arms outstretched. This woman who was not so toxic, so desperate.

This new Tam might even make a wild stab at happiness. Maybe even love, if pigs flew, if the sky fell, if she was insanely lucky.

Or at the very least, peace. If nothing else.

Peace. Something she'd never dared to hope for. Never thought she deserved. She asked the ghosts in her heart to forgive her for not avenging them. Her soul lightened as they granted it.

Children sang in her head. She was euphoric. She'd gone nuts.

Get a grip, Steele, she reminded herself. *Look sharp. You're not in the clear yet. Don't float off into la-la land. You're being irresponsible.*

No one challenged her at the exit. She walked out into the brilliant clarity of the winter evening. The setting sun made the sea glow, the wind blew through the pines, whipping and bending them.

She was astonished by how beautiful it was. Tears blurred her eyes. Her mind was blown by its grandeur. It hurt. She liked the pain.

Bring it on. She was bigger now. She could take it in.

First order of business: take those damned tongue studs out of her mouth. She didn't need them now. Then she would run to the nearest place that sold prepaid cell phones, buy one, call to check on Rachel, and then call Val. Tell him that he'd been right, she'd been wrong, and she was sorry. That she loved him. That she'd pursue him until he gave in out of sheer exhaustion. His anger was huge, but so was her love.

And she was tough. Let him yell and scream and be pissed at her. She'd wait him out. Let Stengl rot. Let Novak and Georg kill each other.

Fuck them all. In the face of all the bastards who wished her ill, she was going to live. With her kid—and her man. She really was. Oh, God.

The urgency she felt to get away from there was building up to a frantic level. She yanked open the door of the Opel—and heard the muted pop of another car door opening behind her. *No.*

She spun, flinging up her arm to block the blow that she instinctively knew was aimed at the back of her head. It connected with her forearm. White hot, fiery pain shot up her arm.

Broken. *Shit*, a useless right arm.

She scrambled back, hit the car, bounced. Dragged in air, tried to block the sickening pain. She'd deserved that one, floating around in a fucking cloud, drunk on beauty and hopes of love.

She would pay for it now. András loomed, his face wild and grinning. Wet-lipped and sharp-toothed, like an evil hobgoblin from one of her grandmother's scarier stories.

Her knee jerked up toward his groin, and hit hard. *Yes.* Air escaped from him in a grunting whoosh. She scooted away, but he scooped her right off her feet with a swipe of his leg at knee level. She lost her center, teetering on those fucking spike-heeled Manolos, goddamnit, betrayed by vanity and fashion—

She fell against the Opel again, jarring the broken arm, and almost screamed. It cost her the split second she needed to wind up for another blow or block. The entire weight of András's body slammed into her, squashing her against the car, dragging her down, down, first to her knees, and then thudding heavily, flat onto her face.

He sat on her back, squashing out air, light, everything. Her face was ground against the asphalt. Pebbles scratched her cheek.

"Bitch," he panted. "You'll pay for that. Screaming." His hoarse, grating voice rasped in her ears. "You can start paying right now." He stuck his wet, meaty tongue into her ear, wiggled it. "Guess what pretty little toddler is on her way to visit benevolent old Daddy Novak right now, as we speak?"

"*No!*" Horror exploded inside her. She convulsed in instinctive denial, but his weight made the movement barely a wiggle.

András laughed nastily. "Ah, yes. We'll get there about the same time she does. A touching family reunion. I can hardly wait." His hand clamped around her mouth and nose, pressing over both with a damp gauze pad that had a sharp, acrid smell. "Little ones never last long. . . ."

Her blood pressure plummeted, pulling her into a sucking hole of despair. An express elevator to hell and the lightless oblivion beyond it.

Chapter
26

The Opel's driver's side door hung open as Val pulled the Fiat up next to it. The car subsided into ominous silence after a rattling death cough.

Val's heart stuck in his throat as he shoved the stiff, creaking door of the Fiat open and stared at the scene. The ignition key peeked out from behind the left wheel tire. A single shoe lay on the asphalt between the two cars. A black, spike-heeled pump. One of the Manolos.

He got out, crouched to pick up the shoe. He hated to think of her barefoot. So vulnerable.

He thudded down onto his knees. Trying to breathe, trying to think. What next. What now. Ah, God.

Get up, Janos. You've got a job to do. Don't just crash like a melodramatic asshole. It sounded like Tam's crisp, merciless voice in his head.

It comforted him. Gave him the impetus he needed to fish up the keys from behind the tire, drag his leaden body off the ground, and slide into the Opel. The laptop and Hegel's cell phone still lay on the passenger side floor, forgotten since that morning.

He reached for the cell phone. It still had some life in the battery. He stared at it for a long, hostile moment, and shook himself to break the paralysis. He pulled up the stored text messages.

348. The room number. Georg's last message to Hegel.

Three steps back. His usual mantra struck him as ludicrous, almost cruel. He could not take three steps anywhere. He was too muddled, too exhausted. He was terrified.

You will have to do somewhat better than your best to get out of this. Imre's dry voice echoed through his head.

Val's chest twisted, to think of Imre. Better than his best might not be enough. It had not been so far, or this would not have happened. Imre, dead. Tamar and Rachel, taken.

Even Georg might do better now. Any variable that could give her another fighting chance, Val had to throw into the mix right now while he still could. While she was alive. He punched "call."

It rang eight times. Someone picked up, and there was a waiting silence on the other end, though he could tell the line was open.

Val tried to speak, but doubt had seized his voice.

Georg got tired of the waiting game. "My curiosity cannot resist a telephone call from a dead man," he said in English. "Do I speak with the spirits from beyond?"

Val cleared his throat with a cough. "No," he said. "Janos here."

"Oh. You." Georg switched to Hungarian. "I am going to kill you when I see you. You know that, eh?"

"Fine. Whenever you like," Val said dully. "I just want to give you some information first. About Tamara Steele."

"Ah. Yes?"

One last moment of frantic wondering, if he was giving her another chance or condemning her to a living death.

No. His Tamar would never languish in a cage for long. Not his man-eating tigress. Not her.

"I am waiting, Janos," Georg prompted. "I am not a patient man. What about her? Let me speak with her."

Val shut his eyes and threw the dice. "I can't," he said. "Novak has her now. András abducted her. Less than an hour ago."

Georg sucked in an audible breath. "You fucking idiot," he hissed. "How could you have allowed this to happen?"

"She exposed herself when she ran from me," he said dully. "She was trying to get back to you. She . . . she wanted you."

Georg was silent.

"She will be in Novak's hands within eight hours," Val added after another minute ticked by. "Dead within twenty-four hours of that, almost certainly. If not sooner."

"If this happens, you do know what will happen to you, Janos?"

Val stared bleakly at the horizon. "Yes," he whispered. God help him. He did.

"Pain," Georg said softly. "For as long as I can inflict it. Pain you cannot imagine. Think about it."

Val broke the connection. There was no point in thinking about it. The threat barely touched him.

If Novak killed Tamar and Rachel, anything Georg did to him afterward would be supremely redundant. He doubted he would even notice.

In fact, he would make a point of being already dead.

Georg clicked the phone closed with a hand that tingled with excitement. His heart thudded with lust and fury.

She wanted him. She had always wanted him. He had known in his deepest heart that they were destined to be together. He was the only one who could accept or understand her dark side, her secret, shameful desires, and she was the only one who could comprehend his.

He would reward her for her loyalty and save her from that blood-drinking monster, Novak. And she would owe him her life. He liked that.

But he had to be quick and lucid. And ruthless.

He walked down the small spiral staircase into the common room of the luxury apartment he had rented in San Vito. His eyes slid over the five men who were there. Someone had betrayed him. Sold him out to Novak, telling the old man about Tamara's continued existence and Georg's search for her. It was one of the men in this room.

It galled him to harbor a traitor, but that same man could be used to feed false information back to Novak.

The traitor would subsequently die a slow and horrible death, once he was identified.

"We're going back to Budapest at once," he announced. "Novak has openly challenged me. Tomorrow at midnight, we mount our attack." He turned to Ferenc. "Call the others. We will conduct a strategy meeting. We must videoconference. Hurry. There is a great deal of planning to do."

Ferenc pulled out his phone and got to work.

Georg strolled out to the terrace of the luxury villa, which was perched right over the roiling sea. He turned up the volume on his telephone. The crashing of the sea served nicely as white noise to cover his voice. He punched in the code to scramble the call, and dialed the PSS man he dealt with now. The defunct Hegel's second in command.

"Yes?" the man asked.

"It happens tomorrow," Georg said without preamble.

There was a startled pause. "Tomorrow? So soon?"

"My men cannot know," Georg said. "They're baiting the trap. Your team will mount the attack. I will call you in two hours and explain the details. You will need an eight-man team in Budapest by tomorrow."

Georg hung up the phone and stared at the heaving waves. There was a great deal of planning to do. Most of his men would probably be dead by tomorrow. He would have to sacrifice them to unmask the traitor, and he would be hard put to replace them. This was going to be expensive.

But his mind was too occupied for planning. Filled with filthy, sweating fantasies that made his crotch ache with eagerness.

Fantasies of fucking Tamara, over and over. While the whole world watched.

Andrea first noticed the curly-headed toddler curled up, thumb in her mouth and sleeping like an angel next to her dad, while passing out the ear phones in the first class cabin. She was the same size as Andrea's two-year-old Liliana back home, currently being spoiled rotten by Grandma. These long runs out and back to Frankfurt were hard. By the time Andrea got back, she was longing for her Lili.

Funny, that the little cutie was already sacked out even before they took off. Usually, the noise and bustle of boarding revved kids up. If they calmed down at all, it was during that high altitude drone of midflight over the Pole. Portland-Frankfurt was a long flight for a toddler, but Andrea had tricks for the kids, over and beyond the usual crayons the airline provided. She'd be ready when this one woke up.

She beamed at the little girl and smiled at her father, a big, bearded dark man. "What a doll," she enthused. "How old?"

The guy blinked a few times before answering. "Two," he said.

"I have a two-year-old at home, too," Andrea confided. "It's a beautiful age. No matter what anybody says."

The man smiled briefly and accepted the beer she'd just poured for him, and looking away as he sipped. Not the chatty type.

Andrea glanced at the kid every time she walked past 10A and 10B. She slept like a rock, in the exact same position, skinny legs curled up, thumb in mouth, arm flung over her head.

Hours later, the little girl had not moved. Her father gazed into space or read a newspaper. Andrea served him his meal. He ate it, folded his hands, dozed without ever touching or looking at the child.

Seven hours into the flight, Andrea served the man a drink and nodded at the little girl. "My, she certainly is a sound sleeper," she commented. "You're lucky, on such a long flight."

The man's eyes flicked up to hers and away. "Guess so," he said.

"Let me know when she wakes up and I'll get her some yogurt and juice," she offered.

He mumbled something and looked back down into his paper.

After ten hours had gone by, Andrea began feeling nervous. She checked the passenger manifest, not even sure exactly why. John and Melissa Esposito. Well, of course, he was her father. What else?

Maybe the little girl had been dosed with antihistamines so that she'd sleep. Some parents did that when they wanted a hassle-free flight, but she was awfully small for that. Maybe she was a heavy sleeper, and this was her full night stretch. Maybe she was jetlagged from a previous leg of their trip. Or maybe Andrea should just mind her own beeswax.

Even so, an hour later when the man got up to stretch his legs and stroll to the bathroom, she slipped over to 10B, and took a peek.

Same position. The kid did not look good. In fact, Andrea was unpleasantly reminded of that bout of rotavirus that had landed Lili in the children's hospital last Thanksgiving, an IV in her tiny arm. That pinched, pale look, the pale, wrinkled skin, sunken eyes, the dry, colorless lips. Dehydration. Her cheek was cold. Her hand felt like ice. Andrea smelled pee. She slid her hand down under the child's body.

Yep. Wet, as was the seat beneath her. No wonder she was cold. At least that meant the dehydration couldn't have gotten to a critical point yet. Still, Andrea was tempted to check her pulse. Just to see if she had one.

"What the hell do you think you're doing?"

The man's low voice made her jump. Andrea spun around and faced him. "Ah. Sorry. I was just, ah, checking on your little girl—"

"That's not necessary," the man said.

"But she's wet," Andrea protested. "She'll get chilled. And she—"

"Her mother will change her when we get to Frankfurt."

To *Frankfurt?* Andrea stared at him. That was three hours from now. Four, by the time he disembarked, got through the lines and slogged through that enormous airport.

She glanced down at that poor little girl and flagrantly broke airline regulations with her next words. "If you give me a diaper and fresh clothes, I'll change her for you," she offered.

"No, thank you. Don't worry about it," the man growled.

"It's no trouble. She really should wake up anyway, just so she can take in some fluids," Andrea said earnestly. "The air in here can really dry out a little—"

"Miss?" The man leaned right up to her ear and murmured, "Why don't you fuck off and leave us alone? That way, I won't have to make a formal complaint to the airline about your inappropriate questions, and the fact that I found you touching my daughter's private parts when I got back from the rest room. Hmm?"

Andrea jerked away. Her heart thudded, her face reddened. She scurried away, tears of shock and hurt indignation clogging her throat.

She conferred with her colleagues, but it was almost time to serve breakfast, it was a very full flight, everyone was waking up and stretching their legs, and none of the rest of the flight crew wanted to tangle with a crazy guy. Certainly not when they were all so close to landing the plane and letting the problem just walk away.

The next two and a half hours crawled by. Andrea ignored him, but she felt his eyes on her. Hot, nasty little pinpricks, burning into her neck. The little girl did not move, even during the shudder and roar of landing. When the doors opened, John Esposito tossed the child over his shoulder so that her head and arms dangled limply down his back, and waited in line to exit, impassive. He held only a briefcase.

A briefcase? He didn't even have a baby bag. What kind of father took a two-year-old on a fifteen-hour flight with no bag? Not a book, not a toy, not a snack. No wet wipes, bottle, sippy cup, nose tissues. To say nothing of diapers, a change of clothing. Like, what the hell?

Something was off. Something was really wrong with this picture.

Her stomach fluttered. She stood with her colleagues as the passengers filed out, chirping "Buh-bye! Buh-bye!" like a trained parrot. She didn't look at John Esposito as he walked by with his limp burden, but she peeked as he unfolded the stroller in the icy cold jetway and dropped the child in it. He did not fasten the little girl in. Or tuck any sort of cover over her.

He turned, looked. He'd known she'd look. He was ready with a triumphant smile that said, *I won, you cowardly, ineffectual bitch.*

"Buh-bye," he taunted softly, with a waggle of his fingers.

He disappeared down the jetway. Andrea wrenched her faltering smile back into alignment and longed for Lili so hard it hurt.

She needed to grab her little girl. Hug her and snuggle her. Right now. But Lili was on the wrong side of the world. It was night back in Portland. She couldn't even call. It would be hours before Lili woke up.

Until then, Andrea was going to stare at the airport hotel room ceiling and wait. Feeling scared.

She could already be dead.

Val wrestled his mind back to blankness as he moored the small, inflatable motorboat to a huge vine that clung to the side of the ancient stonework bridge. The road that ran over it led to Novak's crumbling eighteenth-century palace on the river. The McClouds had texted Rachel's radio frequency to him, and her icon had come to rest here some hours before. Val had been unsurprised that the revenge orgy would take place at Novak's favorite residence. The old man felt like an aristocrat here. It pumped up his vanity.

He knew the place well. He'd spent lonely years here, in the old days, once it was discovered that he had a knack for computers and technological devices. He'd made it his business back then to learn every detail about the ancient palace, having nothing better to do in his leisure time. The grounds were honeycombed with dungeons, wells, cisterns and drains, and he'd spent long hours studying antique floor plans he'd found in the library, hand-drafted in elegant cursive script. He'd wriggled through miles of culverts, tunnels and various other lightless, dripping holes, just out of curiosity. And since knowledge was power, his policy was to share what he learned only when his colleagues or employer had a pressing need to know it.

No one had ever asked.

He could only hope that no one else had made such a thorough study of the estate since then. It was unlikely. Crawling through dank, rat-infested eighteenth-century sewer pipes was the kind of thing only unbalanced teenagers did voluntarily.

And desperate, luckless bastards like himself, of course.

He opened the computer and checked Rachel's icon. It remained stationary. The satellite photograph on his screen showed a bird's-eye view of the place, which he remembered well. The icon blinked in what looked like one of the outbuildings, garages that used to be the stables. He slid the computer into his pack and climbed carefully out of the boat.

Keeping his mind focused on the task. Not letting it wander to what they might be doing to her right—

No. He picked his way over moss-slimed rocks, blanked out his mind with manufactured white noise.

In the flickering twilight dimness beneath the bridge, he shone the flashlight on the rusty iron grate bolted over the sewer hole in the wall. It dated back to the first World War, from the looks of it. He rattled the thing, examined the corroded bolts. He wouldn't even need the welding equipment. A few wrenches with the crowbar—

this one for Rachel, *oof,* this one for Tam—and ah, *fuck.* A fresh, hot wet spot in his shoulder. He'd ripped open the wound again. But the grate was loose.

She could be dead. Or worse.

He stepped savagely on the thought. Look straight ahead. Not productive, to think of it. Not useful to them.

Yes, and neither are you, testa di cazzo. He'd been buzzing around this problem for almost twenty-four hours like a fly around a turd. Endless precious hours wasted in inefficient, infuriating means of travel. No time to equip, no time to assemble a team or plan something brilliant. András had certainly had the use of a private plane waiting at the Naples airport. He'd probably gotten to Budapest during the night, and to Novak's estate by the small hours of the morning with his prize. Hours for them to play with her if they'd wanted to. If Novak had been in a hurry.

Whereas Val himself had been forced to drive like a maniac to the Roma airport at Fiumicino and abandon the rental car in the taxi lane, door hanging open, keys in the ignition. He'd sprinted up to the ticketing area, waiting on line after line, trying desperately to find a seat on a commercial flight.

He was spoiled, by all the high budget shortcuts of PSS and the obscenely rich corporations and military operations that they serviced. *Cristo,* how did normal people survive the nightmarish frustration?

Normal people didn't usually have their lovers chained under a torturer's knife.

One last wrench, one last blaze of agony to take his mind off his troubles, and the grate came loose from the mouth of the sewer pipe. Thud, clang, and it rolled into the water with a sullen splash.

He clutched the flashlight in his teeth and scooped out armfuls of trash, twigs, leaves and sludge that had drifted down with the rainwater overflow for decades. It had lodged against the grate into a sludgy wall, making the opening too small for a man to crawl through.

He wished he had a team, but it took time to coordinate a team. The McClouds were fierce and competent and well meaning, but they were hours behind him, having to cross two continents and an ocean. He could not hope for help from them. By the time they followed their beacons to the source, whatever was going to happen would have long since happened. So be it.

He tightened his teeth on the pen flashlight and launched himself headfirst into the dark, wet hole. It was like crawling into his own grave.

Which did not bother him. He was not afraid of death. It was life without her that he could not face. The blankness of it, the dull, flat emptiness that he had mistaken for calm. Detachment.

Cold, slimy mud squelched between his fingers. He should have thought of rubber gloves, but he'd been too frantic to do more than procure the most basic things that occurred to him: backpack, boat, crowbar, welding gear, guns, ammunition. His black clothing was now covered with stinking mud. At least he wasn't immersed in icy water. But then again, the evening was still young.

A couple hundred meters brought him to the main tunnel, a larger and still older one. Here he no longer had to crawl but only crouch, doubled over. He started to run, splashing through the dripping tunnel, the flashlight bobbing wildly between his teeth.

The tunnel was long, with various forks and twists. Overflow from old rainwater cisterns at several points on the estate all found their way here, and he had to dig into his ironclad long-term memory, concentrate and count to remember which one led where he meant to go. He gave thanks for Imre's rigorous training.

He crawled, face first, through the last hundred meters of the overflow pipe. He barely fit inside it. His shoulders had not been quite as broad the last time he'd crawled through, years ago.

The space before him suddenly opened up into a black void. He stuck his head carefully out and peered up. The cistern had been out of use for a hundred and fifty years or so, the area above ground having been turned into a conservatory at some point in the middle of the nineteenth century. The greenhouse above remained, but in Val's time of servitude, it had been abandoned, used largely as a storage room and weapons dump. Gabor Novak was not a man with any interest in nurturing life, be it animal or vegetable.

But the conservatory was inside the security perimeter.

The overflow hole was in the narrow upper shaft of the well. Three meters above his head had been the opening. Val had remembered there being a little light inside the well, shining down from the pattern of holes drilled in the iron plate covering the access.

He could barely make out those little holes. The fading light of evening did not penetrate them. Beneath him, the narrow tube of stonework yawned out wide into the huge antique rainwater cistern. Ten, twelve meters deep. Falling into it would be a very bad, slow, lonely death if one did not have the luck to break one's neck outright.

He groped on the wall in the darkness for the corroded iron ladder steps bolted to the wall, hoping that whatever lay over the iron plate would not be too heavy for him to lift. Hoping that Tamar was still—

No. Straight ahead. Move.

He gritted his teeth around the flashlight, wriggled his upper body out even further, and reached for the first rung.

It snapped off the wall. In his wild flailing for purchase, the flashlight slid from his mouth. He clutched the far side of the wall with his shaking, rigid fingers, legs splayed in the overflow tube, the hand with the throbbing shoulder groping desperately for another rung. A part of his brain that was cool and detached counted the many, many seconds that passed. The iron rung, *plop*. The flashlight, *plop*.

So. There was water in the cistern. Who knew how much or from what source. Perhaps it would be drowning for him, rather than a broken neck. No matter. He had no preference.

He reached, clasped the next rung. He would have to pull his entire upper body out of the overflow hole to test this one. There would be no way to keep from falling if this one gave out. He had no reason to think it would be any stronger than the one beneath it.

He had even less reason to turn around and go back.

He realized, bemused, that he was muttering something under his breath. An old prayer he had learned from his grandmother in his early childhood in Romania, before his mother had gotten bored with the man Val had known as his father, and their tiny rural village, and run off with her fancy city boyfriend to Budapest. Taking her luckless little boy with her.

The prayer was in a dialect he barely remembered. Something he'd recited at bedtime, verses to ward off monsters, beasts, vampires.

He gave the rung his weight. It bowed, ever so slightly—and held.

He pulled himself up. Dangled from it with his entire weight, clenched his teeth. Waited stoically to fall and die.

It didn't happen. Not yet. Not his moment. Maybe later.

He dragged himself upward and began to climb.

Chapter
27

"You've removed every last bit of jewelry from her body, András?"

The cool, dragging voice sliced through the hideous dreams and the ever-present consciousness of pain, echoing strangely in her throbbing skull, volume cutting in and out. She ran the words back, trying to dredge some meaning out of them. It sank in slowly.

Hungarian. Not her best language, but she managed in it.

"Of course, Boss. I'm tying her hand and foot. Nothing to worry about. Besides, I inspected every centimeter of her body. Repeatedly. Nothing on it but what God gave her."

"Do not underestimate this woman." She tried not to shudder at the sound of that voice, like the cool, dry scales of a venomous snake sliding over her skin. "She is extremely dangerous."

"I know." András's voice was long-suffering. "My balls are still sore. But I promise she won't give us any trouble. Not when I do *this*."

A rope jerked tight around her wrists, the right one of which was swollen and hot, and the blur of pain suddenly became horribly specific. She kept her eyes shut, feigning unconsciousness while she tried to remember how her arm had come to be broken.

Then it slammed into her mind, full force. András. Novak. *Rachel*.

Her eyes popped open just in time to see András take in the slack of a rope he'd tossed over a huge, menacing iron hook that was set high into the wall.

He looked down, smiled to find her eyes open, and yanked.

She shrieked. The rope wrenched her up until she dangled by her wrists, the tips of her toes barely touching the ground. Agony. Her ankles were tied, making it impossible to widen her stance, keep her balance, and take weight off her broken arm. She keened between gritted teeth, jerking until she managed to grip the rope with her left hand. Her vision was going dark. The maw of unconsciousness yawned, and she was tempted to tip herself into it.

But no way could it be that easy. They would have a way to revive her. András was a professional, after all, and besides—*Rachel*.

Where the fuck was Rachel? She had to know.

The two men swam into view. Her eyes streamed. She blinked, sniffed, tasted blood. Her face was swollen from a blow she did not remember receiving. Her heart forced blood through inflamed tissue, slamming painfully with each throb.

There was that prick András, dressed in executioner's black, holding the rope, his cobra face expressionless, his eyes strangely dead and empty. And Daddy Novak's hideous, grinning face.

His son Kurt, four years dead, was rotting in his coffin, and his corpse probably looked much like the skeletal man who stood before her now. The zombie king. His pale, bright eyes were identical to those of his dead son. The same strange, poisonous green color.

She glanced around the lavish baroque salon. The windows looked out on a vast, terraced garden, and beyond it, the winding curves of a river, fading into the twilight. Candelabra were lit on several tables, and the opulent gilded molding and trim gleamed in the flickering candlelight. Subtle track lights installed in the vaulted ceilings lit up the frescoes. Chubby, smiling cupids flanked gruesome depictions of martyred saints. There was one being pierced with a multitude of arrows, one being flayed alive, another holding her chopped-off breasts on a plate as if serving them up. One unlucky saint held both of her gouged-out eyes in her hands, mouth wide and screaming, eye sockets bleeding. The eyes in her clutching hands looked bloodshot, shocked and terrified. As if they still could see.

Tam looked away before she had to take in the images on the

other panels. Novak followed the direction of her gaze and chuckled.

"Pretty, aren't they?" he asked, switching to heavily accented English. "I'm so fond of my frescoes. Seventeenth century. The artist was anonymous but very gifted, in my opinion."

Very fucked up in hers, Tam thought. She noticed two huge flat-screen TVs, set on tables to either side of her. Their blank fifty-inch screens were dark and empty. They were incongruous in the dim room, otherwise full of priceless baroque era art and furniture. Then the air moved on her shivering body, and a huge, gold-framed standing mirror right in front of her brought her attention to another unpleasant fact.

She was naked.

She was not surprised. She had learned young how vulnerable nakedness made a person feel, how easily controlled. It was a quick and dirty instant weapon for sadists and bullies, and she'd met too many of those in her lifetime. But she was tough as an old boot. Nakedness was not a problem. No, that fucking broken arm was the problem.

Novak clapped his clawlike hands together. "I was beginning to wonder if you would ever wake up. I've been so impatient to meet you, Tamara Steele. What a pleasure."

He paused. Did he expect her to say that the pleasure was all hers? But even if she was disposed to play word games with him, she was shaking too hard to breathe enough to speak. All she could manage were shallow, squeaking drags for air.

Novak studied her thoughtfully, eyes hooded. "Let her down, András," he said. "Onto her feet."

András scowled and gave the rope an agonizing jerk. "But she—"

"She will faint," the old man said harshly. "I want her conscious. I want this to last."

András let up so abruptly she thudded down, legs buckling. She sagged to the side and was brought up short by her tortured wrists.

The two men watched impassively as she struggled to get her feet beneath her body again.

"Is that better, my dear?" The fake solicitude in Novak's voice oozed over her like slime. Her mouth was so dry, she was choking.

She tried to swallow. Tried to cough. Regretted it. Coughing jarred everything, and everything hurt like pure, flaming hell.

"What do you want from me?" she whispered.

Novak's smile curled thinly upward. "Something special. Something intimate. Something only you can give me."

Her body clenched at the implications of those words. "Be more specific," she croaked.

He leaned forward, close enough so that his fetid breath almost made her gag. "Pain," he hissed.

Ah, yes. Great. Why was she not surprised. She almost rolled her eyes, but that sort of flip defiance could make her fate worse.

Or rather, Rachel's. It was all about Rachel now.

"I never used to have such a passion for torture," Novak confided. "It was just a means to an end. I am not like András, who is a true aficionado. An artist of pain. Then I discovered I had a disease the doctors were pleased to call terminal, and one day, while punishing a man who had wronged me, I noticed something odd. I felt restored by the experience. It literally gave me energy. I tried it a second time. The phenomenon repeated itself. It was therapeutic. Amazing, no?"

She was speechless. Not surprised, though, at the total self-absorption. The mark of a true psychopath.

"Really," he said earnestly, as if she had argued with him. "I absorb the life force of the person I am punishing. Particularly if they have robbed or insulted me, as you have, my dear. It is so perfect, so appropriate. You were responsible for the death of my son. And now I have your daughter. Symmetrical, no?"

Her heart raced, her stomach rolled. Her ears rang, with some deafening inner noise. Rifle shots crackling from a distance. Screams from the tortured prisoners in the basement cells. Death all around her.

He looked hurt, at her failure to respond. "It's true," he protested. "Every time I indulge my test values show a marked improvement. My doctors want to know my secret, but they wouldn't understand if I told them. I'm intrigued to see what effect playing my games on a three-year-old should have on my health. I suspect it will be a potent tonic."

He stared into her eyes as he said it, avid for her reaction. She was too raw with pain and fear to hide it. His face creased with delight.

"Ah, yes," he muttered between wheezing chuckles. "This will be good. This will give me months. A year, maybe. Delicious."

She vibrated with pure fear. Her fuck-you-in-your-face bravado was torn away completely. He had her, and they both knew it. Even the tongue stud was pointless now. He would never get close enough to her for her to use it, not until after he had finished with Rachel. At which point, whether she lived or died would be no longer relevant.

Perhaps breaking the capsule and dying first would take the fun out of hurting Rachel for them, but then probably not. And she could not abandon her baby here while Rachel was still alive.

He might still come close enough to her before he started in on her baby. Close enough to gloat. She could hope for that.

"Where is she?" Tam forced the question out through shaking lips.

"Near, very near," Novak assured her. "We've been waiting for her to wake up. The idiot who brought her overdid the sedative dosage for the airplane flight. Not used to dealing with small children, evidently. The child was practically comatose when she finally arrived, but my people tell me she's come around nicely in the past couple of hours. In fact, she never stops screaming. I shall send András to fetch her in a few minutes, and we can begin."

The pressure increased in Tam's chest. An iron claw of fear gripped her lungs, her heart. Squeezing, crushing. She had always thought that she had seen the worst, felt the worst there was to feel.

How innocent of her. How naive. How lacking in imagination.

"We kept you under for the duration," Novak went on. "Mostly because of your reputation for clever escapes and non-linear thinking. You should be flattered."

He sounded like he was conferring a compliment. The fragment of her mind still capable of rational thought marveled at the kinky weirdness of it. Flattering a woman who was dangling from a hook by her wrists. What, was she supposed to simper? Thank him?

She had to lure him close enough to spit. It would be better to kiss him and get the stuff inside his mouth, but even spraying it onto his face might be enough to carry him off, sick as he was.

Tam dragged in air, gathering her energy. Her lips were trembling. She had to steady them. She had to work up some spit. He had to move closer. Just a little bit. *Please.*

"Thank God I don't have to worry about fucking you, at least," she taunted him. "Your breath is so foul, it smells like something crawled down your throat and died there. Please don't breathe on me, for the love of God. Step back. It makes me gag."

Novak's eyes were wide, weirdly empty. "Ah, yes," he whispered. "You are strong. You'll last a long time. Strong ones are the best. Who knows? Maybe what I do to your daughter will actually revive me to the point of sexual arousal. We shall see, hmm?"

But he did not step closer, no matter how desperately she willed him to. He was too alert to fall for it, even though he considered her defenseless. His resistance to being manipulated was automatic.

And he had no sexual energy at all. She should have made her play on a different level. *Shit.* She'd gone with sex by sheer force of habit, it being what worked for most men, but not him. She'd fucked up, and her sweet baby would pay for her mistake.

He was speaking again.

Pay attention. Stay sharp. For as long as you can. Stay sharp for Rachel.

". . . wait for Janos to bring you to me," Novak was saying. "He was taking too long, so I sent András to speed things up. But I thought you might enjoy this video memento of your mad love affair."

That confused her for a minute. Was he talking about Val? Yes. Val had been sent to collect her. Imre was the hostage. And Imre was dead, so they had changed tactics. Yes. That tracked.

Memento of her mad love affair? What the hell? Images began to flicker on the TV screens. She could not make them out with the tears and sweat in her eyes. The light in both screens were dim, and it seemed like—those frantic, rhythmic movements—oh, for the love of God, was this possible? Porn, to accompany her torture? The sheer, banal stupidity of it was insulting. Even in the face of this much pain, this much fear.

Fuck it. Her arm hurt too much to bother contemplating the sewer of the man's mind. She was far too busy calculating the best possible second for a murder-suicide. *Focus.*

". . . no, look at it!" Novak was insisting. "Don't you recognize yourself? Pay attention, Tamara."

Herself? She squeezed the hot, stinging moisture out of her eyes, and looked again.

And looked and looked. It was . . . oh, hell, no. It was not possible.

It was their room in San Vito. The graceful triple loggia that looked out over the sea, the dim light of dawn, the tender glow of pink.

And on the bed, behind the fronds of some blurry plant in the foreground, herself and Val. Her, mounted and moving over him, head thrown back, making soft moans of pleasure.

How? How had they been found so soon after they arrived? When could the cameras have been planted? When they were out to dinner?

She looked at the other one, but it took over a half minute of horrified squinting to force that dim, writhing snarl of erotic images to resolve into something comprehensible. Mostly because she didn't want to take the information in. Her mind resisted it desperately.

Herself, pinned against the door of the tiny staff kitchen of the Huxley. Moaning like a cat in heat as she let herself get good and nailed by Val Janos. The camera looked down at them, godlike from on high, judging her for being so stupid. It focused on her face, flushed with pleasure and excitement. And drugs, she remembered. She'd been as high as a kite, on the mystery drug, plus chianti.

The thought was a nasty icicle stab. She cringed, shuddered, and steeled herself. Forced herself to reason it through. Step by step.

There was no way they could have anticipated Janos and planted a camera to watch him without his knowledge. No way they could have connected her to Nick and Becca's wedding before she actually went there. The only one who could have planted that camera was Val himself.

He'd chosen the place, prepared it, drugged her into a sexed-up daze, dragged her to it, and fucked her there. To entertain the beast. That was the truth. There was no other explanation.

Novak followed her train of thought step for step, his eyes hot and avid. "Yes, I see you understand now. Shocked, are you? He did what I paid him for. He got you to fall in love with him. It's his professional specialty. I'm acquainted with PSS, you see. I've used them in the past. I've been told that Val Janos is always the operative of choice when it is necessary to fuck one's way into the target's confidence. What a coup for his CV. He can persuade any woman of his undying passion. Even an ice-hearted bitch like you."

"No," she whispered.

"Oh, yes. And they said you were so suspicious, so intelligent. But you fell. Legs wide open. Like magic." He cackled and wheezed. Blood spattered over his lips and chin.

She had not thought it possible to feel worse than she did, but it was. One more thing wrenched from her, one more bleeding wound. And she felt so alone, more than ever before. Abandoned in hell.

Imre. The foolish, girlish part of her mind latched onto the vain hope that maybe, just maybe, that video footage was all about keeping Imre in one piece, something Val had been forced to do. Maybe . . .

But Novak was shaking his head, waving an admonitory finger. "I know what you're thinking," he said, from behind his blood-spotted handkerchief. "Forget your romantic notions. He told you the heart-wrenching tale of how I held his old patron hostage and threatened to cut him to pieces if he did not deliver you?"

She did not rreply.

"We concocted that scenario together. And yesterday, he did as I commanded and told you of Imre's valiant sacrifice? Did he beg you to run away with him to live in romantic bliss on some green island on the Aegean? I see that he did. That bad boy. He'll definitely get that fat bonus that I promised him. He's earned every penny of it." He took a step closer, staring at her as if he wanted to eat her alive. "Let me show you how much Vajda loves you, Tamara." He glanced at András. "Pull the rope," he commanded. "Off her feet. Ten seconds."

András complied eagerly. The rope wrenched her up off her feet.

She hated herself for the shriek that scorched her throat. And for being so vulnerable. For having loved Val for even an instant, for having believed him. For getting caught. For everything. All of it. Rachel. Oh, Rachel.

She struggled to get a better grip on the rope with her left hand. Ten seconds. Ten centuries of lightning stabbing through her nerves.

She sobbed in air and hung on, delirious with pain—

Thud, down she went onto her floppy tied ankles. She clung to consciousness, and attempted the agonizing task of trying to stand again.

"Enough chatter." The old man suddenly sounded irritable and exhausted. "András, go get the child. I want to begin."

András wound the rope around a hook set into the wall at waist level, knotting it with a jerk. She gasped at a blaze of fresh agony. He strode purposefully out of the room, leaving her alone with Novak.

"The stupidity of women is always a fresh surprise," Novak mused. "You are very beautiful, it is true, but even so, it is obvious to what you are, what you exist for. You are a disposable toy, Tamara. How could a man declare love for a thing like yourself? Men don't love women like you. They use them and discard them like the trash that they are." He took a step closer. "But still, I'm surprised you were taken in so easily."

Part of her was on her knees, no, on the ground, writhing and wailing *yes, it's true, yes, just kill me please and have done with it.*

The other part whispered, *come a little closer, you sick filthy fuck.*

She moved the tongue studs in her mouth, positioning the poison capsule between her molars and trying to work up enough spit to deliver it. Difficult, with such a parched mouth. She would have to be spot-on accurate. She tried to sniff down her useless tears of terror and agony and make them good for something.

Come on, old man. Two more steps. Just two, and I'll melt the organs inside your body into slop.

Faster. She snorted, sniffed. Novak's weight shifted. Time slowed. She was so tuned in, she sensed his every tiny movement as if her own body was making it.

Finally. The mix of tears and saliva in her mouth was ready to spit as he moved closer . . . jaws ready to chomp, lungs ready to provide air to propel her liquid projectile . . . closer—

Ding, ding. A soft, musical chiming sound shattered the moment.

Novak broke eye contact, turned to look at the intercom on the table.

She almost screamed her disappointment. So fucking close!

Novak punched the button. "I told you I was not to be disturbed!"

"They've brought in Luksch," a male voice on the intercom informed him.

Novak's face changed. "Oh. Excellent. Bring him in, then."

He turned back to Tam, rubbing his hands together. Too far away from her. The moment had slipped away. She wanted to wail, shriek.

"Georg has been bad," Novak confided. "Wanting you for himself, even knowing how you had wronged me. Then I discovered that he was planning to murder me and take over my business! Can you imagine it? Millions spent grooming him to take over Kurt's place! Ingrate! He will watch his toy smashed. That's what happens to little boys who grab, grab, grab. I taught my Kurt that lesson, too. He learned it early. That's what made him so strong, so unusual. Do you remember how strong he was, Tamara? Ah, Georg, my dear. There you are."

Two large men hustled Georg into the room. The man's face was battered, his lip split. Older bruises decorated him as well, relics from his fight with Val in the hotel blooming under both his eyes, purple and blue. His teeth were clenched, except for the gaps where two of them had been knocked out by Val in the hotel. His eyes were wild with rage.

There had to be some way that Tam could turn this new wrinkle to her advantage, but if there was, she could not see it. She was too scared, too crazed with pain to crunch the data.

"There she is, Georg," the old man crooned. "Your heart's desire. The woman who plotted your best friend's murder. But perhaps he was not quite such a friend as we all thought, eh?"

Georg's thin, scabbed lips drew back like a snarling dog's.

No. This could not possibly help, she concluded bleakly. Georg was bound hand and foot, a gun to his head. As badly off as she was herself. No, she needed a miracle. On the scale of an earthquake, a volcano, a tornado, a bomb, a meteor—

"Ey!" Georg shouted. He sagged to the ground between the two men who clutched his arms—and the room exploded.

Windows shattered with an enormous crash and glass flew, peppering her face and body with stinging shards. The mirror exploded and toppled backward. One of the men who had been holding Georg was hurled down onto his back. His jaw was torn away, a red, raw mess of torn meat, white glints from shattered bone and teeth showing through. He pawed at himself, eyes white-rimmed, rolling with panic.

Bam. The other man holding Georg clapped his hand to his throat. Blood jetted, black in the candlelight. It gushed through his fingers. His gun thudded to the carpet. He toppled, bounced, lay still.

The sudden silence was deafening. Georg sat up in a leisurely, unhurried way. He reached for the nearest gun, scanning the room through narrowed eyes. Cold air swirled through the empty window frames. The flames in the candelabra flared hellishly high. Tam watched the tableau, soul shaking with shock . . . and astonished hope.

Novak was curled on the ground, shaking. Blood spread quickly beneath his wasted body. His hand was pressed to his midriff. Gut shot.

Good, she thought viciously. *Die in agony, scum.*

Georg aimed the gun at the man whose jaw had been shot off.

"So you are the one," he said. "Traitor and spy. I had to let all of my men be killed in order to identify you, Ferenc. This grieves me."

The man gurgled, eyes bugging over his shattered lower face.

"I told the sniper to aim for your mouth," Georg told him. "I thought it appropriate. Don't you?"

Blood sprayed as the man shook his head. He clutched at Georg's leg. Georg kicked him away. "The real punishment would be to leave you alive with that face," Georg said. "But alas, it is not practical."

He pulled the trigger. *Bam.* The contents of the man's skull exploded from the back in a pink, splattering fan, over the carpet, wall.

Black-clad men bulked up with Kevlar, masked with helmets and bristling with equipment and weaponry were sliding into the room like shadows. One through the door and two through the space where the windows had been. Broken glass glittered everywhere.

Georg bent over to Novak's shriveled form. He slid the barrel of the gun into the old man's gaping mouth and jerked his face up with it.

"You're not the only one who had an inside man," he said. "I had one, too. Someone to take out your security at just the right moment. You got soft, old man. Complacent. Now you die, and I'll take back my toy. And everything else you have, as well. It's mine now. All mine."

Novak struggled to speak. Georg jabbed the gun sharply, knocking the old man to the ground again. Then Georg turned and looked at Tam. That persistent white froth of bubbly spit dangled from his grimacing lips. His eyes dragged over her, lit up with unholy lust.

He licked his wet, foamy lips and started toward her.

Chapter
28

The first sentry's eyes barely had time to widen before Val grabbed the side of his head, whipped it down, and smashed the man's temple into his jerked up knee. The sentry thudded to the floor. A swift, brutal kick to the nose to make sure he was out, and Val darted on.

He felt a detached sense of unreality to be slipping through the corridors of this hellish place again. The palace was drafty and cold, with a pervasive stench of damp and mold. He'd found the place crushingly depressing when forced to live and work there in his youth, like the dismal castle of an absentee vampire. He almost expected to run into himself as he passed silently by the mildewed library with its treasure trove of rotting antique books.

He stopped, listened. Heartbeat slowing, time slowing. Battle ready.

A sentry rounded the corner. Val jabbed a punch into his face, grabbed his neck. A headbutt, an elbow raked across the the throat, a knee jab to the groin, and the man was felled. In relative silence, but for the grunts and thuds.

He froze in an agony of indecision at the top of the staircase.

Crash, gunshots, glass shattering. The noise broke his paralysis. He sprinted down the stairs. The Saints Salon, then. Novak's favorite room with its baroque splendor and its creepy frescoes. Typical.

Georg had arrived and made his move. It was about fucking time. He experienced a flash of what almost amounted to warmth for the bloodsucking freak. Not that it would keep Val from killing the man at the first opportunity.

He began stepping over bodies, skirting puddles of blood. Novak's staff, he assumed, taken by surprise by Georg's attack force. Blood-spattered, water-damaged walls, and rolled in dark rivulets across the cracked antique tilework.

So he'd missed the first wave. Just as well. Not his fight.

The next corner he turned would put him outside the Saints Salon. With his sixth sense, he picked up the inaudible shush of fabric-clad thighs rubbing together, squeaks of rubber-soled boots against tile. The man turned the corner, whipping up his gun—

Thunk, Val's knife sank into the man's eye, before the shout had time to flash from the man's brain down his nerve fibers to his throat.

He staggered, fell. Val sprinted forward and grabbed him under the armpits, dragging him out of sight of anyone around the corner.

Black-clad, heavy, slung with gear. The dead man was shorter and slighter, but the bulky vest might camouflage that for the brief moment that mattered. He whipped the helmet off the dead man—and gasped in a short, shocked breath. Staring at the corpse.

Cristo. He knew this man. Knew his name. A PSS agent, young, hired less than five years ago. Efficient, capable. Professional.

Val dragged his eyes from the accusing gaze of the pale, staring blue eye that remained. Unfortunate, but if he had not killed, he would have been killed, and Tamar had no time for moral ambiguity.

This man had made his choice. He had known the risks.

The fastenings of the Kevlar vest made a loud *scritch* as he wrenched them loose. He stilled, ready to shoot whoever might poke his head around the corner to investigate.

Seconds ticked by. Nothing. No one.

He donned the vest, ignoring the blood that stained it, put on the helmet, strapped on the chin guard. He angled his head for maximum shadow on his face and walked toward the other black-clad man stationed in front of the Saints Salon.

A gun crashed from inside. The man turned to look, distracted.

Val leaped, grabbed, wrenched. *Crunch*, the man's vertebrae gave. The man flopped to the ground, neck snapped, shitting himself.

He did not recognize this one. Thank God.

The door to the Saints Salon was ajar. Val prodded it with the gun barrel until it swung further open. He peered around the door frame.

His breath froze in his lungs. Tamar hung from a rope by her arms in the corner of the room, her tangled hair falling like a dark curtain around her battered, beautiful face, a stark mask of pain and mute endurance. Still alive.

It wrenched something inside of him loose. Grief, rage, and terrified hope. He had been trying to brace himself against finding her dead. Trying and failing. But hope was more cruel than despair.

Three men were down on the ground. Four were on their feet, one of them Luksch. Val's knife flew into the throat of the nearest man, and he spun, arms windmilling, glass crunching beneath his boots before he crashed to the ground.

Val dove, tucked, and rolled to dodge the bullets, but when he somersaulted back up into a crouch, still more bullets thudded into his chest, *bam, bam*, and flung him backward, like huge, punching fists. He slammed to the ground, wind knocked out, and rolled onto his knees without air, gasping for oxygen. He brought the gun up, took aim at—

Henry. Blue eyes and square jaw. Henry. Holding a gun on him. Val's muscles locked for a fraction of a second—

Bam. His weapon spun uselessly out of his hand into space. It sailed in a high arc, bounced, skidded across the carpet.

Then, the numb, cold burn. The trickling heat of blood. Shot in the arm. Fucking shit. Henry had shot him. His friend.

"Valery." Henry's face looked distant, sad.

Val focused on the gun muzzle in the foreground. Henry's face faded to a blur. "You?" he whispered.

"You weren't supposed to be here," Henry said dully. "I wasn't supposed to have to face off with you, buddy. There was no reason for it." Henry's eyes flicked past him, focusing on someone behind Val. His voice muted. "But I can't change things now."

"Why?" Val demanded, his voice hard.

"Money," Henry said matter-of-factly. "A lot of it. Hegel told you. We would have been happy to share, but it just didn't work out. Your dick prevailed, man. But no woman is worth millions."

Val's eyes flicked up to Tamar's bright gaze. It blazed down, unquenched. An instant injection of passion, of power, straight into his muscle fibers, his nerves, his mind.

So beautiful. So precious. Her intelligence, her courage, the steely endurance beneath the smooth, seductive curves of her tortured body.

Tears slid down her cheeks. She rubbed them angrily against her stretched arms. So tough around her secret core of tenderness.

Worth millions. Worth anything, everything. His life, his soul, his heart. But Henry would never understand that.

Not this Henry who he had really never known at all.

". . . would have helped you save Imre," Henry was saying.

"Imre is dead," Val informed him. "I am here for her now."

Henry shook his head. "You can't save everybody, Val. I'm sorry. I was hoping you would stay the hell away from here, but you just had to poke your nose in. It's just business. My friendship for you was real."

Val glanced pointedly at Henry's gun. "Do not talk of friendship and hold a gun to my head."

Henry's mouth tightened to a colorless line. "It's just business," he repeated, his voice hard. "Good-bye, Val."

Val stared up at Tamar, locking eyes with her. He had never feared death before and did not fear it now. What he felt was piercing grief for the life he had thought he might live with her. An improbable fantasy, destined to end with a bullet to the brain, but even so. That fleeting fantasy, that brief hope had been the sweetest, finest thing he had ever known. Even so, he was grateful.

He braced himself. Waited for it, his eyes fixed on Tamar's.

"No," said Georg suddenly. Glass crunched under his feet as he started walking toward them.

Henry glanced at the other man, alarmed. "What?"

"Don't shoot," Georg said slowly. He gazed at Val, an expression of discovery on his face. "Not quite yet. I want him to watch first."

Henry frowned. "Watch what? Do you mean . . . oh, no. For God's sake, you can't be serious. Now?"

"Yes. It's perfect." Georg's eyes were gleaming with wild excitement. "He's the perfect audience. It will be the sexual experience of a lifetime. Here, bring him closer so he can see everything. Hold him. He watches. Kill him when I come. Exactly when I come."

Henry's mouth twisted in distaste. He gestured with his chin for to the other black-clad man to approach. "Hold your gun to his head," he ordered the man curtly. "If he moves, blow his brains out."

The man held his gun up to Val's temple. Henry stepped behind him and wrenched Val's wounded arm back, then the other one, hyperextending the mangled, wounded shoulder. Torquing them into a tense, shaking hammerlock of pure pain.

Val's lungs jerked, in hard, shuddering gasps. Blood ran down, dripping off his fingertips. The wound in his shoulder had torn open again. He felt the warmth, the sting. Hot liquid, spreading.

Henry dragged him toward the corner where Tamar was hanging. The man with the gun to Val's head accompanied them, step for step.

He was a couple of meters from her now. Henry behind him, the gunman to the side, and Tamar before him, staring down, eyes blazing.

"This is your life, from now on," Val said to his former friend. "Pandering to that crazy sadist's whims. Kneeling to kiss his stinking ass for your money. Enjoy it, Henry. You deserve it."

"Do not fuck with me," Henry hissed. "I did not choose this."

"Yes, you did," Val said. "You bought it. And you will pay for it."

But all thoughts of Henry vanished from his head as Georg started toward Tamar, massaging his crotch.

As if she needed more of a fucking challenge. As if things were still a bit too tame around here, too easy. Now Val had to show up and put himself in mortal danger.

Damn him for complicating things. She would rather have died with her feelings hurt, hating his guts, thinking him a backstabbing traitor, than be forced to watch him die trying to save her. Much rather.

How many more pieces of her heart were going to be torn out of her chest and stomped to death before her eyes? There was no end to it.

At least Novak was down. Maybe Rachel had gotten her miracle. Then again, maybe not. András had her, and András loved to hurt just for hurting's sake. And Georg was walking toward her, Tam, his face a tight mask of lust. Her body recoiled. Her ordeal had only just begun.

Imagine. The man was turned on by a woman hanging from a hook, a woman with a broken arm. She shook with a mix of tears and hysterical laughter. What was it about her and sadistic madmen? Why were they so attracted to her? She must have been a bad girl in a past life to deserve this insanity. Not once, not twice, but repeatedly.

When András came back with Rachel, bullets would start to sing again with her baby right in the middle of it. Val was immobilized, a gun to his head. She was hanging up like a cow in a meat locker—helpless.

Except for one thing. She rolled the tongue studs in her mouth as Georg touched her breasts, eyes shiny and rolling with hot excitement. His hands were stickily damp as they clamped over her breasts and squeezed. He groped at her crotch. Gripped it painfully hard.

She marshaled her self-control to put a look of heavy-lidded longing on her face. "Kiss me," she whispered. "Please. You saved me. Kiss me before you do it. I have been dreaming of your kiss."

He jerked her toward him, pulling her off balance again. *The arm, oh God, the arm* . . . she clamped down on a shriek of pain to not waste spit.

His face came closer, filling her field of vision, distorted, grotesque in every lurid detail. His breath was sour and damp, pulsing wetly against her face, stealing all the air.

She placed the poison capsule between her molars, estimating distance, velocities, counting seconds, crunching data. Cold and sharp. Robot Bitch. Not yet . . . not yet . . . three . . . two . . . one . . . *crunch*.

The capsule broke.

Her mouth filled with a granular, metallic bitterness. His lips touched hers, hideously slippery with mucus. His mouth yawned.

She spat the poison wad into it.

Georg reeled back, spitting, pawing at his mouth and tongue as the corrosive burn began to spread. He lunged forward, slapped her. She did not feel it. He slapped her again and again. Her cheek was numb. He was screaming, bellowing, but she could not hear his voice.

The calculating machine in her head reminded her that she had less than fifteen seconds . . . thirteen . . . twelve, before it was too late to bother with the antidote, but she couldn't coordinate her jaw muscles to bite again. She'd gone limp, spent her strength . . . nine . . . eight . . . seven . . . the icy tingle, the numbness of impending death crept through her . . . five . . . four . . . blood trickled from her nose . . .

Rachel.

She bit down on the other capsule. The antidote was bitter too. She needed more spit to swallow the stuff, but she was dry, her mouth full of sand and dust. She flung her head back so that the blood streaming from her nose would run down her throat.

Come on, Steele. You're good at swallowing bitter pills.

Georg was falling, writhing, twitching. She saw it as if through the wrong end of a telescope. She could not enjoy her victory. It was too far away, too long ago. It had happened to someone else.

She gulped her own blood and fought the darkness.

It was Imre who saved him, in the end. Imre, who had taught him to use his brain like the high-functioning machine that it was.

Val cut loose from the fear battering at him like a hurricane wind. He took the three steps back and floated free. He still smelled Henry's sweat. Still felt the cold circle of steel the other man pressed against the pulse point of his throbbing temple. Still felt the burning agony of his wounded arm and shoulder.

Still saw Georg, slavering and groping the woman Val loved.

But he floated apart from it. Waiting in the vast stillness inside his mind for his opportunity. There was always a split-second opening, if the mind was wide open and soft enough to sense it, flexible enough to recognize it for what it was. And quick enough to exploit it.

... *he's kissing her, fucking pig rapist* ...

No. That thought would shatter his focus. He let the thought go, wrenched his concentration back to the matrix. Wait. Just ... *wait.*

Georg reeled back and began a strange dance, screaming and pawing at his mouth. He slapped Tamar, once, twice.

"What is it? What is it? Where's the antidote?" he bellowed. "What is the antidote, you fucking bitch?"

Antidote? Poison. Oh, God, no. Tamar. *No.*

The shocked gaze of the man holding the gun on him skittered over to the spectacle. Val felt the relentless pressure of the gun barrel against his head waver for an instant—

Val flung himself backward against Henry, ignoring the flare of pain, forcing the man to shift his bulk, brace himself—

Now!

Val ran up the wall in three big steps, and flipped his body over Henry's head. Henry shouted, and tumbled backward. They crashed to the ground together. The impact knocked Henry's grip loose.

He grappled for Val, flipping him over with a roar of rage, and pinned Val beneath his huge, muscular bulk. Val heaved, struggled ... and pushed with his thumb against the stone on the ring he wore, Tamar's ring, that released the spike. Short, but razor sharp and wickedly pointed.

Henry's grip slipped on Val's bloody wrist. Val wrenched it loose with a shout—and stabbed the small spike into Henry's carotid artery.

Gouts of hot blood splattered him, rhythmically. Henry choked, convulsed, stared down into his face, a look of betrayal in his eyes.

Val crawled out from under him, grabbed Henry's gun, and clambered to his feet, blood-drenched and swaying.

He pointed it at the man whose job it had been to hold the gun to his head and asked a silent question with his eyes.

The gunman shook his head in reply. His wide eyes darted, from Georg's corpse to Henry's, to Tamar, and back to the gun in Val's hand. The place was silent, but for Val's breath sawing in and out of his mouth, and the moaning whisper of the wind. Heavy brocade drapes billowed and swirled. Candle flames leaped and flared.

He lifted his hands, pointing his gun in the air, and began to back warily toward the door, boots crunching and sliding on the broken glass. He stumbled over his colleague's dead, bloody body. Caught himself, without even looking down.

"I'm gone," the gunman said. "I'm out of here. I was never even here at all."

Val nodded, and waited until the other man had slunk out the door. His running footsteps retreated. The silence was absolute.

Val turned to Tamar. She sagged in her ropes, eyes closed, face deathly pale. Blood streamed from her nose. More trickled from the corners of her mouth. Georg lay still, though his feet still twitched. Bloody froth foamed from his mouth. His face was blue, tongue protruding.

She'd pulled some poison trick. A kamikaze move. Ah, God.

All the times in his life that he had numbed himself to endure some atrocious thing had not prepared him for this. He was a helpless child again. Staring at the end of the world, lying on the bathroom floor.

Then, to his astonishment, her eyes fluttered open. They focused somewhere beyond him, and widened. She sucked in a bubbling breath.

"Watch out!" she cried.

He jerked to the side, and the bullet grazed his hip, plowing a deep furrow to join his other wounds. Novak grinned from his pool of blood on the floor, thin neck straining, and lifted his Walther PPK to try again.

Val emptied Henry's Taurus into the old man and kept pulling the trigger compulsively even after the gun was empty.

He glanced wildly around the room. "Anyone else? Anyone?"

No one moved. No one spoke.

Val stumbled over to the dead man, the young one, who lay on his back with Val's knife sticking out of his throat. He yanked it out and lunged toward Tamar.

He put his arm around her slender body as he reached up to saw at the rope. Just a few passes of the blade severed it, and her slight weight dropped into his arms. She was covered with tiny rivulets of blood. Small wounds, from the shards of flying glass.

He gathered her up, looking around for a place to lay her down that was not strewn with glass. There was none.

He dropped to his knees and cradled her.

Her eyes opened. Her gaze was still sharp. "Don't . . . k-kiss me," she croaked in a halting whisper. "I'm poisonous."

Despair slammed through him. "Oh, fuck," he said, his voice high and shaking. "You are killing me, Tamar."

Her lips twitched. "Melodramatic," she whispered. "Idiot."

Their eyes met, full of pain and longing. She hitched in a shallow breath and said her daughter's name with a whispering sigh. "Rachel," she said. "András has her."

Her eyes commanded him back into action.

"Yes," he said thickly, smoothing back her sweat-stiffened hair. "I understand." He pressed a kiss to her damp, icy forehead. "There's glass everywhere," he said, helpless. "I don't know where to put you."

"Fuck the glass," she croaked. "Get . . . Rachel. Move your ass."

He cleared a spot on the rug as best he could with his boot and laid her down gently. Then he forced his shaking legs to bear him over to the bloody carnage on the ground to scrounge for loaded weapons.

Rachel. The last thing that he could do for her.

Chapter 29

Connor stared out the windshield. His eyes burned like coals. The atmosphere in the taxi had the tension of a bomb countdown.

There was nothing to say. It had already been said, repeated, hashed out, torn apart, attacked, picked to pieces. They were so on edge that anything anyone said annoyed the shit out of all the others, so they had collectively subsided into a gloomy, self-protective silence.

Connor sat in the front, clutching the monitor with the satellite map. Their driver sensed the weirdness, despite the language barrier, and kept casting nervous looks at him and the others, in the rearview mirror. Seth, Sean and Davy were crowded into the backseat, everyone red-eyed, grim, and tense from the strain of suppressing the thoughts of what might already have happened to Rachel, considering her ten-hour head start.

All they could do now was throw themselves at the location of the beacon in Rachel's red coat and see what happened. Connor had called the FBI liaison in Budapest when they got to Hungary, and told him what was going on, just so that someone would be sure to follow up should the worst happen. They had been strictly forbidden to go anywhere near Novak.

What the fuck. To a man, not one of them had ever learned to do what they were told. And they were the only ones whose prime agenda was Rachel's safety. They needed to be the first ones on the scene.

They were almost there, bumping over a narrow, ancient stone bridge over a narrow river and then down a long avenue next to a tall stone wall. All of them noted the cameras mounted at regular intervals along the top of it. The cab driver came to a stop at a big wrought iron gate. It was yawning wide open. Weird.

"We are arrive," the driver ventured timidly.

As they watched, two men came sprinting out of the gate. They didn't even look at the car, just ran, hell for leather, toward the bridge.

OK. Weirder.

The meter read 155 euros. Connor handed the guy two hundred-euro bills. They piled out and the cab peeled away, tires squealing. Connor didn't blame him. It was very clearly a bad scene.

Then another guy came pounding out the gate. Davy grabbed him, slamming one of his thick forearms across the guy's throat.

"What's happening in there?" he demanded.

The guy gibbered in Hungarian. Davy gave him a shake and tried the same question in French, then in German. The guy just struggled and squawked, voice high. Finally, Davy flung him away in disgust.

"Get out of here," he muttered.

The man stumbled, flailing, caught himself and ran.

"Rats leaving the ship," Sean said. "Got a fix on Rachel?"

Connor peered at the handheld. "Got her. Let's just go for it. They're not manning the cameras now. The shit's hit the fan. It's every man for himself."

They took off running, swift and silent, down the long, curving avenue of trees. No one challenged them; no one shot at them. A huge, decaying eighteenth-century palace came into view.

They veered around it to follow the signal, and found a long, low building that must once have been a stable. Getting closer. Forty meters. Thirty. The icon blipped on the screen, tantalizing them.

They burst into the building, peering around, guns at the ready.

No one was there, just a long row of covered parking slots. Fifteen meters, ten, eight. Dead silence.

The beacon was inside one of the cars. Connor's heart pounded with dread. Five meters, four, three . . . there it was. A Mercedes coupe.

No one was inside it. They flashed their penlights in every direction. No one. The doors were locked.

They crowded around to the back of the vehicle, and stared at the trunk. The beacon was there. Connor tried it. Of course, it was locked.

He swallowed hard and pounded on it. "Rachel? Honey?"

No one answered. Seth elbowed through them, carrying a big, rusty garden implement, like heavy hedge clippers. "Everybody get the fuck out of the way."

They all moved back, and Seth went berserk, smashing and pounding and cursing, until the back of the car was unrecognizable.

He finally jolted the lock loose. They wrenched the trunk open.

A puffy red child's ski jacket lay there. No Rachel. Connor smelled urine. He put his hand on the carpeting under the coat, felt around.

Yes, there it was. Dampness. Pee.

"Baby piss," he said. "They put her in the trunk. They put a three-year-old into the fucking trunk of a fucking car."

There were about three seconds of appalled silence. Sean broke it.

"Let's move," he said harshly. "Let's go hunt. I need to kill something. Now."

"Right on," Seth growled.

A ragged burst of gunfire came from the direction of the mansion. They took off running again.

He would recognize Rachel's screaming anywhere. It would cut throught any kind of noise, a gun fight, an air raid, even the roaring and ringing of his ears. Val followed the sound, lurching forward in an unsteady, limping run fueled by unmixed adrenaline. He left a trail of blood behind him, but he didn't care. If his blood supply lasted long enough to kill András, that was all he asked of it.

He lost the sound and stopped, straining to hear her again. The wounds throbbed and burned, all of them, the old ones and the new. There was a burning hole in his chest. Every panting breath hurt. Broken ribs, from the bullets that had punched into the Kevlar.

He rounded a corner. The shrill, faraway wail crescendoed. He launched himself forward again. Blood ran from the gouge in his hip, down his leg, into his boot. His foot squelched with every step.

The layout of the place was coming back. The sound seemed to come from above him, though it could be an aural illusion. He ran toward the grand staircase and took the steps three at a time, driven by terror. He would hang on as long as he could for Tamar's sake, but he knew what his body could and could not do, wounded as he was. He knew that feeling: the faintness, the cold, the nasty tingle.

He had only minutes before his body failed him.

He stopped at the top to listen, guts sinking at the silence. There it was, a squeak, quickly cut off—to the left. He stumbled down the corridor toward the sound, abandoning all effort at stealth.

András rounded the corner, clutching a writhing, squirming Rachel under one arm, brandishing his gun with the other hand.

He stopped cold when he saw Val, jerking Rachel up so that she shielded his chest, neck and head.

Val dove for the nearest doorway as András opened fire on him, tearing the rotten door loose from its antique, rusty hinges. He pitched forward into the stifling darkness. Bullets crashed into walls, the floor, sending splinters and shards of wood, tile, and stucco flying.

At the first moment of silence, Val called out over the ringing in his ears. "It's over, András. They're dead. Put her down."

"Who's dead?" András demanded.

"Everyone," Val said. "Dead, or else running. Didn't you hear the guns?"

András paused. He had heard them, and not known what to make of them. "I'll judge when it's over, dickhead," András growled, but there was uncertainty in his voice.

Rachel let loose with another piercing ultrahigh shriek that rattled all the molecules in his body. Val heard a slap, muffled cursing. "Shut up, you squeaking brat, or I'll—"

His words were obscured by another shriek, more ear-shattering than the last. Val lunged for the door, peered around the frame.

Zing, a bullet flicked past his ear, ruffling his hair. He jerked back, having ascertained that Rachel's squirming body still shielded all the good target points. *Merde.* Trapped, like a fucking rat in a cage. He couldn't return fire, couldn't give chase. He was useless.

"I've got the gun to her head," said András, his voice taunting. "Throw your guns out into the corridor, and step out of the room with your hands before you. We're going to talk to the boss."

"He's dead," Val said wearily.

"Of course he is," András crooned. "And this screaming little darling will be, too. It can't be too soon for me."

"It's all over. Novak is dead. They're all dead," Val repeated.

"Really? If the boss is dead, what reason is there for me not to kill her right now? Or better yet, I could shoot something off her, a hand, a foot. It would be a pleasure, after the trouble she's given me. At this range, I could probably blow her leg right off at the knee. Shall we see? Should I try it?"

"No," Val said swiftly. "Don't."

"No? You don't like that idea? Then throw out your guns, fuck-head. Now."

The gun stocks were sticky with his drying blood. Val peeled them loose from his hand, the Beretta and the SIG he'd gleaned from the dead PSS agents.

"Did you hear what I said, you cocksucking man whore?" András's voice sharpened with tension. "On the count of five, she loses a foot. One. Two. Three—"

Val let the guns drop. They clattered onto the tiles.

"Kick them out into the corridor," András directed, pitching his voice over Rachel's shrieks. "Then put out your hands."

Val kicked the guns. They slid over the tiles with a clatter.

His hands were dripping blood. He held them out the door, fingers splayed wide, turning them to show that they were empty.

"Step out, and put them on top of your head."

Val walked slowly out into the corridor, lifted his arms, placed his hands on his head.

András's arm was clasped around Rachel's waist, in a cruelly tight grip. Rachel kept struggling, undaunted.

Val wanted to applaud. The child did her mother proud. He stared at András, balancing like a tightrope walker suspended over a boiling lava pit. Blood trickled down his arm, slow and hot and ticklish.

Checkmate. *Three steps back. Detached. Floating. Wait for it.*

Rachel flailed, flopped, shrieked. András had to struggle to hold her. "Get down on your knees," he growled. "Stay still, you little shit, or I'll peel you like a grape."

Val sank slowly to his knees. Waiting, watching for his opening. Widening out his senses, softening. *Wait for it. Wait.*

András adjusted his grip, lifting her higher. Rachel flung herself forward against his face, almost as if she were kissing him. Suddenly András yanked her away from his face and flung her to the ground. A red bite wound flamed on his cheek. Broken skin. Blood

Now!

Val let the Walther PPK slide from the sleeve of his jacket and into his hand as Rachel skittered on hands and knees, and darted into the door he had broken through. András shot after her, bullets pumping out, screaming something unintelligible, his hand to his distorted, bleeding face.

Val opened fire with the Walther. *Bam, bam, bam.* Head, throat, chest.

András toppled across the threshhold, a look of stupid surprise on his face. There was a hole in the center of his forehead.

The sudden silence was disorienting. Val's cool detachment evaporated the instant there was no desperate use for it. He began shaking convulsively. He almost fell. Caught himself.

He lurched to his feet, limped over to András. Kneeled by him to make sure he was dead. He prodded the man with his gun. The condition of András's skull convinced him. There was very little left inside it. Good.

He blundered into the room, bumping painfully into various obstacles and trying to intuit where a light source might be. The darkness was so dense. The room appeared to be crowded with bulky furniture covered with canvas dropcloths.

There might be no light source at all. Back in his time, entire wings of the old palace had been left to fall into decay just as they had been in the eighteenth century. No wiring, no modern plumbing.

"Rachel?" He got down to his knees with a grunt of pain, putting himself in the glow of twilight from the door so that she could see him, wherever she was. If she was alive. If András had not shot her.

"Rachel?" He tried to pitch his voice normally, but it rasped and quavered, barely recognizable. "It's Val, remember? Your Mamma's friend? It's all right now. Come out to me."

She did, to his astonishment. He heard a rustle, a squeak, and a tiny body scrabbled across the floor toward him. Rachel ran into him full on, knocking him onto his ass, and wound her arms around his neck. He grabbed her, held her, chest shaking uncontrollably. She was alive.

Ah, no. Not yet. Please. He could not fall apart. Not yet.

He picked her up, swaying dangerously. He didn't have much time left. He had to find someone to care for her, to make the phone calls, the arrangements. He could not slide down into oblivion and leave Rachel alone in this slaughterhouse just because all his blood had drained out of his body.

That was no fucking excuse. He had promised Tamar.

He lurched out into the corridor, gasping for air.

"Mamma?" Rachel asked, her voice breathless.

His chest tightened around his heart like a fist. "I'm sorry. I don't know about Mamma, baby," he whispered. "We'll see about Mamma."

Rachel squeezed her eyes shut, digging her fingers into the blood-soaked fabric of his coat. "Mamma. Mamma. Mamma. Mamma," she repeated. Like a mantra. Blocking out the world with the magic word.

He envied her the trick.

He scooped up the guns and staggered back toward the Saints Salon, following his own trail of blood. He was not sure what the fuck to do now. He couldn't show Rachel her mamma naked and covered in blood, not if the unspeakable had happened. Yet Tamar's vibe dragged at him like a steel cable attached to his insides. Someone was reeling it mercilessly in.

He had a bad moment when he turned the corner outside the Saints Salon and saw the two men, but as soon as he focused his eyes, the shock of blond hair struck an instant chord of recognition.

Connor McCloud, Seth Mackey. Val was so relieved, he might even have wept. He didn't care.

Connor hurried toward them, his face gray with strain. "Oh, thank God, thank God," he muttered. "Rachel? Honey? You OK? Holy Jesus, Janos, what's all this blood? Is she—"

"Not hers," he said, exhausted. "She's all right."

Connor reached out. The little girl relinquished her grip on Val and transferred it willingly enough to the other man. "Mamma?" she asked.

"Oh, honey, I don't know," Connor said helplessly.

Rachel began to sob. Val turned away from the sound, and shuffled like one of the living dead into the blood-drenched Saints Salon.

The place was cold and dark. Wind whispered through it. Davy and Sean were bent over Tamar's still form, muttering to each other. A thermal blanket was thrown over her. Davy was pumping on her chest.

Val fell to his knees next to them, only dimly aware of the glass shards digging into his flesh. "How is she?"

"Alive," Sean said. "I don't know how, or for how long, considering the condition he's in." He indicated Georg's gruesome corpse, bent backward in a contorted arc. The man's mouth, nose and bulging eyes all streamed blood. "She must have taken the same poison he did."

"She kissed him, and he died," Val said.

"That's what I figured." Sean's voice was grim. "She has a tongue stud in. Some kind of poison capsule. The chick is a fucking head case. She makes me tired."

Val cupped her jaw, tried to open her mouth. Sean batted his hand away. "Don't touch her, for Christ's sake! Some of the stuff she uses goes right through the skin. We can't even do mouth to mouth."

"I don't care about the poison," Val said. "I will give her mouth to mouth."

Davy gave him a steely glance. "Like hell you will. Things suck enough without you croaking on us, too. Try it and I'll knock you out."

It would hardly be necessary, Val thought, swaying. He caught himself against the floor as he stared down at Tamar's still form.

Her face looked like a pale, delicate wax effigy.

"I must call someone," he said, shaking himself. "Medics, doctors. For Rachel, too. Someone give me a cell phone. An ambulance—"

"Connor's already on it," Davy interrupted him. "The FBI liaison's taking care of it. Everybody's on their way. So, these bodies . . . uh, what the hell happened here? Did you waste them all?"

"No. Just a few of them," he said vaguely. "Seven or eight, maybe. They mostly killed each other. What are you doing to her arm?"

"It's broken," Sean said roughly. "Those filthy pigfuckers had her hanging from a goddamn rope with a broken arm. I can't do shit about her crazy poisons, but at least I can splint her arm."

Glass crunched as Val thudded down onto his ass. He caught himself with a bloody hand. The dim room was fading away.

He struggled to stay awake, alert. He didn't want to leave Tamar while she still breathed. What a waste of precious moments with her.

But he could not support the weight of consciousness any longer. He was collapsing under it. On his way down the long slippery slide.

Oh, for fuck's sake, he's shot, he heard one of them say in an exasperated tone, before he pitched face first into nothing.

Chapter
30

Cray's Cove, five weeks later . . .

Val pulled his motorcycle to a stop at the road that led to Tamar's house. It was different than the last time he had seen it. It was now a road, not a camouflaged deer track. The driveway was freshly asphalted. A plain whitewashed post boasted a large, shiny silver mailbox with STEELE stenciled on in in bold black letters. There was a plastic box for the *Washingtonian* and another box for the local paper.

It disoriented him. For a moment, he doubted his own bulletproof, iron-riveted memory, but just for a moment. He'd been intensely aware of the exact latitudinal and longitudinal coordinates of Tamar's physical presence on earth since he learned of her existence. He could not be mistaken about this. He gunned the motor again with a muttered curse.

He was just afraid, after these endless weeks of enigmatic silence. Afraid to speculate what the silence meant. So fucking afraid, he could barely eat. Or breathe, for that matter.

It was Tamar's way to let a man sweat, but it seemed particularly cruel to him now, after lingering for weeks near death, to be left alone to doubt, to wonder. Should he reach out to her? Was it better to wait?

But he could not wait forever. It was killing him. He had to know.

And besides, he knew Tamar. She liked strength. Needed it. He had to be strong. Fear was weakening him, so he had to be fearless.

Hah. A stiff challenge. But he would try with everything he had.

Doubts nagged and stung him. She had never actually said that she loved him, except for that time that he remembered like a dream after she'd cuffed and drugged him at the *agriturismo*. And that may have been just a chemical fantasy. Questionable at every level.

He'd hoped that trying to save her and Rachel would have been a point in his favor but evidently not. She had ignored his very existence ever since.

He jerked to a stop at the electronic gate. There was a vidcam mounted above it. He buzzed the button and waited for a response.

This simple gate was nothing like the high-tech camouflaged facsimile of the falling-down barn that had stood here before. She'd ripped out all of her space age security, and put the plain, simple basics in their place. In other words, she'd lowered her defenses.

He wondered what that meant about her change in mood. He hoped it was good news for him. He was afraid to speculate.

No one was responding to his buzz, but he was going in anyway.

He was ready to face anything, even a loaded gun. Nothing could be worse than this blank emptiness. The boredom and pain of convalescence, then the intensive debriefing and subsequent negotiations with PSS. Then the quiet, endless days, one after the other, alone and dazed in his apartment in Rome. Slumped in a chair, staring at shadows moving on the wall for hours. Unable to eat, sleep, move.

Everything he tried to do felt like useless playacting, empty of all significance. No connection to anything that counted. How could there be? What counted had been ripped out of him.

What counted was walking around, living and breathing a half a world away from him. His heart, walking around outside his body. Ignoring him.

The intercom finally beeped. "Who is it?"

It was a female voice, but not Tamar's. "Is this the home of Tamar Steele?" he asked.

A cautious pause, and someone said, "Who wants to know?"

"Valery Janos. Is she home?" He stepped up to the camera, stared into it, and let whoever was looking at the monitor inside get a good, long look.

The gate clicked and hummed open. He accelerated on through, and headed up the long, winding road that led up to the crest of a mountain that plunged steeply down to the Pacific Ocean. The hillside was dark with towering conifers and draped with a ragged mantle of mist. The broad, shining beach was lashed with surges of white foam. Dramatically beautiful, as befitted the home of a woman like Tamar.

The closer he got to her, the more his chest ached.

Had it just been his wishful fantasy projected onto her, that dawn interlude in the hotel room in San Vito? He had seen something in her eyes that had changed the nature of his existence. His soul had awakened, and so had his heart, his brain, and other parts he didn't even know how to name. They had risen from a deathlike sleep, and now they would give him no peace.

Had it been real, that half-remembered 'I love you'?

The garage was open when he pulled up. A young woman with a mop of curly red hair stood in the opening, holding a squirming baby in her arms. Margot McCloud. The name floated back to him. Davy's wife. She was not smiling.

Val could politely initiate a conversation in ten different languages, but he just stood there, swallowing over the dry lump in his throat. "Is she here?" he asked when he could finally speak.

Margot jiggled her baby, studying him solemnly. "Yes. She's working. In her studio."

His stomach sank. "So she doesn't know that I'm here yet?"

Margot shook her head. Her red curls floated and swirled in the air. "Not yet. She blasts music into her headphones when she works. Come on in."

He followed her through a security room filled with cutting edge surveillance equipment and noticed that most of it was deactivated. Snarls of disconnected electrical wire were everywhere.

At the top of the stairs, he looked around, fascinated. Tamar's living space was exactly as he would have expected. Minimalist, severe, and yet subtly opulent. The lines were clean, the grain in the blond wood paneling swirled voluptuously. There were incredible vistas outside each of the huge triangular windows. He had never seen it, but he felt as if he recognized it. Like her, it was uncompromising, stark, and beautiful.

He passed a room crowded with an uncharacteristic clutter of color: toys, books, mobiles, pictures. A small form hurled itself out the door and smacked into his legs.

"Val! Val!" Rachel crowed, clutching at his thigh.

He was gratified at the warmth of her welcome, and the sudden upwelling of tenderness he felt for the little girl took him by surprise. He picked her up and hid his face against her curly head for a few seconds, until the shaky, misty feeling passed. "Hello, little sweet," he whispered.

A stocky older woman with a black and white bun stopped at the threshold, staring at him with wide-eyed curiosity. Had to be Rosalia.

"Rachel and I are old friends, Senhora," he explained in Portuguese, kissing the top of Rachel's head.

Rosalia was charmed. "Ah! So you are this Val that they tell me about, eh?" She shot Margot a delighted look and winked broadly. "Good, then! Go up and talk to her. She is too sad. She needs cheering up from a handsome young man like you."

That remained to be seen, he reflected bleakly. He passed Rachel to Rosalia, soothing her protests with a promise to come back and play later. A promise he desperately hoped he would be able to keep.

"Come on. I'll show you the way," Margot said.

He followed Margot down the hallway, leaving Rachel's loud squawks of disapproval behind. They climbed up a spiral staircase. The cells in his body were shaking apart in fear and dread, and he spoke just to distract himself from the feeling. "How has she been?"

Margo glanced back over her shoulder. "Hmm. Not great, in my book. You'd better ask her yourself. We've been taking turns, parking our butts here to keep an eye on her, and she hasn't had the energy to kick us out yet. I think she's working up to it, though." Margot stopped in front of a carved wooden door, and gave him a speculative look over the flame-colored curls on her daughter's head.

"Don't startle her if you can help it," she advised. "She's jumpy these days. Not sleeping much."

"You mean, she might kill me by mistake?"

She smiled as she pulled open the door. "You said it, not me."

Tamar was wearing headphones and bending over a jeweler's bench, her back to them. She wore drawstring pants of undyed linen that hung low over her hips and a shrunken black T-shirt that did not cover her navel or conceal the deep, feminine curve of her hips. Her feet were bare. Her hair hung in a thick, loose mahogany braid.

She was lost in her work, swaying sinuously to music only she could hear. So thin. Her arms, so narrow. There were livid surgical scars on her right arm. The McClouds had told him about the surgeries to repair torn, mangled tissues, ripped tendons.

He stared at the scars, tight-lipped. His throat ached.

Margot cleared her throat. "I guess I'll just leave you, then. You'll want to talk to her in private, I'm sure."

"Yes, it's best," he said. "That way, we don't both have to die."

Margot choked on a short burst of laughter. "Good luck."

The door clicked shut behind her.

Val just stared. After weeks, his eyes were starved for the sight of her. Every perfect detail. The upright straightness of her back, the creamy texture of her skin, the perfect lines of her cheekbone, the way her plain work clothes draped and clung to her graceful curves.

He felt helpless, lost. He had no plan of action, just hunger, and incoherent longing. He could think of no way to get her attention without giving her an unpleasant adrenaline jolt, so he elected to wait. She had a sixth sense, just as he did. She would feel his gaze soon enough and turn around.

And he would know if life held any hope of happiness for him.

No. It was not a matter of hope, he told himself, resolute. It was a battle of wills. She could accept his love, or she could kill him. Killing him was the only way she would be able to get him out of her hair. Those were her options. It was very simple.

He was not leaving this place unsatisfied.

How could a man declare love for a thing like yourself? Men don't love women like you. They use them and discard them, like the trash that they are. Tam tuned the insidious ghostly voice out with effort. *Fuck off, Novak*, she whispered silently. *You're dead. You lost the game.*

Evil old bastard. At it again. Chipping away at her, from the inside. None of it is true, she reminded herself. Don't be fooled. Don't fall for it. Don't let him win. He would not drag her down with him now, when she was home free.

On the outside, anyway. On the inside, she was a ragged mess.

She dragged her attention back to the music blasting into her headphones and focused on the bracelet she was working on. The evil, whispering voice was backing off with time, but oh, so slightly and oh, so slowly. Every time she spaced out and stared blankly into space, which was often, Novak's raspy voice was there to fill the gap, whispering his constant stream of cruelty and filth.

Damn. She had to get over this. Rachel was traumatized, too, and Tam had to be strong for her. She could not afford to whine and mope.

But oh, God, it was hard. She weighed two tons. She felt so tired, so sad and empty. The fucked-up arm and the near-lethal dose of poison on top of it all had wiped her out. So did pining for Val. Not twenty seconds passed that she was not thinking of him, dreaming of him. Lusting for him, too, now that the worst of the poison had worked itself out of her system. She was starting to feel almost human again, even a little bit female, which meant that erotic dreams of him had begun to torment her, along with the hideous nightmares. She'd be hard put to say which type of dream was the most upsetting.

He had not called or texted or e-mailed. Granted, neither had she. She'd grabbed Rachel and run, over oceans and continents, as soon as she'd been capable of standing. Well before the doctors had wanted to let her go.

She could not bear to see him. She'd been in overload. Poisoned, polluted, sickened by everything, herself included. It had overcome her. The poison she'd swallowed, being slimed by Georg, having Rachel taken, threatened. The mental poison that Novak had force-fed her. Those videos, playing and playing in her head.

And that last awful conversation she'd had with Val. He, spitting with rage and betrayal, handcuffed to the bed. She, spraying a drug into his face so she could run off and murder someone.

All things considered, they had issues.

She couldn't bear the thought of him looking at her the way she felt. She flinched from being seen by anyone. It hurt, it burned. The only reason she permitted it at all was for Rachel's sake.

That was why she allowed the McCloud contingent to hang out here, always underfoot and driving her slowly but surely bugfuck. So that Rachel would have one more healthy, sane point of reference, besides the long-suffering Rosalia. She could not trust herself to be one. On the contrary.

She'd thought about contacting Val by e-mail, with the electronic distance giving her a little emotional protection. Had even gone so far as to pull up the Capriccio Consulting Web site contact page on her computer screen, even typing a few words.

Something had always laid a heavy, smothering hand over each attempt. The same something that kept playing the erotic footage of San Vito and the Huxley hotel over and over in her head, the images cheapened by the camera's cold, unfriendly eye into porn.

She saw glowing, malevolent green eyes watching her in the dark when she lay in bed not sleeping. When she did get to sleep, she dreamed of herself, skim milk pale and covered with goosebumps, cold, wearing soiled, limp, red silk lingerie. Alone, shivering in the snow. All the many monsters of her life circling round, licking their lips.

And that voice, whispering. That evil voice. *Men don't love women like you. They use them and discard them, like the trash that they are.*

This wasn't her usual horror of being made a fool of. This was worse. The stakes were so much higher. If she called it wrong, if she opened herself up, offered herself to Val, and proved to be mistaken, she wouldn't just feel like a fool. Not this time.

She would be dead. Destroyed. It would be the end. She didn't have the courage to risk it. Her reserves of courage were all used up.

Hah. Now who was being melodramatic? She slid her hand up under the goggles to wipe the tears away. What would she say to him if she got him on e-mail anyway? *Hi, what's up? How do you feel?*

God help her. Did she really want to know?

Even now, she imagined that she could feel his presence. Her skin prickled with warmth. If she turned, there he'd be, gazing at her out of those dark, smoldering eyes filled with speechless longing.

But she would not give in to the urge to turn. The blankness she felt when she saw the empty space where he wasn't was too fucking depressing. She had to stop doing that to herself.

But her neck itched madly, hairs prickling. She took off the headphones, and hesitated for a moment. Her heart thudded.

Ah, what the hell. Why not compound her misery?

She turned, looked . . . and gasped.

The world shifted on its axis. Her blush started from the very soles of her feet, or even deeper. From some other lost dimension of her being: the molten core of her soul, the bottom of the ocean of her heart.

She felt naked. Inside out. Sweet, shivering chills chased themselves across her skin. Part terror, part astonished joy.

He said nothing, just gazed at her. His hair was longer, too long for the cool style he had before. It dangled over his eyes and ears in unkempt waves, streaked with threads of stark white.

He was thinner, more compact than before. His eyes shadowed, his skin paler, his jaw sharp. His cheekbones jutted out like they'd been carved with a dull knife. But it was him.

God, how he filled the space he occupied. How he dominated it. He took the place he inhabited and claimed it utterly, made it his own.

The way he had claimed her. By some freak miracle.

She cleared her throat. "Aren't you going to say something?" The words burst past the aching block in her throat.

His mouth twitched. "I was waiting for you to start."

She snorted out of sheer force of habit. "Typical. Men always shrug off the responsibility."

"No, Tamar. It is you who are being typical," he said calmly. "Hiding behind your sarcasm the way a child hides behind her mother's legs. Traveling across the world to you is a statement in itself. I am awaiting a response to it."

Her blush got hotter. She didn't know what to look at, what to do with her hands, with her mouth. She felt . . . fluttery. A speechless ditz.

"My response," she repeated. "What am I supposed to respond?"

His lips twitched, a wicked ghost of a smile hinting at how much he was enjoying her flustered state. She wanted to smack him for it, the uppity bastard. Condescending to her.

"Anything you like," he said blandly. "But if you need suggestions, I will gladly give them to you."

She clenched her jaw, forbidding herself to weep. "No one tells me what to say or think," she said inanely. Gah. As if it needed to be said.

His deep-grooved, blindingly beautiful grin rocked her back, gasping for breath. "Certainly not," he said. "The very idea."

"What do you want from me, Janos?" she demanded.

"Everything," he said simply. "And call me Val. I have earned that much from you, by now."

She squeezed her eyes shut. "Back off. Too much, too soon."

He was silent for a moment. "If you wish. I am in no hurry. I am not going anywhere. We can go as slowly as you like."

"This is my place," she flared. "I say who stays and who goes."

"Of course, of course," he soothed. "Let us talk of things that do not make you anxious. Neutral topics."

She was irritated afresh. Condescending to her again. "We have no neutral topics," she snapped.

He sighed. "You are a difficult woman," he said plaintively.

She gave him a tight, falsely sweet smile. "Oh? Do ya think?"

He flicked his gaze upward, praying for patience, no doubt. "How about the weather?" he suggested, his voice even.

She waved her hand toward the window. "Take a look," she said. "It's gray. There's fog. It's the Washington coast. End of conversation. Nice try. No dice."

"All right, moving on," he murmured. "How is Rachel?"

That was far from a neutral subject. "She's better," Tam said cautiously. "She still has screaming nightmares every night. But she's started to talk again, and she's eating a little more and going outside the house, at least when I'm with her."

He nodded. "Good, then. I am glad. And your health?"

She shrugged. "Fine."

He let his waiting silence speak for him, insisting.

Tam made a rude, impatient sound. "Really. I'm not lying to you. The last time I had liver function tests, there was definite improvement. The tissue is regenerating. There's some organ damage, of course, but nothing that'll kill me any time soon. I'm not going to climb Everest or run any marathons for a while, that's all. It was just the month-long mother of all hangovers."

"And the arm?" he persisted. "The McClouds told me you had surgeries."

"The McClouds talk way too much," Tam muttered. "And one in particular takes quite a lot upon herself to open my door to uninvited guests. That McCloud is going to hear from me about it."

His mouth tightened. "Ah. That's all I am to you, Tamar? An uninvited guest?"

She crossed her arms over her chest. "Do not guilt trip me, Janos."

"Why not?" he said. "I have nothing to lose. I might as well see if guilt will work with you, since nothing else does. I saw what that poison did to Georg. I thought you were dying. Why did you not tell me that you had taken the antidote?"

She gave him a sideways look. "I had a lot on my mind."

His mouth hardened. "You really are a bitch, Tamar."

"And that's a surprise to you? That's not liable to change, Janos. If it puts you off—"

"It does not put me off," he said. "On the contrary."

She floundered for a moment. "I—I—what do you—"

"I know you now, Tamar," he said. "The more acid you are, the more tender the place you are trying to protect. The crueler you are to me, the more I have cause to hope."

Cause to hope. His words made her heart shake in her chest.

"I told you once before not to pin a softer side onto me," she said, but her unsteady voice betrayed her.

He let his silence speak for him once again—for such a long time, she began to twitch. "You are lying because you are afraid," he said finally. "But you need not be afraid of me."

"Um." She decided to ignore that loaded statement, and groped for a neutral topic to replace it with. "So how's your health, Janos?"

The bastard had the nerve to look as if he was trying not to smile. "What about it?" he said lightly. "What do you care? I am no one to you. I am just an uninvited guest, no? You do not even call me by my name."

"Cut the crap and answer the question," she snapped.

He shrugged. "There were many holes to mend," he said matter-of-factly. "I lost a great deal of blood. My convalescence would have gone more quickly if you had been near me."

"I'm glad to see it went just fine anyway," she said crisply.

The silence lengthened. Tam was on the verge of flinging herself at him when he looked around her studio with a rueful smile.

"I almost didn't recognize the road to your house," he said.

She sniffed. "Ah, yes. That. I changed the look of everything in the interests of getting the hell over my own paranoid bullshit. It was just overcompensation, anyway. I started feeling embarrassed by it."

"You have less to be afraid of now," Val said. "With Georg and Novak dead. And PSS is working on making you disappear from all the Most Wanted databases of the world."

"They are?" She was startled. "Why on earth would they do that?"

He shrugged. "Because I told them to."

The edge in his voice made her look at him more closely. "I didn't know you had that kind of clout with them," she said.

He waved his hand dismissively. "They were embarrassed about Hegel and Berne's involvement in a mafiya turf war," he said. "Bad for the company's image. I told them I would be pleased to keep my mouth shut—if they did what they could for you."

She blinked. "Ah. So you're bullying them now? I'm surprised they didn't just kill you."

"Let them try," he said.

She swallowed. "No," she said quietly. "I would rather they didn't."

"Would you? How kind," he said, his voice laced with irony. "In any case, you should not have much trouble now from anyone."

"That is my hope," she said stiffly. "I've lost my taste for trouble."

"I have not," he said, his eyes gleaming. "There is some trouble that I still would welcome."

She broke eye contact quickly and stared down at the jewelry that she'd been working on. She couldn't bear to look at him. Feelings vibrated inside her at a screamingly high frequency.

His footsteps sounded soft and deliberate, moving closer to her. "What are you working on now?" he asked quietly.

She invited him with her hand to take a look at what was on the bench. "See for yourself."

He looked at the items she'd been working on, and carefully picked up a ring. It was a streamlined blend of white and colored gold knotwork, with a blazing sun as the centerpiece, a yellow diamond glittering in its core.

"Very beautiful," he said. "This looks too big for a woman's hand."

"It's not for a woman's hand," she said.

He slanted her a startled glance and then reexamined the ring in his hand. "No? Did you not tell me that you only design jewelry for women? Was that not part of your philosophy?"

"I did, and it was," she admitted. "But this ring is not for a woman."

He slid it onto his left hand, and admired the effect. "It fits."

She shrugged. "It's part of a matched set."

"Ah, *sì*? Show me the other pieces."

She picked up the other ring, a smaller one. "For the woman," she said. She put it in his outstretched hand. This one was white gold knotwork, with tiny accents of yellow gold, with a crescent moon curled around a small white diamond.

He stared down at the pieces, a frown of concentration on his face. "They are perfect," he said. "What are their defense applications?"

Her blush began to rise again. "There are none."

He swiveled his head toward her, taken aback. "None?"

She shook her head.

Val closed his hand over the woman's ring. "I want them." His voice rang fiercely. "These rings are mine."

She bit her lip, still unable to look into his face. "They'll cost you."

"I'll give you everything I have," he said promptly.

She lifted an eyebrow. "You're not a very shrewd bargainer, Janos."

"Do not play with me. Do not be flip. Not about something so important," he said roughly. "Be silent if you cannot control yourself."

He grabbed her left hand and slid the woman's ring onto her ring finger. It fit, of course. He put her hand up to his lips, and kissed it. "Beauty for beauty's sake alone?"

She covered her shaking mouth, embarrassed. "I suppose so."

"No more deadly secrets?"

She started to shake with silent, helpless laughter. "I don't have any secrets from you," she said at last. "I've tried to keep them, but it just never seems to work out. I'm giving up the effort. Go ahead, Val. Know all my nasty, deadly, dangerous secrets if you feel like it. Knock yourself out."

He kissed her hand again. "I am honored to know them."

"Nice, nice," she scoffed. "You're good at putting a pretty spin on things, Janos. Did they teach you that in gigolo school?"

He winced. "Ouch. Must you always deflate me?"

"Always," she warned. "I'm hardwired that way. Don't delude yourself into thinking that love will change me."

His grin went suddenly incandescent. "I could weep for joy to hear you say the word love for the first time. But for the fact that it would frighten you into fits if I did."

"Frightened? Me? Hah." She glared at him, but could not maintain the expression when he touched her face with his fingertip that way, as if she were a flower. Rare, precious, and delicate.

He leaned his forehead against hers, and the hot point of contact was so sweet, as intimate as a kiss but more oblique, more secret. She did not flinch away from it. She melted into it, softening.

He slid his hands down, over her shoulders, over her ribs, to the warm, bare skin of her waist, and then skimmed them upward, pulling the black T-shirt with them. Tam raised her arms, let him tug it over her head, pulling wisps of hair loose and dangling around her face.

She gazed at him, naked to the waist. "It's not the first time," she said. "I said the word once before."

He froze. A muscle in his jaw pulsed. "After you drugged me? So it wasn't just a dream?"

"No. It wasn't a dream. I said it." She shivered, feeling exposed. The pants hung low on her hips. He drew the drawstring bow loose, with a slow, deliberate pull. The soft, crumpled linen garment puddled around her feet, leaving her entirely naked. "And I meant it," she finished in a whisper.

"Ah, Tamar," he whispered back.

She flinched violently at the gentle touch of his hands span-
ning her waist. For a moment, it was just as she had feared it
would be.

She cringed, her body going hard and tight with self-loathing at
his touch. Still hearing that low, rasping voice, droning endlessly.
*Men don't love women like you. They use them and discard them like the
trash that they are.*

But she closed her eyes and breathed. Covered his hands with
her own, holding them motionless at her waist, and waited for a miracle.

Val himself was the miracle, a living, breathing miracle. His gentleness, his tender patience, melted her, healed her instantly.

The feeling bloomed from deep inside her, soft and sweet and intensely alive. Surprised, moved. Every moment a deeper revelation,
a new level of tenderness, of longing. Her body was soft, hot, intensely sensitive. His every tiny touch burst like fireworks, tingling
through her nerves. When he put his arms around her and pulled
her against himself, an earthquake of accumulated tension shuddered through her.

He felt thinner, harder, his arms as tight and taut as piano wire.
He vibrated with emotion, desire. He was rigid with the tension of
holding back. Waiting for as long as she needed him to wait.

Amazingly, she felt safe in the circle of his arms. She pressed her
face against him, breathed in his delicious scent. Listening to his
heart, pounding strong and fast.

Safe. The feeling was so unfamiliar, it frightened her. To think
that she could feel safe with him after all that had happened between them. All the ugliness, all the violence and betrayal.

"Why did you do that to me?" she blurted out and hid her face
against his chest again. Afraid to hear the answer.

He stroked her hair, gripping her thick braid to tug her head back
so she would look into his eyes again. "The video, you mean?"

She waited, eyes locked with his.

A long, careful sigh escaped him. "It was the deal I made with
Novak," he said. "Or rather, the deal he made with me. I was to de-

liver those videos to him every three days, and in return, he would refrain from carving a piece off of Imre while I watched on the videophone."

She winced. "Oh, God."

"I was desperate," he said. "I hated myself for it, every time. I would never have chosen to do such a thing to anyone, let alone you. I am sorry. It's over. Can we leave it behind? Can you forgive me?"

She nodded.

Val closed his eyes, sagging with evident relief. "He wanted me motivated," he said. "He did not expect me to fall in love with you. Nor did I, though it happened before we even met."

She glanced up, startled. "How could you—"

"I watched you and Rachel for ten days. That was enough for me," he said forcefully. "You were so gentle with her, so patient. You were so strong. And *bella maladetta*. My wildest fantasy in flesh and blood. I did not even know that I had a fantasy woman. But you were—are her."

He cupped her bottom and lifted her up onto the table. "My turn, now, Tamar. How could you do what you did to me?"

Her fingers tightened on his shoulders, then she remembered his wound and let go as if she'd been burned. "What are you referring to?"

"Ah, but where do I begin. The handcuffs, the drugs?" Anger hardened in his voice. "Running away while I was practically comatose? As if you did not care, as if there was nothing between us?"

The impulse to shove his accusation away from herself in anger was almost automatic, but she short-circuited it. She breathed, deep and slow, and swallowed the sharp words back.

They were no longer true, in any case, and she did not truly want to say them. It was just a reflex. A tic.

What she really wanted was for him to understand. She concentrated on the buttons of his black shirt, unbuttoning them one by one as she spoke to give her hands something to do, her eyes some place to rest.

"You know why," she said fiercely. "I had to settle accounts with

Stengl. He murdered my family, destroyed my village, my home. He killed my childhood, raped me, turned me into something that I was never meant to be. I'd been waiting my whole life for payback."

His eyes narrowed. "Than why did you not kill him? I know that you did not. Santarini would have sent the Camorra for me by now if you had, and I was in no condition to defend myself from them. Did you fail to get close enough to him? Or did Ana—"

"No. I . . . changed my mind," she said, her voice halting. She undid the last button, spread the shirt out over his chest.

He frowned. "Changed your mind?" he repeated. "When?"

"When I got into his room," she said. "When I looked into his eyes. That was when I realized—"

"What?" he prompted impatiently.

"That you were right," she admitted. "He wasn't worth it. He was nothing compared to what I had to lose. Even though I thought that I had already lost it after what I'd done to you. I thought you'd never want to see me again."

Val lifted her right arm, bent low, and pressed a gentle kiss against the scar. Then another and another.

She took courage from that. "I was running out of the clinic to find you when András got me." She closed her eyes tightly, feeling every warm, soft butterfly kiss so intensely against her flesh. "You must think I am so stupid."

"Not at all," he said. "But explain this to me. Why did you change your mind about us and leave me all alone? Did living in bliss with me in a tropical paradise no longer appeal to you?"

She shook her head. She couldn't bear to talk about it. The core of the problem. Her secret shame, the weakness in herself that she despised so violently. She was not made of gemstones or metal. She could not wash away the stains. Not anymore.

He took her face in both his hands. "Answer me, Tamar."

She swallowed, tasting the bitterness of the poison. A bitterness she still tasted faintly every moment of every day. "I couldn't," she whispered.

"Why not?" he demanded, unrelenting.

She squeezed her eyes shut, and searched herself for the courage she needed to say it. "I felt . . . soiled," she whispered. "Poisoned, damaged. I felt like a black hole. Like I didn't deserve—oh, God. I thought it was better to get away, stay away. I didn't want to inflict myself on anyone. Certainly not you."

His face was blank with astonishment. "Oh, God, Tamar," he said helplessly.

"I'm sorry." Her voice was fogging up with tears, to her distress. "I couldn't get past it. I'm not as strong as you think I am."

He gave her a short, hard shake. "What bullshit," he said roughly. "You should have known better."

"Well, I didn't," she flung back. "And maybe I never will."

"Oh, you will. You should have come to me, Tamar. I would have convinced you. You are a queen. A goddess. Shining and perfect."

She snorted. "Oh, please. Don't overdo it, Janos," she said tartly.

"I cannot help it," he said. "It is my nature. And you inspire me to flowery excess."

"Oh, God," she muttered. "I am so in for it. I can't stand flowery excess."

"You will learn," he promised solemnly.

"Will I?" She yanked the shirt down over his shoulders, his arms, and stopped to stare at the angry scars.

She stopped to kiss each one. Then she moved on to the older scars. There were many of them, and by the time she had kissed her way through everything she could see, he was fully aroused. She wrenched his belt open, shoved down his jeans. Took him in hand, squeezing with a shuddering sigh of delighted satisfaction. Ah, yes.

"So, did this interview with me work out to your satisfaction?" she asked breathlessly.

He kissed her throat as he pushed her thighs wide, then teased her clit tenderly, circling it with his fingertip. "Oh, yes. But there was never any question of you refusing me," he said.

She blinked at him. "Really?"

He nuzzled her ear. "I had decided. You agreed to love me, or you would have had to kill me to get rid of me. Either way, I won."

"Oh?" She suppressed a crack of laughter. "How do you figure, loverboy?"

"Killing me would be a long, difficult process," he informed her solemnly. "I am very hard to kill. It could take your whole lifetime. And in the meantime, while you plotted and schemed and made attempt after attempt, I would at least be with you, no? So I win."

She snorted with laughter and pressed a hot kiss against his chest. "Melodramatic idiot."

"Admit it," he said. "You love that about me."

"I love everything about you," she said rashly. "But it's been so long. Remind me why, Val. Go ahead, blow my mind. Bowl me over. Show me exactly why I love you so much."

He gave her that radiant grin that made her heart jump with unbelieving joy, and got right down to it.